A Rage of Regents

Nigel Tranter

CORONET BOOKS
Hodder and Stoughton

First published in Great Britain in 1996 by Hodder and Stoughton
a division of Hodder Headline PLC
First published in paperback in 1996 by Hodder and Stoughton
A Coronet paperback

10 9 8 7 6 5 4 3 2

British Library Cataloguing in Publication Data

Tranter, Nigel, 1909 –
    A rage of regents
    1. English fiction – 20th century –
    Scottish authors
    2. Scottish fiction – 20th century
    I. Title
    823.9'12 [F]

ISBN 0 340 65997 1

Printed and bound in Great Britain by
Caledonian International Book Manufacturing Ltd, Glasgow

Hodder and Stoughton
A division of Hodder Headline PLC
338 Euston Road
London NW1 3BH

"I have no desire to rise to heights at such a cost! To wed some stranger, to be tied to a woman I know naught of. Here is shame! Folly! I will not do it!"

"Watch your words, John! And to *me*! You will do as I say. Have you forgotten? You are not yet of full age, for two years. Even if you were, you would obey your father. You cannot refuse. But, see you, here is none so ill a fate. Margaret Douglas is a personable young woman. Fair. Agreeable. Well made. She limps a little, but that is nothing. You will – "

"Limps! Limps, you say? You would have me to wed a cripple!"

"Do not be a fool, boy. She is no cripple. She will make you a good wife."

"I would choose my own wife! Not be harnessed to some lame female, whom no one else will marry, I take it!"

"Quiet! Enough of this. You are of nineteen years, and you will do as I say. Your marriage is in *my* hands. I know what is best. For you, and for us all."

His father turned and left him standing. Lady Carmichael looked at her son, head ashake, and went after her husband.

Also by Nigel Tranter
(in chronological order)

Columba
Druid Sacrifice
Kenneth
MacBeth the King
Margaret the Queen
David the Prince
Lord of the Isles
Tapestry of the Boar
Crusader
The Bruce Trilogy (in one volume)
The Wallace
True Thomas
Flowers of Chivalry
The Stewart Trilogy:
Lords of Misrule
A Folly of Princes
The Captive Crown

Lion Let Loose
Black Douglas
Lord in Waiting
Price of a Princess
Chain of Destiny
The Master of Gray Trilogy (in one volume)
A Stake in the Kingdom
The James V Trilogy (in one volume)
Warden of the Queen's March
Children of the Mist
The Wisest Fool
Mail Royal
Unicorn Rampant
The Young Montrose
Montrose: The Captain General
Honours Even
The Patriot
The MacGregor Trilogy (in one volume)

Principal Characters in order of appearance

John Carmichael, Younger of that Ilk: Elder son of Sir John, of that Ilk.

James, Lord Somerville: Uncle of above.

Sir John Carmichael: Lanarkshire laird.

Lady Douglas of Pittendreich: Former Countess of Angus.

Lady Margaret Douglas: Daughter of above.

Archibald Douglas, Earl of Angus: Young chief of the Red Douglases.

James Douglas, Earl of Morton: Uncle of Angus and brother of Lady Margaret; chancellor of the realm. Black Douglas chief.

Janet Kirkcaldy, Lady Kerr: Daughter of Sir William Kirkcaldy.

Sir Thomas Kerr of Ferniehirst: Border chieftain, whom Mary Queen of Scots had called her protector.

James Hamilton, Duke of Chatelherault: Chief of the Hamiltons.

Archibald Campbell, Earl of Argyll: Chief of Clan Campbell.

George, Earl of Huntly: Chief of the Gordons.

Sir William Kirkcaldy of Grange: Leading soldier. Keeper of Edinburgh Castle.

Master John Knox: Leading Kirk reformer.

Lord Claud Hamilton: Son of the Duke of Chatelherault.

John Erskine, Earl of Mar: Regent of Scotland.

William Maitland of Lethington: Secretary of State.

Sir Walter Scott of Buccleuch: Great Border baron.

Lord Hunsdon: English governor of Berwick-on-Tweed.

Lord Home: Great Scots Border baron.

Annabella, Countess of Mar: Foster-mother of the king.

James the Sixth: King of Scots.

Johnnie Mar: The king's foster-brother.

Lady Mary Erskine: Sister of above.

Sir Walter Ker of Cessford: Border laird. Chief of separate branch of the Kerrs.

Master George Buchanan: Reformist minister and tutor of King James.

Sir John Foster: English Warden of the Middle March.

Elizabeth Tudor, Queen of England.

Lord John Hamilton: Second son of the Duke of Chatelherault.

Master Andrew Melville: Prominent divine. Principal of Glasgow University.

Esmé Stewart, Lord of Aubigny: Kinsman of the king.

PART ONE

1

John Carmichael was shaken, as never before in his twenty years, shaken, bewildered, downcast – and blood-spattered. The blood was not his own, at least; partly his uncle's and partly, probably, that of one of Moray's men who, attacking him, he had managed to best, cutting him down with the sword which he had somehow lost thereafter, as he sought to raise and support his wounded uncle, the Lord Somerville, who had fallen off his horse. So John had had to dismount also, and both horses had bolted. Now he stood, on a low spur of Cathcart Hill above Langside and the Clyde, the older man slumped on the ground and alean against him, moaning and muttering incoherently, clearly seriously injured, and he stared around him, at a loss. What, in the good Lord's name, was he to do?

John's staring alternated between the scene of carnage and chaos of the battlefield which he had just left, to the north, past all the fleeing soldiery around him, some mounted but most on foot; but mainly southwards where at least the flight was more orderly, if scarcely organised, a compact and quite large body of men, all mounted, and well mounted, and one woman in their midst, the queen, fleeing the disastrous field. There went, in fact, the surviving leadership, such as were not slain or captured, of the loyalist army. Ought he, Carmichael Younger of that Ilk, to be fleeing with them? After all, he had come to fight for Mary against her wretched half-brother, the Regent Moray. They had most clearly lost the battle; but that was not to say that the queen's *cause* was lost. Should he have fled with them, with her, found another

3

horse amongst the many riderless, and ridden off? But that would have meant leaving his wounded uncle, his mother's brother. He could not do that. Admittedly there were Somerville men-at-arms in flight amongst the others, whose duty undoubtedly was to help look after their lord. But all who had survived seemed to be intent on saving their own skins. Many had fallen in the fighting; there had been three hundred of them, mainly horsed. Where were they now?

He just could not leave his Uncle James lying there. This was John Carmichael's first taste of real war, and for all the flourish at the start, he was not relishing it, any more than really comprehending it and what had happened. Confusion was his main state of mind.

With the queen's party disappearing over a ridge to the south, John recognised that standing there staring was going to achieve nothing for either of them, end in their capture or cutting down almost certainly, payment of the price of being on the losing side, imprisoned at the best, possibly his uncle's death from wounds. No enemy appeared to be coming up this hillock meantime from the battle area; but it was only a question of time, and probably short time. The sooner he was off the better.

Horses, therefore. Where their own were now he had no notion, probably grabbed by other decampers. He could see riderless beasts here and there, none so far off. He must try to win two of these. That meant leaving Lord Somerville there meantime, but there was no help for it.

"Uncle," he said urgently, stooping. "Wait you here." Not that the poor man could do anything else. "I must get horses. To escape. See, there are some over there. Wait. I will be back with mounts." He hoped that was true.

Only moans greeted that. The other was grievously stricken, barely conscious.

John laid him flat on the grass, and hurried off. There were three animals standing, reins hanging loose, about two hundred yards away, evidently as bewildered by the situation as he had been, although one bent head to crop grass now and again. He saw one man running up to them, whereupon the beasts trotted away. The man evidently thought better of it and hurried off afoot.

John, brought up with horses since childhood at Carmichael in the Lanarkshire hills and moors, could surely improve on that. The creatures could get as frightened and upset by battle and bloodshed as could men, and these, having lost their masters, would be in a highly nervous state. A soothing approach was called for. The animals had halted again, not far off, and he walked slowly towards them. When they began to move away again, he called out, but calmly, reassuringly. He kept this up as he went, pacing over the rough ground unhurriedly; and although the horses moved also, they went not as a group but one and then another, and not far, only a few uncertain yards.

John continued to talk and walk, forcing himself to seem calm, confident, all but authoritative – despite the fact that he was anything but, very aware of fleeing men and the cries of the wounded, and fear that at any moment the regent's victorious troops might come up here pursuing stragglers.

His quiet, assured approach worked, at least for one of the beasts, a sorrel mare, which turned head to look back at him, and then edged away only slightly, where the other two went further. John actually hummed a gentle melody now, hoping that this would help to allay fears in the mare; he had done this often when grooming horses, and found that they tended to like it.

Whether it was that or not, the creature did allow him to come up with it. And once he had grasped the trailing reins, all was well. The mare did not sidle nor shy, and patting its flank, John was able to hoist himself up into the saddle without difficulty.

And, once mounted, the effect on the other two horses was evident. They accepted that here was normalcy again, after the fright and clash of battle and loss of their owners; and as John reined his mare over towards them, they awaited him unmoving, although one tossed its head and actually whinnied, whether in welcome, relief or complaint. Used to acting as cavalry mounts and in company, they accepted this new master's authority, and he was able to reach over and take their reins without them shying away. He had intended to find two mounts but it seemed that he had gained three.

He trotted them over to where his uncle lay, and dismounted.

Now the next and major problem. How to get the inert man up into the saddle? Somerville, a middle-aged man, was no lightweight, and wearing half armour. He made no response to John's urgings to try to rise. No way could the young man lift the other high enough to get him on to the mare's back. Moreover clearly, once there, he would not be able to stay upright in the saddle. He would have to be held in front of John himself, sharing one beast. Here was a coil indeed.

He must have help. At least there was no lack of men to call on, other fugitives passing nearby all the time. A pair hurrying past he called to, but they ignored him. Then a single man, who also looked the other way, trying to run. Four came by. John decided that something of a bribe was necessary.

"You – see you!" he called. "Horses! Come, two of you. Aid me. Aid this wounded lord up. And you can ride. A beast each."

That had its effect, an improved means of escape. But not two, all four came over to him.

John did not argue. If he was sharing a mount with his uncle, these four could ride in pairs also.

"See, the Lord Somerville is sore hurt. I will mount, then you lift him up to me. You can take the other horses. Ride pillion."

Nothing loth, the four picked up the wounded man, less than gently, as John mounted the mare again. Somehow they got his uncle up and settled slumped before him, where he would have to be held securely. Then, arguing over who should sit where, the others climbed on to the remaining horses. John gathered that they were Hamilton men-at-arms. The Lord Claud Hamilton and his elderly father, the Duke of Chatelherault, had been prominent amongst the leaders of the queen's army.

They set off without delay. At least all knew approximately where to ride, for the White Cart was there below to guide them, and then the great River Clyde. Following this up, south-eastwards, they would come to Hamilton town in some ten miles. Cowthally Castle, Somerville's main seat, was much further, twenty miles at least, but in the same general direction, a long way to ride double-mounted with a wounded man – but that was for the future. Meantime, down Cart to Cathcart, then over to the Clyde in the Carmyle area.

John led the way, for these Hamilton men were obviously foot, not cavalry, no expert riders, especially when two to a beast. Burdened thus, the horses could not go fast, but with no pursuit as yet evident, speed was not of the essence. Covering the miles was what mattered.

John found holding his uncle approximately upright and secure at the front of his saddle, on a trotting mare, less than easy, and tiring on the arms. But it was possible, and every mile saw them further from that grim battlefield and all that it meant.

They duly went by the Cart to the Clyde, passing fleeing men all the way. John wondered where the queen was now, where she was being taken. Beautiful, unfortunate Mary Stewart; how grievous had been her short reign in Scotland, so far. She had only come back from France in 1561, seven years before, a young widow of his own age, eighteen years, had remarried here twice, unhappily both times, produced a child, James, but had fallen foul of her so-called Lords of the Congregation, the extreme Protestant leadership, which condemned her as an arrant Catholic, imprisoned her in the Douglas castle of Lochleven, forced her to sign a form of abdication, and crowned her infant son king as James the Sixth, with her illegitimate half-brother James Stewart, Earl of Moray, as regent for the child. She had escaped from her captors, renounced the alleged abdication, and returned to her throne, challenging the Protestant Lords. And now this disaster. But she still would have much support in her divided realm, irrespective of the religious question. Loyal men would rally to Mary, their rightful monarch. All was not lost, in one lost battle. Where would those escaping lords be taking her? Where would she raise her standard anew?

At Carmyle, they turned up Clyde, their road avoiding the river's coils and twists, by Cambuslang and Blantyre to Hamilton, that journey taking them just two hours. Entering the town, without remark or farewell, John's four companions left him, to turn up a winding side-street and disappear. So much for gratitude. He rode on alone, stiff, saddle-sore and weary, arms aching with holding his uncle in place, the older man seeming to drift in and out of consciousness.

They were almost halfway to Carnwath here, he recognised. Could he keep going all that way, another dozen miles? But what option had he? An inn? A tavern? His uncle required the services of a physician, he judged, care and nursing, and as quickly as possible. He would not get that at any roadside inn. He must get him home to Cowthally even if they must ride until the mare dropped — or his own arms lost their power to hold up his burden.

Presently the mare was ceasing to trot, scarcely to be wondered at.

He followed the Clyde right to Lanark. It would have made a shorter journey to have borne off to the left, north-eastwards by Carluke; but that would have meant crossing higher broken ground of low hills, in the circumstances inadvisable. Four miles on, with the dusk settling on the land, he did leave the great river, near Carstairs, to head due north now, and up on to the moorland by a drove-road. Fortunately May nights are never very dark in Scotland, and he was able to avoid bogs and difficult patches. Passing the little White Loch, thankfully he reckoned that he had only another mile to go. Cowthally Castle was a strange choice to be the Lord Somerville's chief messuage, when they owned large lands and houses elsewhere; but it was its comparative impregnability which accounted for this, a highly defensive site, even if not obviously so at any distance – and the Somervilles in the past, and possibly still, had been apt to require safe and secure establishments.

The castle was set in the middle of a marsh, undrained deliberately, thus permitting no fewer than four wide moats of water which had to be crossed before access could be gained. There were drawbridges, which could be raised and lowered, over narrowed parts of these; also underwater flagged causeways zigzagged for those in the know. Otherwise the place was unapproachable, and even cannon kept beyond effective range; not the most comfortable of residences perhaps, but comforting in unruly days, and of a winter's night.

Fortunately John knew the whereabouts and chosen contortions of the causeways, for he had been here frequently; at night the drawbridges were all raised; and he splashed across on the weary mare. Even so, he had to ring a great hanging, clanging bell when he reached the high and parapet-crowned outer walling, with its gatehouse, and clang it again, before he gained attention from the presumably dozing guards.

"The Lord Somerville and Young Carmichael!" he shouted, when a voice demanded who came to Cowthally at this hour; and added, "And open swiftly, see you! My lord is wounded."

That did produce results. With a great clanking the iron portcullis was raised, and the creaking, massive door swung open. John rode in through the gatehouse arch, where two men, armed with sword and spear, scrutinised him in the half-dark. Recognising him, and exclaiming over the collapsed and unconscious figure he held between his arms, they preceded him into the cobbled courtyard.

He ordered them to come and support their lord while he dismounted.

That getting down of his uncle from the saddle was almost as difficult as had been the lifting of him thereto, the three of them fearful indeed that he might fall, his sprawling weight leaden. Then between them they had to part carry, part drag the body over the cobbles to the doorway of the main keep of the castle, and up the wooden steps to the entry platform, for the doorway was on the first, not the ground floor, reached across a gangway which could be withdrawn for further security. It was in place, fortunately, that night. Surely never had a Lord Somerville returned to his fastness in this fashion.

It might seem strange that they had to beat on the door timbers to gain attention and entry, the fortalice's occupants not aroused by the noises of bell-ringing, portcullis clanking and shouting; but the walls of that hold were ten feet in thickness, and the windows small and shuttered of a night. Sounds, as well as visitors, did not penetrate easily.

But the rasping of the door's steel tirling-pin did result in a servant opening to them, with consequent exclamations and cries. A maid, hand to mouth behind him and holding a lamp, was sent hurrying upstairs to inform the family.

They laid the unconscious man on a bench, shaking heads over him.

Lady Somerville came down in haste, stared, and then went to kneel beside her husband, silent.

She was much younger than her lord, who had married comparatively late. Behind her came a girl in her early teens, Margaret, the older of two daughters. The other, with her two brothers, were seemingly abed.

John began to give some account to the Lady Agnes's back, trying to explain the situation, she demanding help to remove the armoured heraldically painted breastplate her spouse wore, the servants stooping to aid her, the daughter beginning to weep.

The woman presently rose, and turned on John almost

10

fiercely. "James should have been taken to a physician," she declared, all but accused. "He is grievously hurt. You have brought him far? From near Cathcart, you say? All that way, requiring succour."

"I thought it best, Aunt. To get him home to your care."

"Hours on a horse in that condition. Many hours. Folly!"

"We could have been pursued by Moray, the victor of the battle. The queen fled. The regent's men cutting down escapers . . ."

"I must send to Lanark for our physician. None nearer. You would pass Lanark?" That was more indictment than question.

He shook his head, unhappily. "I had not thought on that. Only to get him here . . ."

She ignored him now, telling the manservant to get Dod Hutcheon and have him ride at once for Lanark. Get him out of his bed, if need be. And the same with the physician, Crawford. Have him back here. No delay. She swung on the maid, and her tearful daughter. "Fetch hot water. Clean cloths. My box of salves. Do not stand there staring. Quickly." To the guards, "See you, carry him upstairs. Heedfully. John, help them. In God's name, take care! Come!"

Agnes Hamilton, Lady Somerville, was a masterful woman, as became the daughter of the late and famous Sir James Hamilton of Finnart, who had been one of the foremost men in the land, Privy Councillor, Steward and Master of Works to King James the Fifth, builder of castles, and rich, although an illegitimate son of the Earl of Arran, one of the many such. But he had been especial. And he had been executed at the late king's command, allegedly because of concocting a plot against the royal life, but actually because the monarch, chronically impoverished, coveted the fortune he had amassed. His daughter had been much affected and distressed by this, needless to say, as well as impoverished; and her already strong character

11

hardened into imperiousness. John Carmichael was not alone in being wary of her, although she could be kind enough and good company also.

He did as he was told, and with great care and no little manoeuvring, they got his uncle up the narrow and twisting defensive turnpike stair, not only to the first floor where was the great hall and the living quarters, but on up to the next landing and the principal bedchambers. There the injured man was laid on a bed, and the men dismissed.

John, downstairs, realised how weary he was, and sore, his arms and back aching with the awkward position he had had to hold for so many difficult hours, sitting on the back of his saddle not its dipped centre, and holding up that heavy, armour-plated body for perhaps twenty-five miles, and that after the stress and trauma of the battle and flight. And he was hungry – he had not eaten since breakfast. He said so, and was brought cold meat and wine, at the great table in the hall.

Left alone, he presently fell asleep in front of the smouldering hall fire.

Some indeterminate time later he was roused by the maid, to be informed that his aunt had not wholly forgotten her hostess's duties, that the bed for him was ready up in an attic-floor room, and hot water to bathe in. The physician had not yet arrived from Lanark.

John's bathing that night was superficial, to say the least; and bedded, he fell asleep again all but immediately, his first day of warfare thankfully behind him.

He slept late next morning; indeed it was early forenoon before he was roused, with more hot water and a tankard of honey wine to aid the waking process. He washed rather more comprehensively this time, and went down to eat a solitary breakfast in the withdrawing-room off the hall. There presently he was joined by his young Somerville cousins, two girls and two boys, the latter agog to hear about the battle and the queen, and whether their father was going to die, Margaret still somewhat weepy. He sought to reassure them.

It was some time before Lady Somerville appeared, looking a little drawn, for she had been up all night, but none the less in command of the situation. She promptly dismissed the children, informed that the physician, Crawford, was still with her husband, who had been bled, and was conscious intermittently but talking no sense. She wanted full details of the battle and its consequences.

John did his best to enlighten her.

"That Moray is the devil!" she declared. The earl was an illegitimate son of the monarch who had executed her father. She was not entirely consistent in this for, to be sure, Queen Mary was also James the Fifth's offspring, although legitimate, the only such. "Our good queen? Where is she now? And what of my Hamilton kin? Have they escaped?"

"That I do not know, Aunt. Chatelherault, the duke, yes. For he was never down in the battle, watching, with the queen, from the higher ground. Argyll, the chancellor, was in command, but he fainted before the onset. He was – "

"The Campbell fainted! MacCailean Mor! Save us, is that the best Her Grace could do for commander!"

"The duke was old, and less than well. His sons, the Lords John and Claud, did well, winning on the flanks. The Lord Herries commanded the cavalry, being largely Border mosstroopers. The Earl of Eglinton the foot. But Kirkcaldy of Grange was with Moray, and he is the finest soldier in the land. He made a feint, and drew away much of the Highlandmen. Then his cavalry rode down our foot. We were outwitted, I fear . . ." His voice tailed away.

"Moray and his damnable Reformers will be crowing. Aye, and pecking like the carrion crows they are!" the Lady Agnes commented. "Grabbing decent folk's lands and moneys. And Holy Church's. I know them!" She was a good Catholic. "But the queen? She is foolish but honest.

13

Most of the land will support her still. Why did she have to wed those two scoundrels, the weak Darnley and that ruffian Bothwell? If she had wed a Hamilton now . . ." She shook her dark head. "But there is time for that, yet. If she will be well guided, for once. Now, I must return to my husband. I am against more blood-letting, as the physicians ever advise. He had, I think, lost enough blood already! You, John Carmichael, what do you intend? Will you bide here meantime? Or . . .?"

"No, Aunt. I will be off for home. My mother and father will be anxious. If they have heard of the defeat."

"Very well. My thanks for bringing my lord back – even though you did not bring the physician from Lanark! You will learn, perhaps!" She left him.

John was not long in making his departure, and on the mare he seemed to have won, not a bad beast if less well bred than his own lost mount.

He had no great distance to go, a dozen miles or so, south by west, through low hills, by the Medwyn Water to the Clyde again, with ever the majestic mass of the great Tinto Hills rising before him, going between Carnwath and Carstairs and Ravenstruther, to cross Clyde at Hyndford, and so into Carmichael parish. All these Car-names, like Carluke and Carmyle passed the day before, indicated how important this area of the upper Clyde had been to their Celtic predecessors, for the car was *caer*, meaning a fort in that language. John could not actually trace his ancestry back as far as that, but he could, directly, to a Robert de Carmichael in 1226, and he was not the first of the line allegedly. His father often chaffed his mother on that fact, that the Carmichaels were much the more ancient line than were the Somervilles, even though they had not buttered up King James the First to make them lords of parliament.

Rounding the isolated Carmichael Hill, quite lofty, however overshadowed by mighty Tinto, on a projecting spur of its southern shoulder he came to his home. Carmichael Tower was a much more typical fortalice than

Cowthally, although smaller, tall, square in the Borderland fashion, set on a green shelf of the hill, rising to four storeys and an attic, this within a wallhead parapet and walk, no moat possible on this site, but a deep dry ditch guarding the only approach. No real courtyard was feasible either, but an irregular enclosure to the rear contained stabling, storehouses and brewhouse. Its castleton, if so it could be called, consisted of a few cottages and barns on lower ground before the twisting track up. The Carmichaels, although ancient and with a stirring background, were not a rich and powerful house; and the Lord Somerville had rather thought that his sister was marrying beneath her when she wed Sir John Carmichael of that Ilk – hence the chaffing over comparatively ancient blood.

John's welcome home was warm with relief, word of the defeat and the slaughter at Langside having reached here by some of their own returning men at the castleton, but who had no information as to the fate of the young laird. Also, they knew of Queen Mary's escape and riding south, for she and her party had crossed the Douglas Water on their way, which river passed only four miles west of Carmichael, Douglas town itself ten miles. Lady Elizabeth threw her arms round her son, choking back tears over his deliverance; and Sir John gripped his shoulder convulsively, wordless. Young Archibald, his brother, and Mary still younger, were less moved, but very vocal. They said that they thought that he might have fled with the queen.

Questioning followed, needless to say. What had happened to Uncle James? Where was Queen Mary now? Who was responsible for this grievous débâcle? What of the other loyalist great ones, especially the Hamiltons? And Maxwell, Lord Herries, with his Border mosstroopers, to which grouping the Carmichael and Somerville contingents had been attached? John answered as best he could, while being plied with food and drink, acknowledging that he was very ignorant as to details, having found real warfare a confusing business indeed, and nothing

15

like what the ballads and story-tellers made of it. Looking to one's own little part in it all, one's own confrontations and assaults, aye and welfare amidst dangers, was apt to preoccupy the mind. But he had managed to cut down one enemy rider, whether slain or not he did not know.

That last pleased his small brother, at least, who too demanded details, who was he, where and how had he struck him, and with sword or lance? John was afraid that in his answers he sorely disappointed Archie.

His mother insisted that Sir John at once took her over to visit her brother at Cowthally. Thankfully, she did not urge her son to go back with them.

It was good to be home again, although repercussions from that sorry defeat would not be long in affecting their lives, even here at Carmichael, that was all but certain; the Regent Moray and the Lords of the Congregation would see to that against all who had supported the queen.

2

It took five days for the extraordinary and dire news to reach Carmichael Tower. Mary the queen had gone, had left Scotland, fled into England, to throw herself on the mercy of Elizabeth Tudor, her sister-monarch. She had ridden with her faithful supporters down to the Lord Herries's castle of Terregles, near Dumfries, and there, despite the advice and pleadings of all, she had made up her mind. Her seven tragic and desperate years of reigning had become too much for her. She would go and seek the refuge, care and aid of Elizabeth, whose heir actually she was. One day, God willing, she would come back, and with English help, resume her throne.

Unhappily her company had escorted her to Dundrennan on the Solway shore, where, after emotional farewells, she had embarked on a small boat and had been rowed across the firth for the Cumbrian coast and Carlisle, leaving her dismayed adherents to face a future grim and frightening indeed.

All but stunned by these tidings, the Carmichaels, like so many others in Scotland, faced a completely new situation, in the nation and in their personal reactions and positions. Young James Stewart was now undisputed monarch, which meant that his uncle, the Regent Moray, was as undoubtedly ruler of the land, a hard and able man who, had he been legitimately born, might well have made a strong and effective king. But in the circumstances he would be ruthless, backed by the militant Protestant lords; and all supporters of his half-sister would be endangered and assailed, nothing more sure. And without the queen as figurehead to rally to there was no least hope of keeping her royal banner flying, of maintaining her rightful claim to the crown in any practical way, especially as she was putting herself in the care of the hated English. Mary Queen of Scots, beautiful, attractive and usually courageous, was maintaining her lack of good judgment to the end.

What, then, was to be the course for her more prominent and known upholders to follow? Lying low would avail them little against the new regime. Any attempt to maintain a pro-Mary party would be treated as high treason against King James. Realities had to be faced. Co-operation with the regent, then? Many, undoubtedly, would so choose, however unpalatable. But would such co-operation be accepted? Much more was to be gained by the Lords of the Congregation in damning them, as Catholics and traitors, having parliament condemn them and forfeit their lands and wealth – which in effect would mean to the lords and chiefs, although ostensibly to the crown. Only the very powerful in manpower of the Marian supporters, such as the Hamiltons, the Campbells, the Maxwells and the Setons, would be apt to retain their properties and position, although not their influence. For the others . . .!

Sir John Carmichael was an eminently practical man, and saw that decisions must be made if he was going to save himself, his family and people from ruin and trouble. He sat down at table with his wife, elder son and Carmichael of Nemphlay, a nearby lairdly kinsman. Something must be done, and quickly, before they found themselves arraigned before either the Privy Council or parliament, and charged with rising in arms against King James, something short of going cap in hand to Moray. What?

His three hearers eyed each other, silent.

"Douglas!" Sir John said, then. "There lies possible hope for us. Always we Carmichaels have had links with the Douglases, perhaps the most powerful family in the land. Placed where we are, almost on the Douglas Water and within a few miles of Douglas-town itself, this has been inevitable. And the Douglases have now supported

Moray, not very actively but in name at least. The Black Douglases, under the Earl of Morton, Dalkeith, Lochleven and the rest, always backed the so-called Reformers. Lochleven was indeed the queen's gaoler at his castle in the loch. And the Reds, under the new Earl of Angus, Morton's nephew, Pittendreich, Whittingehame, Kilspindie and the others, have chosen to hold to Moray. Our links with them all could be used to some effect, perhaps."

"How that?" Nemphlay demanded. "What would make them favour us, act on our behalf?"

"We Somervilles have married into the Douglas line," John's mother added.

"As have we Carmichaels. And remember our Carmichael crest, the Broken Spear! That was won on the field of Bauge, in France, under Archibald Douglas, Earl of Wigtown and Lord of Galloway, fighting for the French in the Auld Alliance against the English, when our Carmichael ancestor unhorsed and slew the English commander, the Duke of Clarence, suffering only a broken spear in the process and winning the day. Thus our proud crest. That was a sufficient link with Douglas, was it not?"

"A long time ago," Nemphlay observed. "In 1421, no?"

"Perhaps. So was the barony granted to us by the first Earl of Douglas, who died at Otterburn, with Carmichael fighting for him. And *his* son married the daughter of George Douglas, Earl of Angus. He was my grandsire, three times removed. I say that it is time that the Carmichaels renewed their close links with Douglas."

"How would you do that, John?" his wife wondered.

"I shall think more on it, but I judge that I might pay a visit to Pittendreich."

"Where is that?"

"In Lothian. Near to Lasswade. None so far from Edinburgh. George Douglas of Pittendreich, kin to Lochleven, has died. He became important through marriage.

I knew him well. By that marriage his two sons succeeded to the two Douglas earldoms of Angus and Morton. I could approach his widow and younger son. The elder is dead."

"What have you to offer them?" Nemphlay enquired.

"Offer? Little enough. But I knew her, and her husband, when we were both younger." He glanced at his wife. "We both sought the same woman. He won her!"

"Ha, and this was the Douglas female you have told me of. Before you courted me! Myself only your second choice!"

"Scarcely that, my dear. I was young. *I* did the better in the end."

"But if you had won her, then would not your sons have been the Earls of Angus and Morton?"

"Not so, since I am not a Douglas. She was, to be sure, herself; but the earldoms would only pass through her to male Douglases, never to a Carmichael. No doubt why she was married to Pittendreich."

John, listening to all this, and getting lost in the details, shook his head. "I do not see what is to be gained by it."

"Links, son – links! Renew the links with Douglas. Pittendreich's widow will have much influence with her earl son. And Carmichael of that Ilk, he of the Broken Spear, who once courted her, will not go unheard, I judge. Aye, and wed to Lord Somerville's sister. If I offer her the hand of friendship."

None of his hearers was greatly impressed or convinced, but they did not actually say so – especially as they had no practical suggestions to offer for the betterment of the Carmichael position in this dangerous new situation created by the queen's defeat and flight.

They left it at that.

Two days later, Sir John, typically wasting no time, was off for Lothian.

John, for his part, had a visit to pay less distant than Pittendreich, indeed only on the far side of Tinto, at

Lamington, a mere ten miles away. It was a little journey which he was increasingly liking to make.

He chose to go over the eastern shoulder of the great hill, Tintock Tap as the locals called it, although by following the Clyde up around north-abouts, by Thankerton and Symington, he would have had a much easier ride. But he always enjoyed the challenge of Tinto, which so dominated all that area, otherwise hilly as it was, and the magnificent vistas to be seen from its heights in every direction save due eastwards, where Culter Fell rather blocked the view; fifty and more miles wherever otherwise he looked, west down Clyde past where that grievous battle had been fought, south-west to Ayrshire, south towards Dumfries-shire, whence the queen had fled, and north over the seemingly endless moors to the Pentland Hills of Lothian, where his father would be pursuing his strange quest.

Down the south-eastern side of the hill he came, in some three more miles, to the Tower of Lamington, a building very similar to that of Carmichael itself, slightly larger in that its site was more spacious for courtyard and outbuildings, if rather less defensive. There was room too for a pleasance or orchard-cum-garden; and here, in the May sunshine, he found two women tending the new growth, one of later middle years, the other young. He went no further, for it was these, or one of them, whom he had come to see.

Lady Baillie was a handsome woman, of loftier degree than was her husband, Sir William, daughter of the fourth Lord Maxwell, and former Countess of Angus, no less – although it was the death of her sickly son by Angus which had resulted in the present earl, of the Pittendreich line, gaining the title and lands. Her husband also dying, she had married Sir William Baillie, a reduction in status, and produced offspring, of which this young woman, Marion, or Mirren, was the youngest. She was less striking in looks than was her mother, but was a saucy, cheerful and attractive creature, and well thought of by John Carmichael.

He was greeted pleasantly by the ladies, and was not long in getting down on his knees beside them to help them transfer iris plants from under the apple trees to a more suitable bed with more light. Marion told him that he should be wearing gloves, as she was, and offered to go fetch him a pair; but he pooh-poohed that.

Lady Baillie was not long in asking him about that terrible battle for, being a Maxwell herself, indeed sister of the present Lord Herries, she was firmly on the queen's side, whatever the Angus alignment. Will Baillie, her son, had in fact been with the Herries company, which had escorted the fleeing Mary southwards, and had only got back to Lamington two days previously. Marion added that he had had no news of John, and they had been anxious that he had come to no harm.

They were given some account of the battle, such of it as was seen from John's point of view, and were told of the Lord Somerville's wounding, and something of the problem of getting him home, without making too much of it. They were duly concerned, and he received their commendations modestly.

Distress was declared over the queen's flight to England, and anxiety over the situation which would follow in Scotland, trouble possibly for the Baillies almost equally with the Carmichaels. John thought it best not to mention meantime his father's odd mission to Pittendreich.

Presently Lady Baillie announced that Sir William and their son Will were off visiting their secondary property of Hardington, and that she would go indoors to see that the midday meal was being suitably prepared. Nothing loth, the young people were left together.

It was pleasant just to be kneeling beside Marion there in the spring sunshine, working at the iris; but, rising to transfer the roots to their new setting, John assisted the girl up, and somehow managed to retain his hold of her in the lifting and carrying process – and was not shaken off. There was, as yet, no accepted relationship between these two, however much John was beginning to wish that there was. Marion was a year younger than he was, and he was still two years short of full age.

"Mirren," he said, "I thought of you in the battle. Just before we charged, the Somerville and Carmichael troop. A man . . . wonders. It was a strange moment. I had not done the like before. Wonders whether he will come out of it. Seeing the flash of steel in lances and swords ahead, hearing the cries and trumpet calls. I had a thought of *you*! Wondered whether I should ever see you again!"

"Did you, John! That was . . . kind. I am glad that you did. And that you escaped, thus to come to me again."

"Are you? Glad? Then so am I." He recognised that this was no very profound declaration, but he gripped her arm the more firmly. "Glad, Mirren."

He always called her Mirren rather than Marion. There was this tradition in the Lamington family that Marion Braidfoot, wife to the nation's greatest hero, William Wallace, had been born and reared here, her father then the laird; and Wallace had always called her Mirren. The name, and its diminutive, pronounced Mirn, one syllable, not the three of Marion, had continued on in the succeeding Ballie family, the more determinedly in that Baillie was but a corruption of Balliol, who had all taken the wrong side in the Wars of Independence, the Wallace and Bruce campaigns, so this ancient association was the more to be cherished.

They worked together with the plants congenially until a call from a maid announced that the meal was ready, and they repaired to the tower to partake, hand in hand.

After an excellent repast, John had the notion of suggesting that he and Mirren should go riding together up the Thriple Burn and on to Culter Fell, that eastern rival to Tintock Tap, when, unfortunately, Sir William and his son arrived back from Hardington sooner than expected. Immediately men's talk of battle and warfare, tactics and follies, the national situation, fears and apprehensions, took over; to suggest breaking it up and taking the young woman for a ride was just not to be considered. John had to swallow his disappointment and act the man of action. He liked Sir William and young Will well enough, but . . .

No more gardening was suggested either.

With ten miles and more to ride home, the visitor could not delay indefinitely, and after more food and drink, he took his reluctant departure. He had wondered whether he could risk a kiss in salutation and farewell, but sadly all the family came out into the courtyard to see him off, and he was insufficiently bold. But he managed to murmur in Mirren's ear that he would be back before long.

He returned home by the round-about Clyde route, pondering future tactics other than military.

Sir John arrived back at Carmichael two days later, and in fairly cheerful mood. He had made, he declared, quite considerable headway with the Lady Pittendreich and her grandson, Archibald, and there were positive signs that the Carmichaels could weather the present storm under the Douglas canopy, if they acted discreetly and advisedly. And the most positive indication of this was to do with John. Elizabeth Douglas and her son were prepared to consider Carmichael the Younger as husband for her daughter, Margaret Douglas!

Utterly appalled at this announcement, John was vehement in his protest. It was unthinkable, not to be contemplated. Marriage! And to someone he had not so much as met!

His mother looked at him, sympathetic; but his father frowned.

"Be not so hasty, John. This is important. For us all. We need some such link if the Carmichaels are to survive as a house, a line. Think what it means, son. You will be uncle and good-brother to the Earls of Angus and Morton! The two great Douglas chiefs. With such close alliance, none will challenge us, not even Moray himself. None would wish to offend both Black and Red Douglases! It will unite us with the greatest houses in the land. Who knows to what heights it might allow you to rise!"

"I have no desire to rise to heights at such a cost! To wed some stranger, to be tied to a woman I know naught of. Here is shame! Folly! I will not do it!"

"Watch your words, John! And to *me*! You will do as I say. Have you forgotten? You are not yet of full age, for two years. Even if you were, you would obey your father. You cannot refuse. But, see you, here is none so ill a fate. Margaret Douglas is a personable young woman. Fair. Agreeable. Well made. She limps a little, but that is nothing. You will – "

"Limps! Limps, you say? You would have me to wed a cripple!"

"Do not be a fool, boy. She is no cripple. She will make you a good wife."

"I would choose my own wife! Not be harnessed to some lame female, whom no one else will marry, I take it!"

"Quiet! Enough of this. You are of nineteen years, and you will do as I say. Your marriage is in *my* hands. I know what is best. For you, and for us all."

His father turned and left him standing. Lady Carmichael looked at her son, head ashake, and went after her husband.

3

Sir John was not one to let the grass grow under his feet. Within a week he announced that he was going to take his son to Pittendreich to visit his future bride, a week in which father and son had, not exactly avoided each other but had as little personal contact as was possible living in the same house, the subject of marriage not raised again between them. Not that John imagined that there would be any weakening of the paternal will; he knew his sire too well for that. He sought to be out of Carmichael Tower as much as was possible, those May days of 1568, and when that was not feasible, spent most of his time in his own room. He thought a lot about Mirren Baillie.

But realities had to be faced, and the morning dawned when they were to be off northwards, John dressed in his best, with two of the castleton men as escort. His mother bade them an anxious and halting farewell.

They rode over the great moors, by Carnwath, passing near Cowthally Castle but not calling in, on by Auchengray, all the southern skirts of the Pentland Hills beginning to loom on their right, by Cobbinshaw to the headwaters of the Water of Leith, Kirknewton, Currie, Colinton, and then, with Arthur's Seat rising out of the smokes of Edinburgh ahead, swung eastwards to round the Pentlands' northern escarpment to make for the North Esk valley wherein, only a few miles south of the city, was the parish of Lasswade, and the not very important estate of Pittendreich. John and his father had conversed but little on that forty-mile journey.

Approaching Pittendreich Tower, a name which he had come to dread, John could not but wonder that this fairly modest fortalice, no larger than Carmichael's, should have come to mean so much to the great line of Douglas, which had cut a wider swath in Scotland's story than any other save perhaps the royal house of Stewart, and had great castles innumerable all over the land. And it was, to be sure, a marriage which had effected this, he recognised – not that this helped him in contemplation of the marriage which was being thrust upon him. It occurred to him, not for the first time, to wonder whether, if he made himself seem quite obnoxious to the Lady Douglas and her daughter, they might reject him as unsuitable? Could he so behave?

On presenting themselves at the keep door, the two Carmichaels were ushered upstairs to the usual first-floor hall, and left to gaze at Douglas portraits decorating the arras-hung walls. There, presently, they were joined by the mistress of the house, alone, who eyed them quizzically but not unwelcomingly.

The former Countess of Angus was indeed a handsome woman, tall, bearing herself superbly, dark and carrying her years as well as she did her person. Sir John kissed her hand, but his son merely bowed, somewhat distantly.

The lady considered him in frank assessment. "So this, Sir John, is the young man who seeks to wed my daughter!" she observed.

Almost John said that he did no such thing; but found that he could not so speak. He inclined his head, instead, if less than eagerly.

"My son is aware of the honour such would bestow on him," his father answered, carefully. "He would, I think, make a good husband for the Lady Margaret. And a fair supporter for the House of Douglas. He has proved himself in battle. And single-handed brought the sorely wounded Lord Somerville, his uncle, whom you know, to his home at Cowthally, at no little risk to himself."

"I commend that, even though it is not in itself a recommendation for a worthy husband!" That was quick, but said with a smile.

27

"Perhaps not, Elizabeth. But it reveals him as courageous and loyal, concerned for others' welfare – which may have some bearing?"

"To be sure." She was still eyeing John assessingly. "Margaret is out on her horse at this moment. But she will be returning shortly, no doubt. Now, refreshment? You have ridden from Carmichael Tower? Today? How many miles? Forty? But that is no great riding for what are almost Border mosstroopers, no? You will be a good horseman?" That was addressed to John directly.

"Fair, lady," he answered, his first brief vocal contribution.

"That would be important. For Margaret," he was told. "She is a great horsewoman, always has been. Her way of . . . making up for it all! But come you into the withdrawing-room, and we shall seek revive the inner man!" She led them through to an inner and smaller chamber off the hall, where she rang a bell to summon a servant.

While waiting, the pair who had once contemplated their own marriage spoke together. John moved over to the window, aware that he was not behaving well. He was hating being used as something of a pawn, a mere useful appendage in a game of family politics.

He gazed down into the courtyard while the others chatted, and wine and oatcakes were brought for them. And as he stood there, the clatter of hooves sounded, and into view rode a young woman on a spirited horse, clearly so in that it sidled and tossed head as a groom came to hold it and to assist the rider to dismount. She slid from the saddle lithely enough, but was obviously careful as she touched down on to the cobblestones, the servant with one hand on the beast's bridle and the other holding her arm to steady her. Standing, she moved to stroke and pat her mount's tossing head, before turning and walking to the keep door, hitching up her long riding-skirts somewhat. And very evidently she limped. She had long fair hair, tied back, and was taller than the groom who led away the testy horse. John smoothed his chin, as he was called over to partake of the provender.

It took some time for the young woman to come and join them, for she had changed out of her riding habit into indoors attire, the skirt of which, although by no means short, was not overlong. And most manifestly she suffered from a club foot, as she all but hobbled in – by which time John had moved back towards the window, tankard in hand.

"Ah, my dear, here is Sir John again. And his son, also John, the Younger of Carmichael," her mother greeted her easily. "You have ridden less far today?"

"Only over to Dalhousie and Cockpen," she was answered. "Greetings, Sir John." But it was on the younger man that her eyes focused.

And they were fine eyes, large, expressive, dark, considering her hair colour, and the expression now almost urgent, enquiring, searching.

John's gaze was equally so, all but a stare. And what he saw could not but affect him. For she was eye-catching indeed, and not only for that bent, misshapen left foot; finely and delicately featured, all but beautiful, and with a notably rounded figure to go with her height, she being approximately the same height as he was. She might be a year or so older than he, and giving the impression of being all woman, not girlish, nothing like Mirren Baillie.

He took a step forward, almost involuntarily, stopped and bowed. He did not speak.

She did. "I have heard well of you, sir," she said, and her voice had a lilt to it. "Perhaps better than you have heard of me?" That was frank at least.

He cleared his throat. "I, ah, salute you, Lady Margaret," he got out and bowed again. He could think of nothing else to say.

His father sought to help bridge the uncomfortable pause. "I know George Ramsay of Dalhousie," he said. "He joined the queen's party. Has he survived the battle?"

"Yes. He won back safely. But I did not call upon them today. All this of the queen and her little son is grievous. For all. Dividing the nation. That blood should be shed over it, in the name of religion, Christ's religion and faith! It is so wrong!"

John blinked. This was unexpected, a young woman speaking her mind on a subject of such controversy, and she the aunt of Angus and Morton, firmly on the regent's side.

"I agree," he found himself saying. And then, "But I did also fight. On the queen's side. So, who am I to speak!"

"Our poor queen!"

They eyed each other.

Her mother intervened. "It has not taken you two long to reach dangerous subjects! Margaret has always had a mind of her own. It looks as though this young man has also! Perhaps, Sir John, we should leave them to their . . . indiscretions? Lest we overhear treason! Think you that we may risk leaving them together?"

The older man nodded, and followed their hostess out of the withdrawing-room.

John drew a long breath. He was being outmanoeuvred, he felt. But perhaps this young woman was also? She could well be no more eager for this match than was he.

"They know their own minds," he jerked. "Whatever may be ours!"

"Yes. Our elders always know best! I take it that you, sir, would not be here if you had your way?" Those fine eyes could have a very direct gaze.

He shrugged. "I was not . . . consulted."

"Oh, but I was. Consulted, and counselled! And given to understand that I am to be fortunate! I wonder?"

What was he to say to that? "I think that you deserve better."

"And you? To be forced to wed a woman deformed!"

So it was out. With this one, he could see that it had to come to this. He swallowed. "That, Lady Margaret, is not important." God forgive him for that

30

lie. "It is this of . . . compulsion." And he added, "For us both."

"It *is* important for me. Think you that I am not aware of the shame of it? For us both. For you to have to marry such as myself, with this foot. For me, to marry an unwilling man. Saddled with a wife to apologise for. How think you I should esteem that?"

He shook his head. "Not that – never that!"

"Do not perjure yourself, John Carmichael. See you, I have had to live with this all my life, was born thus. Think you that I do not know what it results in? I would have been wed years ago, had I been otherwise. Other than disabled. Now you are to be burdened with me. For the sake of what? Some advantage for your family, and possibly mine. You have my sympathy, sir!"

"Do not speak so," John said, almost urgently, surprised as he was to hear himself. "You are . . . well favoured. Do not decry yourself."

"It is not *myself* I decry. I have my pride, even if misplaced! It is my fate. And, it seems, yours."

They considered each other, there by the window, all but assessingly now, a strange situation. Then the young woman mustered something of a smile.

"But I am well enough on a horse! You will have to make the best of that, as I do. Come, we will rejoin our betters, lest they . . . fear for us!"

Silently, biting his lip, he followed her out into the hall.

Their elders were not there. A maid told them that her ladyship and Sir John were taking a walk by the riverside.

"Shall we follow them?" Margaret asked. "Or, think you, they would prefer to be alone? Sir John once favoured my mother, did he not? Perhaps he still does?"

"As to that, I know not. But he is, I judge, happily wed."

"Oh, to be sure. Even though his concern for your marriage is otherwise! We can join them, if you wish. I *can* walk, see you, even if I do hobble."

Uncertain how to deal with this surprising young woman, John certainly did not want to occasion her embarrassment and any distress by having her walking any distance with that bent foot. On the other hand, the prospect of standing or sitting and making difficult conversation indoors did not appeal either, even though that might be the objective of their two parents in leaving them thus.

"Would you prefer to ride?" he asked. "You like riding, you say."

"Would you? Yes, I am well enough on a horse. But you have already ridden far today."

"Not so very far. Forty miles. I could do double that."

"Ha! Of course, the Borders mosstrooper! Your horse will be tired. But I can give you another mount. Yes, let us take to horse. Go none so far, but better than standing here, or my shambling at your side! You will not be going back to Carmichael this night. And our evening meal will not be for some time yet. So, wait you just a short while for me to change back into my riding-gear. I will tell Dod Gillies to have a horse ready for you."

Presently, clad as she had been when he first saw her, John was about to assist her up into the saddle when Margaret demonstrated her agility and expertise, other than in footwork, by hoisting herself in a single lissom spring on to her mount's back, indicating strong arm muscles, adept from much practice, the young man hard put to it to rival her.

She led the way out of the courtyard and turned away from the high riverside spur on which the tower was sited to ride south by east, through level tilled land where the oats were already sprouting green, better land than Carmichael's moors and heaths. But once beyond this and on to open pasture where cattle grazed, the young woman set the pace indeed, kicking her beast into a gallop, and a fast one, and keeping it up. John was not to be left behind, of course, so that it became something of a race, scattering cattle right and left. And although that was no brief spurt but a long continuous pounding career, the man did not overtake the woman although he by no means politely held himself and his mount back. Possibly she was proving something, but if so her back view gave no impression of stressful determination. She rode superbly, in fact.

When eventually she slowed to a canter, they were amongst rolling country with scattered woodland, not really hilly as John knew hills, but with slopes and hollows. "You know this country?" Margaret asked, and when he shook his head, pointed. "Yonder is Upper Dalhousie. You will know the Ramsays, at least. And beyond is Aitkendean. We can go that far."

"You ride well," he told her. "I do not think that I have ever seen a woman ride so well as you do."

"Our sex may not be so well suited for the saddle as you men are," she returned. "Somewhat top-heavy, shall we say? But I have been a-horse since small childhood. I have had to be, you understand. Had I been born a man, and born thus, who knows what I might have achieved? At tournaments. Even in battle. There is my Douglas blood speaking!"

"Better as you are!" That was the least that he could say.

They rode on, at a trot now, by places Margaret named as Whitehill Aisle, Carrington and Parduvine; but after an hour or so had to head back for Pittendreich, with the evening mealtime approaching. They had another gallop, on which, whether deliberately or not, the young woman allowed John to ride more or less alongside. It was a fine mount which she had found for him, even better than the one he had lost at Langside battle; the Douglases would not stint themselves on horseflesh, to be sure. Returning by Capielaw, Gorton and past Hawthornden Castle, they came to the North Esk again, and down its twisting course to the tower-house, well pleased with their ride, sufficiently so for John to leap down swiftly to the courtyard cobbles to be able to assist his companion down from the saddle, without making too much of it, for clearly that club foot would make dismounting more difficult than mounting, however strong her arm muscles. It was the first time that he had actually touched her. She did not thrust away from him.

Lady Douglas commented on her daughter's odd method of entertaining their guest, while Sir John searched his son's face keenly. The couple could not but be aware that their behaviour was under scrutiny, inhibiting as this was. Dinner was about to be served, they were told; and Margaret went to change clothing again, and John to wash.

Over the meal which followed, the present tense situation in Scotland was discussed, the Regent Moray's probable attitudes and policies assessed, and whether and when Queen Mary was likely to return to try to regain her throne.

The evening was passed in the withdrawing-room, the atmosphere less than entirely easeful, although Margaret helped by rendering songs and ballads, accompanying herself on harpsichord and lute; she proved to have a fine singing voice, which John might have guessed at when he noted the lilt in her speech. But she retired early. John was glad when he and his father could do the same.

In the morning, their departure was not unduly delayed. Seeing the two men off, something of tension was evident, at least in the younger couple. Margaret eyed John all but searchingly, unspeaking. He shook his head, very much at a loss for words himself; then, on an impulse, reached to take her hand and raise it to his lips briefly, just why he could scarcely have explained to himself. He bowed stiffly to the Lady Douglas, and turned away to his horse.

His father behaved more normally, but shook his head also, this over his son. They mounted and rode off, the two women watching but not waving.

"So, son, you have seen your bride-to-be," Sir John said, as they left Pittendreich Tower's vicinity. "How think you of her?"

John was in no hurry to answer. "She is a notable woman," he admitted, at length. "And, I think, deserves better than her fate!" And he then reined back his mount a little, to make it clear that he did not wish to pursue the subject in conversation. He spoke instead to their two escorts, asking them if they had fared well in the retainers' hall.

His father had more to say however, presently, for John's benefit. "The Lady Douglas and I have discussed her daughter's dowery," he told him. "Pittendreich has no great lands, however much her grandsons, Angus and Morton, may have. But her daughter will bring with her as her portion three tenements in Edinburgh town, one in Liberton's Wynd, one in the Over Bow and one in the Nether. Also the lands of Wrae in Linlithgowshire, and those of Longhermiston and the Mill of Currie in Lothian. This is no rich heritage, but the tenements will bring in useful rents. And the farms and mill may prove of some value, if they are well placed. We shall go and inspect them, in due course. But, to be sure, the main advantage in this match is not its dowery, but the resultant Carmichael link with the Houses of Douglas. Who knows what that may lead to!"

The recipient-to-be of all this benefit expressed no elation.

Father and son had never been markedly close, but seldom as distant as this, as they rode southwards. His riding yesterday had been a deal more pleasurable, John realised. He did not ask for when the wedding was planned. He did ask as to where was the young Earl of Angus, Lady Douglas's grandson and therefore Margaret's nephew, whom they had not seen, to be told that he was presently with his uncle, Morton the chancellor, at Edinburgh, for a visit.

It seemed a long forty miles to Carmichael.

4

The news which reached Carmichael that May and June certainly emphasised the need for Queen Mary's more active supporters to take any precautions they could for their safety. For the regent and the Lords of the Congregation, if not parliament itself, and all in the infant's king's name, were wreaking vengeance on the losing side at that dire battle, or at least all who did not have private armies at their disposal, such as Argyll, Huntly and the Duke of Chatelherault and his Hamiltons. A parliament was being called for August, this requiring forty days' notice, to enact the forfeiture of lands and estates, these much sought after by greedy lords, and requiring parliamentary authority. But meantime arrests and imprisonment proceeded apace, the regent and his supporters ruthless indeed; and becoming one of the most prominent of these was James Douglas, Earl of Morton, the chancellor, who had clearly seen where his best interest lay and appeared to be intent on promoting himself as Moray's principal lieutenant. He had indeed led the van successfully at Langside, but hitherto had not taken any major part in the rule of the realm.

At any rate, Sir John Carmichael was anxious that the Douglas connection should be firmly forged as soon as possible, certainly before the August parliament, when the forfeitures and charges of treason would be promulgated. His elder son was ordered to prepare himself for an early marriage.

John had no option but to come to terms with this, since he could by no means change the situation. He brooded long over it, but, short of absenting himself, bolting to goodness knew where, he saw no way out of it all. He took it that the Lady Margaret was in a like case.

He had to go and inform Mirren and the Baillies, to be sure. Not that there was anything formal in the young people's relationship, not even any understanding that one day they might wed. But their friendship was years old, and the assumption was that they would very likely come together. How would Mirren take his announcement? Would she and her parents scorn him as a weakling? John dreaded this visit. He and Mirren could, he supposed, run off together, secretly, get wed by some accommodating priest, and so forestall the Douglas match. But he knew very well, being Catholics, that his father would manage to have the marriage annulled – and where would that leave Mirren? A shamed and soiled young woman. That was not to be considered.

He could not put off the unhappy encounter indefinitely, with now less than forty days to the parliament; so one morning, without announcing his intention to his parents, he took to horse, as indeed he was doing more and more those days, to be alone with his thoughts. This time he did not ride over Tintock Tap, glorious views scarcely at the forefront of his mind.

On the way, by Clyde, he debated how best this ordeal was to be got over. Should he seek to see Mirren alone and break it to her gently, get the emotional aspect of it over in private, as it were? And inform her family in more impersonal fashion? Or would it be better to try to keep it all on the latter level, let the girl learn of it in company, and so get her over that first shock? This before they had any private talk. He conjectured that, on the whole, the latter would be the least upsetting. Although, of course, he might be misjudging the entire situation. Mirren might not have so much as contemplated marriage to him, their friendship a pleasant dalliance on her part, no more. She was, after all, very young, eighteen years, and possibly young for her age, especially as compared with Margaret Douglas. And, for that matter her parents might well have other plans for her eventual marriage, as had his for himself.

In the event, John's deliberations proved to be abortive, for when he arrived at Lamington it was to find the Baillie family in a state of some concern and doubts, congregated in the castle's withdrawing-room with Lady Baillie's nephew, William, Master of Herries, son of the Lord Herries, who had just arrived with the news. His father, who was Warden of the West March, and had taken the lead in effecting the queen's escape, was mustering his fullest strength in the great and wild territory of Dumfries-shire and Galloway, Nithsdale, Annandale, Eskdale, Liddesdale, Ewesdale and the rest of the Debateable Land, his own Maxwell and Herries folk, but also the fierce mosstrooping clans of Armstrong, Johnstone, Elliot, Wauchope and the others, some of the wildest and toughest characters in the land. This to create a barrier of Borderers to confound the regent and prevent him from making a raid over to Carlisle, where Queen Mary was still being held by the English West March Warden, while word was being sent to Queen Elizabeth in London to enquire her wishes, Moray eager to capture his half-sister even from English soil. The Master of Herries had come to urge Sir William Baillie to add his strength to this muster, together with any others from these parts who were for Mary; and when he saw John, that pressing included Carmichael and Somerville. He also announced that the arrest and detention of the queen's supporters had commenced with the Masters of Cassillis and Eglinton, the Sheriffs of Ayr and Linlithgow, and many other prominent folk, all being confined in Edinburgh Castle until the parliament voiced their fate. So dissenting measures must be taken, and this of the West March muster-in-arms a useful step in that direction.

Listening, John perceived that this was scarcely the moment to announce his marital problems. Also, he recognised that his father would be highly unlikely to agree to add Carmichael strength to this Borders call to arms, having so clearly and definitely thrown in his lot with the Douglases. He remained more or less silent. The Baillies did not seem altogether enthusiastic either over the Herries appeal.

The talk went on; and during it, it came to John that here might be an opportunity for him to inform of his personal difficulties, as it were sidelong, while using the national situation as relevant. He waited until there was a lull in the talk, with a meal being mentioned as almost due, and made his contribution.

"This of the queen's cause, we must see that there is more than one aspect to it," he said carefully. "Clearly it will be long before Her Grace is in any position to make any real attempt to regain her throne. How are those who support her best able to aid her? This of Lord Herries's muster may well be wise, for some, for the West March clans. But for others less well protected perhaps not so. Moray and his lords have long arms and a harsh grip – as we have just heard."

There were murmurs and some nods at that.

John was by no means used to making speeches, but felt that here was something which had to be said, and the chance to say it in a fashion less awkward than might have been.

"My father believes that the queen's people, or most of them, would be best to lie low, meantime, hold their fire. Not rouse the regent and his followers. Avoid offence, if possible. Even seem to accept the present rule. Possibly act as well disposed on occasion. The better to be able to help Her Grace when she does move. Better that than being imprisoned and forfeited – better for the queen's cause. Indeed, he is having *me* to marry into the Douglas family, the aunt and sister of the Earls of Angus and Morton, who support the regent. It is not my choice, but . . ." He left the rest unsaid. And avoided Mirren's eye.

The stir amongst his hearers had its own eloquence.

"You mean . . . the Lady Margaret!" Lady Baillie

demanded. "She with . . .!" That also was left unfin-ished.

Her nephew had different priorities. "Armed risings, all over the land, would keep Moray and his crew the less aggressive," he said. "Argyll and his Campbells, Huntly and his Gordons. The northern clans. The Ogilvys from Strathmore and the Mearns. The queen has great support all over. Only a small part of it was at Langside. We could show Moray that her cause is still strong. And hasten her return."

"Yet there is much in what John says," Sir William observed. "It may be well enough for Argyll, Huntly and the others, far off. And with great numbers of men. But for those within easier reach of Moray it is different. They would not serve the queen well in prison, or banished. Lying low may be wise. And ready to rise when the call comes."

His son, Will, thought otherwise. "But the call has come. My Lord Herries sounds it. A great rising on the border could set the land alight, give a lead to the Highlanders and others. And bring the queen back from Carlisle, instead of her going to Elizabeth Tudor."

"She is held there, boy, as good as a prisoner! By the English warden."

John risked a glance at Mirren. She was eyeing him, nibbling her lip. But looking questioning rather than appalled.

Her mother was questioning also, and aloud. "This of your Douglas marriage, John? Is it agreed? Final? Not just . . . mooted?"

"I fear so. We were at Pittendreich the other day. All is accepted, it seems. *My* voice unheeded!"

She considered him keenly. "You would have had it otherwise? To be sure she bears the devil's mark, that one!" It was an ancient tradition in Scotland that a club foot was Satan's curse on any sufferer.

John somehow could not let that pass for the sake of the young woman concerned. "She is no more eager than am I. But she is not . . . displeasing in her looks, nor her manner. And she is a notable horsewoman." He glanced over at Mirren again.

"What does Morton say to this?" Sir William asked. "The young Angus is no matter, as yet. But Morton is chancellor. And something of a scoundrel, I judge. He may have other notions."

"I do not know, sir. But presumably he knows of it. The Lady Douglas, his mother, and hers, appeared to be in no doubts."

"Morton may be content to get rid of an awkward sister, thus."

Again John was about to say something in defence of the unfortunate Margaret, but thought better of it.

A servitor came from the kitchen in some agitation about the readiness of the meal, and his mistress announced a move by all into the hall.

John found himself sitting beside Mirren, with her brother on his other side. Now for the testing time, although thus, at table, and with others so close, the girl's reactions and comments would have to be restrained almost certainly.

Without delay she spoke, if low-voiced. "Are you unhappy, John?" she asked.

"I am, yes. This is none of my doing, Mirren. But . . . I have no choice, it seems."

"No. To be under full age is hard on a man. I understand. On a woman, not only then. We can be forced to wed where our parents will. As is this Margaret Douglas, you say? It could be difficult, ill, for you. But perhaps not. It could be none so grievous."

He glanced at her sidelong. Was she being kind? Or indirectly bitter? She did not look nor sound bitter.

"I wonder who I will have to marry, one day!" she went on. "I hope that I can *like* him." She squeezed his arm, below the table. "A man like you, John!"

That left his mind in something of a whirl. This less than distressed acceptance of the situation, when he had

41

feared otherwise. She sounded a little concerned, but for him, rather than for herself. Sympathetic, rather than hurt or greatly grieved. A friend's commiseration, not a lover's pain. Had he been making overmuch of their friendship, then?

"You are kind," he got out.

"We can still be friends, John?"

He took his goose leg up to bite at it before answering that. "Friends, yes. To be sure. I will not let my father say with whom I may be friendly, or whom not! Marriage is one thing, friendship another."

"Good!"

Her brother Will, on his other side, must have heard some of this if not all. Now he added voice. "You will be much constrained, John, wed to Morton's sister? He is chancellor of the realm. Working close with the regent. It means that you will no longer be able to support the queen."

"As to that, I know not. Not openly, I fear. But, at heart . . ."

"Your father will not be aiding Herries in this matter, then?"

"I think not."

"He chooses the safer course! And the Lord Somerville? Your uncle?"

"He is sore wounded. As to his people, who knows?"

The other turned away, his disapproval undisguised, to speak to the Master of Herries at his other side.

Mirren took a different view. "At least you will not be endangered in more fighting, John," she said. "I am glad of that."

John had not thought that his Lamington visit would turn out this way. He was relieved, upset – or even slightly piqued?

The meal progressed, with Mirren chatting companionably, even asking whether she would be invited to the wedding, wondering whether the Lady Margaret was indeed entitled to be called lady when she was not an earl's daughter, even though her brother and nephew were earls. John admitted that he did not really know, although she appeared to be called that by all. He was told, with a giggle, that one day his bride would be styled Lady Carmichael of Carmichael!

The repast over, and young Herries departing for the Peebles area to seek support for his father's efforts there, John also took his leave, amidst varying sorts of farewell, Mirren presenting him with her cheek to kiss, and urgings to come back soon, her parents and brother less urgent.

He rode for home with feelings very mixed.

5

It was nearing the end of June when, one day, a messenger arrived from Pittendreich with a letter from the Lady Douglas. This informed that her son, the Earl of Morton, would be interested to meet Young Carmichael, and suggested that he and his father call upon the chancellor at his castle of Dalkeith, near Edinburgh and none so far from Pittendreich. And this before overlong. They might call in at the latter house on their way home.

This Sir John took to be very much in the nature of an authoritative summons. Almost certainly Morton wished to inspect the proposed bridegroom for his sister before agreeing to the marriage; and with not much more than a month until the so-significant parliament, over which Morton would preside as chancellor, was not to be disregarded or delayed. They would go in a day or two; and John would be very much on his best behaviour, he was instructed.

The younger man wondered whether this would be his opportunity to have the match cancelled, by deliberately displeasing the earl.

It was the same ride northwards which they had made before, Dalkeith being only six miles or so south of Edinburgh, a fair-sized town of some antiquity, with its nearby castle long the seat of a senior branch of the Black Douglases, Lasswade an adjoining parish on the North Esk, wherein lay Pittendreich. His father had sent to inform Lady Douglas that they would be going this day, and would she tell her son? John wondered whether she and her daughter might choose to come over for the occasion. He was not looking forward to the interview.

In the event it was all none so difficult. They found Dalkeith castle, large and strongly sited by the riverside, the Esk providing three different moats to guard it, and no lack of men-at-arms to pass before gaining access to the main keep. It was all fully four times the size of Pittendreich where Morton had been reared – or for that matter, Carmichael. As father and son waited in the inner courtyard for their arrival to be announced, a boy appeared from a side gateway, fishing-rod over his shoulder and three trout on a string, a pleasant-looking lad approaching his teens, who demonstrated his angling skills, first to two of the men-at-arms waiting with the visitors, and then to the Carmichaels, clearly proud of his catch from the Esk. When Sir John, admiring the fish, introduced himself as Carmichael of that Ilk and his son, the boy added that he was Archie Douglas and, almost as an afterthought, Earl of Angus. He declared that he had been lucky this day, for this stretch of the river at Dalkeith was not so good as at Pittendreich where he usually lived, this because it lay downstream of the town and the night-spoil therefrom was all thrown into the Esk, somehow spoiling it for the fish. This declared, he led the new arrivals into the great keep, not waiting for the chamberlain thereof to come and usher them into the earl's presence.

Thus informally admitted, with the boy earl handing over his catch to the door porter and saying that he wanted the fish cooked for him for the evening meal, he led the guests up the twisting turnpike stair, whereon they met the castle chamberlain coming down, who announced that his lordship of Morton would be pleased to receive the visitors in the private hall, young Angus informing of his success at the river.

They had to mount two flights of that stair, for the great hall was on the first floor but the private one directly above. Here they were presented to a severe-looking lady of middle years, unsmiling despite the boy's proud account of his prowess with the trout. This was the Countess of Morton, daughter of the previous earl, whose marriage of some twenty-five years before had undoubtedly been an arranged one, and had produced no children. Yet it was in her right that Morton sat in Dalkeith Castle.

She was scarcely gracious towards the visitors, but she did ask after Lord Somerville, to whom she was distantly related.

Waiting, John talked of angling with young Angus, saying that he often fished in the Clyde, as well as the lesser Medwyn Water, and asking whether salmon was ever caught in the North Esk. The boy was clearly an enthusiast, and admitted that he had never managed to catch a salmon, asking how difficult it was to land one. He had heard that these large fish had to be played with care and cunning once hooked, to tire them out, sometimes for long. Was that true? John agreed that it was, and they got into an animated discussion on the subject, the young earl wondering whether the visitor would one day take him salmon fishing on the Clyde, for he did not think that there were any to be found in this Esk. John expressed himself as entirely ready so to do, if Lord and Lady Morton approved.

It was at this stage, with Sir John making difficult conversation with the countess, that her husband appeared. He was a strange figure to represent the great Black Douglas line, in his early fifties, short and burly, with reddish hair and beard and blunt features, anything but impressive as to stature and presence but with shrewd yet twinkling eyes under bushy brows, and with a ready grin. His arrival was greeted volubly by young Angus with the announcement that this kind man — the boy had obviously not picked up John's name and style — caught salmon in the River Clyde and would take him there and show him how to do it. When could he go?

Sir John began to make not exactly apologies but modifying remarks, interrupted by Morton's guffaw.

"Never heed!" he declared. "So this is the young man who would become my good-brother, hey? A fisher for

46

mair than a wife!" He hooted with a form of mirth. "Archie seems to approve o' him!"

"I regret it if my son has overstepped in this, my lord," Sir John said urgently. "His young lordship had brought trout he had caught . . ."

"Aye, he is the great one for the fishing is Archie. I am a right disappoint to him that I havena the time to be at it wi' him." Morton spoke with a broad accent, and with no attempt at polite address towards his guests, ignoring his wife completely. He seemed to John to be an extraordinary son to have been produced by the handsome and cultured Lady Douglas of Pittendreich, and she looking scarcely old enough to be his mother.

"With all your lordship's many duties in the realm, that is not something to be wondered at."

"Aye. And I'll be off to thae same duties in Edinburgh shortly." That was clear indication that they were not to stay long. But Morton was eyeing John keenly, sizing him up most obviously. That young man did not seek to bow nor scrape for, after all, if the earl did not favour what he saw, this awkward marriage might be avoided. But he found that he could scarcely behave deliberately badly. He inclined his head and said nothing.

In fact, any speech would have interrupted the other earl present, for the boy launched into a description of how his line had got entangled in an overhanging willow branch at the riverside, with his trout hooked, and how difficult it had been to free the line without losing the fish, his aunt, frowning, telling him to be quiet, Morton grinning but not echoing his wife.

It all made a curious encounter.

When the boy, frowning now also, stopped speaking, Morton pointed a thick finger at John. "You were at yon Langside, I heard – and on the wrang side, laddie! Forby, I didna see you!"

"I was with Lord Somerville's troop, my lord. We were fighting for what we believed was the right." It was John's father's turn to frown. But what else was he to say?

"Aye. Somerville was wounded and you carried him off, they say." Morton was clearly well informed. "If he was wounded, at least he fought better than some! Like yon Argyll, who fell faint, I heard!" Another hoot. "You were ill led, boy, and on the wrang side. But, och, you'll learn! Yon was a right shambles!"

John did not reply.

"So now – what? Your cause lost, you look in the other airt? To *my* side, heh? Canny for your prospects! You see Douglas as a right useful shield?"

"My lord," Sir John intervened. "Carmichael has had long association with Douglas. From the Broken Spear fight, and onwards."

"Aye, maybe. But no' sufficiently so to fight on their side at Langside!" But it was at the son that he looked, not the father.

John had to say something. "We had always supported the Queen's Grace, my lord. As did Douglas – once!"

He heard his father's quick indrawn breath.

"Ha! So barks the pup! That was before Lochleven, laddie. The abdication. Mary Stewart wasna guid for this realm. I did what I could to rid her o' some o' her mistakes, mind!" He chuckled. Morton had had a hand in the deaths of both David Rizzio, the queen's Italian secretary of whom she was over-fond, and of Henry, Lord Darnley, her second husband. "But she wouldna learn, and wed yon Bothwell. Scotland needed better rule than that, eh?"

John glanced over at his father, who shook his head warningly. He said nothing.

"So, Young Carmichael, how see you your part now, with Mary Stewart gone and, I would jalouse, no' coming back? Unless fetched! Are you a fighter? Or a seeker o' shelter!"

This was direct questioning indeed, challenge, in the circumstances.

"I will, I think, fight for what I believe is right, my lord. Always."

"Aye, but whose right?"

"In the end, sir, the nation's." Was that pretentious or trite-sounding? Yet he meant it.

The earl was considering him closely from under those bushy brows. "You speak plain, at least," he said. "Maybe you'll learn, with teaching! But who's to teach you?" And he looked less than flatteringly at Sir John.

"I do my best, my lord," that man said.

"You didna guide him aright at Langside, Sir John, even if you werena there yourself! Maybe we'll hae to see what *I* can do!"

It was John's turn to draw quick breath. That sounded almost as though he was going to be accepted, thus swiftly, for good or ill. Morton was evidently a man who made up his mind without delay. Was his fate sealed, then?

Young Angus had been fidgeting during all this exchange, but now spoke in that significant pause.

"Uncle James, the salmon!" he demanded. "When can I go and fish for salmon? In the Clyde river. With, with this . . ." He grabbed John's arm.

"Och, we'll see, Archie. Soon, maybe. Is he auld enough to hae a go at the salmon, Carmichael? I am no hand at the fishing. I've heard they're no' easy to land."

"I could win a small one, perhaps," the boy said.

"No harm in the trying," John answered. "Patience required."

"Aye. Archie could dae wi' a lesson in patience! We'll see . . ."

"Soon!"

With a sniff the countess turned and left the room, disapproval personified. Sir John looked after her somewhat anxiously, but not her husband or the boy.

"There's patience for you! If the salmon will teach him it, you'll no' be wasting your time! Time, aye – it's ay time for something! Time I was off to Edinburgh. A meeting wi' Mar and some o' his Kirk familiars! Great ones for the talk! Aye, then, Archie will show you out." Their dismissal was entirely evident. And a last word, to John. "He seems to favour you, laddie. You teach him patience, just." And he turned and left them.

Father and son eyed each other, expressions at variance. No hospitality was being offered here.

The young earl was single-minded, whatever else. "How many salmon have you caught?" he wondered.

"Oh, I do not know. Many, my lord. Over the years."

"Were you older than I am, when you caught your first, sir? I am twelve years."

"I think so, yes. I do not remember. A little older, probably."

"I am quite strong, see you," they were assured as the boy led them out, the chamberlain waiting for them at the first-floor landing.

Their horses brought to them in the inner courtyard, young Angus did not let them go without evidencing further his Douglas prerogative.

"I will come to your river, sir," he declared. "Will I bring my own rod? Or is it not strong enough for salmon?"

"We have rods enough at Carmichael," Sir John said. "If you do come, my lord."

"I will. And soon." But it was at John that he looked. "What is your name?"

"He is John Carmichael, Younger of that Ilk," the older man informed.

"Just call me John," the boy was told.

"Yes, John. And I am Archie."

They mounted and rode off, to waving.

Once safely over the drawbridges, Sir John shook his head. "I would scarcely have believed it," he said. "So easy! All of it. And for much of it, I judge, we have to thank that child!"

"Is it a matter of thanks? But I like the lad."

"And he likes you. You should indeed give thanks. For this day's good fortune. Morton clearly accepted you, whether because of the young earl, or otherwise. He is a strange man, uncouth. But very powerful. With him behind you, matters will be much better.

For us all. I acted wisely – you must see that now, John."

"For whom?" Was that unfilial reaction?

It did not take them long to ride up Esk, by Lugton and Melville to Pittendreich. There they found Lady Douglas awaiting them and, as before, the Lady Margaret absent, away riding again, her favoured pastime obviously. Their hostess promptly offered them the interim hospitality which they had not received at Dalkeith, with a full meal promised in due course, when Margaret returned. They would stay the night, to be sure.

She was interested to hear of what had transpired with her son, and clearly pleased with Sir John's account, conceding that Morton had his own odd mannerisms, always had, very different from his late brother David, but a man to be reckoned with and far-seeing, shrewd. Her reaction to the account of her grandson's part in it all was amusedly understanding. She said that young Archibald would make a good Red Douglas one day and, she thought, a useful friend. She glanced at the fairly silent younger man frequently, as she and Sir John chatted, but she did not actually question him on his feelings in the matter.

The clatter of hooves presently took John to the window again, tankard in hand, to see Margaret dismounting. This time she had a deerhound with her. She would see the Carmichael horses tethered there. Lady Douglas gave orders for the repast to be made ready.

Margaret was in no hurry to show herself thereafter, but she was more handsomely dressed on this occasion, and when not actually walking presented quite a striking figure. Her glance went to John immediately, a mixture of question, misgiving and a sort of defiance, although she went to greet his father first.

"Our friends have had an agreeable meeting with your brother James, my dear," her mother informed right away. "No difficulties there, it seems. And young Archie making his presence felt, but favourably."

"Ah. That will smooth your road somewhat," the young woman said carefully. Was there just a hint of emphasis on that word *your*?

John inclined his head towards her, in some fellow feeling.

Lady Douglas looked from one to the other and then to Sir John, with her own hint of exasperation. "And a good road," she said. "Now, Sir John and his son will be ready to dine. Apparently they ate nothing at Dalkeith. Your good-sister of Morton is scarcely the eager hostess, I think!"

"We female Douglases can have our failings perhaps, Mama!"

John got the impression that this proposed match, although advanced on one front, was less so on another. And somehow this seemed to place some onus on himself to improve matters. As the four sat down at table, he asked Margaret if she had had a good ride, and where she had ridden. Also he had noted the deerhound; did she find that horse and hound paired well together? It could be otherwise, he had found.

The other replied briefly; and when he persisted, with an account of her nephew's concern with angling and his eagerness to catch a salmon, she became more forthcoming, even animated. Clearly she was fond of young Angus. Thereafter the evening became much less difficult, indeed quite enjoyable, especially when Margaret again entertained them with her music. More than once John found himself not exactly comparing this young woman with Mirren Baillie, but noting how they differed, and not only in a kind of maturity.

When Margaret eventually announced that she would seek her couch, John deemed it fit to rise and go to open the door for her. "Sleep well," he told her.

"You are . . . solicitous!" she said. And added, in something of a rush, "Do not think to aid me upstairs. I am quite able to climb them, despite my unfortunate handicap!"

He shook his head as she turned away and left him.

John lay long before he slept that night, wondering what life held in store for him, how much of difficulty and unease, even though perhaps better prospects in less personal affairs.

In the morning, over breakfast, Margaret was kinder without being effusive; and the men were seen off for home with Lady Douglas declaring significantly that she would be in touch before long, her daughter eyeing John with one raised eyebrow.

Sir John at least rode off southwards well pleased.

6

The Douglas connection was emphasised and reinforced only a week later, and surprisingly, with the arrival at Carmichael of two of the name, with an escort of two more, these at least in the Douglas colours – Archibald, Earl of Angus in the care of Lady Margaret, come fishing. Much excitement was engendered by this visit, Lady Carmichael all in a flutter, Sir John cheered, and the two younger members of the family, another Archibald and Mary, duly impressed, with John somewhat astonished at the young woman's presence, however urgently she pointed out that she had come only at her mother's and brother's command. Not that her assertions were of much avail in the chatter of her nephew, exclaiming over the sport and excitement they were going to have in the catching of salmon, John having to try to tone him down somewhat with warnings that the fish were by no means plentiful and easy to hook on a line, and that netting was apt to be a much more profitable enterprise. This was greeted with scorn by the young earl, who was to be an angler, not a fisherman. When could they start?

It was late afternoon, and the visitors had had that forty-mile ride, so enthusiasm had to yield to practicalities. The morrow would come soon enough. Meantime they could examine the rods available, inspect the artificial flies and choose which river they were to try. The boy declared for the Clyde straight away, the largest in south-west Scotland, and therefore where the best big fish would be apt to be; but John pointed out that the Douglas Water was also famed for its salmon, was equally close to Carmichael, and would it not be suitable for a Douglas to catch his first salmon in the Douglas Water?

That was accepted.

In the evening much time was spent over the choosing of rods and lines but especially the flies, artificial flies, this something new for the boy, who had always used bait on his hooks – new to Margaret also, who was interested, having apparently done quite a lot of angling, but only in the North Esk where salmon were not normally to be found. John had no great collection of flies, but showed them what he had, young Angus fascinated, especially when told that even the ancient Romans had used artificial flies. They were made of silk and feathers and occasional fur, quite large for salmon, less so for trout and sea trout, with a hook at the head. Margaret was particularly interested in the making of these, examining the specimens closely and saying that she could make such, and asking which kind of feather was best.

John explained the difference between wet and dry fly-fishing, for salmon the dry fly best, in other words the fly to remain on or just above the surface to lure the fish up to snap at it, this because the mature salmon returned to their original native rivers to spawn, after two years at sea, and did not feed much during this spawning period but tended to be aggressive towards flies and insects. The wet fly, designed to sink into the water, and under, was usually better for trout, more like bait.

The three of them, poring over the flies and comparing them, begot a pleasant companionship and enthusiasm.

The rods produced were less interesting, from simple flexible and thin tree boughs of up to six or seven feet, to sectional wands which fitted together, up to ten or eleven feet, these last for salmon. The lines were of fine, twisted horse-hair, tied to the head of the rod. Also, for salmon there was a wooden spool used, to be held at the angler's thumb, to make possible the winding-in process of line in the constant casting.

Nothing would do for Archie but that they must

forthwith go and practise this casting and winding; so out into the courtyard the three of them went, for John to demonstrate the art of it, the cast, the swing, the surface skimming and hovering, and the reeling-in without the line getting into a tangle. The other two young Carmichaels came to watch, although they could have been done without.

The boy was much too vigorous and impatient with it all at first, and had to be calmed down and his arms and wrists controlled and directed; Margaret's also turned out to require some physical guidance, which the instructor found not unpleasant, necessitating a certain amount of delicate encircling of a rounded female figure. Laughter from the other Archie and Mary had to be ignored.

John said that out on the river normal breezes would actually assist the process, these not available in the sheltered courtyard.

It all made for a stimulating evening.

Margaret was first to retire, Lady Carmichael conducting her to her room, young Angus more reluctant to bed down. John advised him to pray for fair weather and a slight breeze, the boy however asserting that even if it poured with rain they would go fishing.

Happily the morning dawned fine and clear, although with rather more gusty wind than required, which might complicate the casting. With Archie acting very much the earl, there was no delay about setting off for the Douglas Water, with a bag of scones and oatcakes to satisfy the inner man. John was glad to see that the young woman had not lost her interest in the venture, and was not to be left behind. He, however, discouraged his brother and sister from accompanying them, as sure to be a distraction.

Rods carefully held up like lances, they rode due westwards between Carmichael and Whitecastle Hills to the Carmichael Burn, which, after four miles or so led them down to the Clyde at one of its major bends, almost U-shaped indeed and called the Crook of Sandilands, where the Douglas Water came in. Archie had never been here, and was intrigued to view a river bearing his own name, although Margaret pointed out to him that it was really the other way round, and that he, and she, bore the river's name, that it had been called the *dubh glas*, or dark grey-green stream, long before there was any family there called Douglas. That spurred on the boy to ask where John's name came from, to be told that there had been a Celtic Church cell or chapel dedicated to St Michael, and *caer* meant fort; so there must have been a Pictish stronghold nearby, indeed there were green ramparts to be seen on Carmichael Hill.

The Douglas Water proved to be quite a major river and no mere stream as Archie had obviously been fearing. Margaret, who seemed to know her topography, said that it was twenty miles long, rising on the side of the great hill of Cairntable, on the borders of Ayrshire and Dumfries-shire.

Her nephew was only moderately interested in this, now being all agog to find pools where salmon might lurk, and pointing to this stretch and that as possible. John told him that good as these reaches might be, their banks were too much overhung by trees – alder, birch and willow – and this could greatly hamper casting. They would move on upstream to clearer stretches of which he knew.

John was also concerned for Margaret's footwork along the banks, which tended to be broken and often steep, difficult enough for even the agile and sure of stance but trying indeed for the lame, especially when the playing of a catch meant quite complicated movement on the part of the angler to counteract the fish's dartings and runs. He did not actually announce this, but kept it in mind.

They rode on for fully a mile up the twisting course of the river until they reached a fairly straight and open stretch which was reasonably devoid of trees and bushes close to the banks. In fact, pools were more readily found within the bends and loops than on straight lengths, where the current flowed more directly and smoothly; but for novices, the latter probably were best for the handling of rods and lines. He was not anticipating any notable catches, but did not say so.

Dismounting, they tethered the horses to a group of hawthorn trees and made for the river, rods over shoulders, Archie hurrying on ahead and Margaret waving John after him, over-conscious of her disability as to walking, he shaking his head. At the bank the boy was complaining that here seemed to be no pools; but was told that there could be depths and hollows below the surface where the water's currents made surges, and fish could lurk; but this was the best place for them learning to cast with dry fly.

So, finding a fairly level bank and placing his pupils well apart, the young woman actually on a stretch of shingle at the water's edge, John had them practising the casting, both finding it very different from the previous evening's efforts in the tower's courtyard, this because of the breeze, which much affected the fling and direction of the so-light line and fly. But quickly the boy and woman learned to place themselves so as to use the wind to assist, not entangle, even though their flies did not always drop approximately where aimed. These longer rods, too, took some getting used to; but before long, John thought it best to leave them to it, about one hundred yards apart, he telling them to stand as far back from the edge as was possible, for the fish were fairly keen-sighted and could probably see anglers on the bank, and their reflections on the water. He had been told, when he was learning the craft himself, that the salmon were wise, in that they did not fear animals on the banks, cattle, sheep, even horses, but mankind they tended to find alarming. He also said that if they saw a fish rise, surface or make a stir, they should try to drop their fly upstream a yard or two above it, so that it drifted down, thus appearing more natural.

He went off some way downstream, letting them fend for themselves.

He gave them the best part of an hour, frequently glancing upstream but seeing no signs of excitement, and himself gaining not so much as a nibble the while.

Then, returning to the boy, he was greeted by complaints that there were no fish in this Douglas Water, that not a leap, a spout nor so much as a swirl had he seen. Archie thought that they should go and try the Clyde.

John said that perhaps it might be too sunny, which could be unhelpful. Let them go and see how his aunt was getting on.

They found Margaret casting now quite expertly, but also lacking any catch. She pointed.

"There is, I think, a fish out there," she said. "I keep seeing a turning, a swirling, on the surface. I once even saw something dark in it for a moment, I think a nose. I keep casting upstream of it, but cannot get the fly in quite the right place. It is this wind . . ."

John saw the swirl, and nodded. "See you, this breeze is from the south-west. Cast more to the south, there, and let the wind together with the current carry the fly in the right direction. Cast further out."

"I have tried that. *You* see if you can place it better." And she handed him the rod.

He chose a slightly different stance, and made three or four casts. At one, there was a distinct flurry in the water beside the fly, but that was all. He passed back the rod.

"There is a fish there," he declared. "*Your* fish. Try again. The way that I did it. Stand further back. It perhaps sees us."

"I have not your reach and strength of arm," she said. But she wielded her rod in a fair swing, and cast again, a third time, the fly descending and floating close to the swirl. And then there was a splash and the line jerked, the young woman gasping an exclamation as her rod was all but pulled from her grasp.

"A catch! A catch!" John cried. "Let it run. Give more line. The spool." He reached over, to grab and shake the wooden spool so that the horse-hair unwound swiftly. "More. It will turn."

"How much? How much?"

"All the way. When it feels the tug of the hook in its

mouth, it will turn. There! There you are!" This as the rod bent to a strong pull. "Now, it will swim back. And turn this way and that. Play it, lass, play it! A little pull and then ease it. Then pull again. And again."

Archie was dancing with agitation. "Oh, look – it jumped! It is big, big!"

"You had better do it, John," the girl said. "I may lose it . . ."

"No, no. *Your* fish. Keep on playing it until it tires."

"I will do it, if you like!" her nephew volunteered eagerly; but John waved him back.

Margaret did as she was directed, and played that fish back and forth, time and time again, her hobbling stance forgotten in the excitement. The man feared that she would tire before the salmon did, for clearly it was a sizeable fish. But she kept on with it, and gradually, very gradually, the runs and dartings got shorter and shorter. Presently the catch was close enough inshore for them to see the white of its belly as it tossed and turned and twisted, the young woman's main problem now the coiling in of the line, John deliberately not helping with this, not in any way to spoil her triumph.

At length it was Archie who plunged knee-deep into the shallows, to reach down and grasp the fish by its gills and hoist it, wriggling and flapping, ashore, heavy, slippery and active enough to all but overbalance him. Panting, he brought it to his aunt.

"Ten pounds, if an ounce!" John cried. "Well done, lass, well done!" And he took the fish and aimed expertly to kill the thrashing creature with the heel of his spurred riding-boot, Margaret turning to look away at this necessary stage. Then he stooped to extract the fly, with its hook caught deep inside the mouth.

Much admiration and congratulation expressed had Archie getting into a ferment that *he* had not yet caught a salmon, and he must, he must! Margaret agreed with John that this was highly desirable but scarcely to be assured. They must concentrate on the endeavour.

John said that they would proceed very slowly upstream, well back, but eyeing the water keenly for another of the tell-tale swirls, hopefully. Margaret left her rod beside her fish meantime.

They went, peering, as far up-river as the straightish stretch lasted, and bends and overhanging trees began again, this without seeing a sign of fish, to the boy's grievous disappointment. Turning back, they moved downstream, with no more success; Archie was declaring that he must just try a general testing of the water, and John advising that this was scarcely worth while, when a smacking splash interrupted him. They turned their heads to look, but saw only spreading rings of water; but at least these were wide enough to indicate that a fairly large fish had jumped, almost certainly a salmon, or possibly a big sea trout. The position was fairly far out, but not impossibly so to reach from this bank. There was no need to advise the boy what to do.

Archie was hastily unwinding his line, fumbling in his hurry, eyes on water rather than on his spool and rod.

"Not to hurry," John counselled. "That fish will not change position greatly, I think. Take your time, and cast upwind."

The youngster heeded him, took up a stance, and cast. His fly fell short. He reeled in, and cast again. This time he overshot. He tried to pull the fly back over the area of the rings, but it drifted downstream. John almost spoke again, but restrained himself. The boy made a third cast, and this time the fly fell perhaps six feet above where aimed. And it had barely touched water when there was a commotion beside it, and they saw the fish's back as it snapped. The line jerked, and then was dragged off.

"You have it! You have it!" Margaret exclaimed. "Oh, Archie – good!"

"I . . . I . . ." The boy was too excited for any words.

"Give it line! More line!" John urged. "Your spool. Let it run. You have the fish. Play it. Take time."

Archie managed to master his fervour and take heed

of advice. In fact he played that fish very well, back and forward, time and again, and over a lengthy spell. It took longer, much longer, than Margaret's had done to tire, but it was firmly hooked; and gradually the runs grew shorter. When at last it was fully visible in the shallows, the young earl thrust his rod at John and ran to plunge in again to be first to grab his catch. He all but sat down in the water in his haste, feet slipping on slimy pebbles, but recovered himself, and clutching the salmon to him, for salmon it was, flapping and flailing in his arms, he turned to grin exultantly at his companions, standing there in the river.

They hailed him with due esteem and felicitations.

"Splendid!" John said. "You played that well indeed. I could not have done better. Your first salmon! We were fortunate to hear that first splash. A notable chance. But you did it all ably. I salute the Red Douglas!"

Wading to the bank with his awkward armful, the boy asked, "How . . . how do I kill it? Too big to slap on a stone. Like a trout . . ."

"I will do it." John took the jerking fish. Actually it was smaller than Margaret's, perhaps eight pounds, but none commented on that, the young woman giving her nephew a hug.

Thereafter all decided that it was the man's turn. But although they proceeded to cast for another hour or so, no further bites, nor even signs of fish, were forthcoming. John was not concerned. The desired success had been achieved. He decided that they should go back to Carmichael Tower to display their prowess.

Collecting their catches they returned to the horses, and Margaret allowed herself to be assisted up into the saddle, no longer demonstrating her ability. Both the salmon were put into Archie's saddle-bag.

That evening the climate of feeling prevailing at Carmichael was much easier all round, notably with Margaret herself. Marriage was never actually mentioned, but otherwise talk ranged freely, even over the national situation and prospects, salmon fishing by no means dominating the conversation despite Archie's preoccupation – however significant had been the day's activities.

In the morning the Douglas party was for off homewards however much young Angus would have liked to remain for more sport. John accompanied his guests approximately halfway to their destination, turning back only in the Cobbinshaws area. At the parting, he leaned over to clap the boy's shoulder, telling him to come back before long and they would try the Clyde. There were even reaches on that river where they could fish from a boat, and perhaps catch even larger fish. At Margaret he looked questioningly.

"It has been . . . good?" he said. "You have found it all none so trying? Other than the salmon!"

She nodded. "You have been kind. Did it cost you dear?"

"Cost, no. I learned much, I think."

"As well as teaching. More than fly-fishing, it may be?"

They eyed each other.

"So long as any lesson was of some help."

"Time will tell, no? But, yes, I judge that I learned also. Thanks to your forbearance. Poor John Carmichael! You hooked no salmon, but you are hooked with a wife! You will have to play her . . . patiently!"

He did not answer that, but she found a smile as she reined round and rode off, Archie looking from one to the other mystified, before following her.

They carried the two salmon trophies with them.

7

Sir John was worried. It was mid-July and the crucial parliament was to be held in just under a month's time. He urgently desired this vital marriage to be held before then. If the chancellor's sister was wed to John, it was scarcely conceivable that the Regent Moray and lords could forfeit or otherwise take action against Carmichael. But if it was only a proposal, even a betrothal, that could be different. Pressure on Morton could be brought to bear, and he might change his attitude.

Yet they could hardly approach the earl or Lady Douglas requesting haste. That would be likely only to defeat the objective.

Then, fortunately – or otherwise as far as the couple involved were concerned – a letter reached Carmichael on 13th July, declaring that if the date was suitable to bridegroom and family, the wedding should take place in the Church of St Nicholas, Dalkeith on St Mary Magdalene's Day – this was considered to be appropriate by Lady Douglas. Since it was traditional that bride and groom should not see each other before the nuptials, and the Lady Morton was not notable for her hospitality, it was suggested that the Carmichael party should go and spend the previous night at Sheriffhall, a small barony of Morton's a mile or so west of Dalkeith, where they would be welcome. The wedding would be at noon.

Even though his father's relief scarcely applied to John, he had had to become more or less reconciled to this match – he could hardly look on it as a union – and little was to be gained by delay. He wondered how Margaret was feeling? Nine days, then . . .

Those days were made the more significant for them by the news reaching Carmichael of dire measures, arrests and imprisonments of prominent Marian supporters, prior to the parliament. Baillie of Lamington sent word that he and his were going down to their lesser house of Watstounhead on the West March, safe within Herries territory, meantime. The Herries muster was in force, the barrier formed, and so far Moray had not sought to challenge it.

So the day dawned when they must ride, with presents for the bride, best clothing packed, Lady Carmichael and daughter being much exercised over how it would look after being transported by pack-horse, the men less concerned.

They made a slower journey of it this time inevitably, but were in no hurry to arrive at the Douglas house of Sheriffhall, unknown to them all. It lay just over a mile west of Dalkeith Castle, across Esk, a small barony, and Sir John approached it with mixed feelings. For he was informed that it was where the eldest of Morton's quite numerous illegitimate sons, James Douglas, was quartered, with a lady, Agnes Home of Spott, to whom he was not married; and to be lodged there might be looked upon as scarcely complimentary but, on the other hand, it was probably better than having to keep company with the sour Countess of Morton.

Sheriffhall proved to be a fairly modest tower-house, on no very defensive site but with open views towards Edinburgh, unlike Dalkeith Castle down in the Esk valley. And any doubts about their reception were quickly dispelled by them being greeted by none other than Archibald, Earl of Angus, who it seemed had demanded to be allowed to welcome his friend John on this special occasion. There was no sign of James Douglas, but his leman, Agnes Home, a bold-eyed but cheerful young woman, received them well enough, and had a substantial meal ready for them after their long riding. Archie acted the host with much enthusiasm.

The boy took John down to the Esk that evening, to show him his favourite pools, talk being almost solely about fishing, and discussion on why salmon came to some rivers and not others, marriage scarcely mentioned, except to say that Archie was going to stand beside his friend in the church.

John shared a room with his brother and the boy that night, Sheriffhall not being very commodious – and wondered about the next night, but not aloud.

In the morning, the females made much more fuss than did the males, including the bridegroom, part of the to-do being that they could not possibly ride to the church clad in their finery of silks and satins, and so must walk the mile or so, this seemingly a matter of some moment. And since they could not be left to walk alone, it meant that the men had to walk also, an odd situation in the circumstances.

Fortunately it was not far to the bridge over the Esk; but the walking up the hill to the town, and along the High Street, was something of a trial, dressed as they were, and gazed at by all. The citizenry knew young Angus, of course, and were suitably respectful, but stares were inevitable.

St Nicholas's Church was on the main street, and this forenoon, even though the Sheriffhall party had come fairly early, the churchyard already held its quota of tethered horses. It was an ancient and handsome building, unusually so for a comparatively small town church, it having been quite an important collegiate establishment before the Reformation, with a provost, five canons and five prebends. It boasted both a tall steeple and a clock tower, its outer walls enhanced with many decorative buttresses and canopied niches, the saintly statuary therefrom removed, of course.

The parish minister was fetched to receive the new arrivals, paying more attention to the boy earl than to the bridegroom perhaps, and leading them to the baptistry, to wait. Here John was left with the two Archies, for his brother had been appointed groom's attendant before the boy earl had claimed that position. The others were taking their places in the church itself.

The trio had quite a lengthy wait, having arrived early on account of miscalculating how long it would take to walk from Sheriffhall. It is to be feared that the conversation was scarcely relevant to the occasion, matters piscatorial rather than religious or nuptial predominating, although John did ask if the boy had any idea as to how long the ceremony would last, and what would happen thereafter. Archie did not know about timing, but said that he hoped that it would not go on for long, for a great feast was awaiting them down at the castle, with his mother, not the countess, seeing to it. They were to be given swans, geese and wild boar to eat. He did not think that he had ever tasted a swan before. The other Archie said that they sometimes had swans from the Clyde marshes, but he preferred wild goose, pinkfoot or greylag, not barnacle.

This interesting preliminary to marriage was cut short by the return of the black-gowned minister, who announced that the bride's carriage was approaching, and that his lordship and the bridegroom should perhaps take their places beneath the chancel arch. He led the way out of the baptistry.

The nave of the church itself was by no means full, despite those horses outside. The interior of the building was rather extraordinary, highly decorative in carved stonework, with galleries in tiers behind the pulpit, more niches devoid of figures, and lofts above the two side chapels bearing the escutcheons and badges of Dalkeith's craft guilds, tanners, weavers, hammermen and the like. Douglas heraldry was prominent everywhere, and there was a recumbent double effigy, presumably of an earlier Earl and Countess of Morton, close to where the trio were conducted beneath the high carved archway, part of the stone-vaulted ceiling. It was all very different from the small and simple parish church of Carmichael.

They were left to stand, while a choir of singing boys chanted. Young Angus turned round to survey the company, to pick out whom he knew; but the brothers faced firmly forward.

Soon John was being asked why they had to wait? Was his aunt late? It would not be because she was lame – she could walk quickly enough usually. John thought that it was the privilege of brides to be tardy, why he knew not.

Presently a halt in the choir's singing, and then a new chant signalled the arrival of the bridal party, Archie turning to gaze, but the Carmichael brothers keeping their eyes firmly on the communion table ahead which had replaced the altar. John drew a deep breath. This was it, then!

There followed some slight commotion at John's left side, this because the boy Archie was standing where Margaret should be, the young woman, limping up on Morton's arm, smiling as her nephew had to be moved back by her brother. She darted the remainder of her smile at her fellow victim.

It was John's turn not exactly to gaze but to eye his bride with more than sympathy. For she was looking notably attractive, calmly assured and, once stationary, holding herself superbly, dressed in a beautifully cut gown of damassin, bodice of silver and gold, which did full justice to her fine figure, with a long flowing silken skirt, and her fair hair part covered with a lace wimple. At his side she gave no hint of stress nor disquiet, save that he could not but notice that her bosom stirred in quiet rhythm. They did not speak.

The minister and an assistant emerged from the vestry beyond one of the side chapels to stand before them, on the chancel step, waiting for the singing to cease. When it did, the minister launched into a lengthy prayer.

John did not really take in most of what was said and done thereafter, however much it was to his concern, aware as he was of a sense of inevitability. Something of his fate was being fashioned here, in the droning on of this black-robed and sombre-visaged cleric, and being witnessed and confirmed by all present; but it was difficult to relate it to actuality. He wondered whether the same unreality applied to Margaret Douglas at his side.

The service seemed to be mainly prayers and admonitions, with little of the flourish and all but pageantry of the now discredited Catholic ceremonial; but it probably went on for longer – for John, certainly too long. He was brought back to reality by a nudge from his brother, who was holding out the ring for him, a family heirloom, which he hoped would fit the young woman's slender finger; not something which could have been tried on earlier. When Morton raised hand to indicate his authority to bestow the bride on this fortunate petitioner, the minister gestured for the ring, and Margaret, turning to John with something like a sympathetic expression, held out her hand, nodding as he slipped it on the appropriate finger. It was on the large side, but not so much so that it would fall off. Almost without thinking, he gave that hand a little reassuring squeeze, for his companion in this plight of troth-plighting.

As though suddenly wearied of it all, the celebrant promptly declared the couple man and wife, in the sight of God and all men, raised his hand in benediction upon the congregation, and bowed, this towards the two earls rather than to the united pair, and turning to the choir in one of the side chapels, signed for the chanting to resume.

It was done, for better or for worse. They must now make the best of it. Taking Margaret's arm, John turned to face the company, a married man, however little different he felt.

Morton stood back to wave the couple forward in their progress down to the door, having to pull young Archie aside, who looked as though he meant to proceed with them, alongside. Due documentation, signing of marriage contract and other clerkly procedures could be dealt with later. To the regular cadence of the psalm's verses they paced, the husband heedfully adjusting his pace to his wife's limping gait, still holding her arm, his brother and the two earls following.

Outside in the street they found three carriages awaiting them, with Lady Douglas superintending all. She gave Margaret a hug and a kiss, and glanced quizzically at John, before directing them into the first of the carriages.

There they sat, waiting. Apparently they were to occupy it alone, for when Archie came towards them calling something, he was sent to the second carriage, which Morton and his countess were already entering, to his obvious disappointment.

"My mother has it all arranged," Margaret said. "Even my brother has to do what he is told, chancellor and Lord High Admiral as he is!"

"But not his countess, I think!"

"No-o-o."

By this time the folk of Dalkeith had all heard that their lord's sister was being wed, and the High Street was packed to watch as the three carriages, the rest of the Carmichael family in the third, set off for the castle, other guests riding or walking. John felt, somehow, a fraud, sitting there as it were in state. Margaret achieved a smile or two, right and left.

At the castle all was in readiness for the banquet. It certainly came up to young Archie's expectations, swans and all. There were no speeches on this occasion, Morton making no gesture in that direction, and no one else venturing to do so in his house, for which John, for one, was thankful, since anything such would have called for a reply by himself. Indeed the earl let it be known that he himself could not delay there overlong, at table or otherwise, for he had to get back to Edinburgh for an important if unspecified meeting.

This intimation gave John a thought. He was not looking forward to spending the rest of the day – for it was only mid-afternoon – making conversation after receiving the required congratulations from the guests, and he doubted if his bride was either. So, nearing the end of the repast, to which neither of them had done real justice, he murmured to his companion. "If your noble brother can depart early, so perhaps could we?"

"Ah," Margaret said. "That might be advisable. And possible. But where?"

"To Carmichael – where else?"

"M'mm. Well, we must come there in the end!"

"It is not too far for you? At this time? From here. Four hours, five at most. You are a horsewoman."

"Oh, yes, I am that, at least! So be it. I will tell my mother."

"*I* will do so. Play the husband, no? In this respect!"

She nodded.

Lady Douglas was sitting nearby, chatting with Sir John. Rising, John went to them.

"Margaret and I have decided not to linger for long," he told her quietly, with a sidelong glance at his father. "We prefer to be on our way. To Carmichael. Rather than biding here, or at Sheriffhall to make small talk! We could be there before dark."

"Ha! So that is the way of it! Haste!"

"Better than waiting. And overmuch talk."

"Perhaps. Margaret agrees?"

She looked at Sir John. "How say you?"

"If it is what they want . . ."

"Will your ladyship order our horses to be brought? Mine from Sheriffhall. Margaret will have to change to riding-clothes meanwhile."

"To be sure. Wait a small while longer. When the feasting is over and the entertainers come in, you can move then and be little noticed."

"My thanks."

They sat through the remainder of the feasting, the company becoming the more noisy and forward as the wine continued to flow. When a couple of gypsy jugglers put in an appearance, with an acrobat, and space was cleared for them in the centre of the great hall, Margaret told John that she would slip away first. Go to change garb. He to sit on a little longer. It would not be so evident. They could meet at the porter's lodge, by the keep door. Let them hope that their horses were there by then.

Acceding, John stayed sitting when she rose and limped off.

While he waited, Archie came to him – which was as well. "Where is my aunt gone?" he wondered.

"She changes clothes for riding. We are for off, Archie. Quietly. None to know."

"Off? Where? Can I come?" He sat on Margaret's seat.

"No, not today, lad. This is a . . . special day, see you. When we go alone."

"Where to?"

"To Carmichael, just. You look after my family, will you? At Sheriffhall."

"Can I come to Carmichael afterwards? Soon?"

"Well, yes, do that. And we will go fishing again. See, look at those jugglers . . ."

They waited, admiring the gypsies' expertise. And when presently John rose, the boy rose also.

"I will come and see you go," he announced.

Would that draw attention to his exit? John wondered. He decided that if it did it would be to no harm, the young earl's company good screening. Without taking any farewell of his family, or even Morton, the man and boy left the hall.

They went downstairs to the small porter's lodge, in the vaulted basement of the keep's ten-foot-thick walling. Margaret was not there yet. They went outside, and found the two horses ready awaiting them. Archie wanted to know if they needed an escort, but was told that they would ride the more quickly without.

Margaret was not long in joining them, smiling to see the boy there. He told her that John said that he could come to Carmichael soon and they would go after salmon again. How soon?

Glancing at the man, she said, "That is for my husband to say, Archie."

"Give us a day or two," John requested, and led her out to the horses.

As she mounted, Margaret said to her nephew, "Have my mother send on my baggage from Pittendreich. It will be needful. It is already packed. Tomorrow. Do not forget, Archie."

"I could bring it myself?"

"I think not. Over-soon perhaps." And she looked at John.

"Yes. Give us a day or two."

"I have got a new long rod. I will bring it."

Waving, they reined round their horses and trotted off.

They rode southwards fast, almost as though they might be pursued, not quite sure why, since what lay ahead was uncertain, to say the least. But some urge was there, and they were both well mounted. They spoke but little, in consequence.

Resting and watering their mounts at Cobbinshaws Loch, halfway, John did venture some comment. "We are making good time," he said. "We will be there by sundown. And . . . you will be tired. There will be no need to . . . concern yourself. With me." That was the best that he could make of it.

She did not answer and, remounting, they rode on.

They arrived at Carmichael, as foretold, as the sun was sinking, and promptly threw Peg Maclellan, the motherly housemaid, into a fluster, she not having expected anyone back until the next night at the earliest. She pretended not to notice Margaret's handicap. John told her not to worry about any special feeding, for they had already eaten more than enough at Dalkeith. Honey wine and oaten cakes would serve them very well this evening. And plenty of hot water to wash in, above, after their long riding.

There was a problem, of course. The newly-wed couple

would be expected to share room and bed; but John wanted Margaret to feel free, this first night at least, to maintain her privacy. However, he could scarcely announce that to Peg, that he would leave his bedchamber on the third floor to the young woman and bed down for the night in one of the little-used attic rooms above, within the parapet walk. He would just have to leave his bride, as it were secretly, after goodnights were said.

So, presently, after Peg declared that there was plenty of hot water in John's room, and roguishly wished the pair a good night and pleasing dreams, they had reached the stage of awkwardness.

"You will be weary, after your so trying day," John told Margaret. "I will take you to your chamber now. If you are ready to retire?" He realised that he was saying that stiffly.

"*My* chamber?"

"Well, it is my own room Peg will have prepared. And the water there. But once I have shown you all, the garderobe and the like, then . . ." He left the rest unsaid.

"Are you being heedful? For me? Or for yourself?" she asked.

He blinked. "I hope . . . for you. I well realise . . ." He shook his head. "Come you, then." And he led the way upstairs, not hurrying, climbing steps obviously being difficult for her, although even at Pittendreich she would have to mount twisting stairs to her own room, tower-houses being built that way.

On the third-floor landing the door stood open to his candle-lit chamber, steam rising from a great tub near the large double bed, and even a small fire burning on the hearth, welcoming rather than necessary in July. He ushered her in and closed the door behind them. The bedcovers were duly turned back.

"Fortunately she has brought a pail with more water. For me," he said, pointing. "Yonder, in that corner, behind the hanging, is the garderobe. All will be in order. Peg is ever good, caring . . ."

"Yes. All taken care of, indeed." She turned to him. "And you? Your caring, John? There is care, and care!"

"My care, this night, is for you."

"Is it? Not for yourself?"

"No. Not myself, no."

"Yet I think that you intend to leave me here?"

He swallowed, and inclined his head.

"Does that mean that we are wed – but only in name? That you do not *want* me. Lame as I am!"

"Not that – no, never that! It is that this has been forced upon you, Margaret. No will of yours. I seek to give you time. To compose yourself. To come to like me a little, before, before . . ."

"And you me, perhaps?"

He walked over to the fire and stared down into the flames. "I think that I have come to like you already. Not a little."

"So-o-o! Yet you leave me tonight? Why? I am your wife now. Will putting off this night's . . . company, coming together, help either of us?"

He turned to look at her. "You would have it so?" he demanded.

"I have . . . prepared myself," she said simply. "As well tonight as tomorrow. Or thereafter."

He went over to her, and reached out to grasp her shoulders. "I think . . . I think that I have married a notable woman!" he said.

"So long as my notability does not affront you!" And hitching up her riding-skirt, she thrust out her club foot. "The devil's mark."

Gazing at her for moments, on impulse he sank down on his knees and took that crooked foot in his hands, bending to kiss the ankle.

He heard her draw a quick breath and, as he rose again, she spoke.

"I think, John Carmichael, that I have wed better than I could have hoped! May you feel the same, one day!"

"Not now?"

"We shall see." She turned away. "I shall discover your garderobe," she announced.

He went to draw aside the tapestry hanging for her, to reveal the little L-shaped closet within the thickness of the walling, with its stone seat and drain and shelf and tiny slit window. A candle guttered on that shelf. She entered, and he went back to the fire, his thoughts and feelings in turmoil.

He was not given very long to gather and direct those turbulent wits before the hanging was drawn aside and Margaret emerged from the garderobe, a sight to see indeed, and not calculated to calm his emotions. For her clothing no longer covered her, but was held in a bundle before her. Nor was it so bulky as to hide one of her full and shapely breasts, nor the long, white, trimly moulded legs.

It is to be feared that the man did stare now.

She hesitated there for a moment or two, before walking over to a chest, to lay her clothes thereon – and her back view, wholly available for his inspection, was such as to hold the male eye, all but challenging, her strange walk nowise detracting.

She made rather an activity of arranging her gear on that chest, having to bend over in the process – which produced its own impact – before at length turning to face him. And she did not now attempt to hide any part of her but stood there, as it were waiting.

He found words, at last. "You . . . are . . . most beautiful!" he said throatily.

"I am as God made me," she told him, "Not Satan!" and moved over to the water-tub. "I think that to stand in it will be best, no?"

He went to hold her arm as she stepped over into the still-steaming water, and was very much aware of the warm, alluring femininity, even the faint scent of her, so close.

When she stooped to take a cloth hanging over the tub's side, and dipped it in the water, she also glanced round at him, one eyebrow raised. "I can stand, unaided!" she observed, but sounding almost amused rather than critical.

He realised that he was still clutching her. Releasing his hold but encouraged by the sound of her, he said, "May I wash your back? Since *you* cannot!"

"You are kind!" That also held a hint of mockery, but she handed him the cloth.

John had never washed a woman's back before. He found the exercise enjoyable and, to be sure, stimulating, sufficiently so for him to take some time over it so as not to miss any area or hollow or cleft, high or low – and as has been said, hers was a well-built figure. He would have gone down as far as her thighs had she not turned to take the cloth from him, saying that she could reach there well enough, thank you!

She added, "Fetch me the towel, if you will. And then, ought you not to be preparing yourself to wash? Or the water will be cold."

"M'mm. Yes. Perhaps." He went for the towel. "I think that you are quite splendid, Margaret. I, I salute you!"

"Was that what you were doing? There is more than one sort of salutation, then. Off with you!"

Obediently he went over to the garderobe, wondering that it should be the young woman who was unexpectedly all but taking the lead in this bridal-night proceeding. Was that the Douglas blood revealing itself?

He did not undress in the cramped confines of the garderobe, something that he had never done; this was his own bedchamber, after all. Blowing out the candle there, and leaving, he found Margaret already in the bed. She was silent now.

John discarded his clothing quickly, the sight of her sitting up awaiting him there effectively arousing his masculinity sufficiently to complicate the process slightly. He almost forgot to go to the tub and wash in his preoccupation. It was very much a superficial cleansing that he gave himself that night, and the towelling thereafter as brief, before he strode to the bedside.

"You did not offer to wash *my* back!" he said. He was very much aware of his male virility, standing there, as no doubt was she; but somehow the next step of getting in beside her seemed to demand some overture.

"I am . . . concerned for you!" he got out. "Still."

"Yes. You are understanding. I thank you. To be sure, you will know it all. Have been thus before, no doubt. But I have not! So . . ."

"I will seek to be . . . as gentle as I may. But . . ." He shook his head, and climbed in beside her.

She stiffened just a little as he promptly took her in his arms, but she did not draw away. And she made a warm and luscious armful, all curves and smooth prominences – which did not help him. Although he was determined to take his time, he could not keep his hands from running over her person, stroking, fondling, caressing, her back, her buttocks, her shoulders, her breasts; but he forbore, somehow, to keep those busy fingers from reaching down to her thighs and between her legs, seeking to have her relax – while he himself was in the reverse state. Her deep breathing and stir against him was no aid either.

He kissed her, of course, on the brows first and eyelids and cheeks, before the lips. Then going down to her bosom, tongue busy in attempted arousal. And it was then that he began to worry about himself. Could he continue with this, contain himself, for much longer? Need was stirring up within him. He reverted to kissing her lips, and when these moved somewhat and then opening beneath his own, he found himself in greater stress than ever.

"Margaret!" he panted. "I . . . I must! Or, or . . ."

He felt her head nod.

His hand slid down now, over her belly and the silky hair below, and on between her legs – and those fingers felt moistness. The breath he had been holding came out in a degree of relief, even if hers did not. He dared not wait for any lengthy play of fingers or he would disgrace himself.

78

He rolled over on top of her, and was sufficiently aware and grateful that she had widened her legs for him.

Thereafter there was no holding back – not on the man's part, at any rate. Nature took its course, and all too swiftly. The woman's small gasp did not long precede John's moaning ejaculation, as he reared and then slumped down upon her, panting, muttering, and then murmuring apologies.

After a moment or two of tenseness, she found spirit to stroke his back.

He lay, reaching to hold her hand.

"Is that . . . all?" she asked, presently.

It took John a little while to answer that, in the state that he was in then. "Not, not unless you so . . . desire. Give me a little time and, and we may do better."

"Better?"

"Aye, better. For us both, I hope."

"I think that I should wash again," she declared, and got out of bed to go over to the tub.

He lay watching her pale figure in the half-dark, and this time did not rise to assist her into the water and out again.

Margaret came to the bedside, to stand looking down at him. "Why should more be better?" she asked. "Forgive you my ignorance!"

"It is that I reached it too soon," he sought to explain. "I was . . . over-ready. You too desirable. I could have served you better. Made *you* more ready. Had I been less eager, less speedy."

"If there is to be more, then how shall it be better?"

"Wait you. Give me time, and I think that I can help you."

"Help me to what?"

"To some satisfaction. Or, leastways, I hope so."

Distinctly doubtfully she got back into bed beside him, to lie less closely.

"Let me hold you, lass. You are good to hold. Very good. All of you." And he edged nearer.

79

Lying on her back, she gazed up at the ceiling. "We sleep eventually?" she asked, as a hand reached out for her breast to fondle it slowly, and went on doing so, before doing the same for the other – and attaining some slight reaction.

She stirred, and turned head to look at him. She did not speak.

That hand of his was not so much busy as gently searching, enquiring almost, and moving lower, the young woman quiet, passive, patient with him, tolerant rather than expectant. Once or twice she sighed.

When one of those sighs was longer, deeper, and with the suggestion of a quiver in it, he leaned over, on one elbow.

"You do not too greatly . . . mislike this?"

She shook her head, wordless.

"Then I think, I think . . . Yes, I am coming to be myself again!" He took one of her hands and placed it on himself. "You see?"

She still did not answer, but that could be because he was kissing her lips again. She did not snatch back that hand.

It was he who removed the hand, this by hoisting himself on top of her again, neither his hand nor hers any longer necessary. And now he played the man so very differently than before, heedfully, controlledly, attentively but insistently, able now to take all the time required. And he gained some response, the more positive as he maintained the rhythm. And at last she stiffened for a moment, twisted beneath him, and then uttered a little groan.

Satisfied, he did not relax but allowed his own physical ardour to have its head, the better for the long restraint. He went all the way now to male gratification, masterful yet considerate, caring.

The woman beneath him was sighing again.

"Better?" he panted, as he did come to relaxation, sinking on her, however heavily.

"Yes," she breathed. "I thank you, John!"

Soon after, they slept.

8

They rose late next morning, even though they had both
been awake for some time, enjoying the companionship of
lying there together, close, in more than physical contact,
John concerned not to overdo the fostering and coaching
process, but not failing in mild caressing, Margaret now
the relaxed one. It was Peg Maclellan's tapping on the
door and calling that the water she had brought earlier,
much earlier, would be getting cold, and that breakfast
was more than ready, that got them up and into a mutual
washing process, this with no tension about it, indeed some
laughter.

As wedding nights were apt to go, John suggested, theirs
had been a success, and his bride did not deny it. Indeed
she endorsed it by showing signs of positive affection.

John sought further to earn Margaret's approval, that
forenoon, by taking her on his favourite ride, that to
the summit of Tintock Tap, a stiff climb for the horses
but a rewarding one for their riders, with a quarter of
southern Scotland spread out for their delectation. The
man pointed out all the features of significance almost
proudly, Margaret admitting that although she had ridden
to the tops of some of the Lothian Pentland Hills, they
could show nothing like the vistas from this isolated
mountain – save that *they* did have distant sea views.

They rode on down the far side and, while they were at it,
made a quite prolonged circuit southwards and westwards,
John just a little disturbed as they passed near Lamington, and thought of Mirren Baillie. They proceeded to
Douglasdale, indeed right to Douglas-town itself, where
they visited the ancient St Bride's Kirk, burial place of

the old Earls of Douglas, where Margaret recounted the
story of James the Gross, the seventh earl, whose funeral
was enlivened by the coffin somehow coming adrift from
its bearers and hurtling down the steep stairs into the
underground crypt before all the mourners, in premature
interment. They also had a look at the ruins of the ancient
castle of Douglas, demolished on the orders of King James
the Second in 1450, although the lands still belonged to the
earldom of Angus. They talked of the turbulent history
of the Douglas line and how it had grown so powerful
as to rival the royal house itself, sufficiently so for the
extraordinary event of the said James the Second actually
stabbing to death in Stirling Castle with his own hand the
sixth Earl of Douglas, the only such regal assassination
ever recorded.

This prolonged tour around meant that the couple did
not arrive back at Carmichael until early evening, to
discover that the rest of the family had just got back
from Dalkeith.

Out of much talk that ensued, and considerable interest
into how the new bride was taking her changed circumstances, quite a lot of significant news was forthcoming
from Sir John. First of all, the Lady Margaret's dowery.
Morton was bestowing on her, and therefore her husband,
the lands of Wrae, near to Linlithgow, in the west of
Lothian. Neither Margaret nor John had ever so much as
visited the Linlithgow vicinity, and were interested in this
announcement, needless to say. The Black Douglas lands
were widespread, to be sure, and there would be many of
them but little known to the family; West Lothian was
unfamiliar territory to them both. They would have to
go and inspect this new holding, however inconveniently
situated in relation to Carmichael.

On a wider front the tidings brought back were noteworthy, as retailed to Sir John by Morton. First of all, the
parliament was called for 18th August, at Edinburgh, and
indubitably momentous would be its outcome. Meanwhile
much had been happening on the national scene. Moray

had led a large army northwards, to bring under control those great areas, largely held by Marian supporters and mainly still Catholic, under the Earls of Argyll, Huntly, Ross and Rothes; but had turned back without major clash, it seeming more of a demonstration than anything more dire. Something of a naked struggle for power was going on amongst the Lords of the Congregation, and the regent no doubt saw this as demanding his prior attention. Secretary of State Maitland of Lethington, a clever man, was leading a party which was manoeuvring to gain the ascendancy; and Sir John had the feeling that Morton himself was involved in this. It looked as though Mary Stewart's departure by no means signalled peace in Scotland.

On the queen's front, the word was that Herries had left his muster on the West March to go to her at Workington, in Cumberland, where she was being held until Elizabeth Tudor's will was known, this in order to aid her with advice, for it was known that the English monarch was sending up Sir Francis Knollys and the Lady Scrope, sister of the Duke of Norfolk, to interview her and decide on her fate, for Mary was as good as a captive now, it seemed, despite her faith in her sister-queen. What Herries thought that he could do was uncertain; but Morton conceived it possible that he might be spying out the land and the situation to see whether a swift dash in force over the border with his mustered mosstroopers might not be able to effect the queen's rescue, to bring her back to Scotland; after all, Workington was only some forty miles south of the borderline. Morton was now off to inform the regent of this danger, and to propose that Moray lead an expedition southwards, not northwards, to assail the western Borderers and prevent any such attempt.

It all sounded ominous – and typical of the Scots, who much preferred to fight amongst themselves than to face any common foe in unity.

Sir John was congratulating himself on having successfully extricated the Carmichaels from one cause, without effectively committing them to any other. His son wondered.

That night he and Margaret achieved a greater degree of mutual satisfaction together, the young woman clearly resolved to make the best of this marriage which she had not chosen, and evidently not finding it too difficult.

The presence of the rest of the family in the not notably commodious confines of Carmichael Tower, of course, did have a limiting effect, certainly as far as John was concerned; and he quickly came to the conclusion that he had no desire just to incorporate his wifely acquisition into the family life there. He was, in fact, enjoying Margaret's company, and not only in bed; and sharing her with the others did not commend itself to him. As a consequence, they spent much of their time off on horseback, exploring the countryside far and wide – with suitable pauses in quiet woodlands, by loch-sides and in empty hills – Margaret learning much, not only topographical, historical and anecdotal, and imparting not a little to her companion also. They were, in fact, becoming good friends, whatever else.

They did some fishing too, and recognised that it probably would not be long before they would have to put up with company on this activity, if young Angus had his way. John wondered, selfishly, whether this might be avoided by them paying their visit of inspection to the dowery property of Wrae?

That was not to be, however, for the very next day after the suggestion was made, the young earl arrived at Carmichael, with his escort and his fine new salmon-rod, enthusiasm the more vehement for the unfortunate delay. Not that they could be anything but welcoming towards the boy, both fond of him. So they had two days of intensive angling on the Clyde, and with quite rewarding results, however much the visit interfered with marital togetherness. The boy was ecstatic.

When John had had enough of this, he produced the need for a visit to Wrae to see what this property was like; and they would take young Archie back home to Pittendreich on the way, where Margaret desired to collect some of her belongings anyway; then on to Linlithgow. Reluctantly, this was accepted.

On the first day of August the trio and escort set off northwards.

Lady Douglas welcomed them at Pittendreich, and was as interested as had been the Carmichael family as to how her daughter was adapting to her new life. Margaret did not wax lyrical on the joys of matrimony; but no doubt the older woman perceived clearly enough that the new wife was by no means unhappy over it, and the husband likewise – her impressions admittedly having to be gained through the chatter and enthusiasms of Earl Archie on the delights of salmon angling, the infinite superiority of the Clyde and even the Douglas Water over the North Esk, and the promise by John to take him netting for fish on some long stretch of the Clyde at, at – John had to supply the name, Lamington – and had told him that there were even two lochs to net in on his own land at Douglas Castle.

When they had got the boy off to bed, Lady Douglas gave them some news of state affairs which they had not heard at Carmichael.

Parliament was scheduled to be held at Edinburgh.

Elizabeth of England was justifying her all-but-imprisonment of Queen Mary, who was now moved to Bolton Castle in North Yorkshire, deeper into England, the seat of Lord Scrope, by claiming that she might have been implicated in the murder of her second husband, Darnley; and since he had Tudor as well as Stewart connections, and had borne the crown matrimonial, this charge Elizabeth felt it to be her royal duty to investigate. She was requesting evidence from the Regent Moray, in the shape of the notorious Casket Letters, written by Mary to Bothwell, her third husband. How Moray would respond to this was unclear; but Morton was distinctly concerned, for undoubtedly he knew not a little about that sensational murder, indeed was rumoured to have been an instigator.

The regent's demonstration into parts of the north did not seem to have had any lasting effects, for it was reported that the northern lords Argyll, Huntly and some Highland chiefs had had a conference with the Duke of Chatelherault and his Hamiltons at Largs, near Ayr, in Hamilton country, which they could reach by sea to be sure, and were confirming their support for the captured queen, with Herries as their link.

John and Margaret sought to take all this in; but while grieved over the fate of their unfortunate and attractive monarch – they could not really think of the infant James, now two years old, as their king – and concerned for her cause, they could scarcely feel in any way involved. Sir John was distancing the Carmichaels from any further connection with the Marian party; and Morton seemed to be playing a watchful, waiting game. John knew that his father would not be risking attending the parliament in Edinburgh, although he was entitled to do so. The newly-weds were well content to leave the stresses and strains of the nation's rule and governance to others, Lady Douglas obviously seeing that as wise.

In the morning they were off for Linlithgow, some twenty-four miles to the west. Avoiding Edinburgh town by crossing the Burgh Muir to its south, traditional assembly place of Scots armies, they rode on by Corstorphine and Gogar to cross the River Almond near Kirkliston, and so beyond to Winchburgh, passing the great Seton castle of Niddry, where the queen had been brought by Lord Seton after her escape from Lochleven Castle those dramatic months before. Further, Kingscavil was only another five miles, and they reached there just before noon. Enquiring at the village as to where was Wrae, they were directed back a mile or so whence they had come, to where the road crossed a stream called the Haugh Burn; due south of this half a mile lay Wrae under the grassy ridge of Ochiltree.

Turning, they soon found the fair-sized burn, and heading up from it on the long slope presently came to a spread of quite wide fields, not the normal cultivation rigs and common grazing of most of the countryside, clearly a large and unusual farmery, with at its centre a rambling and part ruinous house, no mere farm cottage this, yet not a laird's house either, lacking any defensive features or fortifications.

John was interested, intrigued indeed as to this property, now his, and made a shrewd guess that this had been Church land, probably fallen to Morton and his Douglases at the Reformation. The monks knew how to get the best out of the land, going in for wide fields not narrow strips, and draining the ground to make it possible to grow crops, and fertilising it with dung and seaweeds. Now, here, two of five fields or parks were untended and growing only weeds and thistles, two others were yellow with oats, all but ready to harvest.

"Your brother Morton has presented us with a worthy messuage here, I think," he told Margaret. "Good land, and capable of producing rich crops. He never told you how he acquired it?"

"No. I had never heard of Wrae before. That is a strange house, is it not?"

"My guess is that it was a grange, the farmery of a monastery or abbey. Perhaps part of my lord earl's reward for supporting the Reformers! And now yours, or ours!"

"Is that wrong? Sinful? To be gaining the property of Holy Church?"

John shrugged. "If sin it was, the fault is not ours. The Church owned half the best land in Scotland. How did *it* acquire it all? Best not to ask! But I may be wrong as to this." He pointed. "See, that further side of the house is occupied, smoke coming from the chimney. We shall discover what is to do here."

Dismounting, they went to the house door, Margaret taking John's arm as she limped.

An elderly woman answered their knocking, and became

distinctly flushed and concerned when she was told that here was the Lady Margaret Douglas and her husband, and that this property of Wrae was now theirs. She said that her husband, tenant here, Tom Hogg, was away at market at Linlithgow and would not be back for some time.

They gathered that this Hogg held the farm for Morton, paying for his tenancy in crops, hides and wool; and it became clear that his wife's obvious anxiety was that its new owners would either appoint new tenants or come and dwell here themselves. Margaret told her not to worry about this meantime; they were only inspecting the property. Relieved, the woman said that she and her husband had been there for nearly a score of years, before which the monks of the Priory of St Mary at South Queensferry had farmed the land. Some of the fields or parks were still named after the churchmen, Brothers' Dyke, Easter and Wester Monklands and there was a Friar's Well.

The couple made a survey of the farmery, mounted as easier for Margaret, and saw it as quite a valuable acquisition, although they would not wish to live there, pleasant as the surroundings were. The shire of Linlithgow was not the most peaceful part of Lowland Scotland to live in. Mainly Livingstone and Hamilton country, it was very much Marian territory, with Mary Livingstone one of the queen's Marys and with the captive in England; yet Linlithgow Palace, where Mary and other monarchs had been born, was the royal dower-house for Scots queens, and now held by the regent and his lords, so confrontations were to be expected.

They took their leave of Mistress Hogg without undue delay, and chose to ride back eastwards along the higher Ochiltree ridge above Wrae, where they passed the Hamilton tower of Ochiltree Castle, wondering how it got that name, since Ochiltree was in Ayrshire. It was a new-looking little fortalice, so this had probably also been Church lands, and the Hamiltons, winning it at the Reformation, had given it the name of one of their

Ayrshire estates. Kingscavil was also Hamilton property, so it was evident that John and Margaret must not fall out with that powerful family, with their Wrae sandwiched between them.

For the remainder of their way back to Pittendreich, they returned as they had come. They were back in good time for the evening meal. Thereat, Lady Douglas admitted that both her sons had gained considerable Church lands, thanks to the Reformers. She did not know Wrae but had heard of one property near Linlithgow held by Morton with the odd name of Woodcockdale, presumably nearby.

John said that, on the morrow, if Margaret agreed, they would go to inspect their other marriage-settlement land, given by his father, at Longherdmanston, near to Haddington, a small East Lothian holding which Sir John had been going to bestow on his son when he came of full age, but which was now allotted as marriage jointure. As at Wrae, it would be interesting to see what it was like. When young Archie heard of this, he was swift to demand that he be taken with them on this occasion, for it must be near his great castle of Tantallon, not far from Haddington.

So it was a trio again that set off next morning, on a somewhat shorter journey, Haddington lying only some dozen miles east of Dalkeith, and this Longherdmanston before that. They passed through very different country from that of the previous day, mounting to the high ground of Falsyde, its prominent castle destroyed by the English twenty years before, after their victory at the Battle of Pinkie, fought between it and the Firth of Forth; and thereafter noting the coal-heughs of Tranent, where the enterprising Abbot Mark Kerr of Newbattle Abbey had developed some of the first coal-mining in Lothian, first to his abbey's considerable wealth, and then to his own, for he had chosen to adhere to the winning side at the Reformation, and gained his abbey's lands, plus the coal-heughs with them, his Border reiving stock very much in evidence, for he came of the Ferniehirst Kerrs from Jedburgh.

Entertaining Margaret and the boy with all this, John led them into the vale of the upper Tyne, the only major East Lothian river, which had Archie wondering as to its angling possibilities. Reaching the village of Pencaitland, where the Lord Seton had his Winton Castle, where Mary Seton, the senior of the queen's Marys, had been reared, they crossed Tyne by the Spilmersford and soon thereafter came to Longherdmanston, set directly on the south bank of the river, in cattle-dotted haughland and meadows – this in well under two hours' riding.

The place proved to be no more than another quite large farmery, with a tenant's house much smaller than that at Wrae, cultivation, by rigs, much less in evidence, cattle country evidently, although, with some drainage, John thought that quite good grain fields could be created here. But pleasing as the situation was in the gentle river valley, it was again no place for them to dwell in, however useful as a source of addition to their very modest fortune. John was determined to be an improver of land, and so enhance their prosperity, learning from those monks.

Early in the day as it still was, Archie was clamant that they should go on to the main seat of the Angus earldom, Tantallon, near to North Berwick. He had been taken there a number of times, of course, and was very proud of it, much finer than the ruined Douglas Castle they had visited that time. Margaret also had been there before, but John never. She agreed that it was well worth a visit.

They rode on down Tyne, to pass the town of Haddington within its walls, these part derelict now from English demolitions after Pinkie, and saw its great cathedral-like church of St Mary, Secretary Maitland's house of Lethington nearby. A mile further and they crossed Tyne by a stone bridge said to have been erected by the famous Countess Ada, mother of the Kings Malcolm the Maiden and William the Lion, daughter-in-law of the great David the First who, when her husband had died early, before his father, had retired here to be abbess of the nearby nunnery. Margaret it was who now recounted all this. And she had more to announce thereafter, as they climbed the quite high Garleton Ridge northwards, and then over and down into a parallel wide valley to that of Tyne, the Vale of Peffer, undrained marshland mainly, but with some rocky heights thrusting up on the far side, with the Firth of Forth and Aberlady Bay beyond. Here the young woman pointed out the site of the great and significant Battle of Athelstaneford where, it could almost be said, Scotland had begun, this in the early ninth century, for before that it had been only the land of the Picts of Alba and the Scots of Dalriada. But that battle, with a joint raiding expedition of Picts and Scots into Anglian Northumbria returning laden with booty, having been caught up with by a large Saxon force under one Athelstan, they had been forced to fight at a ford over the Peffer. The struggle had been going against them when Angus mac Fergus, High King of Alba, and Kenneth mac Alpin, grandson of the Dalriadan king, had seen a curious white cloud formation in the blue sky, in the X-shape of the St Andrew's Cross. They had judged that St Andrew, Peter's brother, was watching over them, and prayed that if he would intercede for them with Almighty God and give them the victory, they would appoint him patron saint of both the realms, instead of St Columba. The fighting turned in their favour and the day was won, Athelstan slain; and thereafter Andrew was the land's patron and his white cross on blue, the Saltire, the joint nation's flag, as it still was.

John knew vaguely of this but had never heard the details; and Archie was spellbound.

Beyond Athelstaneford they climbed out of the Vale of Peffer and passed a craggy knoll on which perched the ruins of a small tower, no doubt also demolished by the invading English. What a site for a house, John declared, with magnificent views all around, almost as good as Tintock Tap, to the Norse Sea on the east, the

91

vale and the Lammermuir Hills to the south, and right to Edinburgh's towering Arthur's Seat hill on the west, immediately overlooking the scene where Scotland was born. One day, if he had the wherewithal, he would like to build a house on this knoll.

Now they had not far to go, still eastwards making for the coast, to Tantallon, passing behind the strange and isolated conical peak of North Berwick Law, with its Pictish fort on top. Soon thereafter they were in sight of the mighty red-stone towers of the Angus fortalice, vivid against the blue of the sea, the proud seat of the earldom, which one day would be Archie's home, one of the greatest strongholds in all Scotland, a fortress rather than a castle, set on the very edge of a high cliff above the surging tides.

The boy, excited, presently was pointing out the successive lines of ramparts and ditches raised and dug landwards, to keep cannon out of effective range. And then the three great towers, connected by fifty-foot-high curtain walls topped by parapet walks, the central and largest tower acting as gatehouse, with drawbridge and portcullis, the side towers soaring directly over sheer cliffs. King James the Fifth, Mary's father, had tried to capture Tantallon and failed, Archie boasted, even having his cannon stormed and taken by the Douglases. John was duly impressed. It all made Carmichael Tower seem of very small account.

Admission to the castle was gained by shouts from Archie up to the gatehouse guards that here was the Earl of Angus come to his own house. Open the wicket gate!

The no doubt surprised attendants were not long in obeying, and the three rode in over the drawbridge and under the great vaulted archway of the main keep into an enormous courtyard, really only a spread of open cliff-top, part cobbled, part grassgrown, flanked on two sides by lower buildings, a chapel, kitchens, brewhouses, stabling and the like, with the fourth and longest side, save for a low wall, open to the sea. The castle was in fact a vast wall, cutting off a high, narrow headland of cliffs, making it all but impregnable on three sides, with its landward aspect amply defended. A deep well was sunk in the middle of the courtyard.

Nothing would do but that, dismounted, Archie must hurry them over to the seaward edge, to gaze down at the surging waves far below where, save for one narrow, twisting channel, rocks and reefs and skerries set the seas boiling, and prevented any access by boat except by one who knew that channel, thus enabling the castle to be supplied by sea in the event of a prolonged siege. Archie said that sometimes seals could be seen on those rocks below, although there was none visible today.

While they viewed all this, a middle-aged man came over to them from the south tower, and was introduced to John by Archie as Cousin Glenbervie, actually Sir Archibald Douglas of Glenbervie, who acted as keeper of Tantallon for young Angus meantime. Margaret knew him, of course, a second cousin of her own. He welcomed them, and declared that refreshment was available within when desired.

But the boy would have none of that until John had seen much more. They must climb up to the high parapet walk crowning the curtain walls, and the still higher tower-tops, by many narrow winding turnpike stairways – which Margaret managed surprisingly well, using the ropes which hung down the central newels to help pull her up, the boy racing on ahead. On the dizzy paved walks and parapets aloft they gazed around admiringly over land and sea, the soaring mass of the Bass Rock thrusting out of the waves a couple of miles to the north and taking the eye, its precipices white with the droppings of its thousands of gannets or solan geese.

Between the Bass and Tantallon two small boats were to be seen, clearly fishing. Would that be good sport? Archie asked. How was it done? Was it by lines or nets? John said that it could be by both, although probably those local fishermen would be using nets, set overnight and drawn up by day, with their catch. What fish? Herring and haddock mainly, he thought, although they might get cod occasionally. And there would always be lobster-creels to set and harvest. No salmon, the boy wondered, but John doubted whether they were near enough to the mouth of the Tyne, five miles away probably, for that. Archie said that they must come back one day and try sea fishing. There would be boats for them at North Berwick harbour.

After a quite substantial meal provided by one more Lady Douglas, the trio took their departure.

They headed back for Dalkeith by a different route, more southerly, going by the Whitekirk of Hamer, once a place of pilgrimage founded by a Countess of Dunbar in gratitude for her miraculous cure by taking the water of a spring there, the requirement being that pilgrims should visit it barefoot. One such, Margaret said, had been none so grateful; this was Aeneas Sylvius Piccolomini, from Sienna, papal nuncio, who later became Pope Pius the Second and having walked from his ship at Dunbar haven, in damp weather, cursed this Whitekirk ever after for giving him rheumatism.

Soon thereafter they could see the high whaleback ridge of Traprain Law, a companion feature to North Berwick Law, on the forty-acre summit of which, they were told, King Loth of the Southern Picts, who gave his name to Lothian, had had his capital, and where his daughter Thanea was born, who had a son who became St Mungo, or Kentigern, who eventually founded Glasgow.

Greatly admiring of Margaret's knowledge of all this colourful historical information, John led them by more devious ways back to the North Esk and Pittendreich.

It was farewell to Archie and Lady Douglas the next day, and return to Carmichael. On the way the couple reverted to the subject of their future abode. They agreed that they should have a house to themselves rather than quarters in Carmichael Tower, but that neither Wrae or Longherdmanston seemed suitable for any permanent dwelling. John looked upon himself as a Borderer of sorts, and felt the pull of that storied area. The Carmichaels had a secondary tower-house known as Eastend of Carmichael, and although it was normally reserved for a second son of the house, after the older brother succeeded to the tower itself, it therefore would come to brother Archie. But at present it was standing empty, Sir John having had no brother and his uncle dead. If they could install themselves there, that might be the answer.

So, on the road home, John took Margaret to see Eastend. It was pleasingly situated about two miles south-east of Carmichael, on the Cleuch Burn at the northern foot of Tintock Tap, a small square tower-house of three storeys with an attic floor above within a parapet and wall walk with open rounds at three angles and a conical caphouse to top the stairway access thereto. After Tantallon it seemed a modest establishment indeed – but then so would most laird's houses, even Pittendreich.

Two cottages at a stableyard nearby were occupied by a cattleman and a shepherd and their families, and the former kept the key to the empty tower. Obtaining this was only the first stage of gaining admittance however, for the door, protected by two shot-holes, was at first-floor level and only reachable by a detached flight of stone steps ending in a little platform, from which a removable plank gangway connected with the entry. This was normally kept within the tower, to be pushed out and withdrawn as necessary, a quite usual and useful defensive feature; but when the building was empty, as now, the gangway was kept in the cattleman's cottage, and had to be carried over to the steps and pushed across to rest one end on a stone below the doorstep, this only projecting a few inches from the walling, making a precarious approach. John knew it of old, of course, and carrying up the planking, was very cautious about placing its far end, for if it became detached as he crossed he would fall over twenty feet. Margaret, on the platform, was urgent in her warnings to be careful, declaring this to be a device of the devil and saying that if they did come to live here she would demand a better entry than this. John assured that when, if ever, they were there, this expedient would never be necessary, for the gangway would be held within the tower, and run out easily enough as required.

Gingerly, then, he pushed the planking over the gap, ascertained that it was securely bedded on that projection, and crossed over with the key, Margaret holding her breath. The outer iron grating, or yett, swung out, and the inner wooden door unlocked, he stepped safely inside and was able to pull the gangway end in and settle it securely on the doorstep, going back to lead the young woman over.

There was a little closet in the thickness of the walling just within, for the door porter, with lamp bracket and drain. Across from this, also in the walling, was a narrow straight stair leading down to the vaulted basement at ground level, containing storerooms and the pit or prison, also a well sunk in the flooring earth. At entrance level was the kitchen, also stone-vaulted, with its great arched fireplace and oven, slop drain and shelving. At the far side of this, a turnpike stair rose, in the thick walling, to the upper floors.

They climbed this to the hall or main living-room on the second floor, a fair-sized chamber, again with a large fireplace but no withdrawing-room off, as at Carmichael and Pittendreich. It was sparsely furnished with long table and benches and wooden chests, but at least the fireplace did have stone seats within the ingoing ingleneuks, for comfort of a winter's night, and old deer and sheep skins served as rugs on the stone-flagged floor, while somewhat tattered hangings helped to cover the whitewashed walling. Margaret scrutinised all heedfully and declared that she thought, with a little work, they could make it liveable in.

Upstairs there were two bedchambers on the third floor and another two in the attics above.

All looked distinctly unused and in need of attention and

care, but basically capable of being made into a reasonably comfortable home, or so said Margaret Douglas, although John himself was a little doubtful now over introducing the sister of two earls to this as a possible residence.

They departed, locking the door but leaving the gangway in position and taking the key with them.

At Carmichael they were welcomed back, interest shown in their reactions to the properties of Wrae and Longherdmanston. Explaining that neither, however worthy as farmland, offered suitable quarters in which to install his wife, John asked his father to allow them to occupy Eastend meantime for, although there was enough accommodation for them here in the tower, they were surely entitled to set up house on their own. Sir John proved to have no objection, so long as it was understood that it was not to be a permanent arrangement, for Eastend would be Archibald's eventually.

John's mother was less than enthusiastic about this, for clearly she would have enjoyed Margaret's company about the house. But she accepted it, and did not object to the couple pillaging a certain amount of furnishings, carpeting, bedding, utensils and the like, to make Eastend more habitable.

John perceived that he was going to be busy for the next week or two, even with his brother and sister offering to assist.

9

In the event, Margaret had, or chose, to do much of the refurbishing of Eastend herself, aided by the younger Carmichaels, for John received a summons from her brother, the Earl of Morton, to attend on him at his Edinburgh lodging without delay, soon after the Edinburgh parliament, no reasons given. He had, to be sure, rather guessed that his "gift" of the earl's sister might have to be paid for in some measure of service, just what remained to be seen. His father was eager that he made himself useful to the realm's chancellor, for attachment to so influential a personage could be very rewarding; but Margaret warned her husband to be careful as to what he agreed to take on, for she recognised that her noble brother was less scrupulous and principled than she would have liked.

So leaving the house-bettering in what was proving to be his wife's capable hands, John set off, on the second day of September, for Edinburgh.

Morton proved to have a handsome town-house in the capital, even though with Dalkeith only six miles off he seemed hardly to require such. John found his way to Blackfriars Wynd, off the city's High Street near where it joined the Canongate, and halfway down this quite steep alleyway to the lower Cowgate was the tall tenement, with its own yard behind where horses could be stabled, precious indeed in Edinburgh's cramped space, a town built on a mile-long spine of ridge running down from the great fortress-castle on the west to the Abbey of Holyrood on the east, this last under soaring Arthur's Seat. Places to leave horses were a great problem in the city, these often having to be left considerable distances off, outside the walls indeed. Not so for Chancellor Morton.

John found the earl absent meantime, where undisclosed, his house in the care of one of his numerous mistresses, Jean Crichton, a hearty creature very different from the countess at Dalkeith. She entertained the visitor almost over-warmly for his comfort while he partook of generous provision.

Fortunately, perhaps, Morton was not long in appearing. He greeted John with a sort of shrewd sizing-up inspection, and was apparently satisfied for he did not delay in making his requirements known. He had a task for his new brother-in-law – for that, to be sure, was now John's relationship.

"Do you know Ferniehirst? The Kerr castle near to Jedburgh in the Middle March?" he asked. "I want you to go there, young man, and see Sir Thomas Kerr. He was much in the confidence of Queen Mary, indeed she called him her protector I'm told. He is wed to the daughter of Kirkcaldy of Grange, keeper of Edinburgh Castle."

John admitted that he had seen Sir Thomas, before the Battle of Langside, but had never spoken with him.

"He may well have information which could be of value," Morton went on. "Value to himself, now, as well as to others for he, so close to Mary, could be endangered now. So he will need a voice to speak for him!" That was said almost grimly. "The queen, also. See you, this is for your ear alone, not to be bruited abroad. The regent, Lethington and myself are to visit Elizabeth Tudor in London. We have a proposal to put to her anent Mary Stewart. She, Elizabeth, is holding Mary on the excuse of suspicions that she was implicated in the death of her husband, Henry Darnley. And she was, God knows! But best for all that this is not brought out, that she can be declared innocent. And I judge that Kerr can help here."

John stared. This was heady stuff to become involved in, indeed.

"We have sent to Mary, at Bolton in Yorkshire, Sir Robert Melville, to tell her that if she will renounce all claims to our Scots throne, acknowledging her son James as king, and go to live meantime in France, where she was queen once, we will assert her innocence of Darnley's death to Elizabeth, seek so to gain Mary's release from captivity, and be given English moneys to maintain her royal dignity in France. Mary, we have now heard, has accepted this, and we believe that Elizabeth will be glad to do so also, for she is in a difficult position in it all now."

"Queen Elizabeth in difficulties! How can that be?"

"Well may you ask, lad! It is largely a matter of religion, like so much else. The Catholic party is stirring in England, to overturn their Reformation. Led by the Duke of Norfolk and the Earls of Cumberland and Northumberland. Norfolk sees opportunity. He seeks to have Mary's marriage to that fool Bothwell, now gone to Denmark, annulled, and himself to marry Mary, with the Pope's blessing, and so unite the Catholic strength in England and Scotland and with French help unseat Elizabeth and put Mary on both thrones. Mary, after all, is granddaughter of Henry the Eighth's sister, Margaret Tudor, Elizabeth's aunt, and so nearest heir to that throne."

"Lord!" John wagged his head. "This is beyond all! Can it be true?"

"It can and is, man. So our problem is to counter that. Our policy is good, important. Best for both realms. And Mary says that she will accept it, if Elizabeth will. She has had enough of trouble, war and battle. But we need evidence to give Elizabeth that Mary was not responsible for Darnley's death. And that is difficult to produce!"

"Her royal word, surely?"

Morton hooted. "Think you *that* would serve? Na, na, we need more than that, a deal more! And Kerr of Ferniehirst may give us what we want. Moray has copies of those casket o' letters, *copies* mind, written by Mary to Bothwell while she was in Glasgow at Darnley's bedside, sick he was. They were written in French, see you, and these copies are translations made by yon Master George Buchanan at Stirling, he who's to teach young King Jamie. But there is at least the one missing, a right important one we judge. The second one. Lethington thinks that Kerr may have it. He is close to Kirkcaldy of Grange, his good-father, and the casket with the letters was found in Edinburgh Castle here after Bothwell fled to Denmark. Kirkcaldy may have given it to Kerr for safe keeping, knowing that he was Mary's man."

"And think you, my lord, that he would give it to me, if he has it?"

"He might – to be saving his own skin! For he is forfeited by the parliament, and endangered. If this would buy his safety."

"M'mm . . ."

"There is something else, forby. It was from Ferniehirst that Mary made yon long ride ower the Border hills to Hermitage, to see Bothwell when he had been wounded, and back the same day. Seventy miles and more. And she was fell sick thereafter. At Ferniehirst. For long after. There are tales as to her sickness. See you, if we could prove that she was sick in her mind, just, as well as in her body – as belike she was, then and after – we could win her off the charge of aiding in Darnley's death. As not competent. You have it? Kerr will know the way of it. We would have brought him in for questioning, but yon Borderers are strong for Mary, and look after each other. So, although he is forfeited, we are sweirt to try to take him, for he could have an army of mosstroopers protecting him and his castle before we got there! So you, a Borderer who fought for her at Langside, go visit him. And forthwith. For we are for London in days."

John was still doubtful. "He, Sir Thomas Kerr, may send me packing! I am no important man . . ."

"You are my good-brother! That is enough for you." Morton turned away, the matter evidently settled, shouting for Jean Crichton.

There was no suggestion thereafter that John should stay

the night in Blackfriars Wynd, nor indeed remain there any longer. It was much too far to return to Carmichael that day, so he decided to go to Pittendreich, where at least he was always welcome. He took his leave.

John spent a pleasant evening with Lady Douglas and young Archie, wondering – and not for the first time – how such a strong-minded and yet amiable woman could have produced a son like James, Earl of Morton. When the boy was in bed, John told her of this mission on which he was being sent, and found her interested and supportive. This project of her son's was probably favourable for Queen Mary in her present circumstances, she thought, even though also for the regent, chancellor and secretary. If the unwed Elizabeth could be convinced that her sister-monarch, and at this stage, heir, was absolved from blame over her husband's murder, and set Mary free to return to France, this would be the best outcome meantime. If she thought to try to recover her throne thereafter – for she was still only twenty-six years – then that was something for the future. John felt easier in his mind about it all, for this comment.

His ride next day was due southwards some forty-odd miles, by the Path-head of Ford over the upper Tyne and up Soutra Hill, where the great Augustinian hospice and hospital establishment had been situated, abandoned since the Reformation, and on down Lauderdale to the Tweed near Melrose and St Boswells, and so to the Teviot and its tributary the Jed Water. Beyond the town of Jedburgh and its great part-demolished abbey, he came to Ferniehirst Castle on its high mound above a bend of the river, a strong position, save for assault by cannon-fire, and not to be advanced upon lightly now even without that armament, for its two castletons, to north and south, protected its only practicable approaches. John was confronted by tough mosstroopers, guards, before ever he came in sight of the fortalice, and was escorted thereto in no very friendly fashion.

It was a fairly typical L-shaped tower-house, with high stair tower and angle-turrets, larger than many Border holds but still modest compared with, say, Tantallon. The Kerrs were one of the most prominent Border families, having two branches as it were, Ferniehirst and Cessford, the former being the senior, the two apt to hold the wardenship of the Middle March in turn.

However suspiciously escorted by the guards, John was received kindly at the castle itself by Lady Janet, an attractive woman in her late twenties. She told him that Sir Thomas was out at their other tower of Smailholm meantime but she expected him back before evening. She had heard of the Carmichaels and knew John's uncle Lord Somerville, good supporter of the queen; but she did not enquire into John's reasons for calling. Nor did she mention that her father, possibly the ablest soldier in the land, Sir William Kirkcaldy of Grange, had fought on the other side at Langside. Nor did her guest indicate that he now seemed to be in the camp of Morton and the Regent Moray. Scotland was like that in 1568.

Well fed, he was taken to a bedchamber in the top of the stair tower, and told that this was the room which the queen had occupied on many occasions when she visited Ferniehirst; and thereafter was conducted by his hostess and her small son on a walk down by the riverside.

Sir Thomas duly arrived in the late afternoon, a good-looking youngish man with a keen eye and an easy authority, suitable for the Warden of the Middle March. When he heard that John had been sent by the chancellor, he eyed him the more keenly but made no comment.

Later, after the evening meal, they moved alone into the withdrawing-room off the long hall, and John, just a little hesitantly, announced his mission, declaring that he had been assured that it was all to Queen Mary's benefit and advantage.

He spoke about the so-called Casket Letters first, explaining the forthcoming visit of the regent, Morton and Lethington to London, and their anxiety to have something to present to Elizabeth Tudor which could either absolve Mary from accusations of involvement in Darnley's murder at least, or make her position acceptable. Apparently one of the said letters, written by Mary to Bothwell from Darnley's sick-bedside not long before his death, was amissing. The Earl of Morton thought that it might be with Sir Thomas? It could prove useful, it seemed, on the queen's behalf.

Kerr shook his head. "No, Carmichael, I have none of these letters. If indeed they ever existed, and are not forgeries, drawn up by the queen's enemies! Why should Morton think that I might have one?"

"He believes that you were close to the queen. And that Sir William Kirkcaldy might have given you it. From Edinburgh Castle, where he is keeper, perhaps to give back to the queen."

"No. Nothing such. Sir William is my good-sire, yes. But we see each other but little." The other frowned. "I do not see what the chancellor and regent want with this alleged letter. You say to present to Queen Elizabeth? What would that serve?"

"I am unsure, myself. The earl did not fully explain to me. But he believes that it would be helpful in gaining our queen's release. They would have her freed, to go to France. And with some sort of moneys from Elizabeth."

"I would be in favour of that, yes. And for her to come back to Scotland thereafter, in due course, when she has gathered strength, aid from the King of France and we, her friends, have readied her loyal subjects here to rise strongly in her cause."

John nodded. "Then, my Lord Morton spoke of a sickness of the queen. When she was here at Ferniehirst. Which, it seems, could be of some relevance to her case. I am not sure how this could be. But he, the earl, was quite strong on it. Know you, sir, what he is at?"

"Ah, yes, I think that I do, in this. The queen, when she was here those years ago, before Darnley's death, her marriage to Bothwell, Carberry Hill defeat and shameful Lochleven imprisonment, was very ill. Grievously so. She feared that she had the leprosy!"

"Leprosy! The queen?" John stared. "This is scarcely to be believed!"

"It is true, nevertheless. Not that she had leprosy, but that she feared that she had. It was a dire affair. She had had that long ride to Hermitage Castle in Liddesdale, and back, to see the wounded Bothwell. I rode with her. She was very tired. And sorely sick the next day. Her skin blotched and red. Numbness. She feared that she had contracted the leprosy. There are two sorts, you will understand, the white, which is the most grievous, and the red. She was afraid that she had got it from Darnley. For he was a wretched husband for her, a catamite amongst his other failings. He shared beds with other men and boys. Including the Lord Ruthven – who died of leprosy. The queen feared that this was the source of her sickness, given her by Darnley, and that this was what he was sick of, in Glasgow."

"Lord, here's a pickle! It was not true?"

"No. But she greatly feared it. Feared it sufficiently for her to send me, first to France, then to Rome, and finally to Dalmatia!"

"Rome! For the Pope's blessing?"

"No, no. France first. A place called Boigny. You see, there is an Order of Chivalry, the Military and Hospitaller Order of St Lazarus of Jerusalem. You may have heard of it, very ancient. Established during the Crusades, especially to treat leprosy contracted by the crusading knights. They are still knowledgeable about the treatment of this plague. The queen knew of them from her French days. Their main establishment is at Boigny, near to Orléans. She would have me to go there, to the knights. To bring one back with me to treat her sickness."

"She was so sure of it? And you went?"

"Aye, it was a royal command, although I did not

believe that she had the dread disease, but only some skin infection. But she said that her great ancestor, Robert the Bruce, had had red leprosy. He had kept it a secret, because lepers were, and still are, outcasts of the law, held to be unworthy of any office or place in society, banished by Holy Church, the finger of God upon them. Indeed officially dead. Driven out of the company of men. Not to enter any town, to remain a mile from any habitation of folk. Even lepers' husbands and wives permitted to remarry while the sufferer is still alive. That is the curse of the leper! So for a queen to have leprosy! I had to go, if only to give her some peace of mind."

"To Dalmatia, you said?"

"Aye. First to France, to gain the authority of the Grand Master of the Order of St Lazarus. Lazarus, in Holy Writ, was a leper, you will mind. But when I got to this Boigny it was to discover that the Grand Master was away in Rome. No knight could be sent to Scotland without the Grand Master's permission. So I had to go on to Rome, for they said that he would not be returning to Boigny for some time, negotiating with the Pope on some matter. So there I went, far journey as it was. But from Rome, the Grand Master de Seure sent me to Dubrovnik in Dalmatia, across the Adriatic Sea. There, it seemed, was established the greatest of leper hospices, had been for centuries, where all knowledge of the disease, from all over the world, was gathered and taught, the ablest physicians for the plague. Dubrovnik itself, an independent city-state under the Dinaric Alps, has many lazarettes or leper-houses where sea-water treatment is much used. But over on a nearby island, Lokrum, is the principal leprosarium, as they call it, a college and monastery for the study and relief of the pestilence. There, on the Grand Master's authority, I was given the services of the Chevalier Alain Montfleurie, a Frenchman, who would return to Scotland with me, with his salves, ointments and salts to add to sea water, for the treatment of the disease. So I brought him here, that long voyage, for we came back mainly by sea. These knights carry much authority, all over, for leprosy is a worldwide curse."

"And he found . . .?"

"No sign of leprosy. Some skin affliction, but only that. Her own physicians, whom she had not dared to consult, could treat her for that, and then did."

"So all that, for nothing!"

"Not nothing, for it set Her Grace's mind at rest. She had been distracted, beside herself. The Chevalier Alain did not consider his journey valueless. Nor did I."

"Distracted, you say, sir? All but out of her right mind? And lepers are outcasts, considered dead indeed, their marriages ended. I, I think that I begin to see what Lord Morton was reaching for. Her Grace not responsible for her actions, then? To put this before Elizabeth."

"It could be that. She was not a leper, but yes, she was for a time scarcely herself. She was not privy to Darnley's murder, I am sure, but if Morton and Moray cannot prove that, then this of her distraction might serve their case. They must have heard some word of it. Some of the queen's servants, or even mine, could have talked."

"Strange, if it all may aid in Her Grace's cause now!"

"As you say. And strange that Morton should be thinking to use it! For undoubtedly *he* was involved in Darnley's death. It was plotted at Whittingehame, a Douglas seat in Lothian, when Morton was biding there. Bothwell also."

"As to that, I know not. But he will be interested to hear this. And grateful, it may be."

Kerr grimaced, and they left it at that, to return to Lady Janet.

In the morning, thanking the Kerrs for their hospitality and wishing them well, John returned to Edinburgh.

When he saw Morton, that man was disappointed over the letter situation, but much heartened over the confirmation of the leprosy story. This was what he wanted, all the details required to make their case valid, believable, before Elizabeth Tudor. Mary had not been responsible for her actions. And if those other letter translations did implicate her in her husband's death, here was reason and excuse. If he had become a leper, and she feared that he had passed it on to herself, then he was better actually dead as well as legally. Elizabeth would perceive that. The earl even commended the younger man for his efforts. John put in a good word for Sir Thomas Kerr, stressing his helpfulness.

He rode back to Pittendreich for the night, and on to Carmichael next day.

10

The work of preparation of Eastend for their habitation had a notable effect on John's and Margaret's relationship, bringing them ever closer together in mutual esteem and growing affection. The young woman very much took the lead in the transformation of a fairly bare and stark tower-house into a comfortable and pleasing home, with many features being added which the man would never have thought of, however willingly and effectively he carried out her instructions. Sometimes she shook her head over his efforts, but with fondness. Their appreciation of each other was reflected, of a night, in bed. John now never thought of his wife as lame or in any way disabled.

Working at Eastend, he had ample opportunity to wonder how Moray, Morton and Lethington were faring in London.

It was not all domestic labour and plenishing however, for something in the nature of a command came to them from Pittendreich to attend on the Earl of Angus with a view for a fishing expedition at Tantallon Castle, this while the golden autumn weather lasted and the seas were not too rough. Nothing loth, the couple set off in early October, picked up young Archie, and proceeded on to their coastal destination, Lady Douglas mildly relieved to be spared her grandson's enthusiasms for a space.

They were well received at Tantallon by Sir Archibald, who told them that he had arranged for a North Berwick fisherman to take them out in his boat and show them how net-fishing at sea was done. John had had no experience of this. They would do some line-fishing also.

On the morrow, then, they rode the couple of miles

westwards to the little town and fishing haven of North Berwick, along the cliff-tops, with the mighty Craig of Bass rearing offshore a mile or so but dominating the scene. Sir Archibald told them about St Baldred of the Bass, a Celtic missionary, disciple of St Mungo in the sixth century, who had his retreat or deseart there, for contemplation and communion with his Maker — although how he climbed the rock's precipitous sides was not explained. He was renowned also for his communion with the seals, and for arranging to have his body, on death, multiplied into three, so that the three parishes he had founded, with their little churches, Hamer or Whitekirk, Auldhame and Tyninghame, could have one each for relic purposes, a man of initiative obviously.

North Berwick, nestling beneath its green pyramid of the Law at a small low headland, was very much concerned with salt water, rocks and islets, great and small, everywhere offshore, this at the very mouth of the Firth of Forth, the harbour its fundamental feature, filled with boats and fishing-craft. Indeed it had been founded as the southern terminal necessary for a ferry used by the ancient Celtic Earls of Fife to visit their Lothian lands, the northern opposite base being Earlsferry near Elie on the Fife coast. A castle on the site of the present Tantallon had been theirs.

Down at the harbour, which was tidal, drying out at low water, which was something of a handicap, they duly found Rob Ritchie, the fisherman, mending his nets, along with others at the quayside, a spare, weatherbeaten man. He eyed the newcomers with a mixture of due respect and doubts, as it were sizing them up. The reason for the latter proved to be the need for oarsmen for his boat, which admittedly only required two actually to row it, but another had to take an oar when Ritchie was handling the nets. Sir Archibald was not coming with them, and probably would have considered any such activity beneath him anyway; but John announced that he had rowed on the Clyde frequently and could, he thought, serve for this task.

Archie had never rowed a boat, but declared that he could learn. The fisherman however had a sixteen-year-old son there amongst the others at the pier, and he would man the other oar. So, Sir Archibald wishing them well, although clearly thinking this to be a crazy activity for such as themselves, especially for Margaret, he left them to it.

They were led down to one of the many boats moored in the haven, and Margaret aided aboard. There was a single mast to carry a small square sail, and the craft was filled with wicker baskets, which had Archie asking whether it was expected to fill all these with fish. He was told no indeed, that these were for the indrawn nets; they would be fortunate to fill one of them with their catch – the boy disappointed.

John and Margaret seated at the stern, Archie up in the bows, the Ritchies put out their oars and, watched by their grinning colleagues on the pier, pulled out of the harbour, to turn away eastwards, soon pausing to hoist the sail. The man explained that the prevailing wind was south-westerly, and this would carry them in the desired direction. They still used the oars, but more to hold their direction than to propel them. Archie observed sagely that they would have to pull back against the wind.

He observed something else – the Bass Rock half-left ahead of them a couple of miles. Could they go there, do their fishing around that? He had been told that there were lots of seals there, and a boat could get quite close to them; all sorts of strange birds too. Ritchie had to point out that this was not where his nets were set. The Bass rose out of very deep water, much too deep for set nets, too deep for successful line-fishing also. They could trawl nets there; but that was not how he usually fished. It needed two or even three boats to trawl, the nets near the surface and linked between them. He found set-netting more profitable. It so happened that landward of the Bass a short distance, the sea floor suddenly rose, almost in submerged cliffs, this notably shallowing the water to a suitable depth. This did have the effect of producing very rough seas when easterly gales drove the tides against these underwater cliffs, but it would not trouble them in this weather.

Sailing for over a mile from the harbour, Ritchie pointed out a float bobbing about on the waves, apparently made out of an inflated pig's bladder, with a scrap of red rag tied to it. This was the beginning of his net chain, the various sections set in half-circles hopefully to trap the swimming fish shoals, the red to show which were his, other fishermen having their own beats. They made for this float, which was evidently anchored to the bottom by a rope and weight, and this had to be drawn up inboard, the boat held steady and the sail downed. Ritchie handed over his oar to John, and untied another stout cord attached to the float-rope, and tossed back the bladder into the water.

As his son and John sought to hold the craft in place with their oars, Ritchie, dispatching Archie from the bows, started to pull in on that cord. After a few yards of it, netting began to appear, to be coiled inboard in one of the baskets, scraps of seaweed entangled in the meshes. It was like a long curtain, perhaps five feet in depth and seemingly endless. Hand over hand the fisherman pulled it in, soaking as it was, seeking to shake the weed loose.

"The fish!" Archie cried. "There are no fish! Only horrible seaweed!"

"Wait you, my young lord," he was advised. "This is a coil, see you, hauf a bit loop. The haddies swim into the open end o' it. They swim to the far end o' it, along the netting. When they reach the end, maist will turn and swim back along the other side, but some will likely try to push on through the mesh, and get caught by the gills. Yon's the catch. It's no' until I draw in the centre o' each net that we see what we've gotten." He was continuing to pull in wet netting as he spoke, splashing himself and them all in the process.

"But there is *miles* of net!" the boy complained.

"Aye. Has to be, or the critturs would swim oot ower easy."

112

There was a shout of joy presently, as a single, silvery flapping object came up in the net, but moans as no more appeared.

"Never heed," the earl was told. "Yon's just an odd yin, tried to get oot early. We're no' at the right bit yet."

Presently the man was obviously having to pull much more strongly over the bows, and soon it was evident why, with a bunch of struggling haddocks trapped in a loop of the net, flicking more water over the watchers.

"How many?" Archie demanded. "They are not very big, are they!"

"They're just haddies. Inshore yins. Aboot a dozen, just. No' bad for the first net." Ritchie began to disentangle the fish, and tossed them, still flapping, into another of the baskets.

"How do we kill them?"

"Nae need. They'll dae fine there. Let them be, lord."

Two more fish came up, as the boat was rowed round in a half-circle, making for another red-tagged float, which now could be seen some way off, nearer the shore.

When they reached this, there was more untying of knotted cord, and that first net detached to fill the basket, a new basket brought forward and the process of hauling up and in recommenced. Apparently there were five nets in all sunk in a long series of loops.

They caught very few fish in the second net, but the third produced over a score, and the fourth almost as many, the last being disappointing. But all in all, Ritchie was well satisfied with the day's catch, and his passengers much interested. They were told that he would put out his nets again on the morrow and harvest them the next day; so he looked for three catches each week.

Archie and John were set to work to bail out the bottom of the boat, for all the baskets of soaking net produced much slopping water, their feet already wet. They were rowing inshore now, none so far from Tantallon's cliffs, making for sandy shallows Ritchie knew of, where they could fish for flukies, as he called them, flounders, with lines.

This proved to be a very different exercise, involving much messy baiting with lug-worms, messy in that when the worms, dug earlier on the town sands by Ritchie's son Jamie and kept in a pail, had to be threaded on to hooks, they tended to burst open, and covered fingers with brown ooze, which Margaret decided to leave to the others. The hooks hung from foot-long bars, weighted with lead to take them down, on long lines, to the bottom, three to each bar; and once the weight touched the sandy floor, the line had to be raised about one foot so that the lug-worm bait lay at just the right level for the fish to bite at it. Flounders, flat-fish, lay on the surface of the sand, or just below it, and fed on lug-worms. The fishers held their lines over the side of the boat, looped over one finger; and when a fish bit they could feel the tug on the line. This then had to be jerked, to ensure that the hook caught securely in the flounder's mouth, and the catch was hauled up. Sometimes the fish sucked the bait off the hooks without being caught, and sometimes they were insufficiently firmly hooked, and wriggled off on the way up to the boat. The fishers had to be guided to keep their different lines far enough apart, otherwise they were apt to get entangled, with the motion of the boat and the tide.

In fact, Margaret gained the first tug on her line, felt it clearly, and drew up a fair-sized flat-fish, flailing, brown on one side, white on the other, which Archie declared was unfair, since she had not done the hook-baiting. Also, she let John do the unhooking of the wriggling catch. There were three hooks on her bar, but one had already lost its bait, presumably by a sucker, so two more lug-worms had to be skewered on, and not by her, and the line let down again.

While this was in process, young Jamie felt a tug on his line, and drew up a smaller flounder. Archie cried that he had a bite, but when he pulled up the bait was gone from two of the hooks and nothing caught on the third. These wretched flukies were wicked suckers, he declared.

Ritchie himself gained the next fish, and then John felt a tug, and drawing up, found that he had actually hooked two fish, each flapping wildly and getting the line entangled. He was told that he was lucky, it being unusual to catch two at a time.

Archie was much put out, and making it known, the creatures avoiding his hooks, when his complaint changed to a yell and he announced that he had a big tug. Hauling up eagerly, he proved to have the largest flounder caught so far, to his glee, but almost lost it in his haste to get it unhooked before it was properly inboard. After that, he announced that flukie fishing was quite the best sport yet, even better than salmon angling perhaps, and he was glad that Tantallon was his, and he would be able to do it often.

Their boat was drifting slightly all the time, and presently they began to have trouble with their hooks catching on seaweed, so presumably they were now over rocks, and had strayed away from the sandy bottom. So they had to row back, and were rewarded with a few more bites, but not so many as before, Ritchie announcing that they had probably exhausted the supply for the day. But they had between them caught fourteen flounders, Archie three, and all were well content – and beginning to feel somewhat chilly from wet feet and clothing. So a return was made to North Berwick while the tide still allowed – always a preoccupation of the local fishermen – where the Tantallon party were presented with as many assorted fish as they desired, Archie proudly saying that he would have his big flukie for supper that night.

Thanks were expressed to father and son, and a return made to the castle. They would do this again, one day.

In the morning they returned to Pittendreich, there to learn that Morton, the regent and Lethington had got back from London, and two of them at least none too happy over their visit. Apparently Elizabeth Tudor and her advisers, Cecil, Bacon and Throckmorton, had not been impressed by the evidence produced, either the translations of the letters or the leprosy story, and were refusing to release the captive queen. Elizabeth had heard that Norfolk was aiming to marry Mary and then head a great united Catholic rising and Counter-Reformation in the two nations, and that must by no means happen. Morton had told his mother, however, that Moray had done none so badly out of the interview, for he had come back with five thousand pounds from Elizabeth to ensure that he remained sympathetic to her cause. No such bribery for his two colleagues apparently. However, Lady Douglas thought that the regent would have been wise to share this booty with his companions, for he would be as well to keep her son, the chancellor, as, if not his friend, at least his supporter. John gathered that Morton was resenting not so much the failing of Queen Mary's cause and the succumbing to financial inducement, as Moray's keeping it all to himself.

Clearly, if he, John, was going to have to continue to serve Morton's interests, he would have to watch his step carefully, and seek to steer an honourable course in affairs as far as possible. Margaret shook her head over her brother and those he worked with.

11

The couple at Eastend were spared further entanglements in affairs of state for quite some time, months indeed, Morton apparently deliberately holding back from the regent's activities, as much as was possible for a chancellor of the realm. So they passed a quiet but fulfilling autumn and early winter, settling into their new home, with visits to Pittendreich and Tantallon, and one, in November, to Wrae, to plan with Tom Hogg, the tenant farmer, the best and most profitable use of the land.

They learned, through Lady Douglas, quite a lot of what went on in the nation. The Marian party were still determined to rescue the queen, if possible, and were planning an armed muster at Perth. Moray was countering by calling a muster at Stirling. Morton was lying fairly low but talking of playing the broker between the two sides, a strange development for that man. Thankfully John was not called upon to serve in any difficult balancing act.

Sadly, they learned that his uncle, the Lord Somerville, who had never fully recovered from his wounds, had died at Cowthally.

The Carmichaels passed Yuletide pleasantly, with young Archie coming to join them in the festivities. It was scarcely weather for fishing, but one brief sally was attempted, with scant success.

Then, in January, they heard that the two armies had indeed assembled: Chatelherault, Cassillis, Argyll, Huntly and the mainly Catholic lords and chiefs at Perth; Moray, with the Lords of the Congregation, at Stirling, a score of miles apart. Scotland waited tensely.

It was early February when Morton sent for John, to

appear at Dalkeith. Distinctly apprehensively he prepared to obey. Margaret counselled not to allow himself to be saddled with any activity which went against his conscience. Her brother could not force him to do anything. John was less confident. Morton, as chancellor, that is senior minister under the regent, as well as being one of the great earls of Scotland and chief of the Black Douglases, wielded enormous power. If he was defied he could trump up some charge to have the defier imprisoned until he might yield to pressure.

In the event, however, at Dalkeith Castle, the earl's requirements were not such as to upset his brother-in-law unduly. Morton came to the point with his usual directness.

"You, young man, are still thirled to the queen's cause, I think? Aye, well, you can make yourself useful, see you. You'll ken well enough what to do. Moray and his army are at Stirling, facing the queen's men, the duke and his Hamiltons, Argyll and his Campbells, Huntly and his Gordons, and the rest, but facing them at a distance, near twenty miles! They're at Perth. They've been there for nigh on two weeks already, in right wintry weather, neither side making a move. Folly, eh? I'm for making some sense out o' it."

John nodded. Nothing he could not agree with there.

"I've seen Moray and Lethington. They are willing to call off the contest, disperse their force, if the others will do likewise. On conditions, mind. We have sure word that Queen Mary wishes it so. No fighting. She says that it will aid her case with Elizabeth Tudor if she is not arousing battle in Scotland. So, if Duke Hamilton and the others will but acknowledge young James as king, and send their mustered men back where they came from, their forfeitures by parliament will be called off, and those imprisoned released. You have it?"

"And they know of this? Chatelherault and the Catholic lords?"

"Some of it. The pardon and releases and the recognition

o' the King Jamie. But not Mary Stewart's wishes in the matter. And that Elizabeth has ordered the arrest o' Norfolk. That could alter matters, and the hopes of a united Catholic rising in the two realms."

"And you will go tell them so, my lord?"

"Na, na – no' myself. They'd likely no' have any dealings with me, the chancellor. They'd see me as the regent's man, belike. No, *you* to go. To Perth. They'll heed you, who fought for Mary at Langside. And kin – no' that near, but kin – to the Maxwells and Herries."

"But, my lord, why should they heed me? I am a man of no importance. How can I claim any authority in this matter? Even to know of this of the queen's wishes. And of Norfolk to be arrested?"

"Herries is in England. No' a captive, but able to see Mary Stewart. He it was sent the word. To me. And you are to be my voice in this."

"Will these great ones, Hamilton, the Duke of Chatel-herault, the Earls of Argyll, Huntly, Cassillis and the rest, accept that?"

"They will, if you show them this." Morton delved into a doublet pocket and produced a heavy gold signet ring bearing the arms of Douglas, three mullets or stars in chief and the Bruce's crowned heart below, under an earl's coronet. "I'll need it back, mind," he added, as he handed it to John.

Doubtfully it was accepted. "I still fear that they will not credit me with any authority."

"You *have* no authority, man – save as my repre-sentative."

"Then why not go yourself, my lord?"

"Have you no wits, man Carmichael! We are as good as at war, Mary's men, and her son Jamie's. I am the chancellor o' the parliament. If they could take and hold me, at Perth, as hostage, they might think to gain much. It's no' for me to act the courier, but you. And if I took a large guard, see you, there could be fighting. And no agreement. I ken what I'm at." He

119

half turned away. "Now, enough o' this. You're to be off."

"Now?"

"Aye, now. It's over sixty miles to Perth. You're a horseman, my sister tells me. You'll get a good score o' those miles this night, and be in St John's Town by noon tomorrow. So, off with you. And mind, bring back yon ring!" That was typical Morton.

It was the road for John, again.

Fortunately the road from Edinburgh to Linlithgow was now familiar, even though the last ten miles were covered in darkness. He made for Wrae, to spend what was left of the night there, having to wake up the surprised Hoggs. Then on in the morning by Falkirk and Larbert, the Somerville castle of Plane, then through the edges of the great Tor Wood, past famed Bannockburn, to Stirling.

Here, outside the town and its towering citadel where young King James was immured, the regent's army was encamped by the meanders of Forth and the vicinity of Cambuskenneth Abbey. Carefully skirting this, with no wish to become involved in questioning, John rode on over the historic and strategic bridge, only crossing place between south and north save for the very doubtful Fords of Frew, and on by the causeway where Wallace had won his renowned victory of Stirling Bridge, to Causewayhead and so to the Allan Water valley. Up this he rode for many miles, eventually to cross over into Strathearn, with the Highland hills looming ahead, to cross the shoulder of Moncrieffe Hill and down to St John's Town of Perth, by the winding but wide Tay. As Morton had predicted, he was there by midday.

Here again there was an army to be coped with, avoidance impossible, a large proportion of its manpower hereabouts proving to be Highlandmen, of whom John was wary, like most Lowlanders. He could not speak their language but at least he knew Argyll's Gaelic name and style, so he kept on addressing the kilted ones, asking for

MacCailean Mor, the Son of the Great Colin Campbell, and with this encountered no difficulty in winning through the encamped host to the town walls where, at one of the guarded gates, he gained admission by saying that he had a mission to the Duke of Chatelherault. He was told that the Marian leadership lords were lodged in the Blackfriars Monastery, the same wherein King James the First had been assassinated.

There, in one of the network of narrow streets, he found the men he had come to see, or some of them. He had no difficulty in entering what had been the refectory of the monastery, the large eating-chamber, where now men lounged round the tabling consuming their midday meal, for there was much coming and going of servitors with the viands, and he merely walked in with these unannounced.

Within, John stood for a minute or two uncertainly, none looking in his direction. He recognised Chatelherault, Argyll and Huntly, all seen at Langside, but felt that he could not just go up to any of these and introduce himself. Then, scanning the diners, he saw another whom he knew, less lofty perhaps, but approachable, Sir Thomas Kerr of Ferniehirst, Warden of the Middle March, he who had told him of the queen's leprosy fears, a friendly man. He risked going forward to him.

Kerr recognised him at once, and greeted him easily, even moving aside a little on the bench he shared with others to offer John a seat at table, thankfully accepted.

"You have come to join us, Carmichael?" the other asked. "Not that we appear to be achieving much here! There are mixed notions as to the way forward. Much debate."

"Well, no, Sir Thomas, not really joining you," John admitted. "I am here as a messenger. From the Earl of Morton. With tidings. And suggestions." This was not an easy introduction.

"Ha, Morton again! That crafty one! Ah, forgive me, your good-brother, to be sure. The queen's leprosy dread and my journey did not serve him and his friends to effect, I gather?"

"No. But it is not that, now. He sends me with word which he believes will concern you here, all of you, affect your plans. Sends me to the Duke Hamilton of Chatelherault, my lords of Argyll and Huntly and the others. Can I speak with them? Here? Now?"

"So you are something of an envoy, then? To be sure, I will take you to Chatelherault. I hope that your tidings are good?" He rose.

John followed him up to the head of the table, where the Hamilton chief sat with the earls; Kerr, head of an important Borders clan and warden, nowise diffident. He stooped over the elderly ducal shoulder and announced that here was Carmichael, Younger of that Ilk, come with tidings from the chancellor, Earl of Morton.

Chatelherault blinked in surprise, fork of meat to mouth; but it was Argyll, sitting next to him, who could not fail to hear what was said, who spoke.

"Morton! That rogue! What has *he* to say to us!"

"Tidings of some import, Carmichael declares." Shrugging, Kerr left the rest to the visitor.

John cleared his throat. "My lords, I come from my lord of Morton. With greetings. And, and this as my authority." And he produced the Douglas ring from a pocket, to hand to the duke, who examined it casually and passed it to the Campbell chief, who with scarcely a glance gave it to the Gordon, Huntly, next to him.

"What is all this?" Chatelherault wondered. He was a somewhat vague and uncertain individual, unlikely leader of the queen's cause and this armed uprising.

"Do you wish me to speak now, my lord Duke? Before all. Or . . .?"

"Out with it, man!" Argyll exclaimed. "If indeed you have anything to say worth the hearing! What is Morton at now?"

"His lordship would have you to know of word which

he has received from the Lord Herries, in England. Some kin to myself, my lords."

"Why should Herries send *Morton* word?" That was Huntly. "A man against the Queen's Grace."

"That is not for me to say. But I judge it is because he knows of this of the regent's offer of peace between the two warring factions, my lords. If you, for the queen, will accept the child James Stewart as king meantime. Forfeitures to be revoked, prisoners released and lands returned to owners."

"Nothing new in that," Argyll said. "We do not need Morton's efforts to move us to such folly!"

"Is it such folly, my lord?" John found courage to demand. "When the Lord Herries sends word that it is the queen's wish that you should so agree. That she desires peace in Scotland. That this will aid her case with Queen Elizabeth. And hasten her release from captivity and her return to France."

There was silence as men digested that, eyeing each other.

John took advantage of the pause to add, "Her Grace sees this peace as necessary. For Elizabeth has learned of the Duke of Norfolk's petition to the Pope to annul our queen's marriage to the Earl of Bothwell, now in Denmark, and allow her to wed himself, Norfolk. And she, Elizabeth, has ordered the arrest of that duke, and his imprisonment in the Tower of London."

That had the assembled chiefs, mainly Catholics, much concerned, since it was putting an end to any projected united rising in the two nations. There was murmuring round the table.

"Is this truth?" Argyll questioned. "Not Morton's scoundrelly schemings!"

"Truth, yes, my lord." John hoped that indeed it was. "It is from Lord Herries, who is able to speak with Queen Mary, at Bolton. It is her royal wish. And he is in a position to know the English situation."

Again silence. Then the duke spoke.

"We must consider this. Consider well . . ."

"Aye," Huntly said. "Here's a pickle! We need to take counsel."

"The queen is not under pressure to say this?" That was Sir Thomas Kerr, still at John's side. "Pressure by her gaolers?"

"Lord Herries would not have sent such urgent message had it been so, surely?"

"No-o-o. And we can trust Herries."

"But not Morton!" Argyll jerked.

There were more murmurs and talk.

"We will consider this," Chatelherault repeated, and Argyll waved John away.

"Yes, my lords. May I have the ring back?"

The Earl of Cassillis handed the token over, and John was led down the table again to where Kerr had been seated. A servant was ordered to bring him food.

The senior lords now had their heads together in urgent discussion. Presently they rose and left the chamber, while others finished their meal amidst much talk.

Kerr took charge of John, conducting him out of the monastery to a former hospice of the Order of St John of Jerusalem now being used as lodgings for the lesser commanders of the army. He said that he would send to inform of developments.

John did not have long to wait. Sir Thomas returned, to say that the Marian lords would send to inform the chancellor of their decision in due course, but that it was well nigh certain that the verdict would be agreement to some sort of peace, meantime, with the regent and Lords of the Congregation. But they certainly would not commit themselves to never seeking to restore Mary to her throne in days to come.

That was as much as John could hope for; and with nothing to wait for, it being still only mid-afternoon, he bade Kerr farewell, and set off on the long road to Dalkeith.

He got as far as Wrae again, for the night.

When he reported to Morton thereafter, omitting to mention that he had been named scoundrel and rogue, that man seemed reasonably satisfied. They would do as Mary urged, he asserted. He would have Moray to call a meeting with Chatelherault and the others, to have all sign some sort of pact or treaty, and they would have peace in Scotland – at least for some time. For Mary was young yet, and he judged that she would not be put off from seeking to regain her throne for overlong. But that would have to be dealt with hereafter. Meantime a truce, at the least.

John was dismissed, without thanks but at least without criticism, and the comment that he had been suitably expeditious about the business. He went to spend a pleasant night at Pittendreich.

Two weeks later all Scotland learned of the outcome. At Glasgow, in early March, considered presumably to be something of a neutral venue, unlike Stirling, Perth or Edinburgh, representatives of the Marians under the duke met the regent and his lords, and signed an agreement to accept young King James and end hostilities; also to send a message to Elizabeth Tudor urging her to release Mary and allow her to go to France. Apparently all the doubting northern chiefs were there, save for Huntly, who was probably the most fervent Catholic of them all, and had refused to attend. John was not the only one who considered that ominous, for his Gordons were a powerful, numerous and warlike clan, and they controlled Aberdeenshire and much else of the north-east.

But apart from that, folk breathed more freely.

12

That easier breathing-space was short-lived. In April,
the forty days' notice adhered to, a parliament was
called at Stirling – in fact a convention, for strictly it
could only be named a parliament if the monarch was
present in person; and two-year-old James was hardly to
be brought, although he was in that castle, possibly to howl
or whimper throughout. So a convention-of-parliament
it was. Sir James Carmichael again thought it advisable
not to attend. But they were not long in learning of the
outcome. Allegedly at Huntly's urging, Chatelherault,
backed by the others, and surprisingly the Secretary of
State Lethington, had tabled a motion demanding that
Queen Mary, still held captive despite their efforts, be
permitted to return to Scotland – this to bring pressure
on Elizabeth to release her for France, as had been the real
intention. Moray, claiming that this was an infringement
of the terms of the Glasgow pact, and earning that
five thousand pounds of English gold, denounced its
supporters as committing treason against King James
by so moving, whom they had agreed to acknowledge
as monarch, and promptly clapped Chatelherault and
Lethington in prison in Edinburgh Castle. It was thought
that Moray had been resenting the secretary for some time,
and took this opportunity of limiting his activities. Argyll
and Huntly stormed out of Stirling and returned to their
northern fastnesses.

Scotland was in its accustomed state of trauma and
unease once more.

John lay low at Eastend, hoping that Morton would not
find the situation as requiring *his* services.

Word then reached them at Carmichael that the regent was determined to put an end to the Marian and Catholic opposition once and for all. He was assembling another and larger army, to march north to deal with Huntly, Argyll and the Highland chiefs. More breaths were held, in case the Carmichaels were expected to contribute to this force. But mid-May passed, and they heard with relief that Moray had already marched.

Their thankfulness was the greater in that this period of tension coincided with John's twenty-first birthday and his coming of full age, with its celebrations, modest but important. Now he was his own man; and although his father had not constrained him overmuch these past two years, it made a difference to have to pay only suitable filial heed to parental wishes, and to be able to plot his own course – that is, except for the ever-present preoccupation with Morton's requirements. That problem had been of his father's making but, on the other hand, it had gained him a wife to whom he had become devoted, and well worth the price paid, he told himself.

And as well as lands at Wiston, the final part of his inheritance as heir to Carmichael, he gained another gift at this time, when Margaret gave him the information that she believed that she was pregnant, almost sure of it. Here was joy, except that John immediately became concerned that she did not over-exert herself, took no risks in her riding, rested for lengthy periods, and the like, at all of which the young woman laughed, and told him not to be foolish. There were six or seven months before they need worry about that.

They were in fact fairly actively engaged at Tantallon with Archie, in fishing expeditions and riding the sheep-strewn heights of the Lammermuir Hills, when Sir Archibald Douglas informed them that the regent and his force were returned to Stirling from the north, having defeated Huntly and some other Highland chiefs in a major engagement, Argyll and his Campbells apparently having failed to link up with the others. So now, with the Gordon chief fled and the north-east and Highlands in disarray, Chatelherault and Lethington imprisoned in Edinburgh, Moray was undoubted master of Scotland, for better or worse. Another convention-of-parliament was called for August, in Perth this time, to emphasise that mastery.

Sir John Carmichael, when he heard, decided that it might be wise to attend, in the circumstances, further absenting himself likely now to look as though he was in opposition to the powerful regent.

The news that he brought back in due course was that Elizabeth of England was still refusing to free Mary Stewart, although her sister-queen had now promised never to make claim to the throne of England, always a fear of the Tudor woman, and not to return to Scotland in the foreseeable future. Huntly had been forfeited and banished the realm, although how Moray could enforce that in the wild Highlands was another matter. Morton had acted chancellor, presiding over the convention carefully throughout, nowise opposing the regent but as it were keeping his distance, a man clearly ploughing his own furrow.

John wondered and waited.

His waiting did not imply inactivity. If he was now his own man, he had to support his wife and the family-to-be in suitable fashion; and he had now four properties to look after and in some measure seek to develop – Wrae, Longherdmanston, Wiston and a small holding near the latter, on the far side of Tinto, called Kylesmuir. Eastend was not his own, he only having the use of the house meantime. These lands kept him busy, for he had learned something of the monkish ways of land improvement, particularly at Wrae, drainage, crop management and rotation, fertilisation with manure, stock-rearing and so on. Most lairds considered such preoccupation beneath their dignity and left the land to be tilled by their tenants and herdsmen. John saw it differently, and was encouraged in this by Margaret, who went with him on most of his visits to the properties, making her own suggestions. For instance, she it was who advocated the development of another monkish industry, the large-scale farming of bees, not only for the honey, producing the sweetening required in so much of cookery and food-preparing, but the wax from the combs for candle-making. Everyone required candles for lighting, and the abbeys and monasteries had had almost a monopoly in the production of such, a large source of their revenue. And of course churches used vast amounts of candles in their worship. Since the Reformation there had been a distinct shortage in the land of candles. Here then, said Margaret, was a source of income, and a service to their fellows. She would discover, from sundry former monkish brothers whom she knew, how to make candles out of the melted wax, and build round the wicks; they might even eventually employ candlemakers.

So here was an activity John could encourage his tenants and farm-workers to add to their duties, the setting up of hives and skeps, these something like the pigeon-boxes or nests in dovecotes on a smaller scale, to house the swarms; and the cultivation of plants and flowers particularly attractive to the bees, such as clover, thyme, buttercups and others, to which the wild insects would be drawn, to add to the colonies. In September and October, of course, their own locality was admirable for the production of heather honey, from the slopes of Tintock Tap and Culter Fell.

In all this, John – and Margaret also – had an end in view, other than just improving the land and adding to their income. They had no permanent home; and they did not forget that rocky bluff of Over Sydserf, overlooking the Vale of Peffer between Haddington and North Berwick, with its wonderful prospects of the area where Scotland could be said to have been born, at the Battle of Athelstaneford, a magnificent site if ever there was one, for a tower-house and residence. They passed it every time they went to Tantallon. One day . . .!

National affairs by no means stood still that autumn

and early winter. The Duke of Norfolk in the Tower, chiefest Catholic in England, produced violent reactions from those of that faith, and there were still large numbers of them in Elizabeth's realm, as in Scotland. The Earls of Northumberland and Westmorland in particular, their demand for Norfolk's release being refused, rose in rebellion, and the north-east of England all but fell into their hands. This, so close at hand, produced inevitable repercussions, and there were stirrings amongst the Scots Catholics, especially in the Borderland, where Kerrs, Maxwells, Homes, Elliots, Turnbulls, Armstrongs and the like, grew restive — so much so that Moray was moved to muster another army, at Peebles, as warning. He was not very strong in the Borders.

It was this development which involved John, Morton sending for him at Dalkeith.

"You are friendly with the Kerr man at Jeddart, Ferniehirst, are you no'?" he asked. "He who told you o' the leprosy tale. I heard that you foregathered with him at Perth, yon time." Morton was always well informed. "Well, go you down to him at Ferniehirst. He's Warden o' the Middle March, mind. And that's a crown appointment. You remind him, frae me, the chancellor, that he has his duties! He and his Kerrs are said to be in touch with these English lords risen against Elizabeth. Moray's at Peebles, with a host. We want no trouble in the Borders. You go tell him so. I've my own folk in the West March, Morton and Threave and the rest, and I can have some hold over the folk there, Maxwells, Johnstones, Elliots and siclike. Have you heard, Herries is back from England, and Moray's imprisoned him in Edinburgh Castle with Hamilton and Lethington? But the Middle March is different. Douglas o' Cavers is but a laddie. Go you to Ferniehirst, man Carmichael." It was not often that Morton spoke at such length.

"What am I to say to Sir Thomas, my lord?" John wondered. "To make him heed me. Prevent him from supporting these English lords."

"Tell him that the crown – that's the regent – can appoint a new warden in his place! But, forby, say that his good-father, Kirkcaldy of Grange, could pay the price, if the Middle March rises. He's keeper of Edinburgh Castle, mind, and said to be ower friendly with some of his prisoners! Hamilton and Herries. So . . .!"

"You mean threaten him with Sir William Kirkcaldy in trouble if he does not do as you say, my lord? I could not do that."

"Could you no'? I say that you could, and shall! This is for the realm's welfare, and those who refuse to aid in it, if ordered to do so, can be arraigned for treason! And I'm ordering it!"

John looked away, features set.

"See you, lad," the earl said, changing his tune somewhat, "use your head. This is for your friend's weal, as well as the realm's. Moray has this force at Peebles. On the edge of the Middle March. Any trouble there and he could be at Ferniehirst in an hour or two. Think you Kerr could withstand an army?"

"He will know of this, without me telling him. And threatening his wife's father."

"Maybe. But if you tell him that Home, the East March Warden, is leal, and ready to march, that will have him thinking again, will it no'?"

John was silent.

"He will heed you, lad, his friend. Go, you." He pointed. "You can be at Ferniehirst this night, December as it is. There's no snow on Soutra, I hear."

That was that, then. Would Margaret say that his good conscience would make him refuse to go? What he actually *said* to Sir Thomas was for decision. He would have plenty of time to consider that as he rode those forty miles southwards.

John had some difficulty in gaining admittance to Ferniehirst Castle, shortly after midnight; but when he did it was to find Sir Thomas and his wife Janet not retired but having a bedtime drink of honey wine in the ingle neuk of the great hall fireplace. She was an attractive woman, and although surprised to see their visitor at that hour of night, greeted him kindly and went to get him refreshments.

"Something important must have brought you to Jedforest at such time, my friend," Kerr said. "Ill news? Or otherwise?"

"I am uncertain how you will see it, Sir Thomas," John answered. "In especial, when I tell you that I come at the behest of the Earl of Morton."

"I guessed as much – since it was so the other two times that you have come to me! Your good-brother is very . . . demanding!"

"He is, yes. To my . . . concern. Sometimes."

"And this time?"

John hesitated. "Sir Thomas, this of the English earls' rising. Were you . . .?"

"Thinking of joining them? The answer is – not now."

"M'mm. That is good. But, that is not quite it. There is talk of the Borderers rising. On their own. But in sympathy."

"And that is why Moray is at Peebles, with an army."

"Yes. In warning."

"He need not warn me. Nor your Morton, Carmichael. I have counselled no rising. Not at this time. Whatever it may be in the future. I would not join anything such. It is not the moment. For the queen's sake."

John let out a sigh of relief. "Thanks be!" he said. "Then I need not have feared to come. It was to warn you against anything such that Morton sent me."

"That also I guessed. I am not against some raid into England, to aid our queen. But these Catholic earls, Northumberland and Westmorland and the others, have chosen a bad time to rise. Their concern is not with Queen Mary but for religion, and to gain Norfolk's release. This of Norfolk seeking to marry her was never wise. The present is no time for an uprising. And we are not ready. But the Maxwells want to force the Lord Herries's release."

"So you are not taking to arms."

"No. If, and when, the time is ripe, perhaps. But not now."

"That is well." John paused. "How close are you, Sir Thomas, to Home, the East March Warden?"

"Close? I know him, of course. See him at wardens' meetings and joint assizes. But I would not say close."

"You are not . . . unfriends?"

"No. Why?"

"My Lord of Morton told me that Home is prepared to move against your back if you were to rise against the regent. I think that you ought to know."

"You say so! Ha, that concerns me, yes. Why, I wonder? Does he covet my position here? It is the greater March, yes. But the Homes are very much East March folk, of the Berwickshire Merse."

"Loyalty to the regent and young James?"

"I have never heard him speak to that effect."

Lady Janet arrived back at this juncture with a tray of viands for the traveller, and such talk was discontinued.

When, later, Kerr led John upstairs to the same room in the tower which he had occupied previously, and which a servant had now prepared for him with fresh bedding and hot water, at the door the other turned to him.

"I thank you for telling me this of Home," he said. "It is worth the knowing. A good night to you."

At least John had not had to tell his host about the threat to Kirkcaldy of Grange. But perhaps, in the morning, he should tell him to warn his father-in-law to watch his step at Edinburgh Castle?

That was mid-December 1569. By Christmastide, the English Catholic uprising had been defeated and the Earls of Northumberland and Westmorland and other leaders, who escaped, fled into the south-west Borderland of Scotland, where they aroused sympathy and some concern. Moray, with the wintry weather unsuitable for a waiting army, dispersed his Peebles force. An uneasy peace prevailed.

That is, until the 25th day of January. On that day all was changed. The regent, riding from Stirling to Edinburgh, was assassinated in the town of Linlithgow; and the realm of Scotland reeled.

They learned the details at Carmichael and Eastend in due course. Moray had been shot, with four bullets fired by Hamilton of Bothwellhaugh from a window of his uncle the Archbishop of St Andrews's house, as he rode slowly through the narrow crowded High Street of the town, thus paying the price for imprisoning Chatelherault, the chief of the Hamiltons, who was still in Edinburgh Castle. Bothwellhaugh escaped in the confusion which followed.

Not all the nation mourned Moray, even though he was a son of the late Gudeman of Ballengeich, King James the Fifth, illegitimate admittedly, and so uncle of the young king. But the impact of that shooting on the land was enormous, and apt to be incalculable.

13

Reaction to the regent's death commenced immediately, well before the state funeral, which was delayed for three weeks, the body being taken back to Stirling before being conveyed to Edinburgh's St Giles High Church by boat down Forth, amidst much pomp and ceremony. But well before that, John Carmichael was all too promptly involved, Morton on this occasion not sending for him but actually himself coming to Carmichael to see him. His journey was not wholly for this purpose, to be sure, but to seek to discover the Borderland's responses to this dramatic new situation. Clearly he was much concerned, and inevitably, for as chancellor he was the senior figure in government until a new regent for the little monarch was appointed. And he saw the Borderers' attitudes to be highly significant, all but vital indeed, at this critical juncture.

He had reason to, as he informed John at Eastend. Presumably it had all been brewing well before the assassination, for it could not have been arranged and put in hand in a day or two. But on word of Moray's death, Kerr of Ferniehirst and Scott of Buccleuch, with others, had led a large raiding party over the border into England, taking the refugee Earl of Westmorland with them – Northumberland was wounded – for purposes unknown but most obviously having some relevance to the new circumstances. It was important, it seemed, for Morton to know what lay behind this unexpected move, and its possible impact on the national situation and relations with England. John, as friendly with Kerr, was to go forthwith after the raiders and discover it, and bring back word at the soonest. Morton himself was going on to visit his own West March lands, to make enquiries and test feeling, before returning to Edinburgh for Moray's funeral. It did not take much guessing on John's part to gather that much of it all was connected with the question of who should be the next regent and ruler of the country, Morton surely in the running.

Although scarcely eager for this venture, John was less reluctant than he had been over others, since information was all that he was required to gain. And he was himself interested in it all.

Departing promptly, as ordered, he decided that Ferniehirst Castle itself should be his first call, the Lady Janet possibly willing to inform him as to something of the position. From Carmichael the most direct route to Jedburgh was almost due eastwards, by Biggar to Broughton on the upper Tweed, then down that great river by Peebles to Clovenfords to the Ettrick at Selkirk, this fifty miles. Then across the hills by Lilliesleaf to the Teviot and out of that dale, over Dunion Hill to the Jed Water, another score of miles, this latter Buccleuch country, a long ride in winter even for such as John. Fortunately it was still not snowy weather, and he covered the journey in seven hours.

At Ferniehirst, Janet Kerr was helpful, seemingly seeing no harm in telling her visitor the reasons behind her husband's present venture over the border. It was partly to seek to halt the persecution of the Catholics of the north of England by the victors in the recent uprising, Elizabeth's Protestant lords, to bring pressure on the Tudor woman in Mary's cause, but also to demonstrate to Moray's successor in Edinburgh, whoever that might be – and she suspected that Morton might well be in the running – that the Borderers were to be reckoned with as powerful influence in affairs in Scotland, this without actually mounting an armed challenge to the capital itself. Pressure also to free Herries, Warden of the West March, and Chatelherault from Edinburgh Castle.

This information, John felt, was almost sufficient for

Morton's requirements, and he wondered whether he ought to go back at once with it. But he decided that, since the earl would be in his own lands of Morton and Threave by now, he ought to go on after the raiders and learn more, if possible. Janet Kerr said that, so far as she knew, the party had gone over the Redeswire and Carter Bar pass and down Redesdale beyond into west Northumberland, intending to split up into two thereafter, one to go east into the Earl Percy's lands – he was wounded and recovering at Herries's castle of Terregles – and the other westwards into Neville's Westmorland. It was to be largely a showing of the flag, she understood, and large-scale fighting not anticipated.

John spent the night in which he now looked upon as his room atop Ferniehirst's stair tower; and with his very real thanks was off at first light due southwards for the Redeswire, the actual border crossing, and down English Redesdale, its upper reaches empty country indeed.

It was at Otterburn, where the great Douglas victory had been won against the Percy in 1388, that John learned from villagers that the Scots force had indeed split up here, one section under Buccleuch heading westwards for the upper Tyne and Westmorland, the other, under Kerr, eastwards, by Rothbury and Coquetdale, heading for Alnwick and the great Percy stronghold there, seat of the Northumberland earldom. He turned off to follow the latter.

This was all new territory to John, interested to see it. The relationship between the Scots and English Borderers was a strange one, of much mutual raiding and cattle-stealing, yet of a certain fellow feeling also, little real animosity, in the recognition that they were all Borderers and as such distinct from their own fellow subjects, Scots and English. There was, in fact, considerable intermarriage between the two sides – all tending to complicate the duties of the respective March Wardens.

John spent the night at an inn in Rothbury, a small town where he learned that the Scots party had passed through, without any hostile behaviour, two days previously. There had been no fighting here in the late rising either, apparently, this having been confined, as far as Northumberland was concerned, to the Alnwick area. He rode on thither next day, wondering what he would find. Was he likely to get involved in battle, on this quest? He had scarcely come prepared for that.

It transpired, however, when he reached Alnwick, only a few miles from the sea at Alnmouth, that the fighting was over. It had all been very brief, it seemed, the Elizabethan occupying force lodged in the town, taken by surprise, its leaders in the castle, and so not in any good position to take charge, and the townsfolk, loyal to their absent lord, rising to aid the Scots, their oppressors soon resorting to flight. John found Sir Thomas Kerr in the palatial Percy stronghold, abandoned by the enemy, with his fellow leaders and some of the Percy family.

Surprised as he was to see John again, Kerr knew at once why he was there.

"Ha, Morton wants to know how he stands with us Borderers now that Moray is gone?" he said. "He is the shrewd one! He will rule Scotland if he can! Am I not right, my friend?"

"He has not said so to me. But I dare say that it is so. He is at present gone to his own estate in the West March seeking information there. And sends me after you, Sir Thomas."

"Aye, he would! He knows that we Borderers could make or break his efforts. We, and the northern Catholics, Argyll and the rest. He wants the regency. But I judge that he will not win it. Not yet."

"No? And are you so sure that he wants it?"

"Oh, yes. But he is not to be trusted, by most. _I_ would not trust him! Would you, even though he is your wife's brother?"

"Perhaps not altogether," John admitted cautiously.

"He has played a double game. With Moray. With

Lethington. With the queen, forby. And back with Darnley. No, he has made over-many enemies."

"Who, then, think you, will be the new regent? Someone has to rule for the infant king."

"I would say the Earl of Mar. He is keeper of Stirling Castle, and so holds the child. He is well liked, a Protestant but not harsh against us Catholics. He has not made enemies, like Morton has. And he has never acted against the queen. He could rally much support in parliament."

"Mar! I had never thought of him. What of Atholl? He is a Stewart, and Justiciar of the North, holding one of the greatest earldoms in the land."

"But a Catholic. I would not think that he seeks the office, a quiet man."

John shrugged. "So, what would you have me tell Morton as to your aims and concerns, Sir Thomas?"

"Tell him not to make enemies of the Borderers. To get Herries and Chatelherault released – he could do that, as chancellor, now. To work for Queen Mary's freedom to go to France. To cancel Huntly's forfeiture. Then, if the day comes, he might have our support."

"Might . . .?"

"Aye, might! That one is slippery as any eel! We would have to be sure of him. Hold him to a pledge, an oath. As for this present, we will see Elizabeth's folk out of Northumberland and Westmorland, as warning to her. Tell Morton so."

With that, John had to be content.

Next morning he set off on the long road home, or at least to Dalkeith.

He found that Morton had returned to his town-house in Edinburgh from his West March visits, and so went on from Dalkeith to deliver his carefully worded report. But it seemed that the earl had not exactly lost interest in his mission but had discovered enough in his own lands to inform him, and now had other preoccupations, immediately the funeral of Moray, and thereafter the manoeuvrings as to the appointment of the next regent. John was not in a position to say anything on these issues. And his aim was, of course, to get back home as soon as possible to Margaret at Eastend.

But, it appeared, that was not yet to be. Morton declared that there was much yet to be arranged for the funeral, in suitable pomp and ceremony, and he could use John as his aide in it all. It occurred to that young man, then, that the chancellor, despite his high office and status, seemed to have very few friends and close assistants.

John had emphasised Kerr's concern over the release of Herries and Chatelherault from the citadel; and possibly with the thought that another assassination of their captors by the Hamiltons was to be avoided, the earl almost casually agreed that they should be freed. Lethington also. While there was still no regent, he, as chancellor, was in supreme command; and John's first errand proved to be to go up to the castle on its rock-top, with a written order for Kirkcaldy of Grange to set free the Duke of Chatelherault, the Lord Herries and Secretary Maitland of Lethington, a strange mission this for the younger man to be entrusted with, and to perform it through the person of Kerr's father-in-law.

He had no difficulty in gaining access to the mighty stronghold soaring above the city, by declaring that he came from the chancellor, the Earl of Morton, with important orders for Sir William Kirkcaldy.

The keeper, when reached, proved to be a good-looking, stocky man in his late fifties, who eyed John quizzically, and told him that he knew his father, and understood that *he* knew his daughter Janet.

"So you come from my lord Chancellor," he said, taking the signed paper. "You are now kin, of course."

"Of a sort, sir."

The other searched John's face, raised one shoulder, and opened the letter. Then it was his eyebrows which he raised.

"So, my lord of Morton changes his tune!" he observed.

"Now that the regent is dead . . ." John left the rest unsaid.

"He is to be congratulated on this, at least."

"Shall I tell him that you say so, Sir William?"

"Do that. I think that my lord will be desiring all the friends that he can win, now! No? Tell him also that my lord Duke of Chatelherault and the Lord Herries and the Secretary of State will be free to leave this hold just as soon as they desire."

"I shall, yes. The Lady Janet, your daughter, has been kind to me, sir."

"Then perhaps I should commend her judgment? But watch you my lord of Morton, young man!"

With that warning, John took his leave.

Back at Blackfriars Wynd, he was promptly allotted another task. He was to go to the city's provost, at the tolbooth, and inform him that he, with his magistrates and the chairmen of the guilds and crafts, was to lead the next day's funeral procession from Holyrood up to St Giles High Church. Have them assemble at the abbey at eleven of the clock, the procession to start at noon, robes and chains of office to be worn. They would there take their orders from the Lyon King of Arms. And on John's way back, to call on Colville of Cleish, the late regent's personal herald, who was to carry Moray's coat-armour in the procession. He would be found in his house in Boyd's Close, in the Canongate. He also was to be at Holyrood by eleven.

Here was something of a new aspect of Morton – that of organiser, and concerned with detail. John seemed to have become a runner of errands.

That evening, while the earl was outlining more duties for John on the morrow, in helping to marshal the procession, which seemed to be going to be a most elaborate one, for some unexplained reason, a servant came to announce the arrival of Sir Thomas Randolph and two other gentlemen. Randolph was Queen Elizabeth's resident envoy in Scotland. The earl looked thoughtful, and dismissed John.

It was considerably later and, yawning, John was thinking of bed, when Morton returned after seeing his visitors off. If he had looked thoughtful before, he looked even more so now, and not agreeably so. Indeed he was scowling.

"That woman!" he exclaimed. "That thrice-damned and accursed woman!" And he smashed a clenched fist down on to the other palm. "Does she think that she rules Scotland!"

John assumed that he was referring to Elizabeth Tudor, but did not say so. He said nothing.

"She sends her wretched, arrogant Englishry up to tell me, *me*, what she would have! Her will! She would have Lennox regent! That toady and lickspittle! Her pensioner. The fool Darnley's father. It is insufferable."

"The Earl of Lennox? In England. He has not been in Scotland for years. To be regent? He is the child king's grandfather, of course, if . . ." He did not continue with that. "Need you heed Queen Elizabeth, my lord?"

The older man stamped the floorboards. "Threats if we do not. War, even. Gifts, if we agree! Offers to send her forces to assist us, if there is opposition to her choice. And demands to deliver to her the Earls of Northumberland and Westmorland, who are in our Borders."

"The realm, Scotland, will never accept this."

"She thinks to win Scotland to her rule this way. As her father, Henry the Eighth, sought to do, by trying to wed our Mary to his son. And as all the other English kings have sought, by arms, since Edward Longshanks." Morton glared at John in fury, and then abruptly strode out of the room.

That man thereafter sought a bed in that unwelcoming house.

In the morning, all was bustle and hurry, with Morton not so much as mentioning the evening's concerns and apprehensions, John being sent off to Holyrood Abbey to assist in the preparations for the funeral. He wondered why the earl was so exercised over these obsequies of a man with whom he had often been at odds and whom he probably hoped to replace; but presumably there were reasons. At any rate, he was devising the most elaborate funerary display seen in centuries, much more ambitious than that of the late King James the Fifth; and James the Fourth of course had never returned from Flodden, while James the Third had been feeble and unpopular. Morton made it evident that he was very much in charge; so perhaps it was all part of his self-promotion?

John was kept busy, then, arranging, detailing, marshalling and rounding up, all in the name of the chancellor, although he imagined that this should have been the duty of the Lord Lyon King of Arms and his heralds. Bell-men had been patrolling the town from an early hour, telling the citizens to turn out for the occasion and line the streets. The provost and magistrates turned up in good time, with the guild brothers and craft deacons. The nobility and gentry, or many of them, put in an appearance later, and made themselves something of a nuisance squabbling as to rank and precedence, little sign of mourning being evident there in the wide abbey forecourt. A choir of singing boys was practising in the semi-ruined abbey itself, while the senior lords thronged the palatial abbot's house, long taken over by the crown and governors.

Eventually order of a sort was created out of chaos. The choristers were divided into two parties, one to lead the procession, the other to bring up the rear, with drummers to beat a slow marching rhythm. Then the city fathers were lined up under the provost, in their robes and gowns. Then came the ranks of the gentry and knights, which John was to join once Morton was satisfied that all was in order. The nobility followed, and here there was much dispute and debate as to seniority and prestige. Then came the coffin itself, to be borne by four earls and four lords, Morton, Mar, Glencairn and Cassillis, with Glamis, Lindsay, Ochiltree and Ruthven, with, just in front, Kirkcaldy of Grange bearing aloft the royal standard and

Moray's Stewart banner, and Colville of Cleish carrying the late regent's coat-armour. Behind came the members of the royal household, headed by the Lord Lyon and his pursuivants, these in the main hereditary appointments, the Chamberlain, the Treasurer, the Almoner, the High Constable, the Marischal, the Butler, the Dispenser and the like; and finally the second section of the choir. No doubt a considerable crowd of the common folk would follow on behind; but they would not be admitted to the church service.

When at length Morton was satisfied, the signal was given, the drummers started their beating and the lengthy procession moved off, John hurrying forward to take his place amongst the lesser gentry.

Out from the green skirts of Arthur's Seat they paced, the pall-bearers, four on either side of the coffin, carrying it on firmly attached poles, to commence the ascent to St Giles.

They had over half a mile to pace, up the Canongate thronged with watchers, a separate municipality from Edinburgh proper, relic of the days of an all-powerful Holy Church, with its own tolbooth; and on past innumerable wynds and closes on either side, dropping from the strangely formed, narrow, climbing spine which rose from the abbey right up to the castle, and so into the High Street, packed with the citizenry, so that the procession had some difficulty in winning through. Nearing the head of this and the main tolbooth, combining city hall, council-rooms and gaol, they reached the High Kirk, their destination.

Here there was inevitably some confusion as the long cortège began to fold up on itself as all sought to enter the great church by narrow doorways, the coffin-bearers going first now, and thankfully, to place their burden well forward below the high pulpit, to the choristers' chanting. Others pushed themselves into as good a placing as they could manage, with not a little competition, not to say dispute, lamentation for the deceased scarcely in evidence.

When at length the commotion had subsided sufficiently, a lesser procession of black-robed divines emerged
from a side chapel. They made their way solemnly to
the pulpit area, led by a grey-haired man with a long
trailing beard, stooping and frail-seeming but hot-eyed
and glaring about him – the notable Master John Knox
himself, leader of the Reformist clergy and close colleague
of the late regent. He had recently suffered an apoplectic
stroke, but was not allowing this to curtail his activities.
John had never seen this dominant character; but all
Scotland had reason to know of him and his so vehement
dogmatism, including to be sure Mary the Queen, who
had not been spared his denunciations, both of her
Catholicism and of her femininity and unfitness to rule.
Had he not indeed written a treatise entitled *The Monstrous
Regimen of Women*? He now limped to the pulpit, leaving
his colleagues to dispose themselves where they could,
and hoisted himself up the steep steps to the pulpit by
grasping the rails, and there, from its lofty platform,
turned to stare at the congregation for long moments,
silent. The silence communicated itself to all. Not a
sound was now to be heard inside the mighty stone vaults
of the church, however much noise came in faintly from
the crowd outside.

At length Knox broke the hush by smashing his fist
down on the open Bible which lay on the pulpit's
lectern.

"I heard a voice from heaven saying to me, Write –
blessed are the dead who die in the Lord, from henceforth.
Yea, saith the Spirit, that they may rest from their labours;
and their works shall follow them!" The man's physical
weakness had not yet transmitted itself to his voice, most
assuredly.

Thereafter, pointing down at the coffin, he plunged
into a eulogy on James Stewart, chosen of God to head
their ancient people, with the help of Christ's Kirk, out
of the mire of popery and the follies of a young woman's
reign, into the paths of righteousness and truth. Blessed

had been the realm of Scotland to have had this stalwart defender of the faith in its hours of need; and for ever damned to hell was the miscreant who slew this paragon, and all who supported and favoured him. And bringing down that fist again, he stared at them all, especially, it seemed, at those in the front row nearest the coffin. John wondered how Morton was enjoying this.

There was more of the same, a deal more, until quite suddenly that dominant voice thickened and faltered, and Knox, instead of banging the Bible and lectern, seemed to grip its edges to support himself, clearly having exhausted his strength.

Promptly one of the other ministers half mounted the pulpit steps and announced that they would pray. He proceeded in sonorous tones to urge their Creator to take His servant James into His close keeping, and raise him at the last day further to do His will – Knox meanwhile sinking down on to a seat within the pulpit.

This went on for some time. Then a psalm was chanted, the choristers leading, and those who knew some of the words joining in. While this was going on, Knox was assisted down, and went to lean on the coffin itself, in a sort of proprietorial fashion, his usual challenging look scanning all, despite his evident weakness, and so remained.

Whether the committal service had been meant to go on for much longer, or not, what had undoubtedly become the principal mourner's state probably shortened matters considerably, and, the psalm ended, the other ministers bore down on Knox, two taking his arms, to lead him along the crowded Holy Blood Aisle, to a screened-off area in the south transept, jerking heads in the passing to the lordly coffin-bearers to do their duty, the Kirk here very much in command. Hastily the eight of them went to pick up their poles and raise their burden and follow the divines.

They were led to St Anthony's Aisle, where a cavity had been dug in the stone-slabbed flooring, and here the coffin was lowered to rest, not without difficulty, John imagined – he, like most others in the church, could not see what went on, owing to the building's divisions into aisles – for those poles and their unaccustomed handlers would make the depositing in the grave an awkward business. At any rate, it seemed to take some time and a certain amount of trial and effort. Then Knox's voice rang out again, in the final prayer, strong at first then flagging, and to loud Amens the thing was done. The Earl of Moray, bastard of a monarch, operator of varying policies, strong for the Kirk if perhaps less so for justice and probity, was duly interred, and covered with Kirkcaldy's two banners.

The choir started up again, and the congregation thankfully made for the doors.

But now there was no re-forming of the impressive procession, no attempt made at any organised dispersal. Morton went off with a group of lords, including Mar and Cassillis, whither John did not enquire. He received no instructions now. Without lingering, he made his way down High Street for Blackfriars Wynd. Nothing had been said about further duties, and he desired none. He would wait in Morton's house for only a short while; and if no orders or demands were forthcoming, he would be off for home. After all, he was not Morton's servant, only his brother-in-law. And Margaret's confinement time was drawing near.

He was, in fact, off within the hour, Eastend calling.

14

There was a blessed interval from extraneous involvements and Morton's requirements – as well, for John would have flatly refused any part in them. Margaret's childbirth was somewhat delayed, and when it came about, was not of the easiest. John was all concern and anxiety, seldom leaving her bedside, and having the local midwife roosting in one of the attic chambers to be on call at a moment's notice. His wife assured him that all would be well, and that she would produce the son in due course quite satisfactorily – she was entirely convinced that it would be a boy – and he need have no worries. Early one morning, after a night's labour, John holding her hand much of the time, she proved herself right, in both respects, reminding him of it, exhausted as she was, the midwife hearty in praise and assurances. Hugh Carmichael was lusty as to his lungs, at least.

Joy and relief reigned at Eastend, for, from the first, there was no question that the infant was a healthy one. It was only after a few days that Margaret confessed to her husband that almost her first glance, as the midwife drew their son forth, was not only towards his loins but to his little pink feet, for she had seemingly had a very real dread that her own club-foot handicap could have been transmitted to her offspring.

The mother made a swift recovery, and proved to be an excellent one. But not so doting as to neglect what she conceived to be her other and wifely duties, especially in that matter of the bee farming, which she had adopted as her contribution to their prosperity. She had had John go to Lanark and hire to their service two former monks from the Franciscan friary there, these knowledgeable in the matter, and in the craft of candle-making; and with these two she was apt to be closeted frequently in one of the empty stables of the courtyard, where they built skeps and hives, with frames for the combs, and set up the apparatus of stove for melting the wax, a spinning wheel for making the wicks out of wool, moulds of hollowed-out cattle bone for the tall candles as distinct from the conical ones, and so on. John was sent scouring the neighbourhood to seek out beekeepers and gain stock, the transporting of which did present problems, although fortunately this late winter and early spring period was the best time to do it, with the insects more or less hibernating in their hives and nests. John suffered a few stings nevertheless.

Their tenants had to be sent for from the various properties, to be instructed also, this mainly in the farming and honey-producing side of it rather than in the candle-making and honey wine distilling, particularly the propagation of the clover, thyme, crowsfoot and woodbine, or honeysuckle, with other flowering plants in their seasons, which would attract the wild bees. The former monks explained how these wild ones were to be captured and domesticated. The secret was to find a patch of flowers where the insects were already feeding, then endeavour to follow their flight path back to their nests, wherein would be the queen bees, one to each nest. This discovered, the nest had to have wood burned beside it, for the smoke to eddy around it. Bees do not like smoke, and will not venture out into it, but cluster tightly round their queen to protect her. Then a cloak, or other cover, to be wrapped round the nest, so that it could be detached from the tree trunk or other support, and so carried back in the cloak to a prepared and waiting hive or skep, and inserted. So long as the queen was there, the worker bees would not desert her, and a new colony would become established.

All this, and more, they learned from the Brothers Michael and Thomas, including how to make hives out of straw, almost like thatching a roof. And how to distinguish the workers, which are sterile females, from the drones, larger and male, the queens being midway in size, and living a life of perpetual egg-laying after being fertilised by the drones, the workers eventually killing off the latter. Margaret drew the inevitable lesson for humankind.

John saw all this as satisfying and useful industry, helping to make them more prosperous, and so to be able to contemplate building the house of their dreams near to North Berwick.

In the midst of all the activity, disturbing news reached them from centres of government, although, fortunately, no summons came from Morton. A convention-of-parliament had been called for 4th March, and Sir John Carmichael had gone to attend it, important as it must be, to appoint a new regent. But it was suddenly cancelled, reasons not given. Not that there was much doubt as to these. The Lords of the Congregation and the Reformist party were concerned at the growing strength of the Marian and Catholic opposition; and decided that the appointment of a new regent must be postponed until they could be more sure of a suitable incumbent. A new Catholic rising had taken place in northern England, led by the Dacres, and while this was proceeding no sending back of the Earls of Northumberland and Westmorland was to be considered. Moreover, an envoy from France, one Verac, came to announce promises of aid in moneys, and if necessary in men, for Mary's supporters; and the assertion that Spain was also prepared to assist in the Counter-Reformation. So, with Kirkcaldy of Grange and Secretary Lethington now openly siding with the queen's party, it was no time to risk a parliament where the vote might well go against the faction presently in power.

Sir John returned from Edinburgh bemused, wondering whether he had indeed made the wrong choice as to allegiance. For his part, John wondered where the chancellor stood in all this. What of Elizabeth Tudor's demand that the Earl of Lennox should be regent?

They did not have very long to wait for some answer to this question. Elizabeth sent up two armies that later spring, first to close in on Dacre's rising from east and west; and when this joint assault succeeded, and Dacre, like his predecessors, fled over into the Scots Borders, the two armies followed, ostensibly to bring back the erring Catholic lords but in fact to emphasise Elizabeth's wishes as regards Scotland, Protestantism and the regency.

The Earl of Sussex invaded the East and Middle Marches with seven thousand men; and the Lord Scrope, with perhaps half that number, entered the West March. Despite their alleged mission to capture the rebel refugees, both forces promptly set about terrorising the three Marches, with unrestrained savagery. The Kerr and Scott raids were the first to be avenged, in the Middle March, Ferniehirst and Branxholme Castles being destroyed by Sussex, and even Home Castle not spared in the East March, these as well as over fifty lesser tower-houses demolished and some three hundred townships and villages burned, with much loss of life. In the West March, Terregles, Herries's seat, and other Maxwell, Johnstone and Armstrong towers were laid low.

Scotland reeled under the impact. Argyll, Huntly, Cassillis and the Hamiltons called their folk to arms once again; but with no unified national leadership, no regent or governor, and divided loyalties, no effective army went south to the Borderland to expel the invaders. John wondered anxiously whether his friends Thomas and Janet Kerr had escaped the slaughter. Also whether the aggressors would come in the direction of Carmichael. They might well all have to flee northwards.

Then, at the end of May, there was a new Elizabethan development, none other than the Earl of Lennox himself arriving at Berwick-upon-Tweed with a semi-royal escort of twelve hundred foot and four hundred horse, to assume the regency.

No forty days' notice was possible for the calling of a parliament in these conditions; so the chancellor fell back on the device of saying that the previous and cancelled sitting had only been deferred and should now assemble. A very hasty and unrepresentative meeting was immediately convened, almost entirely Reformist, and this appointed the Earl of Lennox to be lieutenant-governor of the kingdom under King James, his grandson, until a fuller parliament could appoint him regent – this although probably most present did not believe that he was in fact the child's grandsire, the general assumption being that James was David Rizzio's son, Mary's Italian secretary, with whom she had been very close, and whom Darnley had had stabbed to death before the pregnant queen's eyes. Darnley was indeed commonly considered as incapable of fathering a child, this opinion apt to be substantiated by the little king's sallow complexion and dark eyes, unlike the usual fair-skinned and blue-eyed Stewarts. The due forty days' parliament would sit on 12th July, in the tolbooth of Edinburgh.

So an extraordinary situation prevailed in Scotland, English armies in the south, the mainly Catholic north mobilised, the centre, where was the little king and his new governor, largely controlled by the Lords of the Congregation and the Kirk, pretending normalcy, while at Edinburgh Castle with its massed cannon, Kirkcaldy of Grange was able, if he so willed, to batter the city, parliament or none, into submission. It was a breath-holding state of affairs which could not continue for long.

Conditions grew even more dire. There was word that Elizabeth was sending up still another army to reinforce Sussex and Scrope, and was putting to the captive Mary the proposal, all but demand, that the castles of Edinburgh and Dumbarton be handed over to her nominees as the price of the Scots queen's liberty – which that young woman spiritedly refused even to consider. The northern Scots lords and Highland chiefs rejected the calling of the Edinburgh parliament as unlawful, and called one of their own at Linlithgow for 4th August, this in the name of the Duke of Chatelherault, who claimed to be second person of the realm and had been regent for Mary when in France, and of Argyll as Justiciar and Lord Justice-General of Scotland.

Which one would the chancellor attend? Morton represented lawful authority, as chief minister of the crown. The ordinary folk of the realm all but held their breaths, many of the nobility and gentry with them, not least the Carmichaels. Sussex and Scrope stood poised for advance northwards.

On 12th July Morton opened the convention in Edinburgh's tolbooth, with Lennox sitting on a seat beside the throne, to be duly appointed and proclaimed regent. The chancellor himself moved the adoption, Mar seconding. Morton had made his difficult choice. Kirkcaldy's cannon did not open fire.

Surely never had a regent assumed office in such inauspicious circumstances, civil war in progress, plus invasion. Allegedly advised by Morton, Lennox, Elizabeth's nominee, sent word to Sussex to make a gesture westwards by north, towards the Hamilton country, to keep the duke preoccupied, while he himself marched northwards against Argyll, Huntly and the others, with his English nucleus and the Lords of the Congregation's forces. John and his father were concerned that Morton would summon them and their men to join a Douglas contingent in the regent's northwards advance, but happily no such demand was forthcoming, possibly their comparatively small numbers being considered immaterial, and time being short, for it was important not to let the Marian forces assemble at Linlithgow for the alternative convention.

They waited uneasily at Eastend, John finding it difficult to concentrate on land improvement, drainage and planting and bee farming, although Margaret declared that this was much better than worrying about the realm's affairs. She had to admit that Sussex's gestures towards the Hamilton west could possibly bring the English invaders near Carmichael, for Lanarkshire was partly Hamilton country as well as Douglas; but with

153

Morton now supporting Elizabeth's Lennox, the English commander probably had instructions to avoid troubling Douglas territory. At any rate, soon they heard that he had confined his attentions to Dumfries-shire and southern Ayrshire, attacking Dumfries itself with great slaughter, and demolishing the castles of Caerlaverock and Annan and Hoddam, and was said to be boasting that "he had not left a stone house to an ill neighbour within twenty miles of the town".

For his part Lennox, not noted for soldierly activities, but with Morton and the English commanders, took over Linlithgow before the opposition arrived there, and marched on by Stirling, where he picked up Mar, and proceeded on northwards. They evidently decided to deal with Huntly and his north-eastern forces in preference to Argyll and the difficult west Highland terrain. They got as far as Brechin, in Strathmore, where the Gordon chief had based himself. They besieged that town and castle after an initial battle, and these, with Huntly's flight, fell after some time; then Lennox emphasised his regent's authority by hanging all the garrison as example. Presumably hoping that Argyll and the others would take this lesson to heart, the victors returned to the Stirling vicinity, rather than to Edinburgh where Kirkcaldy could menace them from the dominant citadel. By this time it was late autumn, turning into an early winter with bad weather and some snow. Hostilities died down meantime, and it was rumoured that Sussex had gone back to London for further instructions; but he left his army in the Borderland and south-west, and none assumed that any even semi-permanent peace could be looked for once campaigning weather arrived again.

Yuletide festivities were on a very muted scale in Scotland that winter of 1570–71, at Eastend as elsewhere. But at least their first autumnal heather-honey harvest had been a great success, the wax supply abundant, and candle-making and honey wine distilling consequently going ahead satisfactorily. There proved to be no lack of local markets for their products.

Between superintending all this and looking after young Hugh, Margaret was kept busy – and she kept John at it also.

Only one major item of news reached them from the north that hard winter. Dumbarton Castle, near to Loch Lomond, a powerful royal fortress held by the Marian party in Argyll's own territory, fell to the regent, not by storm and siege but by a ruse effected by one of Lennox's own supporters, with some internal co-operation allegedly, a serious blow to the queen's cause.

15

In the event, Lennox proved to be no harsh and oppressive regent, after those first hangings at Brechin, content to rely on the continued pressure of English forces in the land for support, and threat to his enemies. So, although the two sides in Scotland were no nearer mutual acceptance, and discontent and enmity simmered just below the surface, there was no major outbreak of violence and fighting as spring progressed. Lennox remained at Stirling, with his alleged grandson, leaving Edinburgh more or less to the Marians. Kerr of Ferniehirst and his Janet had escaped from their home before it was sacked, and now lodged with her father in the citadel. Scott of Buccleuch was also safe, having other houses in the remote Forest of Ettrick where Sussex and Scrope were unable to reach him in any adequate strength. None thought, however, that these Borderers and their mosstroopers would long remain quiescent.

Tidings of any real impact came, in fact, from England that spring. Queen Mary was removed again even further south, to Chatsworth in Derbyshire. There Elizabeth, worried about possible French aid, and possibly Spanish, with the last's great fleets of warships, sent her Secretary Cecil to put proposals to her sister-monarch. She had assurances, apparently, from Lennox and Morton, that Mary would not be permitted to return to Scotland if released. But if she agreed to instruct the King of France, and the dangerous Duke of Alba, Spanish conqueror of the Netherlands, to call off their proposed aid – and already there were some French captains operating with the Marian faction – then she, Elizabeth, would consider release for her captive to go to France. And Mary, it seemed, was now sufficiently confident of her support, in Scotland and on the Continent, to refuse any such arrangement. Whether this was wise or not, John Carmichael, for one, was not sure. A return *from* France, with a French army and possible Spanish fleet, at the same time as threats against southern England across the Channel, would, he considered, be her more effective course.

While all this was being debated, Sir John Carmichael received a summons to attend a parliament, a true parliament this time, it seemed, not a mere convention, at Stirling; for the five-year-old monarch was to be brought to attend it, this in forty days' time. That meant the beginning of September, this after a reasonably quiet summer in which the Eastend farming ventures had prospered.

Then, as it were in reaction, word came that an alternative convention was being called, in Edinburgh, in the name of the Duke of Chatelherault – who was, to be sure, next heir to the throne of the infant – although the actual caller was none other than Kirkcaldy of Grange, this declaring that Lennox was unlawfully appointed regent, and therefore *his* assembly illegal. This was to be held a couple of days before the Stirling one – a challenge if ever there was one. Sir John was much agitated. At heart a supporter of Mary, he would have preferred to attend this last, but in the present circumstances felt it safer to go to Stirling. Many others must likewise have been in two minds. John at least did not have to make such decision, not being entitled to attend either. The further that he could keep himself from involvement in such matters the better, Margaret only too happy to agree.

They heard no details of the Edinburgh assembly, and how well it was supported – that is, until Sir John eventually arrived back from Stirling over a week later. And then they were told enough to leave them all but dumbfounded, in all conscience. The Regent

Lennox was dead, and the land in greater turmoil than ever.

What had happened was this, they learned. The Edinburgh convention had decided to act rather than merely pass resolutions, and act drastically, on Mary's behalf. They would not only condemn the Stirling one but go there and rubbish it, according to Kirkcaldy, a man of action indeed, he leading. On the evening of 4th September, not an army but a quite large horsed and armed party had set off, heading south as though for the Borders first, to disguise their intentions, but presently swinging round west by north to head for Stirling, nearly forty miles away. It had included Huntly, the Lord Claud Hamilton – his father, the duke, discreetly stayed behind – Kerr of Ferniehirst, Scott of Buccleuch and numerous others, with Spens of Wormiston, an experienced soldier and Fife neighbour of Kirkcaldy's. Riding all night, they had reached Stirling in the very early morning, before most folk were awake. With three hundred and forty Border mosstroopers and sixty hagbutters, they were able to take the sleeping town without difficulty, for it was not large, however important, close all the streets and seek out the hostages they wanted – for it was known that practically all the great ones attending the parliament were lodging not in the castle itself, but in the more comfortable town-houses of the local gentry, the citadel's accommodation being limited and secure rather than easeful. The stronghold itself, of course, was quite beyond the attackers' taking. So they had found their task comparatively easy. Admittedly some of the more enthusiastic mosstroopers found it suitable to set fire to sundry of the houses, in order they said to smoke out the sleepers – this, as it happened, including the one where Morton was lodged. But the objective of capturing the principal figures of the Reformist party was achieved, the prisoners including Lennox himself, as well as Morton, Glencairn, Montrose, Eglinton and other earls, as well as one they had not expected to find there, none other than Argyll, who had chosen to attend this parliament rather than the other, for reasons unexplained. Also, of course, numerous Lords of the Congregation.

It all would have been a dramatic success for the queen's people, had it not been for the enthusiasts' fire-raising activities. For, up in the castle, Mar, its keeper, was wakened to be told that the town below appeared to be ablaze; and hastily arousing his garrison, he sallied forth, by which time the mosstroopers tended to be dispersed, celebrating, looting and raping. As a result, the disciplined castle troops under Mar were able in some measure to reverse the situation and free most of the more illustrious captives. It so happened, however, that Lennox was being held by Kirkcaldy's friend, Spens of Wormiston. One of the Border captains, Calder by name, when opposition appeared, decided that if they could not hold the regent, at least they could get rid of him, and cocking his hagbut, aimed it. Spens, an honourable man, seeing this, threw himself in front of Lennox to protect him and prevent any assassination. But Calder, probably drink-taken, fired nevertheless, the shot at such short range seriously wounding both men. Mar's men, seeing something of this, assumed that Spens had attacked the regent, and promptly cut him to pieces; they also captured Calder, who was thereafter executed, along with others. So a good man was lost, and what had been almost total victory much reduced.

Mar had had Lennox carried back up to the castle, along with the unhurt Morton and the other freed nobles, and the gates shut against all intruders. And there, after a few hours, the regent died – but not before he had nominated the rescuing Earl of Mar, guardian of the little monarch, to be his successor. He was the second of James the Sixth's regents to be assassinated.

The Marian leaders and their force, less casualties, returned to Edinburgh, grievously disappointed, Spens of Wormiston greatly mourned.

Sir John had another and very different tale to tell them at Eastend, less dramatic but with its own significance.

The five-year-old James, brought by Mar to his first parliament, and seated on the throne in the great hall amidst much pomp and ceremonial, had naturally been somewhat bewildered by it all and by the concourse of bowing dignitaries. Presumably he had never before been in the splendid hall built by his grandfather James the Fifth, for gazing around him, the child had piped up in the moments of silence after the ritual prayer by Master George Buchanan, who was to be the boy's tutor, he a colleague of John Knox, to ask what house was this? He was told by Mar that this was the parliament-house, and that this was a parliament, a talk and discussion of his lords, His Grace's first. At which the child, looking upwards at the distinctly ragged and dusty canopy over his throne, observed, "This parliament has a hole in it!" to the hearing of all there. Perhaps James Stewart, despite his years, had something there, Sir John assessed. That was the monarch's only contribution to the proceedings.

Now Scotland had a new ruler. John Erskine, Earl of Mar, was accepted as regent by a reconstituted parliament, with little debate, as an uncontroversial nominee. The chancellor, Morton, had scarcely been able, presiding over the proceedings, to propose himself as regent, and nobody else had put his name forward, although almost certainly he coveted the position. He had many enemies, being the man he was.

Mar himself was very different, of a genial yet strong character, in his later middle years, who had never pushed himself forward in the nation's affairs, but could be relied upon to do his duty. A confirmed Protestant, he was nevertheless not bigoted, and indeed was known to be friendly with not a few Catholics. He had been a loyal and effective keeper of Stirling Castle and guardian of the child monarch; and his own young son, Johnnie, Master of Mar, was of the same age, and constant companion of the young king; indeed his wife, the Countess Annabella Murray, was more or less James's foster-mother, since the

160

boy had never really known his own mother, Mary. Mar had in fact been destined for the Church and given the abbacy of Cambuskenneth, but, his elder brother dying, he had succeeded to the earldom.

Mar was not long in demonstrating that he intended to use his new authority to try to pacify and if possible unite the realm, and get rid of the invading English forces, taking the attitude that Mary, while a prisoner in England, or even an exile in France, could by no means reign in Scotland; and that therefore her son and heir should be accepted by all as king, with the future left to the development of events and consequent negotiations. To John this seemed an eminently suitable and practical stance.

That man did not realise how quickly he would be called upon to assist in this admirable process. Morton sent for him, for the first time for many months. At Dalkeith he was given his instructions.

"Your friend, Kerr of Ferniehirst, is good-son to the man Kirkcaldy," the earl said in his usual abrupt fashion. "Mar, the new regent, wisely or no', reckons that they might come to some agreement. Myself, I doubt it, or the rights of it. But it will cost little to try. Kirkcaldy has Edinburgh in a clenched first, with that castle and its cannon. I'm no' able to use my own house there! Mar wants a quiet meeting with the man, secret, see you. And it comes to me that you could further this, Carmichael."

"Me, my lord? How could that be?"

"Kirkcaldy will no' go to Stirling, that's for sure – any more than Mar will go to Edinburgh! But you could go to Edinburgh Castle to see that Kerr man. He is biding there, we hear, with his good-sire, while Sussex and his Englishry occupy the Marches. And so win to Kirkcaldy's ear."

John drew a deep breath. "Is this honest, my lord?" he forced himself to ask. "I would not be a party to any hurt to Kirkcaldy, through Sir Thomas Kerr, or otherwise. No deception, trickery?"

"Tush, man, mind your words! To who you bespeak! Think you I would hold wi' trickery? Forby, this isna *my* concern, but Mar's. He it is wants words with Kirkcaldy, not me."

"And would Sir William heed me, my lord? In this? A small laird . . ."

"Kerr is your friend, is he not? He will vouch for you. And he knows that you come from me."

"But not from my lord of Mar."

"He will accept my authority to act for Mar. I am the chancellor."

John shrugged. "You wish me to go now? At once?"

"To be sure. Arrange a meeting between them. In some secret place. And come back here to inform me."

So, still doubtful as he tended to be on all Morton's errands, John rode on the six miles to Edinburgh.

In the city, now under the queen's party's control, he faced the problem of gaining admittance to the great rock-top citadel. The tourney-ground leading up to the moat and gatehouse was crowded with what amounted to an encampment of mosstroopers and their horses, through which John had to wend his way, being eyed critically. His announcement that he came to see Sir Thomas Kerr of Ferniehirst allowed him passage, and also gained him admission by the gatehouse guards, with no difficulty.

Up at the palace quarters on the higher portion of the rock, near the little St Margaret's Chapel of ancient fame – although palatial scarcely described the accommodation – he was conducted to apartments where he found Janet and the Kerr children. She greeted him kindly, asked after Margaret, and when he informed of his mission, said that her husband was down in the town meantime; but that her father was in the castle and she would take John to him. Thus easily was the meeting contrived.

Kirkcaldy was with the Lord Claud Hamilton, a good-looking and gallant son of the rather retiring Duke of Chatelherault. He made no bones about accepting John, of whom he had heard, Janet remaining with them meantime. This was all very pleasant of course, but scarcely the conditions for a secret proposal and exchange. At length he had to say, all but apologetically, that he came from the Earl of Morton, at Dalkeith, with, as he put it, "tidings". Janet took the hint, and gesturing to the Lord Claud, she left the chamber with him.

"My lord Chancellor has tidings for *me*?" Sir William asked. "Such must be interesting, I think!" The older man was eyeing John carefully now.

"I have been sent to you by my lord of Morton, yes, sir. He is my wife's brother. But the message is from my lord of Mar, the new regent."

"Ah! More interesting still! What does his lordship have to say to one he considers a rebel, I judge? Scarcely his friend."

"He seeks a meeting with you, Sir William. At this stage a private meeting. Secret. Somewhere to be chosen. As I understand it, the regent is concerned over the divided state of the realm and over the continued English occupation of the Borderland. He conceives that all could be bettered. By some agreement between you and your friends, and himself."

"Agreement? That would be hard to arrange, would it not? Considering our respective aims."

"Perhaps, sir. That is not for me to say. But I understand that he holds that while Queen Mary cannot reign in Scotland while she remains a prisoner in England, or possibly when she is an exile in France, an arrangement could be made whereby her small son James is accepted by both sides as monarch meantime, without prejudice to the queen's return to her throne at some future date, if that was the will of the majority of her people. The nation needs a monarch, so as not to become a mere appendage of English Elizabeth."

"H'mm. That is a point of view, yes. But there could be a host of obstacles to overcome. Not least Elizabeth's aims and requirements."

"I understand that the Earl of Mar believes that a united Scotland could overcome such. As has been proved in the past."

"And the matter of religion? Catholic and Reformist? How is that to be settled? Save, sadly, by force?"

"Mar is a Protestant, sir. But a moderate one. Not one of the Lords of the Congregation. He feels, I think, that both could retain their faiths, and work together. For the national weal . . ."

"That is not the view of the said Lords of the Congregation! Nor yet of your Morton, I judge!"

"They are scarcely winning in this shameful struggle, sir. They might well be prepared for some compromise. Especially if led by the regent himself."

"You are very persuasive, young man! But I do not understand why *Morton* has sent you. Mar, perhaps – but not Morton!"

"Why should my lord not see it similarly, sir?"

"Say that I do not judge him to be strong for peace, concerned with unity, as you make the Earl of Mar to be."

John did not feel that he must defend his brother-in-law's reputation, but he had to say something. "What makes you think that, Sir William?"

"It is scarcely a new thought!" the other admitted. "But this of Argyll, shall we say, confirms it."

"Argyll?"

"Aye, the Campbell. My lord the MacCailean Mor! His change of sides. That is Morton's doing."

John stared. "You mean . . .?"

"I mean that Argyll, who used to be strong for the queen's cause, has gone over to the others. He attended Mar's convention, not ours. At Stirling. We indeed captured him briefly along with the others in the town, but lost him again by some of our people's folly. But, one whom we did hold, another of his Campbells at that, assured us that it was due to Morton's contriving. He had done it by making a bargain. Promising that if Argyll changed sides and supported him, Morton, as new regent, he would appoint him chancellor in his stead, second officer in the kingdom. I take it that if Morton was for Mar's peace and unity, he would scarcely be bargaining thus!"

That had John Carmichael momentarily speechless.

"How think *you*, then?"

"I do not see . . . why he has sent me to you? If it is indeed so?"

"That I cannot tell you. But he can play a deep game, that one. He will be regent, and rule the land, if he can. This of Mar's move may serve him in some way, who knows? But it is not for me to instruct you as to your good-brother!"

There was silence for a space.

"Then . . . you will not meet Mar?" John asked, at length.

"I did not say that. It might be worth my doing so. To hear what he proposes. He is still regent, as yet. Yes, I think that I could usefully see him."

John nodded. "When? Where? It has to be secret, they say, Sir William."

"I recognise that. See you, I know of a place where we could meet privately. Secure. And midway between us. At Linlithgow. There is a small island in the loch there. Near to the palace, but only to be reached by boat. That could serve. But neither side to bring any large party. No attempts at capture! That to be understood."

"I am sure that my lord of Mar would never consider that last . . ."

"But Morton might! I would not put it past him. Could that be why he has sent you? To contrive to capture myself and any whom I bring?"

John swallowed. "I, I did not consider such a thing. But I did ask him if this was all honest. No trickery . . ."

"Ha! So you do deem him capable of it! You also?"

"I said that I would not be party to any ill against you or Sir Thomas Kerr. He assured me that it was all a true mission. I would not have come, otherwise."

"I believe you. But, Morton! Well, Linlithgow, then. When? In one week's time, say? This is Tuesday.

165

Next Tuesday. In the evening. I could lodge for the night at Claud Hamilton's house of Kinneil, near to Linlithgow."

"Yes, then. Next Tuesday evening. I hope that it proves to the good of all, sir."

"To be sure. But watch your good-brother!"

John took his leave, thoughtful indeed.

He saw Janet Kerr and Hamilton again, but did not linger, Sir Thomas not yet returned. On the way back to Dalkeith, he pondered and considered. This of Argyll had shaken him. Was Morton as crooked as that? And Argyll also, to be sure? Could he raise this matter with him? Had he any right to do so? And Morton would not give him any straight answer if, as seemed probable, his intentions were less than honourable. So, was there any point in saying anything? Would he not be wiser to try to keep out of any further involvement?

When face to face with the earl, his self-questioning was scarcely relevant. He informed that Kirkcaldy was prepared to meet Mar, and suggested the following Tuesday evening at the little island in Linlithgow Loch, both parties to be small, and all secret as Mar desired. But Kirkcaldy had not disguised suspicions of guile, deception, treachery. He had assured him that it was all honourable.

"And quite right, man Carmichael! Mar intends nothing false. So Kirkcaldy agrees?"

"Whether he and his colleagues will agree further with the Earl of Mar's proposals is another matter, my lord. But, so far, yes."

"Aye. We shall see. Tuesday next, at Linlithgow. I can be there, then, I jalouse."

"*You* are to attend, my lord?"

"I am. What think you? I am the chancellor, am I not!"

"And . . . will my lord of Argyll also be there?" That was as far as John dared go.

The other looked at him sharply, narrow-eyed. "What has you asking that?" he demanded.

"I heard that he had changed sides. And wondered."

"You did! Folk who ken little should keep their won-
derings to themselves; Argyll has nothing to do with this
matter."

John sought to look suitably chastened.

"Is the man Kerr to be with Kirkcaldy? And Scott o'
Buccleuch? The pair that raided into England."

"I do not know, my lord. He, Sir William, did not
say who would accompany him. Just a small party,
he said."

"Aye. Well, you will be in *my* small party, Carmichael.
I may need you there."

"Me? What, what could I serve? In such secret matter?"

"That is for me to decide. Evening at Linlithgow, you
say? Be you here, then, that morning. Tuesday next."

Dismissed, John set off for Eastend, less than easy in
his mind.

"My brother is a rogue and a villain, however clever!"
Margaret declared. "It is my sorrow that I have inflicted
him upon you thus. But you need not think to do
his bidding in all things, John. Merely because I am
your wife. He finds you useful, clearly. But he cannot
command you."

"Can he not? He is chancellor of the realm, chief
minister, under the regent. Refusal could bring much ill
on me and mine. On my father and family also. He aims
to get his way, does your brother! And has the means to
ensure it."

"It is strange how he is that way. The mischance in our
family. And he to be the head of the Black Douglases!
My other brother, David, of Angus, Archie's father, was
quite otherwise, honest, kindly. Our father also. Where
did James get his character? Why must he be so?"

"Who knows what makes a man? What forms strength
and weakness, good and ill? Morton is able, shrewd,
far-seeing . . ."

"But ambitious above all. He seeks power, always has

done. Uses all to gain it. He used me, to win you and your father!"

"For that, at least, I thank him!"

"As do I. But I would not have you used against your will. If need be, I will go and tell him so."

"That would make me seem a weakling. Not to be telling him myself. Ah, well, we shall see after the Linlithgow meeting. What he wants me there for, I do not know. But I shall find out!"

In due course John rode northwards in company, for he took Margaret and their little son, Hugh, to see his grandmother at Pittendreich. The child, now eighteen months old, Margaret said could be carried a-horse in her arms, even on a journey of that length, if they did not hurry it. Soon they might be able to take him to Tantallon, and see more of Archie, now aged fifteen.

Lady Douglas was charmed with her new grandson.

Margaret must have had a word with her mother, for before John left in the morning for Dalkeith, she drew him aside.

"Do not allow James to be overbearing, John," she said. "He can be so, I know well. Outface him, if need be. To his own good, indeed. Consider it that way. As chancellor, and the Black Douglas, he gains his own way overmuch. Always he has been apt to be demanding, even as a child. He needs others to stand up to him, on occasion."

"But he wields much authority, see you."

"He can be outfaced from the exercising of it where the cause is right. He requires to be. Remember it, John."

That was all very well, of course. But . . .!

At Dalkeith Castle John was surprised to find quite a troop of men-at-arms assembled to escort Morton on this supposedly secret assignment. He had quite some time to wait before the earl was ready to move. John appeared to be his only aide, as distinct from escort. He sometimes wondered why Morton never seemed to use any of his numerous illegitimate sons as messengers and assistants.

Under the Douglas banner they at length moved off

on the twenty-five-mile ride to Linlithgow, skirting Edinburgh to the south by the Burgh Muir. John rode beside his brother-in-law, but there was little converse, the other scarcely one for idle chat.

Passing Wrae, in time, John did mention his farming ventures there, land improvement and Margaret's bee-keeping and candle-making; but his companion seemed less than interested.

Linlithgow, almost four miles on westwards, was a small town dominated by its great red-stone palace, the dower-house of the Scots queens, on its ridge above the quite large loch, with the fine church of St Michael's close by, that wherein the little king's great-grandsire, James the Fourth, had received his allegedly spectral warning not to go on his French-requested invasion of England, which ended in the disaster of Flodden Field. A few retainers hung about the palace courtyard and the town streets, but nothing compared with the Douglas contingent. Presumably the principals were already out on the little island in mid-loch.

John knew of the islet, a favourite retreat of queens, whereon was a bower, as it was called, a summer-house amidst the trees, and something of a private pleasaunce or garden. Here the Bruce had wooed his queen-to-be, Elizabeth de Burgh.

At least Morton did not seek to take his men down to the loch shore, where a boat was waiting, and with only John he was rowed out to the island.

There the first person they saw was Secretary Maitland of Lethington walking with Kerr of Ferniehirst, these eyeing Morton warily, but Sir Thomas greeting John in friendly fashion. Lethington and Morton did not speak. They were led to the bower, where they found the Regent Mar and the Earl of Eglinton, the Montgomery chief, with Kirkcaldy of Grange and Sir Walter Scott of Buccleuch. John felt very much an outsider in this company. If Mar was surprised to see him with Morton, he did not say so. That young man was still wondering why he was here.

It appeared that they were the last to arrive, and no comradely reception for Morton, suspicions rather. There was little delay in commencing the debate, in that summer-house. Mar, Morton, Eglinton, Kirkcaldy and Lethington sat round a table, with Kerr, Scott and John, a little back, on benches, observers.

Mar led off, declaring that the nation required an end to internal war, and to be rid of the English occupation of the Borders. He, as regent, saw no reason why there should not be accord meantime between the factions of Mary and her son, between Catholic and Reformist, certainly while the queen remained outwith Scotland. There had to be a monarch and James had been duly crowned and the regency established. He, Mar, was prepared to be guided by a council of regency containing representatives of both persuasions, this to resolve difficulties and disharmonies. Then, at some future date, should Queen Mary return and claim the throne again, the issue could be put to a parliament, or special assembly of the realm; and if a clear majority were in her favour, she would resume her reign and King James be acknowledged as heir to the throne. There was the style and position of queen consort. There could be a king consort role for James until he succeeded his mother in that eventuality. The late Lord Darnley had been given the crown matrimonial. James could be given the crown consort. But if the majority were for him and the Protestant reign, Mary, his mother, could be queen consort. Meantime, accept James as king. What did they all say to that?

There was silence for a few moments. Then Kirkcaldy spoke. "You make it sound reasonable and acceptable, my lord, in present circumstances. But did we not go through the like at Glasgow, when my Lord of Moray was regent? And what happened thereafter? No promises kept, all as before, strife and conflict . . ."

"Whose fault was that?" Morton grated. "Who changed the terms? Your demand that Mary Stewart should be permitted to return to Scotland, not go to France!"

"It was but a proposal. To force Elizabeth's hand, as you well know, my lord . . ."

"Sufficiently real to make Lethington here change sides!"

Mar intervened, with this acrimony looking as though it might cancel out his initiative. "Conditions change. And now *I* am regent. We can make a new start, in all honesty. These my proposals could greatly serve the realm."

"How many of your party, my lord, the Lords of the Congregation in especial, and Master Knox, would agree to it?" Kirkcaldy asked. And he looked over at Morton.

"I deem most would." That was Eglinton.

"And this of the English invaders?" Lethington put in. "Why *I* could not remain with your party. They are here with Reformist agreement, possibly invitation! Will they concede that they should be sent back to Elizabeth Tudor?"

There was a growl from Buccleuch.

"I shall see that they do," Mar said. "It would be made a royal command."

With more doubtful looks amongst the Marians, Lethington went on. "We have reason to believe that Elizabeth has sent . . . inducements! To my lord of Morton, here. By Sir William Drury."

That produced another all but breath-held silence.

"Idle tales and fables!" that earl said, at length. "The chatter of fools. To be believed by fools!"

Mar cleared his throat. "Such talk should not be continued. Nor credited. To create dissention."

Lethington was not to be silenced. He was, in theory, still Secretary of State, since he had never been formally demoted nor replaced. And he had always been an enemy of Morton. "And Argyll?" he demanded.

Again a pause. It seemed that the secretary was indeed opposed to more than Morton, to this entire initiative.

Mar had to look at Morton again, frowning.

"The Campbell has wisely chosen to aid in this matter," that earl jerked. That was all.

"For a price, perhaps?" Kirkcaldy added.

No reply.

"This of getting the English out of the Borders," Lethington went on. "Without that, no such accord is of any value. Can you, my lords, effect that? With so much . . . acceptance of their presence. My lord of Morton will not deny that he has had dealings with Drury, Marshall of Berwick, and Lord Hunsdon, Elizabeth's envoys."

"I have sought to slacken their grip of our Marches, man!"

"With scant success, then! The Borders scarcely love you and yours, my lord!"

"Then they ought to! Ask Ferniehirst, there. I sent John Carmichael, here present, to him, to have him and Buccleuch lead a raid into England in order to get behind Sussex's force, and give them pause." Morton turned, to look at John.

So that was why he was here! To act go-between with the Border chiefs, who were amongst the strongest of the Marian faction.

"I have visited Sir Thomas on various occasions," he agreed carefully.

"And never to his hurt."

"No."

Kerr spoke up. "Nevertheless, my lord, the English still occupy my land. And Buccleuch's. And should be expelled. But they have the support of the regency. And of the chancellor!"

Another growl from Buccleuch.

"Support! Not so. We have to accept their presence, since we have not the power to expel them, lest *you* assail our backs! Whose is the fault?"

Mar intervened, the peace-maker. "So, the need for, if not unity, at least acting together, is clear. Fighting each other instead of sending the English home is folly. And no help to either King James nor his mother. How say you to that, my friends?"

"This will require much thought," Kirkcaldy said. "Consultation with others, the Duke, my lord of Huntly . . ."

"He who largely wrecked the Glasgow accord!" Eglinton joined in.

Mar raised a restraining hand.

"But not Argyll, it seems!" That was Lethington again, to Morton's dismissive gesture.

This was a difficult ship to steer.

Kirkcaldy turned to his two observers. "The Borderers will be all-important in any decision. How say you?"

Kerr answered. "All will depend on the English leaving. If we can be sure of that, the rest will be accepted, I judge." He looked at Buccleuch, who nodded.

"And with Elizabeth's bribes to those presently in high places, can we expect that?" Lethington again eyed Morton. These two were most evident enemies now, although they had once been close colleagues in government.

"If it will satisfy you, I will send John Carmichael, wed to my sister, to Sussex at Dumfries to urge his retiral. Now that Norfolk has been executed and so cannot wed Mary, there will be the less reason for him and his to stay. No Catholic match, no rising in England." That was longer than Morton's usual interventions.

He had no lack of attention to it. Most evidently none there, even Mar, had heard of Norfolk's end. It may have occurred to more than John to wonder how it was that it was Morton who had gained the information. The news clearly made a major impact. Men eyed each other. It altered much.

After that, there seemed to be little more to discuss, save for some doubts raised as to whether the Gordon chief, Huntly, perhaps the most aggressive of the Marian leaders, would accept this proposed accord, if it could be called that; and if not, whether it could go ahead. Soon the meeting broke up.

John walked down to the boat with Sir Thomas Kerr.

"Your good-brother continues to surprise," the latter said. "Working with him must be . . . taxing!"

"I scarcely work with him," John pointed out. "Say that I serve as his messenger, on occasion. I am seldom consulted as to the message!"

"I guessed as much. Yet you continue to do so? To oblige him?"

"I have little option. James Douglas is, in fact, the continuing power behind the throne, as chancellor, whoever may be regent. At least since Moray died. He has the means to . . . persuade!"

"Aye, that may be so. See you, this of your mission to Sussex that he spoke of. How honest, think you, is that to be? How much, think you, does Morton wish the English out of the Borders? How much of a Reformist is he, in truth?"

"That I cannot tell you, Sir Thomas. Never once has he mentioned his faith, his religious feelings, to me."

"If he has any! Save the promotion of James Douglas! I would be interested to learn of your message to Sussex."

John only shrugged by way of answer to that.

At the boat, which could carry only a few passengers at a time in addition to the oarsmen, Morton and Mar were already aboard. The former beckoned for John to join them. The others could wait.

The regent eyed John interestedly. "You are young, I think, to be entrusted with my lord of Morton's missions," he said. "You must be trustworthy!"

Just what was behind that? John wondered. Did Mar trust Morton, himself? Few others did, it seemed. "I seek to do my best," was all that he could say, and looked at the other earl.

That man produced a sort of grimace and it occurred to John that he had never seen James Douglas actually smile. "Carmichael knows where he stands!" he said.

Was there an opportunity here? "I sometimes wonder!" he dared to observe.

Both men looked at him sharply, the tone of voice perhaps more significant than he realised.

There was no time for more, as the boat grounded.

No lingering and talk took place up at the palace, and farewells were of the briefest. Thereafter the Douglas contingent was trotting back in the Edinburgh direction. The so-important conference had taken little more than one hour.

It was some time, with Morton slightly ahead, that he reined in to speak to John. "Back yonder you said to Mar that you sometimes wondered, John. About what you did for me. What meant you?"

Here was the challenge, then. And it was the first time, he thought, that the earl had ever called him just John. Was that some guide? "My lord, I have my feelings, my concerns, my loyalties. They may not always match with yours. I am wed to your sister, and happily. But I am my own man. You will agree? So, I reserve my right to choose, on occasion!" Was this how Lady Douglas and Margaret would have had him put it? He could hardly add that it was at their advising.

Tight-lipped, Morton pondered that. Then he shrugged. "I can get others to serve my ends, Carmichael. Less . . . delicate!" It was back to surnames. "Are you refusing to go on this assignment to the Earl of Sussex?"

"Not if it is to the realm's benefit. To help get the English to leave."

"Think you that I would do aught that was not to the realm's benefit, man? I will urge that, with Norfolk dead and now no danger of a marriage and a Catholic rising in England, as in Scotland, to put Mary on Elizabeth's throne, as was Norfolk's aim, there is no need for Sussex's occupation of our Marches. Let him retire over the border. And have peace between the two realms. I will give you a letter to him."

That sounded fair enough, naught to baulk over. John nodded.

The ride back to Dalkeith thereafter was, if scarcely

companionable, less stiff as to relations than heretofore. Perhaps the ladies had been right, and Morton needed occasional standing up to.

Somewhat improved rapport or none, John did not think to lodge that night at Dalkeith Castle, nor indeed was invited to, but proceeded on the short distance to Pittendreich. When asked, he gave his hostess some brief indication of his attempt to carry out her counsel, to expressed approval. She was interested in his account of the proceedings at Linlithgow, praised Mar's attitudes and initiatives, but wondered whether, despite his high office, he would be able to carry out all that he aimed for, with the men he had to rely on to aid him. She did not actually name her son amongst them, but that was almost certainly implied.

John got on well with his mother-in-law, and the evening passed pleasantly; but he missed young Archie's presence. He was less and less at Pittendreich these days, but at Tantallon, as was only to be expected with the boy now nearing sixteen years, and beginning to grow into lairdly status.

In the morning John was off for Eastend – but only for two nights, before heading south-westwards for Dumfries.

16

Margaret, although disappointed that she was going to be losing her husband again so soon, was approving of his mission, and still more so of John's account of his assertion of some independence towards her brother, moderate as it had been.

"Perhaps, from now on, you may be spared so much errand-running," she hoped. "James has found you too easy. If we Douglases have to be demanding, *I* have plenty of tasks for you! No? I would wish to see a candle-making manufactory set up, larger than the stable we use here. But since it would have to have much gear, fires and ovens for the melting of the wax, spinning wheels for the wicks, vats, moulds and the like, and storage space, some building of size and substance is required. Also somewhere for our Brothers to reside nearby. Where? If it is to be permanent, it should not be here at Eastend, for we are only here on sufferance. Your brother will want this house if and when he marries. Wrae and Longherdmanston are too far away for us conveniently to visit frequently, as needed. Would Wiston serve? It is none so far off, no large place, with no empty barns, but . . ."

"There are cot-houses there, unused, as I remember. We could make use of a couple of those. Link them together, if need be, with wooden buildings. The Brothers could dwell there. It is but six or seven miles although on the other side of Tinto. An hour's ride, no more."

"Good. Then we could go there tomorrow, before you head for Dumfries." She nodded. "And there is another matter which I have been thinking on, and which I deem we ought to be spending some of our time on instead of devoting it to my brother's interests. That is, this of young Archie of Angus. *You* have no true responsibility for his well-being, I know, but he is greatly fond of you. And he is my nephew. We are not seeing so much of him in these days, and he is growing towards manhood, no longer a child. It is a time when he needs guidance and caring. He will have great responsibilities presently, as Earl of Angus, chief of the Red Douglases."

"To be sure. I have thought as much, myself. We should see more of him, yes. Have him here? Go to Tantallon more often?"

"There, yes. And here. But, more. Most young lordly ones of his age have a tutor, if their father is not alive. Not a teacher but one to guide them towards their future duties. He has only Glenbervie, Sir Archibald. He was appointed keeper of Tantallon by James, a second cousin. I fear that James may seek to step in, seek to mould Archie to *his* will and ways. He is his nephew also, and may well see him as very useful, one day. To use him for his own purposes — which are not always honourable, as we know! And so to control both Black and Red Douglases. It would be shame if Archie was . . . spoiled."

"M'mm. Yes. I see that. Morton has never mentioned Archie to me, in any special way. But, yes. What think you? What can we do? I cannot appoint myself tutor to Angus!"

"No. But we could see much more of him. Talk with him about the future, about his duties to come, his responsibilities as one of the great earls of Scotland. Somehow warn him as to his Uncle James! If he would come to look on us as his guides, as well as his friends, as he grows to manhood, then we might serve him well. And serve others, for one day he will have much power. Is that arrogant, to think so? Prideful?"

"No, no. It is right, wise. I should have considered it. Something that we can do, seek to do. Your mother would approve?"

"I am sure that she would. How it is to be done, to

best effect, I am not sure. But it should not be delayed. Think of it all, John, on your long riding to Dumfries and back."

So, after a day's prospecting and arranging at Wiston, behind Tinto, to their fair satisfaction, John set off southwards on his sixty-odd-mile ride.

He went down Douglasdale to Crawfordjohn, and over the high ground beyond to Sanquhar on the upper Nith, halfway. Then down Nithsdale, by Enterkinfoot and Thornhill and Auldgirth, the remaining thirty miles to Dumfries. He had plenty of time to consider the matter of Earl Archie's tutoring in chiefly responsibilities on the way, although he wondered as to his own adequacies in it all.

He passed many camps of English troops as he went, avoiding any close contact where possible – not that any behaved aggressively towards him. They all seemed to be looking on their occupation of the West March as something like a holiday; presumably the local people were less appreciative. John imagined that the invaders were avoiding the lands of the more assertive mosstrooping clans of Armstrong, Johnstone, Elliot and the like, in Liddesdale, Eskdale, Ewesdale, where their presence would almost certainly have involved constant fighting.

At Dumfries town John learned that his journeying was not yet over, for although the streets were full of soldiery, the Earl of Sussex and his senior commanders were apparently lodging in Caerlaverock Castle some eight miles away on the Solway shore. John had thought that Caerlaverock had been sacked by the invaders, but presumably it was still in a state to be occupied – and certainly it was conveniently positioned for easy communication with the main English base at Carlisle, with a sail of only another eight miles across the Solway Firth to near that city.

When he reached the castle, with the darkening, it was to find it ablaze with lights and swarming with men, clearly but little the worse for its sacking, although one of the angle-towers appeared to be part demolished. A seat of the powerful Maxwell family, it proved to be a very unusual fortalice, triangular in shape within a deep and wide moat, large, with long curtain walls crowned with parapets and wall walks, these rising out of the moat waters, its gatehouse and only entrance at the tip of the triangle, easily defended – but not sufficiently so to have prevented it falling to English cannon brought across Solway by boat.

With so many men coming and going John, dismounting and tethering his mount at the long horse-lines established nearby, had no difficulty in entering the stronghold, indeed doing so with a group of men carrying timber for the fires. Within, when he asked for the Earl of Sussex, these men-at-arms merely shook their heads at him and went on with their own tasks. John had to go in search of somebody more senior, a peculiar situation in an enemy-held castle.

Eventually he found someone who told him that the Lord Sussex was dining in the chapel, of all places – presumably these Protestant English would esteem a Catholic sanctuary as the reverse of sacred; but his informant did not tell him where this was sited, and he had to continue his search. After much climbing of stairs and threading of galleries, it was the sight of servitors carrying steaming meats up from some basement kitchen to the extreme southern end of the extensive building, on the second floor, that guided him to the chapel, in the tail of these providers, ignored by all there.

Not a little bemused by all this, John eyed the seated men in quite a large and ornate chamber, still having a pulpit at one end. These were, to be sure, his enemies, the English invaders, he had to remind himself. Yet they looked no different from any gathering of Scots lords and lairds – indeed more familiar-looking than were Highlandmen.

At least he did not have to seek out Sussex, who could be relied upon to sit at the head of the table, well known as a dominant character, who had been, in fact, governor of Ireland. Thither he made his way, none so much as glancing at him, amidst much talk.

Thomas Radcliffe, third Earl of Sussex, was a slender, beak-nosed, and pointed-chinned man in his later forties, sitting back, tankard in hand. He did not look back when John moved to behind his chair.

Clearing his throat, the visitor said, "You will be my lord of Sussex, in command here?" This over that hunched shoulder. "I come seeking you from my lord Earl of Morton, chancellor of Scotland." He had to repeat that, in the prevailing chatter.

Astonished, the other looked up. The talk continued all around.

"I bring a message. And a letter." John brought out from his doublet the folded paper, tied up with tape and sealed with the Douglas arms under an earl's coronet, and laid it on the table.

"Morton! You?" Sussex jerked. "How come you here? Who are you?"

"I am Carmichael, Younger of that Ilk. Married to my lord's sister. You *are* the Earl of Sussex?"

"I am." The letter was picked up, examined but not opened, and laid down again. "This is unlooked for! Where have you come from?"

"From my lord of Morton. At Dalkeith, in Lothian. But, immediately, from Dumfries, where I was told to seek you here."

The other seemed scarcely able to credit the situation. He toyed with the unopened letter. "And your message, sir?" he said at length.

"Perhaps it would be best delivered in private, my lord?"

The other frowned as though resenting being advised, but thought better of it, and turned to tap the shoulder of the man sitting on his right. "Hunsdon, here is someone from Morton, with word," he said. "Come. We will see him in there." And he jerked his head, picked up the letter and rose, pushing back his chair almost against John. Without waiting for either of them, he strode to a doorway nearby and entered, no doubt the former vestry of the chapel.

A stocky, elderly man eyed John, and waved him on. Hunsdon he had been named. Lord Hunsdon was English governor of Berwick, of whom John had heard much, another hard man. Together they went after Sussex.

"Well, man, your message?" the earl said. "What did you say that your name was?"

"Carmichael." John did not like the other's attitude, and his reception. He himself spoke almost curtly. "The Earl of Morton has sent me."

"You said that. Otherwise I would not be hearing you. What is his message?"

John took a chance. "You know him, my lord?"

"I know him, yes. We met in London, with your Moray."

"I have spoken with him also," Hunsdon said.

"Your message, sir."

"My lord speaks on behalf of the regent, Earl of Mar, and others of the council. They say that now that the Duke of Norfolk is dead, and no marriage with Queen Mary possible, no Catholic rising in England is to be expected. Why your duke was executed, no doubt! So, if our queen is released and permitted to go to France, not come to Scotland meantime, as has been suggested by your Queen Elizabeth, then the adherents of Queen Mary in Scotland will accept King James at present, an end to conflict in Scotland, and no point in this English invasion and occupation."

The Englishmen stared at him.

"Are you telling *us* our courses, young man!" Sussex demanded.

"I am passing on the message entrusted to me. From the King of Scots' regent. And my lord of Morton, the chancellor."

"This is . . . insufferable!" That was Hunsdon.

"Is it, my lords? What good do you serve here? At cost

182

to yourselves. No benefit now for England, and an offence to Scotland. These should be good tidings for you?"

"We are here on the command of our queen. What think you? And Morton? We have reason to believe . . ." Sussex did not finish that.

"The message is clear, my lord. And agreed with by the supporters of Queen Mary. I was at the conference which decided it. But the chancellor's letter you have."

Sussex broke the seal and untied the tape, but turned away a pace or two to open the letter.

When he had read it, he glanced over at John and then looked away again, for a few moments, tapping the paper on a fist. Then he came back, to hand it to Hunsdon without a word, but shaking his head significantly.

The other read, eyebrows raised, looked from John to Sussex and handed back the letter to the latter, unspeaking.

"Well, young man, we have heard your account and read Morton's letter," the earl said. "Your task is done. You . . . may retire."

It was John's turn to stare. No comments, no thanks, no invitation even to partake of the meal, no civilities at all. He bowed stiffly, to turn on his heel. Then he looked back.

"No message for my lord of Morton?"

The other two ignored him, and he went on to leave that chapel.

Offence and resentment did not prevent him from following the train of serving men down to the kitchen premises, where he requested food and drink, of which there was clearly no lack. He was told casually to help himself. He was hungry, after such long riding.

After eating, he wondered what he should do. Why ride those miles back to Dumfries, in the dark, to some inn there? There must be empty rooms a-many in this great castle, where he could sleep. Perhaps no washing facilities, but he could put up with that.

He climbed to the attic storeys beside the parapet walk, far from the chapel, and found a row of unoccupied chambers, some still with beds heaped with blankets as though just abandoned. He wondered where the rightful occupants of these were now, if still alive? Choosing one, he lay down, fully clad, and weary as he was, quickly slept.

In the morning he was awake early, and perceiving nothing to make it worth while speaking again with his inhospitable and involuntary hosts, paid a quick call on the kitchen servants, and then went for his horse.

The sooner that he was on his way home, the better.

"You think, then, that James's letter to Sussex said something different from the message that you were to take?" Margaret put to him.

"I do. I cannot swear to it, but these two, Sussex and Hunsdon, changed in some fashion after they read Morton's letter. They were curt enough before, when I gave them what I was sent to say. But when they read, they somehow were different in their attitudes towards me. Expressions altered. Eyebrows raised. Exchanging glances. And then I was dismissed. As of no importance. All but a fool! I feel that there was something in that letter which made a nonsense out of what I had said."

"I would not put it past James! But what? What would he say, write?"

"That I know not. They made no comments to me. But some different message, tidings. Secret, necessarily. They gave no hint of it, save that they dismissed me, and what I had said, as of no moment. So why did Morton send me?"

"He would have his own reasons. He announced that he was going to send you, did he not? At the meeting, before all the others. A gesture, on his part. Seeming in favour of this move of Mar's. But perhaps he was not? But wished to seem so. He had to do it, then, carry out his offer. But having his own wishes, which were otherwise? The letter."

"Yes. That is how it seems to me."

"What, then? What was in that letter? That sealed and

184

tied letter. You told me that Lethington said that they had reason to believe that James was in receipt of bribes from Elizabeth Tudor. Could it have been something to do with that? That he was assuring Sussex that he was indeed earning his pension, or whatever she sends him? That, in fact, despite the regent's and Kirkcaldy's message, the English need *not* leave Scotland? That he, James Douglas, was in fact working against an accord for his own purposes?"

Husband and wife eyed each other.

"It could be . . . otherwise. Something else," John said, but without conviction.

"If, in fact, he is in Elizabeth's pouch, my fine brother, this would make sense. He desires to rule Scotland, all know. Would be regent himself; and cares not how he becomes it! Therefore bring down Mar. You say that it was declared that he brought Argyll over to his side, by offering him the chancellorship if he supported him as the new regent? So, he could be against this accord, against peace in the land. He could prefer disharmony, upset, Reformists and the Catholic Marians at war still. To discredit and bring down Mar. Therefore the Engiish should stay. That would make sense of it all."

"It could be. Yes, that could be it. So what do *I* do now? What do I say to him, as to my mission?"

"Do you need to say anything? No need to go near him, is there? Indeed, will he want you to do so? If it is as we guess, your part is played. You have given the regent's message. Seemed to prove James as reliable, whether the truth or not. Will he wish any report from you? You have served your turn."

"That could be so. The good Lord knows that I have no wish to see him! The further I distance myself from Morton the happier I will be! No, unless he actually sends for me, I will let it be. Stay here. We shall see what transpires. Whether the English do go."

"My guess is that they will not."

"If they do not, then our reckoning is probably right. A

sorry story! How think you – if your brother does become regent, what then? How will he behave? What sort of rule will Scotland have then?"

"Who knows? James is utterly unscrupulous. But clever. And strong. Stronger, I think, than Mar. And certainly Lennox was, even Moray himself, perhaps. And Scotland has always required a strong ruler to keep order amongst the rival nobles and clans. It might get one! But strong for what? Apart from himself! With the child king in his grip, what might he not achieve?"

John shook his head. "It may not come to that . . ."

Margaret changed the subject. "Have you considered the matter of Archie on your long riding? He might well be affected by all this. The more need guidance, tutoring."

"I did, yes. We must try to lead him towards a worthy future, if we can. How much will Glenbervie serve in this, think you?"

"Not a great deal, I judge. He is none so ill a man, despite being appointed by James as keeper of Tantallon. But only that. Not tutor to Archie. A limited man, I would say. Soldierly, who could be relied upon to maintain Tantallon Castle secure, for James. He is son to Sir William Douglas of Glenbervie, the sixth earl's second son, so second cousin to James and myself. I do not see him serving Archie to much effect. His wife looks to the boy's comfort to be sure, but little more than that. What are your thoughts on the matter, John?"

"See you, if we are to see more of Archie, here is scarcely the best place for us to live. We cannot expect the lad to come down here very often. Or hope to meet him at Pittendreich, now that he is no longer a child. Glenbervie would scarcely agree to that. This Eastend we only have until my brother desires it for himself. And he will be of age in February. So how think you of a move to nearer Tantallon?"

"You mean to Pittendreich? Back to my mother's house? My old home?"

"No, no. A house of our own."

"Longherdmanston is little more than a large cot-house . . ."

"Not that. Over Sydserf. We have always coveted that place, overlooking the Vale of Peffer and the battlefield of Athelstaneford, where Scotland was born. One of the loveliest sites in Scotland, I say. The Lammermuir Hills ahead, North Berwick Law and the Craig of Bass to the east. And only five miles, if that, from Tantallon."

"But it is not ours. And the little tower there on the crag – it is part ruined. We have seen that, often."

"Aye. But I have learned that it belongs to Whitelaw of that Ilk. He does not live there, or very nearby, but at Whitelaw itself, east of Haddington, an old man with only one daughter, no son. He might not sell it, even if we could afford to buy it. But he might lease it to us, the little tower, if not the lands. How would you think to live there until I heir Carmichael, which may be far hence? Nearer to Archie and your mother? For at least some of the time."

"Could we, John? But in the state it is in? The tower."

"We put this house in order. It was not ruinous, but needed much improving. We did a lot here. And Over Sydserf is smaller. What I would like would be to build a fine house there. We could not do that at present. I do not have the moneys. But we could make the little tower fit to live in. And perhaps one day, when our farming and candle-producing and wine-making bring us the siller, buy the place and build our fine house!"

"What have I put into that head of yours with my talk of tutoring Archie?" Margaret demanded, but far from dismissively. "I see work, much work, ahead of me! But, yes, it would be good to live there. We have always said so. If you deem it possible."

"I have long thought of this, wished for it. And the matter of Archie makes it the more to be favoured. And now, the sooner the better. We have the moneys for a lease, at least. We will call on this Whitelaw when we next go to visit Archie."

"Soon that should be . . ."

They left it at that.

17

No word came from Morton, and none wanted; a week after John's return from the south, in late October, they set off for Tantallon, small Hugh now old enough to sit on the saddle-horns in front of mother or father, held secure within their arms.

They went by Biggar, to skirt the southern end of the Pentland Hills, and then north-east by the fringes of the Morthwaite Hills, passing Balantradoch, the former seat of the Knights Templar in Scotland, and so to the third range of green, sheep-strewn hills, the Lammermuirs. They flanked these by the valley of the infant Tyne, some forty miles altogether, the child sleeping most of the way, rocked by the motion of the trotting horses.

Whitelaw, John had ascertained, lay amongst the Lammermuir foothills four miles east of Haddington, the county town. It had taken seven hours to come this far, and they hoped that their reception would be such as to gain them at least some refreshment. They could ride to an inn at Haddington for the night, although small children and inns might not match.

Their destination proved to be a long, low hall-house set pleasantly below Whitelaw itself, amongst undulating grassy slopes, cattle-dotted, above a shallow open valley, not far from the village of Morham. In the event they did rather better than they had anticipated, old Sir Patrick Whitelaw and his unmarried daughter proving to be friendly, and, when they heard of their visitors' errand, and had admired the child, suggested that they stayed the night, which was a hopeful sign, as well as a convenience.

Sir Patrick was not himself famous, but his father had

been, if famous is the word, having been one of the party under the Master of Rothes who slew Cardinal David Beaton at St Andrews, in the early stages of the Reformation; and later in the waylaying and slaughter of Wauchope of Niddry Marischal; indeed alleged to have been privy to the murder of Darnley. But he was dead, and his son and heir seemed a very different kind of man, quiet and retiring. He said that he had once met John's father, and of course knew of the Lady Margaret Douglas and her lordly kin. He was not averse to the notion of leasing Over Sydserf, for his grandfather had gained it as marriage settlement with a daughter of Sydserf of that Ilk, and none of his family had ever occupied the tower. It was in a neglected state, he admitted. If Carmichael was prepared to put it in order, they were welcome to have it at a modest rental. If in time they desired to buy the property, that no doubt could be arranged, for it was not important to the Whitelaw lairdship. It lay on the other side of Tyne, nine miles off, which had its disadvantages. But he mentioned that Sydserf of that Ilk was very proud of his ancient name – it had derived from St Serf, who in the sixth century had nurtured and reared St Mungo, who had founded Glasgow – and he misliked the use of the name of Over Sydserf for the adjacent property. To please him they tended to call it Fenton Tower, for it had come to the Whitelaws through the Fenton connection with the Sydserfs.

John agreed that if they took over the property they would not worry over such name-change. But they would go and inspect the building first, to ensure that it would not be too difficult to make habitable. They would come back on their return from Tantallon, report and seek to come to terms.

That was accepted. After a generous meal, and some account of local history of the Whitelaws, Sydserfs, Fentons and Congaltons of that Ilk and their doings, with a sleepy child, they sought their allotted bed-chamber early.

In the morning they came to recognise why Over Sydserf was a less than convenient adjunct to the Whitelaw property, in that the River Tyne and the parallel Peffer Burn lay between, and there were no crossings nor passable fords over either nearer than the bridge at Haddington and a ford on the Peffer near Prora, the two of these demanding a considerable detour, so that although the two places were only nine miles apart, very considerably longer riding was involved. Not that this would be any handicap to living at Over Sydserf, only making it difficult of access from the Whitelaw vicinity.

When the Carmichaels eventually reached their goal they were, in fact, much cheered by what they found, for the place was in better order than they had feared. It was the stable block and outbuildings of the establishment which, seen from the low ground, had seemed semi-ruinous, the roofing partly fallen in, which had given that impression, the little tower itself all but intact. It was all locked and barred, but they had been lent the keys.

The site was magnificent, an escarpment of rock soaring above green meadows in something of a long fang, a steep drop on either side, yet the fang itself wide enough to provide an overgrown garden and orchard extending from the tower on the crest of it all, a highly defensive situation. They could see the larger house of Nether Sydserf only half a mile to the south, and wondered why the Sydserf family had chosen to dwell there, in a lower and much less imposing site.

The iron yett and massive wooden door behind it unlocked and unbarred, they entered through thick walling into a vaulted basement kitchen, having a wide-arched fireplace, a domed oven and a slop drain, smaller but as good as the Eastend one. A turnpike stair in the thickness of the walling, narrow admittedly, led up to the hall on the first floor, again small but with a good fireplace provided with ingleneuk seats and with fair-sized windows with more seats in the ingoings, all scantily furnished but with a decorative tempera-painted ceiling of wood, showing mixed heraldic and Celtic designs, which much pleased Margaret. There was no withdrawing-room here, since there was only one chamber on each floor, but there were garderobes or closets in the thickness of the walling, just large enough to bed down in, if necessary.

There were two more floors and an attic above, the last within a parapet and wall walk, these providing two large and two small bedrooms, again part furnished with beds and chests and somewhat tattered wall-hangings, and all with fireplaces. John was particularly concerned over the roofing, which could make or mar the prospects for habitation; but once out on the parapet walk, he saw that the roof was in fact sound, covered with massive stone slabs, to his relief; Margaret more interested in pointing out the other prospects, the glorious views, to their little son.

Well satisfied, they agreed that this would make a delightful small home meantime, and with less labour and repair needed than they had feared. They proceeded on the five miles eastwards, to Tantallon.

Archie was vehemently glad to see them, whether or not were Sir Archibald and Lady Douglas, having lost nothing of his enthusiasms as he grew from boyhood to youth, not tall but well built in slender form, complaining only that he did not see enough of them. Little Hugh he eyed somewhat askance, but accepted him as the price he had to pay for the visit. They were barely indoors before he announced a new and exciting development in his activities – leistering. When his aunt and uncle expressed mystification at this, they were told that it was fish-spearing by night from a boat, with a torch-flare. Had they never heard of it? Splendid sport. He would introduce them to it that very night, if it did not rain. The sea was not too rough. The baby would not hinder them, would it?

When they told him about Over Sydserf and their project, he was much elated. Coming to live there, only five miles away! That was a wonder! When? He knew the place vaguely but had never taken much notice of it, just a small tower. They must take him there to see it. Tomorrow? That was Archie Douglas.

John had wondered how to introduce the subject of tutoring, or at least of conveying some understanding as to the duties and responsibilities incumbent on an earl of Scotland and chief of the Red Douglases when he reached manhood. He had come to the conclusion that it would be best just to let the notion and theme of it all emerge gradually, in conversation and everyday discussion, rather than making a feature and point of it, which might put the lad off, Margaret agreeing. So nothing direct was said at this stage, although they did speak of the national situation and the shameful behaviour of some in high places; also the cost to the nation of its weakness for feud and division, Uncle James not actually mentioned by name. Archie declared that if he had his way, those wretched English would be driven out of the Borders by Douglas swords and spears.

A servant was sent off to North Berwick to inform the boatmen that they would be coming for leistering with the darkening.

Fortunately, little Hughie, a good sleeper anyway, weary after all the riding, sank into deep slumber early that evening, and left his mother free to try this new sporting venture.

Riding to the town and harbour, the Glenbervie couple shaking their heads over it all, the trio found all ready for them at a boat provided with a sort of iron basket on a pole, which fitted into a hole in the bows, this filled with dry heather and tow, soaked in oil, to supply the necessary torchlight. There were also three spears, really long-handled forks of five prongs tipped with sharp hooks, these called leisters. Archie explained how they had to be used, remembering always the effects of refraction in the water and the need for balance so as not to fall overboard. It seemed that the light of the flare had the effect of luring the fish to near the surface, where they could be stabbed. Margaret, for one, was very doubtful about it all, but the boatmen seemed to consider it quite practical.

They cast off, heading on this occasion not eastwards towards the Bass Rock area and Tantallon, but westwards, up Forth, for the group of lesser islands called Craigleith, the Lamb and Fetheray, where the sea was shallower and more fish were likely to rise. The water was not rough, but there was a noticeable swell to rock the boat. They had to steer carefully at first, to avoid the inshore rocks of the Hummel and Law skerries.

About a mile out, flint and steel were produced to light the flare, which, oil-soaked, caught readily and produced a violent reddish wavering blaze, this smelling strongly and unfortunately emitting a lot of smoke which set the passengers coughing and, with an easterly breeze, demanded that the craft be turned to face part into the wind so that the fishers were not kippered – which meant that one rower had to remain at the oars to keep the bows from swinging round. The sail was of no use in this venture.

Archie, in urgent demonstration, moved into the bows with one of the spears. He warned that if three of them were at it, all leaning over the one side where the light was best, there was a danger of the craft tipping over when they jabbed, and throwing them into the water. So they must watch each other, as well as the fish. One of the boatmen would sit at the other side, to balance it somewhat.

John wondered whether, in fact, any fish would respond to their flare, and why, but even as Archie was speaking he suddenly leaned over and stabbed downwards. He exclaimed, as he missed, blaming unreadiness and the refraction effect of light on moving water; but at least the fish had appeared.

Taking a spear each, the Carmichaels knelt to peer over the side, Margaret finding the long shaft awkward to handle in the confined space available.

She it was, however, who saw the first fish, and plunged in her leister, all but toppling over in the process and having to grab at the boat's timbers to save herself, thereby almost losing her spear. Clearly this sport had to be pursued with caution. No fish had been impaled.

She was exclaiming about this when there was a further movement, which had her stabbing again, with precisely the same result, her husband, and indeed all the others, urging her to be careful, to be less hasty, she declaring that it was her top-heavy shape which was responsible, her breasts over-large for this activity – which had Archie hooting laughter.

Then John had a sighting, and thrust, but equally to no effect, Archie asserting that they were not allowing for the refraction – obviously a word which he enjoyed using. This had the effect of bending the light rays through the water, slightly displacing and contorting the outline of the moving fish, the more so the deeper it was. Suitably informed and chastened, the new leisterers eyed each other, rather than the glittering, restless water.

There was a period of inactivity.

Then Archie managed to transfix a wriggling haddock, only just getting it inboard before it fell off the single prong by which it was caught, this to much ado, especially as in his efforts the exclaiming sportsman all but lurched over, what with the long spear-shaft and the heaving of the swell. John was instructed to capture the flapping haddock amongst the gear on the floorboards.

Margaret soon saw another fish, thrust and once again missed. Almost certainly her major problem was that club foot, which gave her an uneven stance on the lurching boat when she needed perfect balance. Thereafter she declared that this endeavour was not for her, and that she was quite content to sit and watch others. This put her husband on his mettle, and he concentrated on his peering and care for the refraction problem. He was rewarded, too, by managing to strike a whiting, a small one, but got it in over the side well and truly fixed on two prongs. He gave his wife the task of detaching it from the hooks, little as she thanked him, while he took her leister for further efforts.

Margaret handed over that spear to the idle boatman, and took his place at the other side, to act as balancer, this to avoid further messy and slippery unhookings.

That man, a fisherman to trade, and expert, soon had a couple of haddocks aboard, with seeming ease, which had Archie the more eager. They struck a blank patch after that, and the two oarsmen decided to try further over, nearer to the westwardmost isle of Fetheray, which Archie explained had been something of a holy place in the past, the hermitage of one calling himself St Nicholas, used thereafter as a sanctuary for nuns – that is, until the women grew lazy and corrupt and built a more comfortable retreat on the mainland opposite, at Eldbotle, and hired boatmen to ferry out pilgrims to St Nicholas's cell, at a price. He said that there was not exactly a cave but a sort of corridor through a little rocky headland which a boat could traverse, similar to the larger one on the Craig of Bass.

The fishermen kept well clear of the island, however, making for an area they knew of, and which indeed proved to be worth the reaching, for there they speared over a dozen fish, John getting two of them and Archie three, before their flare had used up the extra fuel brought along, and no more light was available to attract the creatures. So a return had to be made to the harbour, Margaret for one not complaining, for in her inactivity the October night was proving chill out on the water.

Back on land, she was less enthusiastic than were the males on the challenge of leistering.

In the morning, they took Archie back to Over Sydserf. He was not greatly impressed with the place, complaining that it was too small, that Nether Sydserf was too close at hand, and that there was neither sea nor river to fish in. John, for his part, was concerned with water also, but for a different reason – drinking water. There must be a supply somewhere, since no tower-house could subsist without it being readily available; and on a rocky escarpment like this there would be no springs coming up. However, they did find a well and deep shaft in the semi-ruined stableyard, and the water, sampled, proved excellent, far as it had to be hoisted from an underground stream.

They spent some time planning the required repairs, refurbishing and plenishings, Archie volunteering to supply spare furnishings from Tantallon, of which there was no lack, for at earlier stages that great castle had been much fuller of folk. Margaret was busy assessing and measuring for wall-hangings, screens, rugs and the like, for she was a good needlewoman and enjoyed working tapestries. John decided that the stableyard and outbuildings area could await rehabilitation until after they had improved the tower itself and were in residence, Archie offering labour therefor.

On the way back to Tantallon, quite casually John worked the talk round to the state of the realm and the problems of having an infant monarch, the necessity for responsible regency and the duties of lords, clan chiefs and leaders, managing to point out that Archie himself would soon be in the position to play his part in all this, and to show his abilities and skills in leadership; and when the youth took that to refer mainly to the captaincy of armed men, being told that this was the least of it, that the well-doing and prosperity of those who looked to him as lord was much the more important; and that peace and good governance were looked for from the earls of Scotland, the *ri* or lesser kings, however inadequate were some of their present contributions. Margaret backed this up with declaration that the Red Douglases deserved and needed a strong but kind and caring chief, of which they had been deprived by the untimely death of her brother David, Archie's father.

The youngster seemed to take all that in with reasonable attention, and some relevant questioning, indeed wondering about his Uncle James, which had his mentors having to go carefully.

So a start had been made, a basis on which to work hereafter, Archie interested.

They remained two more days at Tantallon, engaging in more conventional fishing and going riding over the vast sheep pastures of the Lammermuirs, wherein the boy earl at least recognised his responsibilities in this aspect of his inheritance, for this of wool-production, not to mention mutton-selling, was the principal source of the earldom's income.

Archie promised to pay them a visit at Eastend before the winter set in, Glenbervie agreeing to provide him with the necessary escort. So the Carmichaels left for home well content – and telling themselves that home would presently be meaning Over Sydserf, or rather, Fenton Tower. They would call in at Whitelaw on the way, and hope to make the necessary arrangements.

18

John had not been long back at Eastend when his father brought him dire news. Peace in Scotland, however much needed and sought for, was again conspicuous by its absence. Huntly had led another Marian rising in the Highlands, not jointly with Argyll this time; and with no sign of an English withdrawal from the Borders, Scott of Buccleuch and Kerr of Ferniehirst had led an expedition into the Middle March in an attempt to hasten the process. And this had given excuse for Morton and Argyll to persuade a reluctant Mar to stage an assault on Edinburgh, to seek to establish the royal authority there. They had been able to use the cannon captured at Dumbarton Castle; and although these had battered down parts of the city walls, when it came to assailing Edinburgh Castle itself, they had proved woefully inadequate, the citadel's own artillery, including the famous Mons Meg of James the Second, directed by Kirkcaldy, being much more powerful and of longer range. So that the attackers had suffered heavily – some of the citizenry also, inevitably – and had to retire back to Stirling. Whether Morton had foreseen this or not, it had a damaging effect on the regent's credit.

So the nation was back in the wilderness of civil war, where it had been before the Mar initiative, and chaos reigned instead of monarchial rule.

John was depressed but scarcely surprised. He had come to assume that the English would not retire, and that all the rest would stem from that.

What now? Was this all as Morton had planned it? Would he be requiring more of John's services? And if so, was he going to be able to refuse them? Margaret declared again that if John felt unable to outface her brother, she would go herself to challenge him. This, her husband said, was not to be considered, making him look a weakling. Which perhaps he was?

No word came from Dalkeith.

They had the expected visit from Archie in November; and as well as going fishing on the Clyde, took him to Wiston to see the bee farming, wax-rendering and candle-making developments, which were proceeding satisfactorily and beginning to bring in rewards. This interested him greatly and set him wondering whether he might attempt the like at Tantallon. Also perhaps at some of his other Angus properties, for he had lands in Douglasdale and Bothwell in this Lanarkshire, as well as the large barony of Abernethy in Perthshire, and other estates in Ettrick and Teviotdale. Would John go with him to inspect these lands, which he had never seen?

That man declared himself as glad to oblige, although not all immediately. As well as being interested, he saw this as opportunity for further schooling of Archie for responsibilities to come.

They started all but at once by making a tour of the Douglas Water vale, not this time on angling expeditions but to investigate the properties, townships and potentialities, and to get to know something of the people, not only the lairds and landholders but the ordinary folk. Margaret had a reliable and motherly local woman who helped in the house, and of whom young Hughie was fond, so she felt no guilt in leaving the child in her care for short periods, and was able to accompany the others on some of their visits.

They all found the exercise rewarding, and educative for more than Archie, the reactions of the Douglasdale residents interesting. All, of course, had reason to be curious and concerned over the character of their young chief; and his friendly and enquiring attitudes towards all sorts clearly pleased. And the visitants saw much to challenge and concern them also in it all, matters which needed attention and improvement, but also possibilities and prospects for development and increased prosperity and well-being – all excellent experience and training for the young earl.

Fortunately this area was comparatively little affected by the prevailing national unrest, on the edge of the Borderland but scarcely of it, separated by the Mennock, Lowther and Tweedsmuir Hills, and of no particular interest to the invading English; and the Douglas name, Red and Black, still meant something in Scotland, not to be provoked unnecessarily, the Morton connection linked thereto. It would be somewhat different in the other Angus properties, no doubt, particularly Ettrick and Teviotdale; but here in Douglasdale conditions maintained a fair degree of normalcy.

When, after ten days of this, Archie returned to Tantallon, his self-appointed advisers felt that they had made a good start, and that he was in fact enjoying and responding to their coaching. They were, of course, anxious that their exhortations and attentions were not over-obvious to the youth.

They had another anxiety, however, at least John did. This was that the ever well-informed Morton would get to hear of the situation and take objection to their activities and concern for his nephew. He was, to be sure, Archie's legal guardian until he came of age, and as such responsible in theory for much of his upbringing; and this included the management of the estates. So John and Margaret had heard quite a lot about the chancellor's requirements during their visits to Douglasdale, mainly in the matter of demands for increased rents and other wealth-production – not that land-improvement and bettering conditions appeared to be his concern, only gainful advance, the which almost certainly went directly into Morton's own pocket, not his nephew's. Margaret, however, held that her brother was too much concerned over the realm's affairs to spare much time and thought to Archie's advantage, however much he might cherish the financial gains. But John remained anxious.

No demands nor messages came from Dalkeith, although indirectly tidings regarding Morton's activities reached them intermittently.

In fact, the chancellor now seemed to be ruling the land. Mar, discouraged and dejected, was undergoing bouts of sickness, just what was not reported. With Argyll's support, Morton called the tune, at least in the central belt of Scotland, although the Highlands and north, save for the Campbell country, were beyond his control; and the Borders still largely dominated by Sussex. The rumour was that he, Morton, was actually advising Elizabeth Tudor to execute Queen Mary – although this even John and Margaret could scarcely credit.

So Yuletide came to an unhappy land; and Margaret gave her husband a Christmas gift with the information that she believed that she was pregnant again. Come later summer or early autumn 1572, Hughie would have a brother or sister.

The new pregnancy, any more than the last, by no means prevented Margaret from engaging in their now all but teeming activities, on the land, the candle-manufacture, honey wine-making, seeing a lot of Archie, and particularly making habitable Fenton Tower. The latter project made demands on more than their time. The Carmichaels were not a rich family, and their moneys had to be harboured fairly carefully. The rental, repairs and furnishing of Fenton demanded considerable outlay of funds, and John just did not have them available, what with the developments at Wiston and elsewhere, even though these were beginning to bring in returns. So the decision was made to sell off Wrae. This was the furthest distant of their properties and therefore the least visited and exploited, despite the fact that John's first notions of land improvement emanated from the monkish examples there. Also, of course, it had come to him as Margaret's dowery, and so was not any traditional Carmichael land. Sir John was much against this, thinking that the Fenton departure was a folly anyway, although Margaret was not. Fortunately, however, they were able to keep it approximately in the family, for they found Carmichael of Edrom, a far-out cousin, prepared to purchase it, this producing much financial relief.

Once the worst of the winter was over and travel became less difficult, they were able to proceed apace with the Fenton work, and to involve Archie on it, so close at hand. This Tantallon connection was a distinct help in their unavoidable association with Sydserf of that Ilk, who was less than happy over this development all but in his back yard, and John and Margaret were at pains to be on as friendly terms as was possible. But with the Earls of Angus and Morton relationship, Sydserf felt bound to be reasonably accepting, although never enthusiastic, and no actual hindrances were put in their way. Archie fulfilled his promise to provide labourers and masons to help rebuild the stable block and cot-houses, and himself came all but daily to aid in the refurbishing work, even trying his hand at the whitewashing of interior walls, and painting designs thereon, the last not always with success. Furniture also was forthcoming from Tantallon.

No doubt Glenbervie transmitted something of all this to Morton, but no evident reaction was forthcoming. It was almost as though the chancellor had forgotten the existence of John Carmichael meantime – which well suited the latter.

Archie was not forgetting, however, especially his pro-jected visits of inspection to his outlying properties, and was urging John to take him. He was keen to see the Ettrick and Teviotdale lands in especial, but was inevitably con-cerned about the English presence in the Middle March. John thought that a Morton nephew was not likely to be interfered with; also that, with Ferniehirst and Buccleuch friendly to himself, it ought not to be too difficult a survey. They planned an expedition for the beginning of May.

But it was not to be, Morton's arrangements otherwise. For in late April, with campaigning weather becoming available, he instituted a series of raids down into the Middle and East Marches, in theory to establish regency control there, although Mar himself appeared to have no hand in it. In fact, John assessed it as directed mainly against Sir Thomas Kerr and Sir Walter Scott, these Kirkcaldy's principal lieutenants at Edinburgh, although the Lord Home, after blowing hot and cold, had finally thrown in his lot with the Marian supporters and joined the others based on Edinburgh's citadel. The fact that Home was Warden of the East March, and Kerr of the Middle, both monarchial appointments, made the situation the more confusing, indeed ridiculous, which Morton made a partial excuse. At any rate, he and Argyll led their forces of Black Douglases, Eglinton Montgomeries and Campbell Highlanders down into the Marches over a period of two months, savage assaults and no mere demonstrations – as indeed they had to be if they were to make any real impact on the warlike mosstrooping Borderers who knew how to defend themselves and their households. The scale and harshness of these raids was such that they became known as the Douglas Wars – much to young Archie's indignation, who declared it shameful that they should be given the name of Douglas when it was only Black Douglas accountable.

John found it noteworthy that, so far, Morton had not called for any Angus reinforcements, which was a blessing. Likewise no demands for his own services. Margaret judged that her strange brother, whatever else, was no fool, and would recognise that warfare against John's friends of Ferniehirst and Buccleuch would make him less useful hereafter; and that calling on the Angus manpower to help devastate the area where the Red Douglases were strong, Ettrick and Teviotdale, would be counter-productive. So, although they greatly deplored the raiding on the Marches, they were not actually involved; but it was certainly no time to go visiting there.

Then, in August, Queen Mary's Catholic cause and party suffered a grievous blow. On the Eve of St Bartholomew, Queen Catherine de Medici of France, with the Pope's blessing, ordered a massacre of French Protestants, in order to lessen the burgeoning power of Henry of Navarre, with over ten thousand men, women and children slain in savage cruelty, five hundred of them claimed to be of the nobility and gentry. Moreover, the Vatican declared Queen Elizabeth Tudor deposed. This resounded throughout Christendom and had the effect of arousing and greatly strengthening the Reformist cause, thus aiding Morton in his campaigning, and further damaging Mar's efforts at rapprochement and unification against the English invaders. Indeed it gave Morton, who was now calling himself Lieutenant-General of the Realm as well as Chancellor and Lord High Admiral, the excuse to request Protestant Elizabeth, via Sussex, to assist in putting down these bloodthirsty Catholics by sending up more powerful cannon than they had in Scotland, to assist in reducing Edinburgh Castle.

The Douglas Wars thereafter took on a different character, with the arrival of the requested heavy artillery in late September, Elizabeth apparently only too happy to oblige, and her armament far outmatching anything that even Edinburgh could use to counter. With a large army, Morton attacked the city; and the English cannoneers, selecting advantageous siting for their pieces, with the streets and market-places in their hands, were able to batter the citadel from out of range of its own weapons, this leading to the eventual surrender negotiations. Kirkcaldy believed that he had obtained honourable terms to yield, but reckoned without the Black Douglas. Lethington, Kerr, Scott and Lord Home were less trusting. Indeed, while the three Borders chiefs managed to effect their escape under cover of darkness, and eventual exile, the Secretary of State actually chose to commit suicide, by poisoning himself, rather than fall into Morton's hands. And Kirkcaldy, taken, was promptly executed, Scotland's most famed and foremost soldier.

Thus, suddenly, the Marian and Catholic cause collapsed in Scotland, as in England. Morton triumphed, and in more than just military victory, for on 9th October the Regent Mar died at Stirling, a dejected and almost pathetic figure, superseded in all but name these past months, a man of vision but lacking the drive and toughness which his position demanded. He had been sickly for some time, to be sure, but that did not prevent many from alleging that "he died not without suspicion of poison".

And, to be equally sure, there was no question as to who would, must, succeed him. The very next day a parliament was called, for November, to appoint the Earl of Morton as regent for James the Sixth, King of Scots.

PART TWO

19

The mighty upheavals in the land did not immediately affect John and Margaret Carmichael, blessedly. They all, in fact, coincided with their moving into residence at Fenton Tower, to their great joy and satisfaction. John was fond of his old home at Carmichael, and recognised that when he eventually succeeded his father as Carmichael of that Ilk, he would have to spend more time there. But meanwhile this was his chosen domicile, although he would miss Tintock Tap for his riding. And Margaret, now nearing her second delivery, was glad to be back in Lothian and none so far from her mother. Archie was a constant visitor.

Although not actually involved in the national affairs, John was much concerned as to future developments, for the realm and also, of course, for himself. As regent, how would Morton act? Would he be the tyrant, the oppressor? And would he make demands on himself, and him scarcely in a position to refuse the country's ruler? Also perhaps seek to use Archie and the Angus power? Margaret was not so anxious. She judged that her brother was ambitious above all else, unscrupulous, yes, and devious. But now that he had attained supreme power in the land, he might make none so ill a regent. For he was strong with it all, and if any nation required a strong ruler, Scotland did. The child monarch was only six years old, and if Morton acted firmly but reasonably effectively, he could have possibly a dozen years of rule ahead of him. After all, there was no higher that he could rise now, so the need for treachery and deceit, intrigue and unnecessary violence, was no longer there. James Douglas would never become a saint, but he might prove a passable ruler; and with the Catholic cause now more or less defeated, save in the Highland north, there would be less call for harsh measures. The crucial time for her brother, as she saw it, would be when King James came of age and took over the reins of government into his own hands. Then, power passing from him, Morton might revert to his former behaviour. But that was far hence, and he might not even live that long. She admitted meantime that he might seek to make use of Archie and his earldom.

John's father wisely attended the parliament which duly appointed the new regent, and condemned and forfeited many for treason, including the Lord Home, Kerr of Ferniehirst and Scott of Buccleuch, declaring their wardenships of the East and Middle Marches consequently vacant, appointments to be made in due course. In a judicious gesture towards the late regent, whose memory he now appeared to revere, Morton had the new chancellor, Argyll, announce that the Earl of Mar's widow should remain the guardian of small King James, and her son, the new Earl of Mar, of the same age as the monarch, act his foster-brother. So the new regent could use subtlety when advisable.

All this John learned when his father and brother came on a visit of inspection to Fenton Tower. These could see no sufficient reason why that move had been made, but assumed that Margaret was responsible for it.

The two former monks who now managed the Wiston farmery and manufactory, still known as the Brothers to all, had told John of a device which they had learned about in one of the granges of their priory, greatly to increase the grazing and hay-making yield of ground for winter feed for cattle, sheep and horses. This required a burn which could be dammed up in late autumn and early spring, in order to flood meadows for short periods. This had the effect of much improving the grass once the water was drained off, first for the beasts to graze and then to make late crops of hay, over and above the single June hay harvest which was usual. No rivers or large streams could be used for this, temporary damming being impracticable, only smaller burns being suitable; and there were none such available on the Wiston land. But at Over Sydserf there were two such burns which ran down either side of the spine of escarpment on which the tower stood, through meadowland dotted with bushes, and there floating the meads, as it was called, was possible. John decided to try it; and when Archie heard about the project, he was eager to assist and, if it proved a success, order the same on some of his own land. He would come and help John construct the dam. The pair were fast becoming land-improvers, however unsuitable a preoccupation for lairds and earls most would consider it, especially to work at with their own hands.

So much clearing of bushes, digging and turf-cutting, stone-gathering and felling of birch saplings and the like to provide an interlaced framework to anchor the loose infill, was the order of the day, and careful design and survey important, for the burns had to run freely at most seasons of the year, with a sort of wooden gate closing the gap when the flooding was required. Also an alternative channel had to be cut to lead the floodwater in the right direction, much debate involved in the planning and routing. Margaret could not do more than advise in this endeavour, for in the midst of it all, rather later than expected, she took quite briefly to bed and was delivered of a girl child, to be named Elizabeth, after a much easier labour than for Hughie. Great was the joy, even if Hughie looked on the new arrival doubtfully at first.

Fenton had become a hive of industry and a tower of satisfaction. Their first Christmastide there was a happy one, even though the early winter was a dry one, and the meadows below were scarcely flooded. Come the spring . . .

That spring of 1573 produced more than the desired rain. There was peace of a sort in the land, and Morton's regency thus far acceptable to most, with no major upheavals, even though a strong hand at the helm was very evident. It was in March that that strong hand beckoned towards East Lothian — for it was not only to Fenton that the call came but to Tantallon also. John Carmichael and nephew Archie were to appear at Stirling Castle forthwith.

John had been dreading this despite his wife's more optimistic attitude, but he could not refuse to go, since Morton's voice now held the authority of a royal command. Archie, for his part, was interested to know what his uncle wanted of him. He wondered whether they would see the small king.

They set out on the fifty-five-mile journey to Stirling with mixed feelings therefore, taking Margaret, Hughie and the new baby with them as far as Pittendreich, to introduce Elizabeth to her grandmother, after whom she was named. They all spent the night there.

Avoiding Edinburgh to the south, they went as usual by Linlithgow, noting that at Wrae in the passing, Carmichael of Edron appeared to be continuing with the land improvements which John had initiated.

Their arrival at Stirling in the late afternoon coincided with a great influx of Kirk ministers, the town seeming to swarm with the black-robed throng. Wondering at this, John was told that now that Master John Knox was dead — which he had not heard of — the regent had summoned a conference of senior clergy, under the Reverend James Lawson, Knox's successor at St Giles, Edinburgh, and the Reverend David Lindsay, of Leith, to discuss the Kirk's greater contribution to the realm's well-being. This had sounded ominous to ministers in general, and they had flocked to Stirling to give support to their leaders.

This intrigued John, who had never thought of Morton as greatly interested in Kirk and worship, however useful Knox had been to him on occasion.

Up at the castle, the announcement that the Earl of Angus had called to see the regent at the latter's request gained them admission without undue delay. Neither John nor Archie had ever been in this traditional and principal seat of the royal line in Scotland, so like Edinburgh's citadel in its rock-top position, but larger and with finer and more palatial buildings. Morton, it appeared, was still in conference with the ministers, so the visitors had time to inspect the great stronghold, and to admire the splendid views in all directions; northwards to the blue mountains of the Highland Line; west over the vast marshy levels of the Flanders Moss, sometimes called the Moat of the North, which had even held up the invading Romans; east down Forth from its narrow meanderings to the wide estuary; and south over the extensive Tor Wood and Campsie Fells, past the sites of the Battles of Bannockburn and Sauchieburn, Bruce's great victory and James the Third's humiliating defeat and death.

With the regent remaining unavailable, it occurred to John that, since Archie was eager to see the young monarch, they might risk calling at the palace block, a magnificent structure built by Queen Mary's father, James the Fifth. After all, as a senior earl of Scotland, Archie was one of the *ri*, the lesser kings of the ancient Celtic polity, and as such surely was entitled to pay his respects to the *Ard Righ*, the High King. Archie was nothing loth, and they approached the palace.

There they had more difficulty of entry, being kept at the door by the royal guards while one of them went to enquire whether admission was permitted, despite John stressing the identity of Angus.

It was a woman of middle years, striking-featured but comely enough, who returned with the guard, to eye them keenly. She introduced herself as Annabella Murray, Countess of Mar.

So this was the widow of the late regent, now proclaimed guardian of the young monarch in room of her late husband. John presented Archie to her, not troubling to mention his own identity, and said that they had called to offer their respects to their liege-lord.

The lady nodded, said that she had met the previous

Earl of Angus many years before, and led the way within.

They threaded various vaulted corridors and climbed a stair to a lesser hall, hung with tapestries, from which youthful voices had sounded. Here they found two young boys and an older girl, she perhaps of sixteen years, good-looking, slender and lively.

The same could scarcely be said of her companions, especially one of them. They had no doubts that this was the king, for James Stewart's appearance was talked of throughout the realm; short, loosely built, knock-kneed and of sallow complexion – an unlikely and graceless son of a beautiful and graceful mother. The other boy was stocky and plain-faced but cheerful-seeming compared with the solemn, great-eyed James, this Johnnie, seventh Earl of Mar.

The callers bowed low to the child monarch, who was eyeing them all but suspiciously, while the countess introduced them as the Earl of Angus and a friend, come to pay their duty to His Grace. Archie, after a brief inspection of his sovereign, had more eyes for the smiling girl.

"Angus?" James said, turning to the other boy. "Angus is one o' the seven first earls, Johnnie. Like you. Mar, Fife, Atholl, Moray, Lennox, Strathearn and Angus. The auld *ri*, you ken. No' like the newer ones – yon Argyll and Huntly and a'. Aye, and Morton!" That ended in a snigger. The words were a little difficult to make out, for the boy's tongue was over-big for his mouth, which affected his speech and made him dribble. But whatever the delivery, that was a remarkable announcement for a six-year-old. Clearly this was a remarkable as well as an extraordinary child.

"What aboot Buchan, Jamie?" Johnnie Mar asked.

"Och, that was a wheen later. Yon Comyns wrought it. An ill lot them, forby."

John had heard that the king always spoke in braid Scots, presumably because the Mar family did, with whom he had been reared – and as was proved by the countess's reproving comment.

"Yon may be richt enough, James, but it's nae way to greet my lord o' Angus," she declared. "Come you, and gie him your hand to kiss."

The girl skirled a laugh.

James shambled forward, licking his dribbling lips, and held out a not-over-clean hand.

Archie knew the required form of obeisance. Sinking on one knee, he took that small hand within his own two palms, and murmured, "Your Grace's leal servant!" before rising and making a pretence at kissing it. John wondered whether to do the same, but since no one looked at him, he hung back.

"Whaur are you frae?" James asked, all but accusingly.

"Tantallon, Sire."

"Yon's no' in Angus. It's in yon Lothian, is it no'?"

"East Lothian, Your Grace. The shire of Haddington."

"I was at Haddington once," the girl said. "Mama took me there, one time. When we went to Lethington's house." She spoke with a less broad accent than the others.

She was then introduced as the Lady Mary Erskine, that being the Mar family name. She bobbed something of a curtsy to Archie and then looked at John, smiling. "And who are you, sir?"

John cleared his throat. "I am John Carmichael, Younger of that Ilk, lady." And added, "Sire," with a glance at James.

"He is wed to my aunt," Archie added.

"That will be my lord o' Morton's sister?" the countess put in. "She with . . .!" She left the rest unsaid.

James looked from John to the speaker, with his great soulful eyes. "Morton's sister?" he asked thickly. "And this Angus's aunt. How comes that, ava'?"

"Their mother married twice," he was told. "Once to an Earl of Angus, and then to Douglas o' Lochleven, whose son gained the earldom o' Morton."

The boy considered that, seemed satisfied, and turned away.

"Jamie's ay asking questions!" Johnnie Mar said, and grinned.

The Lady Mary chuckled also. "If *you* asked mair, Johnnie, you'd learn mair! And Maister Buchanan would spare the rod a wheen!"

With this sort of talk developing, the countess clearly considered that the interview, or audience since it was a royal one, had lasted long enough. "We shall retire, no?" she said, and led the way out, the visitors bowing low again.

The Lady Mary also accompanied them downstairs to the door where, with a giggle, she presented her hand to be kissed by Archie after her mother did, and was given a better salute than had been offered to their liege. John merely bowed as they took their departure.

"That is a well-favoured lass," Archie observed. "But the king . . .!"

"He is clever, that boy," John declared. "At six years to know all that, about the earls. And to be interested in how my wife could be both your aunt and Morton's sister. They say, of course, that his tutor, Master George Buchanan, is a hard task-master and beats knowledge into the boys!"

"That would be what the lassie meant about sparing the rod. But James speaks as do my North Berwick boatmen! As do the others. Why, when we do not?"

"The late regent Mar did so also, I have heard. It must be a conceit of the Erskines."

They went to see whether Morton's meeting with the ministers was over yet. They found the regent in the Chapel Royal, of all places, where the conference had been held apparently, and where he was still conferring with a senior clerk. He eyed them critically as they came in.

"So you are here!" was his greeting.

It was a considerable time since John had seen the earl. He wondered whether to say anything by way of congratulation on attaining the regency, but decided not. "We came, as requested. At the earliest, my lord."

"As well you might! You are growing, Archie! Just as well, maybe! For what you are to be at. More than digging in the earth and painting walls at yon Sydserf!"

The other two exchanged glances at this proof of Morton's renowned knowledge of all that went on, even in their unimportant affairs, which information could only have come via Glenbervie.

The regent turned back to the clerk at the table. "I want the worth of every benefice awarded to these parish ministers from the Auld Kirk's revenues and lands," he said. "A third of each to come to me. For the weal o' the realm. A third, mind! See you to it. Heed not what they said. I do the deciding, not them! And I want it at the earliest. I have my informers all over the land. So . . ." He dismissed the scribe with a flick of the hand. "Now, you two!" He gestured towards a doorway into what was presumably a vestry of the Chapel Royal. "Come."

Unspeaking, nephew and brother-in-law followed him thither, as the clerk, gathering up papers, hurried out.

In what was evidently a robing-room, Morton sat at another table. "See here," he began, without preamble. "I have tasks, duties, for the pair of you, right important duties, not just this of playing the farmer! You're young for it, Archie, but I'll be keeping an eye on you! Aye, and you likewise, Young Carmichael! It's the Borders, those damnable Marches! I've won over Elizabeth of England to agree to withdraw Sussex and the English force. But I'm not having those Marchmen rising against me, thinking that they can gang their ain gait now, reckon that they can do as they please. This realm has got to be ruled – and I will do the ruling!" He pointed at them both. "You have it?"

They eyed him, wondering.

"So, here's the way o' it. The Wardens o' the Marches are responsible for keeping the peace, holding courts of justice and punishing offenders – and there's plenties o' these down there! Little good as the wardens have been at it, this long while. Themselves often the greatest offenders! That's to change. Forby, all three wardens are now forfeited and in exile – Home, Ferniehirst and Herries. So new wardens will be appointed and take their orders from me. The Homes are much the strongest house in the Merse and East March. Lord Home is banished. But there is another branch o' the family, Cowdenknowes, that's been at odds with their lord, firm for reform. Cowdenknowes is just over into the Middle March, but that is of no moment. Sir John Home o' Cowdenknowes will be Warden o' the East March, then. I've had word with him."

No comment from the other two.

"In the West March, Herries has been a right bane. But he's gone. In France, I hear. He was a Maxwell, who married the Herries heiress. But there are senior Maxwells, who did not love him for that. The Lord Maxwell is no' yet twenty years. But there's Maxwell o' Caerlaverock, o' Calderwood, o' Terraughty, and others. One o' them I will make Warden of the West March, aye. So – the Middle March. Kerr o' Ferniehirst was warden there – your ill friend. So *you'll* replace him, Carmichael!"

John stared, swallowing. "Me! Warden! But, but . . .!"

"But nothing, man. You'll do as warden – if you do as I tell you. And if not, then . . .!" His fist slammed down on the table.

"My lord, this cannot be! I have no place there, have no authority."

"You have my authority! That is plenty!"

"But they will not accept such as myself. The Borderers. They are fierce and strong, the mosstroopers. They need one of their own kind, not such as myself, son of a Lanarkshire laird."

"But my sister's husband! I'll give you the authority you need, never fear. So, no more havering! Now, this of authority. I'm that, mind, but I've got a realm to run, not just the Borders. You and the others will do with someone nearer to back you, in lesser matters, someone close to hand. So I'm appointing a Lieutenant of the Border, to aid the three new wardens. And you are it, Archie Douglas!"

It was that youth's turn to gaze, open-mouthed but speechless.

"You're young, aye. But you're the Red Douglas. You're an earl o' Scotland. And you're my nephew. That will serve you. And I will keep you right."

Archie found words, of a sort. "Will anyone heed *me*?"

"I will see that they do, boy! Once you've hanged a few, they'll heed you! You'll be my lieutenant. And at Tantallon you're none so far from the Borders. And with lands in the Middle March."

His two less than eager and almost unbelieving nominees were completely at a loss.

"Now, enough of this. I've plenties to see to in ruling this Scotland without teaching you two what's required of you. Although I'll tell you, mind! You have wits, o' a sort – use them. Better than all this o' farming and candles and the like. This realm has been misruled for long, and I have to right it. I will send you the necessary instructions later. But, now – "

John, in his all but alarm, found words, and courage, actually to interrupt. "My lord, this of my lack of authority. My age, my lack of experience, my comparatively lowly position. We Carmichaels are an ancient family, but of no great standing. I am not an earl! The powerful Border chiefs, the Kerrs, the Scotts, the Elliots, the Turnbulls, the Haigs and the rest, will but scoff at me. I cannot just go about saying that I am wed to your sister! I have no true standing."

"We will have to give you it, then. See, come you." And he rose.

They followed him out, two bemused characters; and of the pair John the more so, with the greater idea of what would be involved in it all.

Morton did not favour them with further details or

information, but in fact led them back whence they had just come, to the palace block. There he had no need to heed the guards but just strode in, merely throwing back over his shoulder, the order, "Go tell Lady Mar that I would have word with His Grace. To bring him."

He conducted the others into a downstairs vaulted chamber, and left them there.

"This is beyond all!" John said to Archie. "It is crazy-mad! Lieutenant and warden! Has your uncle gone out of his mind!"

"He seems to be sure of himself. And he should know. We cannot refuse, can we?"

"I know not! He is the regent. Speaks in the name of the king. But why choose me? You I can, in a way, understand . . ."

Morton came back with the Captain of the Royal Guard, an Erskine kinsman. He did not bother to introduce them. And they were followed, with little delay, by the Countess Annabella leading young James by the hand, and looking enquiring.

"What is this, my lord?" she demanded. "We were about to sit down at table."

"You will not be delayed long, lady." Morton turned to the boy. "Sire, this John Carmichael is to be knighted. You are needed. It will take no time. Erskine, your sword."

As captain, that man wore his sword on all official occasions. He presumably had been told that this was such. He drew the blade and handed it to the regent.

Morton took the small king's hand, the boy drawing back at the sight of the naked steel, but being held firmly.

"Kneel, man!" That was thrown at John.

More overcome than ever, that man glanced from the countess to Archie, and wagging his head, made a rather ungainly business of getting down on his knees on the stone-flagged floor.

Morton drew the small royal hand, to press it on the sword-hilt, however unwilling the boy. Then he raised the weapon, young James hobbling back in his alarm and all but falling over, as the regent brought down the blade on first one shoulder of the kneeling man, and then the other.

"Arise, Sir John Carmichael," he jerked. "And be thou a good knight until thy life's end." And without further ado, handed the sword back to Erskine.

Sir John got to his feet in something of a daze.

Despite the momentous change of status thus enacted, no one present seemed to be in any way affected or impressed. Indeed it was all as though some tedious concern had been got out of the way, and all could now go about their own more urgent affairs. Morton gestured for the countess to take the boy away, which she promptly did, the regent following. Erskine, sheathing his sword, looked a little uncertainly at the remaining pair, and then strode off himself. The young earl and the new knight were left alone in that chamber, in a variety of bewilderments.

Archie spoke first. "Is this . . . good?" he asked. "Has it changed matters? Given you the authority that you asked for? Are you somehow aided in this?"

John wagged his head. "It must be so. Why it was done. Knighthood! It is scarce to be believed. Me! I have done nothing. And now? What is expected of me? Is it really so? Am I now indeed Sir John Carmichael? After that, that play with a sword!"

"He said it. 'Arise, Sir John!' And the king there, little as he is. He had to touch the sword, just touched it."

"He could not have wielded it himself. But . . ." John wagged his head again. "What now?"

"They have left us."

"Aye. As though we no longer signified! Knight and earl we may be, but we seem to matter little here!"

They went out into the evening air. Nobody was there to attend or direct them, certainly no invitations to a meal or beds, no calls from upstairs, no sign of Morton. After looking about them for a while, they decided that there was nothing for it but to go down to one of the town's many inns, to eat and spend the night.

At the castle forecourt they collected their horses, and at the gatehouse informed the guards that the Earl of Angus and Sir John Carmichael would be down at one of the taverns below; and if the regent, or His Grace, required their company, he could send for them there.

That, then, was that. They rode down into the town and put up at the first hostelry which looked sufficiently respectable. After eating, they soon sought beds, for they were weary. It had been a demanding day, and they had ridden over fifty miles. Nevertheless, it was long before John slept that night.

They waited, in the morning, for any summons or word from Morton. But when, in mid-forenoon, nothing of the sort was forthcoming, they paid their lawing, and set off back for Lothian.

20

"Sir John Carmichael, Warden of the Middle March!"
That was Margaret. "Here's a wonder! Are you duly
impressed with yourself, my dear? And what will your
father say? You, suddenly senior to himself!"

"That is of no matter. What is, as I see it, is what am
I to do? How am I to carry this responsibility? Be indeed
the warden. Hold courts. Settle disputes. Treat with the
English wardens. Keep the peace between feuding clans.
Act for the crown. Me!"

"Why not you, as well as any other? You are over-
modest, John. Do not underestimate yourself and your
ability. And you have the necessary backing — however
suspect his behaviour! I mean my brother, not Archie.
His being made lieutenant is ridiculous! Archie is bright,
yes. But at only seventeen years! James is but using his
name and style, as Angus and the Red Douglas, for his
own ends. This will all be no gain for Archie."

"He is appointed to support me, and the other wardens.
He will, as far as he is able. But . . ."

"When are you to take up your duties?"

"That I do not know. Nothing was said on that. Morton
merely said that we would receive our instructions. I would
be glad if they never came!"

"Ah, but you will have to earn your knighthood! And you
may well make an excellent warden, and do the Borderers a
deal of good. You must make the best of it, my love." She
nodded at him. "So, where are you going to be based, in
your Middle March? Shall we have to live there, now?"

"Lord, no! We are but forty miles from the March,
here. I can ride there, by Soutra and Lauderdale, in

six hours. This is now our home, and must remain so, whatever Morton decrees! I suppose that I will have to have some lodging there, some place where I may bide. Where? The only house I know in the March is Ferniehirst. What prevails there now, I know not. Sir Thomas is gone, an exile in France. Janet, his wife — where is she? Kirkcaldy's daughter, and he executed! She has three children. Perhaps she is still at Ferniehirst. If the English have left her alone. A kind and fair woman. How grievous has been her fate!"

"Yes, you have told me of her, often. There, then. That is something that you could do. Without waiting for these instructions of yours. Go and see how Ferniehirst has fared. And make some traverse of the Middle March. I will come with you. Archie also, perhaps. And you will discover something of what lies ahead of you, of us."

"Aye, that would be best. I had something of the sort in mind. To go inspect there, first. Good, we shall do that. Ferniehirst. And then a survey."

"Perhaps you could lodge there? When you need to bide in the March. It is central enough, is it not? So, we shall plan that. Now, tell me about little King James . . ."

No word, in fact, came to Fenton Tower or Tantallon from Stirling meantime. But they heard indirectly not a little of the regent's activities, from various sources, Glenbervie, Sydserf, Whitelaw and, not least, oddly, from their parish minister at Dirleton, the nearest village, who had christened little Elizabeth and who found occasion to visit them. It seemed that, despite — or perhaps because of — the conference with the clergy at Stirling, Morton had gravely offended the Kirk, this by demanding large financial support from it. At the Reformation, part of the riches of the Catholic Church had been allotted to its Presbyterian successor, such as had eluded the clutches of greedy lords, and this had been distributed amongst the parishes of the land in the form of benefices and livings. Now Morton was claiming one-third of all such, as the rightful contribution of the Kirk to the maintenance of law, order and good governance of the state, this to the fury of the ministers. It seemed folly, on the face of it, for the new regent thus to turn the clergy against him; but he was allegedly sending out collectors of his Thirds, as they were called, to all parishes, very large moneys obviously being involved. He was also urging that, if the provision of these revenues was proving difficult, parish ministers, scarcely overworked, should take over the charge of two, three or even four churches.

They also learned, from other sources, that Henry Killigrew, Elizabeth's envoy, had become Morton's constant companion; so that clearly he was in close touch with London, for good or ill, the good being the withdrawal of the force under Sussex, and the ill that allegedly he was urging the return of the captive Queen Mary to Scotland for execution, this over implication in the murder of her husband Darnley, that old story. This, if it was true and the price to be paid for the English withdrawal, would shake the nation, even the most confirmed Protestants, and did not seem the sort of policy which would aid Morton's rule. So there were grave doubts about the rumours, in more ways than one, despite the alleged assertion being widely quoted that he had declared that "so long as Mary lives, there will be treason, troubles and mischief".

There were no doubts abroad about the regency's enrolment of a new army, this of informers, not soldiers. These, in their hundreds apparently, were not only to investigate parish ministers and funds, but to spy out all manner of offences, against the state, against the laws, against individuals, against property. And these offences were to be met with heavy fines, to be imposed not only by sheriffs, provosts and magistrates, but by the holders of baronies, and the moneys transmitted to the regent's treasury. If the said barons and magistrates failed to give adequate proofs of their diligence in this matter, they themselves were to be fined, and with appropriate severity.

Margaret declared that her brother appeared to be

adding avarice to his failings of ambition and unscrupulousness. It would be interesting to learn how much of all this money would be reaching the national coffers and how much sticking to Morton's fingers. No doubt the Wardens of the Marches would be expected to support this new campaign of finings. But at least, she pointed out, it might be said to be an improvement on the previous normal penalties of imprisonment and hanging.

At any rate, with still no direct communication coming from Stirling or Dalkeith, the Borders excursion was duly organised, Archie eager to take part. Baby Elizabeth was now weaned, and able, with Hughie, to be left in the care of their motherly nursemaid, Margaret glad to be able to resume her favoured riding activities.

The three of them, then, with the first hay crops in from the "floating the meads" experiment, and successful, and the flooding renewed, set off southwards through the Lammermuirs for Soutra and Lauderdale, deeming any escort unnecessary. It was good to be riding free and fast, even though there were large questions as to what they would find at their destination.

Where Leader joined Tweed, near Melrose, they crossed the eastern shoulder of the Trimontium, the Roman name for the Eildons, and so on down to cross Teviot at Ancrum. After that it was not far to the Jed Water, and up it to the town of Jedburgh. Here, the most important community of the Middle March, John thought would probably have to be his base for courts of justice and the like. Archie asked where he would have to station himself, as lieutenant; but John reminded him that his uncle had said that Tantallon itself was none so far from the Borders, or at least the East March. So no other place would probably be necessary for his duties, which would be largely advisory surely? When the other asked who was he to advise his elders the wardens, no answer was forthcoming, although Margaret, smiling, observed that time would solve that problem.

They enquired at the fine house which Sir Thomas Kerr had built for Queen Mary in the town, on her frequent visits, not so much for her, it was said, who generally stayed at Ferniehirst itself, but for the members of her entourage who tended to overcrowd the castle. Was that castle still surviving? And was it occupied? They were told that it had been damaged by the English; but that Lady Kerr still dwelt there, with her children. Where Sir Thomas was gone, none knew.

It was only a mile or so further before they had to climb the hill, at a bend of the Jed Water, to reach Ferniehirst, the castle perched on a spur above the river's deep valley. On lower ground nearby they found the castleton cottages partially destroyed, but some being occupied again in patched-up condition. From there the three riders were eyed with suspicion, men bringing out their weapons, but John calling out that they were friends of Lady Kerr's produced the desired effect. The castle itself, built on the L-plan, had its south wing wrecked, its walls intact but its roofing black with fire, and windows gaping; but the taller, turreted stair wing seemed to be comparatively undamaged, and there was smoke coming from one of its chimneys. They dismounted.

Actually it was the sound of children's voices which led the visitors not to the shot-hole-guarded door within the broken-down courtyard wall, but round the side thereof to an orchard where Janet Kerr and her three youngsters were collecting apples.

Janet recognised John at once, and came to greet him, looking wonderingly at his two companions, although carefully not staring at Margaret's hobbling gait. Salutations and introductions followed, John declaring his sorrow and sympathy over what had happened to the Kerr family and to their home.

"Where is your husband now?" he wondered. "Do you hear from him?"

"The last that I heard was that he was in Spain, but intending to go to the Netherlands," she said. "He is with a group of other exiles, selling their swords, as they say! And still seeking to muster aid for Queen Mary's cause."

She looked at Margaret. "So you are the new regent's sister? Perhaps you can tell me whether there is any truth in this terrible talk of him, the regent, urging the English to return the queen for execution? Here in Scotland!"

Thus challenged, Margaret spread her hands. "I have heard the talk also. But know not if it is so. My brother, he is a hard man, yes! I would that I could tell you that it is untrue, that he is incapable of it. But I fear that I cannot. I am sorry."

The two women eyed each other.

"It may not be so," John said. "Morton is devious. It may be but a device. He has obtained the withdrawal of Sussex and the English invaders. This at least must be of some satisfaction to you?"

"That depends, does it not, on what he puts in their place! Now that he rules Scotland, his sway in the Borders could be no less grievous, I think."

John coughed. "I hope not. I judge not. You see, I am . . . he has appointed *me* to be warden of this march. In room of your husband. Scarce believable as this is. And my lord of Angus, here, to be Lieutenant of the Border."

She stared from one to the other.

"It is strange indeed," John went on, anxious to reassure as far as was possible, to lessen any alarm and fear which might be aroused by his announcement. "Why he has done so, we know not. We both were greatly surprised, all but stunned indeed. But at least, so long as we are so placed, we shall endeavour to act as kindly as may be, honestly, not oppressively."

"Yes. We are friends of the Borderers, not enemies," Archie put in.

"It may be that my brother seeks peace in the Borders now," Margaret added. "He has the entire realm to rule, and we know that he was concerned with the unrest here, fears that the Border clans could cause his regency much trouble. He has the Highland north to try to control, to bring under his authority, no light task. He will not wish to saddle himself with more unrest here. So he appoints those he knows are well disposed. I think that it could be that."

The children, a boy and two girls, came up with trays of apples at this juncture, and their elders were glad enough to leave a difficult subject alone for the meantime.

"This is Andrew. And Mary. And Janet," the mother announced. "Wild ones, lacking a father's hand!" But she smiled.

"Ha! *Sir* Andrew!" John said, nodding to the ten-year-old boy. "We both bear the same . . . burden!" For this was quite a famous youngster, in that he was all but unique in the land, having been knighted as a baby by Queen Mary, as an indication of her appreciation and gratitude towards the father, a strange gesture. John had never heard of any other baby knight, in Scotland at least, although it was said that some foreign princes had been knighted at birth.

The boy was more interested in his apples, declaring that the best ones were up at the tops of the trees. He had got them, his silly sisters frightened to climb high. He pointed out the largest ones.

Janet Kerr led them all into the castle.

The signs of damage were evident inside, scorching on some walls, especially in the winding stone staircases, where the draught had carried flames upwards. But the house still held its lived-in appearance and atmosphere, or at least this northern part of it, and the visitors were conducted up to the first-floor hall, and assured that a meal would be ready for them shortly. When Margaret and John protested that there was no need for this, that they would go back to Jedburgh to eat and spend the night there, their hostess would not hear of it. Evidently she was coming round to assess these new appointments, however unexpected, as acceptable and possibly favourable. She had ample supplies and no lack of help from the cottagers, she asserted. They must stay the night. Fortunately they still had a sufficiency of rooms for guests.

So they gratefully settled in at Ferniehirst, the two women quickly forming a friendly relationship. And once the children were despatched to bed, after an adequate meal, an interesting and valuable talk developed, when John admitted his ignorance of much of the duties of a warden, and his doubts as to procedure and priorities. Janet Kerr had been wife to the warden for almost a dozen years, and knew it all. She expressed herself as entirely willing to assist and advise, no doubt seeing this as an opportunity to help ensure as kindly a regime in the March as was possible. She said, indeed, that John could lodge at Ferniehirst whenever his duties brought him to this area, his wife and the Lieutenant also, needless to say. It was convenient for courts at Jedburgh, and fairly centrally placed in the March as a whole.

Much appreciative of this so useful guidance, aid and offer, John went on to seek answer to many points and issues which were concerning him, Archie learning not a little also. The entire wardency problem, which had been looming darkly, became considerably lightened, and indeed began to assume something in the nature of a challenge to be met, an opportunity to achieve something worth the doing.

John asked about his colleague-to-be in the East March, Sir John Home. Janet admitted that although she had met him, she did not know him well. She was aware that he did not get on well with his kinsman, the Lord Home, now also exiled, nor with most of the Merse Home lairds, who were apt to follow where their chief led, and which now would make his task of governing the East March difficult, considerably more difficult probably than John's. His handicap had always been that his lairdship of Cowdenknowes was not in the East March at all, but just over into the Middle one, on the bank of the Leader near where it joined Tweed. And this had the effect of distancing him from the rest of the clan, in more than miles.

John said that they might call in and see this Home on their way back northwards; they must have passed quite close, coming here. But meantime he wanted to know about, and if possible visit, Hermitage Castle, Archie also concerned with this. They had heard that it was in Liddesdale, which they would have thought was in the West March. Yet apparently John's full style was Warden of the Middle March and Keeper of Liddesdale, with Hermitage, a royal castle, also the base of the Lieutenant of the Border. Could Janet explain?

She said that it was strange, yes. Her husband had thought that it had dated from early in the previous century, when there had been great troubles with English raiding over the border, and the West March Wardens had been unable to cope. That March was quite the largest of the three, although not the strongest, with all Galloway included in the responsibility. But it also had the most unruly of all the clans within its eastern bounds, the Armstrongs, Johnstones, Elliots, Wauchopes, Nixons and so on, of Liddesdale, Eskdale, Ewesdale, Dryfsedale and those hilly areas. And such wild mosstroopers of the Debateable Land, as it was called, where the actual borderline was vague indeed, were frequently in league with their opposite numbers on the Cumbrian side, often intermarried, and as a result could not be relied upon always to counter the invaders effectively. So the impulsive James the Second had devised this arrangement whereby Liddesdale, the most troublesome, and full of Armstrongs, should be declared, as it were, in the Middle March, which had greater and more reliable forces at its command, to keep it in order, and thus drive a wedge between the other dalesmen. This was Thomas's assessment of it. He had always found it something of a bugbear, being so far off and holding such ungovernable inhabitants. And it was there, of course, that Queen Mary had made her famous ride from this Ferniehirst, there and back in one day, over seventy miles, to visit Bothwell in Hermitage Castle when he was Lieutenant of the Border and had been wounded by one of the said unruly dalesmen.

If the queen could do it, they could do it, John said, looking at Margaret, who nodded. They would ride next day for Hermitage.

Janet warned that the way was over very wild and hilly terrain; but was assured that it would be no rougher or more taxing than reaching Tintock Tap.

So it was bed for them all, and an early start in the morning.

Their route lay back over into Teviotdale and up the river to Hawick, by Denholm-on-the-Green, easy enough riding. But once beyond the town, still up Teviot, they soon began to rise into hilly country; and once past Teviothead they were into wild territory indeed, over a high pass to the head of Ewesdale, with the Wisp Hill on the one side and Cauldcleuch Head and its lesser summits on the other. A few miles on, past Caerlanrig, where James the Fifth had hanged Armstrong of Gilknockie and a group of his clansmen forty-odd years before, they swung off the Ewes headwaters, at Linhope, to follow a remarkable drove-road of violent twists, turns and heights through the hills of Tudhope and Carlin Tooth, westwards, taxing even for these riders, to reach the headwaters of the Hermitage river itself, down which they went, as it led into Liddesdale.

The castle, when they reached it, looked a grim and stark place indeed, on a knoll above the river under the frowning Hermitage Hill, with a ruined chapel nearby which had given the place its name, once the cell or refuge of some Celtic saint of stern outlook. Quadrangular, with massive high walls and little in the way of external windows, it contained a small central courtyard from which any light had to penetrate to its chambers, a parapet and walk topping the walls. All three riders eyed this most unwelcoming establishment without favour, Archie declaring that if this was to be any seat of his it would not see much of him.

Liddesdale itself, at least this upper part of it, was bare, amidst barren hills, with little sign of habitation and cultivation, although there were shaggy black cattle on the distinctly rocky slopes. Presumably the notorious

Armstrongs and Irvines tended to be based further down in rather more hospitable territory.

Having come thus far, they felt that they had at least to enter the castle, little as it attracted them. Approaching it, there was no sign of life, until, round the back, they did discern a wisp of smoke rising above the curtain walling. So the hold *was* occupied. They returned to the front and the great high-arched and pointed entrance, however small the actual doorway beneath it, this with raised drawbridge across the moat, and iron portcullis lowered to bar all. They raised their voices in halloos. Whether or not they had been observed, there was no evident reaction.

Dismounting, they had to keep up their shouting for some time before they gained any response. At length they heard a voice coming from the parapet walk demanding who came to Hermitage, and why? John called up that he was the new Keeper of Liddesdale, and had come with the Lieutenant of the Border. They requested entrance.

"I ken o' nane such!" came back to them.

"Then, sir, you will have to learn," John told the speaker. "I am Sir John Carmichael, new Warden of the Middle March. Who are you?"

There was no answer.

"I said, who are you? And have the gates opened, that we may enter."

"Is it worth the doing?" Margaret asked. "To go in? It is an unlovely place, this!"

"I am Sandie Armstrong o' Braidley, keeper o' this hold," came down to them.

"Then if you wish to remain keeper, open to us!" John sought to make that sound sufficiently authoritative, his first assertion thereof as warden.

"Then come you roond ahint," he was told. "There's a bit postern." That was all. They had gained no glimpse of the speaker.

The problem now was where was this postern door? And how to reach it, with water-filled moats all round the stronghold?

At the eastern side, they found a section where the moat narrowed, and beyond it a low closed doorway in the blank walling, with an iron yett or grating fronting it. Beside it was a gangway of three planks alean against the wall. Presumably this was the entrance intended. They wondered whether Queen Mary had had a similar reception when she visited here seven years before.

They had to wait there patiently, although Margaret still advised departure, with nothing to be gained by entry. But John felt that he had to show who was master here, otherwise this Armstrong would have even less respect than he was showing now.

When at last a creaking heralded the opening of that door, two men appeared, to peer out through the bars of the yett which still barred the door. Then, with a clanking, this was opened also, and the pair emerged, of early middle years both, to pick up the gangplank and push it across the gap of the moat. John and Archie stooped, to ensure that it was firmly based at their end. No greetings were forthcoming.

Taking his wife's arm to lead her across, for he was concerned for her limping progress, the bridge being not three feet wide, John, making his voice stern, asked which was Armstrong?

"I am Braidley," the burliest one answered. "Here's Willie Kang Irvine."

"Then I cannot congratulate you on your reception, Braidley!" he was told. "In future we will require better. This is the Lady Margaret Douglas, sister to my lord regent, the Earl of Morton. And here is the Red Douglas, Earl of Angus and Lieutenant of the Border."

"Ooh, aye. And what seek ye here?" Clearly the Armstrong was unimpressed.

"I told you. I am Warden, and Keeper of Liddesdale. And this castle is in my care. We require to see it."

The other looked at his companion, and shrugged. They both turned and headed within, leaving the visitors to follow.

Through the great thickness of the walling they passed into the small inner courtyard, a gloomy cavern of a place. Here the pair turned.

"What are ye looking to see?" Armstrong demanded.

"This hold," John said briefly.

"Aye, weel. You're in it!"

"Who appointed you keeper? Or deputy, since *I* am the keeper."

"I've ay been keeper. My father was afore me. Braidleys."

"Well, Braidley, we will . . . examine it."

The other shrugged, and the smaller man, who had a lean and mean look to him, grinned. They both turned again to another door, and left the others there.

"Now we know why Sir Thomas Kerr found Liddesdale something of a bugbear!" Margaret commented. "The sooner that we are away from here, the better I will be pleased."

"We must see something of it," John said. "We need not stay long. There is a door opening on to a staircase, see you. Shall we start there?"

"I suppose that we might look for the pit or prison where one of my less reputable ancestors, Sir William Douglas, the Knight of Liddesdale, starved to death his friend Sir Alexander Ramsay of Dalwolsey, the Flower of Chivalry! I fear that you have married into a grim family, John!"

"What is this?" Archie wondered. "I have not heard of it . . ."

As they climbed into the empty and barren-seeming first-floor hall, Margaret recounted how, in the mid-fourteenth century, the two knights, both renowned for their skills in warfare and tournaments, were close associates. But Douglas became resentful of Ramsay, who had recaptured Roxburgh Castle for the king from the English, after Douglas himself had failed to do so, and had been rewarded by David the Second for doing so with the office of Sheriff of Teviotdale, which had been a

Douglas perquisite. So Ramsay was assaulted, wounded, and taken to be confined here at Hermitage, in a dungeon, and left without food or water. They say that it took him seventeen days to die.

Archie was silent for a while after that.

John said that they would be better looking for the room where Mary had visited the wounded Bothwell. But left alone as they were, they had no idea where to search in that vast, gloomy and fairly empty fortress of echoing chambers, corridors and towers. Where Armstrong and Irvine had gone to they did not know, and had no desire to go and try to find them. Clearly three-quarters of the stronghold was unused and little furnished.

Quite quickly they all agreed that they had had enough of this. They made their way back downstairs to the courtyard, and out of that postern gate, to cross the gangway. They did not seek out the elusive residents to say farewell. Returning to their tethered horses, they mounted and rode off. Enough of Hermitage Castle meantime.

They rode a little way down into Liddesdale itself but, only too well aware of the long and difficult ride back to Ferniehirst, they did not call upon any of the small towers and houses which they began to see. These could await another occasion. They turned back to return whence they had come, scarcely enchanted with the day's doings, although the challenge of the horseback journey held its own satisfactions.

It was dark before they won back to Ferniehirst. Janet Kerr, hearing of their experiences, sympathised and admitted that she had feared something of the sort. Those Armstrongs and the like were a grievous lot. Small wonder that the West March Wardens had been glad to be quit of them. John said that he would have to consider finding a new deputy keeper for Hermitage.

In the morning they took their grateful leave of Janet and her youngsters, John saying that he would certainly be back for advice and hospitality, if he was not going to be a burden. Then they headed off north-westwards for the vast Ettrick Forest area beyond Selkirk, which Archie wanted to see, for he had those lands there. He was, however, very vague as to the names and whereabouts of these Douglas properties, although he did know of two, called Blackhouse and Eldinhope; just where these were placed, he knew not.

They rode the score of miles, by Hawick again, itself in Douglas overlordship, and over low hills and moorland to the Ale Water, and past Ashkirk to Selkirk, which would be another important centre for Middle March administration, a sizeable town near where the Rivers Ettrick and Yarrow joined. Here, introducing themselves to the provost of the burgh, they learned that both Ettrick and Yarrow valleys were over thirty miles in length, and that Eldinhope and Blackhouse Towers about eighteen miles up Yarrow. This information had them reconsidering their proposed plans for the day. Margaret did not want to leave the children, at Fenton, for overlong; and this was merely a preliminary visit of exploration. One more night away from home was as much as she contemplated; and this suited John also. So they would content themselves with a brief inspection of the lower ends of the Ettrick and Yarrow valleys, and then head north by east for Cowdenknowes in Lauderdale, to see Sir John Home.

So they rode up Ettrick for a few miles, past Oakwood Tower, a Scott of Buccleuch place, famed as the seat of Michael Scott the Wizard, a twelfth-century man of parts indeed if all was to be believed, and on to Kirkhope, also Scott's. This was very pleasant country, amongst green rounded hills, cattle-strewn, remarkably more congenial than the heights and dales they had traversed the day before, with scattered woodland and riverside meadows of lush grazing, good riding land. At Kirkhope they turned off northwards to make the four-mile traverse over high ground, of Witchie Knowe and Rough Cairn, to the Yarrow valley at Deuchar, which name Margaret explained to Archie meant that it had once been the house of the custodian of the relics of some Celtic saint, possibly his bones, as was quite usual, deuchar and dewar being the same, which saint she knew not. Then they proceeded down Yarrow and back to Selkirk. This part of that valley was also all Scott property, so Archie was seeing nothing of his own lands, which must lie further up the two long rivers. He was disappointed, but liked what he saw of the Ettrick Forest, so renowned in ancient times, and not so ancient, as the refuge of outlaws, broken men and those hunted by stronger foes, and a sanctuary for William Wallace in his guerilla-warfare campaigns against the invading English.

With no wish to impose themselves on the Homes of Cowdenknowes for hospitality, they made their way, still north-by-east, the eight miles to Melrose on the Tweed, where there were inns to choose from, and where they could inspect the spot in the renowned abbey where Robert the Bruce's heart was buried, before the former high altar, the representation of which featured so prominently in the Douglas coat of arms; the said heart having been brought back from the famed crusading venture by Bruce's friend, the good Sir James Douglas, who had taken it on that chivalric expedition to fulfil the king's vow that if God gave him the kingdom, he would go on crusade, and had never been able to do so.

Archie was learning much on this journey about his ancestors, good and bad.

They passed a reasonably comfortable night in what had formerly been a monkish hospice attached to the abbey.

It was not far next day to reach Cowdenknowes, five miles up Tweed to the ford at Old Melross, which had given the abbey area its name, and once across that wide underwater causeway, another mile up to the confluence with the Leader, after which it was a bare three miles up that river's eastern bank. The Home castle proved to be larger than they had anticipated, a quadrangular establishment with four square towers, situated in a strong position at a bend of the river, below the prominent and isolated Black Hill of Earlston. It looked a pleasing place enough, despite its famed rhyme:

> Vengeance! Vengeance! When and where?
> Upon the House of Cowdenknowes,
> Now and ever mair!

Just what these ominous lines referred to, the callers did not know; but Margaret said that the castle had the reputation of having a remarkable series of pits or dungeons, the first reached only by a hatch in the floor of the main vaulted basement, and a second in the floor of the first, under a trapdoor and chute. Perhaps the verse had something to do with these fearsome holes?

At any rate, when they saw Sir John Home, they gained no impression of harshness, and were interested to learn that he was married to a daughter of the late Sir Andrew Ker of Cessford, a distant kinsman of Ferniehirst. They caught Sir John as he was about to set off for a day's hunting with Haig of Bemersyde on the Black Hill and its outliers, and so they sought not to delay him. He was not unfriendly however, although obviously eager to be gone. He declared that he too had been surprised by his appointment as warden, as, he imagined, would be some of his fellow Homes in the Merse, who probably considered that the position should have come to one of them. He did not, therefore, anticipate an easeful regime. But he would be glad to co-operate, where possible, with Carmichael, for he imagined that they might well have similar problems. He looked somewhat askance at young Archie as Lieutenant of the Border, but made no comment.

They parted on passably friendly terms.

So it was back up Lauderdale and east down Tyne, their survey made, on the whole less apprehensive as to the future than they had been when they set out, for which they had largely to thank Janet Kerr.

21

With still no instructions arriving from the regent, John at least began to feel somewhat uncomfortable over his sheer inactivity as a warden. Ought he not to be presenting himself to the folk of the March, showing a concern, demonstrating authority in some measure? He did not know just how much the wardens were expected to make their presence felt in the area, under unexceptional conditions. Usually they would be living there, of course, and so be fairly evident to all, as had been Sir Thomas Kerr – although admittedly these last difficult years he had spent much of his time at Edinburgh, with his father-in-law, Kirkcaldy, and Scott of Buccleuch. Margaret advised not to worry. Basically the responsibility was her brother's, and if he was not concerning himself, presumably with other and more pressing matters demanding his attention, why should John feel any guilt? He had not asked for the appointment, and could not be expected to go seeking out duties and tasks.

Moreover, they had plenty to do with their time, there at Fenton, and at Longherdmanston and down at Wiston, with the farming and land improvement, their candle industry – which was becoming quite large-scale and profitable – and the honey wine and mead making and distilling, in which Margaret especially interested herself. The way things were going with these ventures, it would not be very long before they were able to think of purchasing Fenton Tower and lands.

In the early autumn they heard a possible reason why Morton had not been concerning himself with the Borders situation, and in touch with John and Archie. He had been making a northern progress, not leading an army as had been apt to be the way in the past, but endeavouring to nullify the threat to his regime of the Gordon and Highland chiefs by using persuasion rather than force. He had gone up to Aberdeen, accompanied, it seemed, by Killigrew the English envoy, and only a small escort of guards, and had held meetings with Huntly and his very active brother, Sir Adam Gordon. This, on the face of it, statesmanlike initiative seemed to have been fairly successful, and the threat of hostilities from the Catholic north appeared to have subsided for the time being. What Killigrew's contribution may have been was not reported, possibly the promise of Elizabethan gold. At any rate, the regent had returned to Stirling with credit enhanced. Even Margaret was moderately impressed.

Killigrew's efforts to increase his queen's influence in Scotland and keep the regent co-operative, this made the more advisable by the French and Spanish armed threats against England, with papal blessing, received something of a setback that autumn, through a series of piratical attacks by English ships on Scottish vessels, particularly those trading with the Netherlands, the wool-carriers in especial, proceeding to and from the staple at Veere. This wool trade was one of the country's greatest sources of revenue, the Lammermuir and Cheviot sheep-runs producing vast quantities of different grades of wool, to be exported to the Continent via Veere and Bruges and Brussels, the Scots vessels coming back laden with exchange goods and moneys, these making tempting targets for the English plunderers. Great was the Scots outcry, anti-English sentiment grew the greater, to the regent's concern. To Archie Douglas's also, since no little part of the Angus revenues came from the Lammermuir sheep. Here was an awkward challenge for Morton, who was reputedly seeking to arrange a formal defensive and religious league with Elizabeth Tudor.

The long-expected summons to Stirling came at the beginning of November, and was for both John and Archie to appear. Morton had made his base at Stirling, where the young king was settled, all but held, reputedly considering Edinburgh as still an untrustworthy city, full of potential rebels. The two of them rode thither, wondering just what was in store for them.

In the event, the instructions they received were quite other than anticipated, especially for Archie. Morton interviewed them, after some delay, in his own quarters of the palace block, Henry Killigrew, his constant companion, greeting them civilly before absenting himself.

The regent eyed them critically. "You two," he said, "I havena seen you this long while." He made that sound as though it was some fault on their part. "Are you keeping those rascally Borderers in order, eh?"

The pair exchanged glances. "We can scarcely claim to be doing that, my lord," John answered. "You have sent us no instructions, as you said that you would. We have made a journey through the Borderland, yes. Visited Jedburgh, Hawick, Hermitage, Selkirk and the Ettrick Forest. Learned not a little. But as to keeping it all in order, we can only say that we saw little *dis*order."

"No? Maybe you didna look that hard!"

"There is no trouble there, Uncle, that we heard of," Archie put in. "You said that you would send us word."

"I have had more to do than teach you your duties!" they were told. "There's ay trouble in those ill parts. But they can slaughter each other to their ain satisfaction and the guid o' this realm, if so they wish! But there is trouble, o' a sort. And you have to see to it. Yon Ker o' Cessford, I hear, is calling himself Warden o' the Middle March now. You'll hae to put him in his place, man Carmichael. And forthwith."

"I do not understand, my lord?"

"He claims that he is entitled to be warden, now that Ferniehirst's gone. Forfeited. He is saying that the Kers and the Kerrs are ay the wardens turn-about, Cessford and Ferniehirst. They're far-back kin, just spelling their names differently. One as big a rogue as the other! It's his turn now, this one says, Walter o' Cessford, the numbskull! He's forgotten that it is a crown appointment and *I* act for the crown. You'll have to go and tell him so, see you. I've made you warden, no' him. And you, the Lieutenant, Archie, will tell him the same."

"If he, Sir Walter Ker, would make a good warden, my lord, why not so appoint him?" John asked. "It would help keep peace in the March. I have no wish to be warden . . ."

"It's no' your wish which signifies, man – it's mine! And I do not trust that Wat Ker. He's been up to mischief enough ere this, raiding over into England, ay at odds with the Homes and the Rutherfords. Na, na, I want them that I can make sure will carry out my wishes in the Borders and I can ensure that you do!" That was pointed. "Forby, I've enough to do picking another new warden for the East March, without finding one to replace you!"

"The East March? But . . . Sir John Home? He is warden."

"Have you no' heard? The man is dead! Thrown from his horse, hunting, the fool! Broke his neck. So I'll have to appoint another. And it will have to be a Home, more's the pity. None other could rule the Homes in the Merse."

They stared. Home dead! And he had been going hunting, that day, at Cowdenknowes.

"I will have a task finding another Home that I can rely on, aye. Now, you!" Morton turned on his nephew. "You, boy, you're eighteen years now. Time that you were wed. You need a wife. And an heir for Angus and your Reds. And I have a wife for you!"

If Archie had stared before, now he did so open-mouthed. John likewise looked dumbfounded.

"A fine lass," the regent went on. "And here, at Stirling. You have met her. Mary Erskine. Daughter of the last regent, Mar. The present young Mar's sister. She will do for you finely. Good blood, well made, and of an age to bear bairns."

"But . . . but . . .!"

"No buts! You're in my ward still. And will do as I say. And be glad to! I have told her, see you. And she says that she likes you fine."

"Marriage! I, I have no wish to marry. And when I do, I would choose my own . . ."

"You should be well content that I have chosen for you, boy. And chosen well. You could scarce do better than the Lady Mary Erskine. Forby, she brings you as her dowery one-third o' the lands o' the lordship o' Duffus, near to Elgin, fine property. And another Pittendreich, thereabouts. And Cauldcotts, and others I mind not the name of. So you are doing well, see you."

Archie turned to John, helplessly.

That man could not aid him. Still under full age, and Morton his legal guardian, his uncle had the right to choose a wife for him, even if he had not been the ruler of the kingdom. But why was the regent doing this now? He would have good reason, that one. Annabella, Countess of Mar, was the king's guardian; and young Mar his foster-brother. The Erskines were hereditary keepers of Stirling Castle. So it was probably all concerned with holding James Stewart close, strengthening his grip on the young monarch. All that could be said, or at least remembered, was that the girl had seemed pleasing, attractive. And Archie had had an eye for her. Arranged marriages were not always to be deplored – had he not reason to know!

"Now, I have more to do than talk to you two!" Morton declared. "I have a pair o' tulchans to see, waiting here. Fat cows would be a better name. But . . . rich!"

"Tulchans?" That was Archie. "Tulchans are stuffed calves, are they not? Skins of dead calves covering straw dummies, to make cows give more milk?"

"Aye. But these tulchans are fat kirk priests willing to be named bishops, to gain the revenues o' the old bishoprics. At a price, mind!" And Morton permitted himself one of his very few chuckles. "This realm is in sair need o' moneys. So, off with you . . ."

They were making for the door when the older man called them back. "You, Carmichael, you go see Cessford. In Tividale. He who reckons he should be warden. You go as warden, from me. He's wed to a daughter o' that scoundrelly Lord Home. I canna mind her name. Tell him that, since he knows the Homes, he should recommend which o' that ill tribe should best be Warden o' the East March. That will please him, give him some bit hold over them! And say, forby, that when I've got other work for you to do, I'll maybe appoint him to the Middle March. Keep him quiet meantime. You have it? Do that." He waved them away.

Preoccupied, the pair went out into the courtyard.

"I do not wish to wed!" Archie burst out. "Why should I have to do so? To this Mary, or other. Just because *he* wills it."

"It is sore, yes. But, I fear that he has the right. While you are under full age, as your lawful guardian. It was the same with me, when I was wed. Against my will. And yet . . . how happy has been my marriage, despite that! Margaret is a joy. It could well be the same with you. She seemed a pleasing girl. And friendly."

Archie looked unconvinced. "What now, then?"

"Should we not go to see her? And her mother. While we are here. We can scarcely leave without doing so."

They went, in distinctly uncertain state, to the royal quarters.

They found the countess and her daughter alone, and stitching at needlework; the king and his foster-brother, Mar, apparently at their studies with Master George Buchanan. They were greeted almost amusedly by the mother, the young woman eyeing Archie rather less frankly than at their previous meeting, but still interestedly, enquiringly. She was a comely creature, with characterful features and expressive eyes.

"So, here is the bridegroom!" the countess said, smiling. "We wondered when we would see you."

Archie cleared his throat, but said nothing.

"My lord Regent has just told us," John informed. "It was a considerable . . . surprise."

"No doubt. But a pleasant one, I hope? You are both, I judge, to be congratulated." And she glanced at her daughter.

Mary rose, laying down her tapestry-work, and came over to them, as before dipping an incipient curtsy. She held out her hand, glancing at the two of them.

When the younger visitor did nothing but look doubtful, John took the proffered hand and kissed it, and bowed. He looked at Archie, who took the hint and did the same. John then went over to salute the countess.

"Douglas and Erskine have been linked before," she said. "No ill match. My young lord will be pleased?"

John summoned up his wits. "The more so, my lady, when he comes to know her the better!" That was the best that he could do.

"Ah! There spoke a careful man, I think! As becomes a Warden of the Marches. Let us hope that such is mutual!"

"My lord of Angus is an admirable young man, Countess. I have known him since his childhood. To my pleasure. To be relied upon."

"And . . . knowledgeable? As to women?" That was shrewd, questioning.

Again John was tested. Archie had never spoken much about his views on the other sex. No doubt he had had some tentative and exploratory ventures with local girls at Tantallon by this time, but not, so far as they knew, been involved to any marked degree.

"Only moderately, I would think. And . . . respectfully."

"Still you are careful, Sir John! Let us hope, then, that they teach each other kindly."

They turned to look at the couple, who were standing silent, but eyeing each other all but assessingly.

"I think that you need have no fears, lady. For your daughter."

246

"I trust not. I made my own modest enquiries, see you, before I agreed to this."

"Ah, yes . . ."

It was at this stage that the door was flung open and young Johnnie Mar came hurtling into the room, followed much less boisterously by the soulful-eyed hobbling James Stewart.

"We are finished!" the former cried, ignoring the visitors. "Over for today. Maister Buchanan skelpit me! Right hard. I didna say the Latin right. Sair! Jamie didna get it, no' today. He read a whole chapter o' the Bible, oot o' the French and into the Latin. Wi' no' a mistake." But he glanced at the other boy almost scornfully as he said it.

The small monarch was paying no heed, but looking at Archie Douglas. "Angus again!" he said, lisping. "I was after learning that the first Earls o' Angus werena Douglases at a'. They just married into it. So they're no' right *ri*. Any mair than the Erskines are. They did the same, aye." And a dirty-nailed finger pointed accusingly at the two young earls.

The countess laughed. "As well that we Murrays are better bred!" she said. "For my children's sake." She had been born a Murray of Tullibardine.

"Ooh, aye." James nodded owlishly. "The Murrays were o' de Moravia. Just Flemings, see you. Yon Freskin son o' Ollec was frae Flanders. He wed the daughter o' the right Albannach Moray, and ca'ed himsel' de Moravia. Mind," he nodded the somewhat over-large head, "the Albannach were in the, the matriarchal succession." The boy had difficulty, with the likewise over-large tongue, in enunciating that. "So it's no' so false-like."

John was astonished again at the knowledge of this royal curiosity, this prodigy. What sort of a king was James going to make?

After more talk along these lines, the countess suggested that she, John and the two boys, should go into another room, to leave the future bride and groom to have some private converse. Whether this would please Archie John did not know, but he could hardly object, and they moved out into a withdrawing-room.

Here the countess encouraged young James to display further his extraordinary knowledge of the roots and origins of the great and powerful families of the land – to the boredom of her son Johnnie. When they had all had enough of this, the monarch was sent off with his foster-brother, who was urgent to play hurly-hacket on the steep slope of a portion of the northern side of the castle rock, while the countess spoke of arrangements for the wedding, which apparently was to be celebrated sooner rather than later, for whatever reason, consultation with Archie evidently nowise necessary.

When the girl and the young man appeared, presently, they seemed to be on quite good terms, constraint gone at least. The countess asked if the visitors had time to have a meal with them, so clearly they were not expected to stay the night. She said that it would be ready shortly. John reckoned that, if they got away in an hour or so, they could win as far as Wrae, to sleep.

As they fed, John was thankful to note that Archie and Mary, sitting side by side, were clearly getting on well together, gurgles of laughter coming frequently from the girl, he talking animatedly, good signs. King James, for his part, ate deliberately, contributing nothing now to the conversation, presumably feeding to be dealt with as heedfully as all else.

Farewells thereafter were amiable but not prolonged, Mary and her mother conducting their guests down to the door. Hand-kissing served well enough for the countess, but when Archie turned to the daughter, it was to plant a kiss first on her cheek and then on her lips, no shrinking back noticeable. John was less forward.

As they went for their horses, Archie turning to wave, John said, "You are none so displeased over the marriage now, I judge? She seems a likely lass. Warm and friendly."

"Yes. I think that I can like her well. She laughs a lot!"

"No ill sign. You could do a deal worse than Mary Erskine."

"So I was reckoning. You think that she will find me to her . . . pleasure. I do not know anything about, about marriage!"

"You will learn, Archie, you will learn! You both will. Your aunt and I will give you some instruction. But, mostly, you will teach each other. As we did. And joy in the learning!"

They left it at that, and rode off, down to the town and out, seeing nothing of the regent.

22

With no further word from Morton, John thought that he had better pay his Borders visit to Ker of Cessford without much delay, to get it over before Yuletide and the worst of the winter. Archie, eager to learn all that he could about being lieutenant, said that he would go also. And Margaret expressed a desire to do the same, but not if John would prefer not to have a female attached to him on such occasions. He assured her that, far from it, he enjoyed her support and advice as well as her presence. He was still very uncertain as to his duties and responsibilities as a warden; and as the sister of the regent, her presence would undoubtedly enhance his authority.

So they set off on St Margaret the Queen's Eve, heading for Ferniehirst in the first place, to obtain Janet's guidance on the best approach to Cessford, whose castle was only a few miles therefrom. That woman had made it clear that she was genuine in her desire to be of help and to provide hospitality.

They went their usual way, through the Lammermuir foothills, over Soutra Hill into Lauderdale, and down it to the dales of Tweed and Teviot. So far there was no snow on the hills, and riding conditions not difficult. So they made it to Ferniehirst in exactly five hours.

Janet was clearly pleased to see them, declaring that she was glad of adult company, and leading a somewhat lonely life since her husband was exiled. Her children kept her busy, but . . .

On learning of the reason behind John's visit, Janet warned him that he would be faced with a distinctly difficult situation at Cessford. There had been trouble between some Kers and neighbouring Turnbulls, and one, Lancy Ker in Oxnam, had stabbed a Turnbull, grievously wounding him. Normally small injuries were not the source of much upset in the Borders, but this wounding was serious, and the victim, being a tenant of Turnbull of Bedrule, that laird had taken up the matter, demanding redress. Ker of Cessford, who by no means loved the Turnbulls, had taken up Lancy Ker's cause and, all but acting warden, had his tenant in custody, as much protective as punitive, lest Lancy was a target for Turnbull retaliation – a fairly typical Marches situation. Only Cessford was not the warden, although he claimed that he ought to be.

John perceived that he would have to go carefully here, an additional complication which he could have done without. Janet's advice was that he must assert his authority in this case, awkward as it was, or Cessford would take it as confirmation that *he* was in charge of the Middle March and Carmichael only a figurehead. John saw that, but it did not lessen his problem. It had occurred to him that wardens could appoint deputies; did Janet think that it would be sensible to offer Ker the deputy wardenship? Or would this merely make his own position the more difficult? Margaret had expressed herself as against the idea.

Janet agreed with her, strongly. That would create a situation where Cessford would be, in effect, the warden, and John all but powerless. No, he would have to show his authority right from the start, or accept a merely nominal status. When he mentioned Morton's suggestion that, to keep Ker reasonably quiet, he could say that he might be the next Warden of the Middle March, after John himself; and that meantime he might think to propose a suitable warden for the East March, preferably one of the innumerable Home lairds, Janet said that, in that case, the chances were that he would name his own nephew, Sunlaws – or, as he now was, Cowdenknowes. Surprised, her guests looked wonderingly at this. Cowdenknowes?

That was the recently appointed but more recently dead incumbent. It fell to be explained that the late Sir John Home had a son, Sir James, of Sunlaws, with whom he had not got on well, but who now had succeeded to his father's greater estate and style. And whose mother, still alive, was Sir Walter Ker's sister.

This information set them all cogitating. They had not heard of this Home of Sunlaws. But surely Morton, who ever made it his business to be knowledgeable about everything which might concern his interests even remotely, would have known not only this Home's identity but his relationship with Cessford, especially as he appeared to have been knighted. And yet he had not nominated him as warden. Why? It would seem the obvious choice, to succeed his father in this, as in all else. The regent had reason behind all that he did or did not do. Yet he had suggested asking Cessford!

John realised that walking warily was the more necessary, in this as in all else to do with this March.

However, they spent a pleasant evening with Janet Kerr and her family.

Next forenoon the three of them rode north-eastwards for just under the hour, over the higher ground of Ulston Muir to Crailinghall and so to Marchcleuch on the upper Cessford Burn, then down this for a couple of miles to the castleton, all but a village, and the castle itself on its mound, a massive square tower within a courtyard. Here, when they won past the guards, they found the Lady Ker of Cessford, to whom they carried a commendation from Janet, for she had been, in fact, Isabella Kerr of Ferniehirst, Sir Thomas's sister. The Kerrs and Kers were like that, much intermarried as well as tending to share the wardenship – although by no means always agreed. This lady said that her husband was over at Caverton, where their son William was seated, not far off; but he should be back shortly. Meantime they were welcome, however carefully John was eyed.

They had not long to wait before Sir Walter arrived, a

powerfully built and thick-set man in his later fifties, who proved to be notably less amiable than his wife when he heard of the identity of his guests, not rude but distinctly stiff. He fairly quickly was asking, bluntly, the reason for this visit?

"My lord Regent sends me, sends us," John said, seeking to sound cordial. "He knows of your contention that you should be warden of this March rather than myself. But, at this stage in the realm's affairs, and especially of the Borders, he feels that an outsider, as it were, would be best for the March; and being married to his sister here, he chose myself. And being kin by marriage to my lord of Angus here, the new Lieutenant." That was as tactful as John could make it.

Ker looked from one to the other of them tight-lipped, saying nothing.

"He, the regent, recognises your family's claim to alternative wardenship with the Ferniehirst Kerrs," John went on. "Of long-standing custom. And he says to tell you, Sir Walter, that when my term of the duty is over – and presumably that will not be overlong hence – he will remember your claim and hope to be able to grant it."

"I was warden until ten years past, when Mary Stewart replaced me by Ferniehirst." That was all, but it was in the nature of an accusation.

"No doubt Her Grace had reasons," John said carefully. "But times change, and frequently we have to change with them, I have found! It was no wish of mine to be warden here. But now that I am, I must play my part to my best endeavour, you will agree?"

If he agreed, Ker did not say so. "This March requires a man who knows it and its folk, to govern it," he declared. "Morton should be aware of that."

"My brother is aware of more than just the Middle March of the Border, Sir Walter," Margaret put in. "He has a realm to govern, in the king's name. And must use his . . . judgment."

"Judgment, is it? Or favouring his own!"

"Favour? Was it favour, sir, to appoint my husband, who had no desire for this duty? Or my lord of Angus, who was no more eager to be lieutenant? But in the rule of a kingdom, someone must make the decisions, without fear or favour. That has to be the regent, with the advice of the Privy Council. As was done here."

"As lieutenant, I have to act the, the arbiter," Archie declared, not very confidently. "Complaints, they are to come to me." And he glanced at John for confirmation.

Cessford's expression was eloquent of what he thought of this young callant, Red Douglas or none.

John felt that this encounter was drifting in the wrong direction. "My lord of Morton, as I say, recognises your position and experience, Sir Walter," he said, conciliatory as to tone. "And he seeks your good offices and advice in the matter of the East March. Sir John Home of Cowdenknowes was appointed warden there. But sadly he has died. So a new warden is required. And with the Merse and that March all but in the hands of the Homes, it almost certainly has to go to one of that house. The Lord Home himself was warden, but he is forfeited and in exile. So who should take his place? Not any of his sons, or close kin, that is for sure. But there are fully thirty Home lairds, in the Merse and nearby. How to choose one, on whom the regent can rely without offence to some of the others? He looks to you to guide him."

The other's expression had markedly changed, as he eyed John assessingly.

"My lord it was who asked for this word from you."

"Then there is no question, Sir John, as to who should be warden there. Sunlaws. Sir James Home, now of Cowdenknowes. A better man than his father! I wonder that the new regent had any doubts. Sunlaws for warden."

"Ah! He is your nephew, is he not?" Margaret observed, smiling slightly. "Favour?"

"Favour, no. He is the best man."

"That is well, then. I shall so inform the regent." John

254

took a deep breath. "So, now, one last matter. There is, I am told, dispute between the Turnbulls and one of your own name, in Oxnam. A Ker. Over an assault. Stabbing with a dirk, no? The Turnbulls demanding justice. You know of this, Sir Walter?"

"I do. And I can, and do, deal with such matters. Amongst my own folk."

"Ah, yes, no doubt. But is this not a matter for the warden? Turnbull of, of Bedrule, is it? He may esteem it so, I think. Since the complaint is against one of your name he, or the injured man, may deem it fairer to be judged by one less . . . involved. Of the same name and lands."

"Then they would be wrong, sir! Young Bedrule is a fool, anyway!"

"Still, it might be wisest for me to hear the case."

"My people will expect me to deal with it."

"I say that Sir John Carmichael should do it." Archie made his first decision as lieutenant.

Ker looked from one to the other grimly. "Very well. You may find your task . . . taxing!"

John took a chance. "Not so much so perhaps, Sir Walter, if I have you sitting at my side, in guidance!"

"M'mmm." The other looked doubtful, then shrugged. "As you will. When do you wish this hearing to take place?"

"So soon as possible. For we have other matters to see to."

"Aye. And where? Here at Cessford?"

"No. Since it is to be a warden's court, it should be held in a place where all who would may attend. To see justice done. The town of Jedburgh would be best. The castle there."

Ker frowned. Jedburgh was very much Kerr territory, not Ker. Kelso he would have preferred. "As you will. I will have Lancy Ker there, at Jeddart Castle, by noon tomorrow. See you to the Turnbulls!" That was almost a challenge.

"Very well. Tomorrow . . ."

The visitors did not linger thereafter, and headed back to Ferniehirst.

"You dealt with that one well," Margaret commended, once they were a-horse. "He was difficult, but you had his measure. That of having him to sit by your side at the court, was well thought on. Thinking to guide you, no doubt, but clear before all in accepting you as warden. The appointing of his nephew, this Sunlaws, helped also. I had to seem to support James, my brother, and his authority. I was not amiss? And then this of favouring – that I could not resist!"

"No. That served well enough. And Archie, you showed your authority, at the right moment."

"Arbiter was the word?"

"Indeed, yes. So now, we have to see this Turnbull of Bedrule."

Back at Ferniehirst, Janet was interested to hear of the Cessford meeting, and said that Sir Walter was none so ill a character although his manner was against him. She told them how to get to Bedrule, about as far to the west as was Cessford to the east. She judged that the Turnbull was a spirited young man, almost fiery, but honest enough. The Turnbulls were not exactly at feud with the Kers, but there was apt to be constant friction. Striking a balance could be difficult.

They rode on over the Dunion Hill into Teviotdale, and on up that valley, under Minto Craigs, on one of which perched the tower of Fatlips Castle, a Turnbull seat, while below it, oddly near, was another, Barnwells. But Bedrule was further, on the other, southern, side of the river, on the steep bank of a tributary, the Rule Water. Here, near an extraordinarily placed church, sited on top of a cliff-like mound, was the seat of the Turnbull chiefs, and from which had come the famous Bishop Turnbull of Glasgow, who had founded Scotland's second university. Here they found Patrick Turnbull helping his men to build a new barn, a good-looking young man save for a slight cast in one eye.

When the callers introduced themselves they were warily indeed considered, and when John explained that he would be holding a warden court next day at Jedburgh, the more so.

"Cessford and the man Lancy Ker will be there, to answer your complaint against the assault of one of your Turnbulls. You should compear. You will speak for your wounded man?"

"Will we win justice, sir?"

"It is my duty to see that justice is done. I do not wish for statements now, nor to make judgments in advance. Just to ensure your presence. And you to come prepared. Will the wounded man be able to appear himself?"

"I will see that he is there, if I have to carry him into Jeddart Castle myself! But will Cessford be playing the warden, whether he is or no? If so, what justice will I win?"

"*I* will be doing the judging, not Cessford. He will be there, yes, but only for guidance."

"Guidance! That one!"

"Guidance as to practice, conduct of affairs, yes. And he will speak for his Ker accused, no doubt. But I will make the decisions." And when Turnbull still looked doubtful, John added, "And the Earl of Angus, here, the new Lieutenant of the Border, will be there to confirm any judgment, or otherwise."

Archie nodded.

Probably Patrick Turnbull was more impressed with having an earl involved than with the new and unknown warden.

"There can be no doubts as to the fault," he asserted. "The two Kers had stolen three of Dod's beasts. From the common grazings of Denholm-on-the-Green, above Honeyburn. The beasts were marked. Herd-laddies saw them being taken and told Dod. He went after them, with three others. They were not for giving them up. There was a fight, and yon Lancy, an ill chiel, stabbed Dod. Could have slain him . . ."

"Yes. But, see you, I do not want to hear it all now. At the trial, yes. I must not make forejudgments."

"You will hear it quite otherwise from that Cessford! I know the Kers."

"Perhaps. But I will use my own wits, and seek to judge fair. And my lord, here, will hear it all also. And consider."

Only half convinced, Bedrule said that he and his Dod Turnbull would be at Jeddart Castle by noon next day. They left him to his barn building, to return to Ferniehirst.

Next forenoon it was four of them rode to Jedburgh Castle, on its hill high above the town, for Janet elected to come with them, interested to see how the affair went, and able possibly to proffer some guidance on matters procedural, for of course she had sat in on many courts when her husband had been warden.

Jedburgh, or Jeddart as the locals called it, Castle was something of an anachronism. It had been a royal stronghold, indeed a favourite residence of early kings, where Alexander the Third had had his death foretold in a vision by Thomas the Rhymer. But although it was still royal property, it had been long unused by the monarchy; and its keeper was now the provost of Jedburgh. It was indeed seldom used, up on its hilltop, save for warden courts and as a prison, the town's tolbooth being apt to be overcrowded. On hearing of this John wondered why this case was to be heard before the warden and not before a local magistrate, such as would be apt to do the filling of the burgh's gaols; to be told that, first, the assault had taken place in Teviotdale, outwith Jedburgh's jurisdiction; and second that the Turnbulls were ever suspicious of Ker or Kerr influence, and no magistrates would be appointed along the Jed Water and tributary valleys who were not partial towards these two houses. Hence the warden court.

John was learning fast about the Borderland.

In what had been the great hall of the castle, they found Bedrule and two muscular mosstroopers already present with, sitting on the floor — for there was no seating in the body of the apartment, only on the raised dais at the far end, with its table and chairs — a bandaged figure, half lying. Hoping that it did not seem to prejudice a fair hearing and verdict, John and the others went over to ask after the victim, who promptly launched into a vehement and prolonged accusation against the damnable Kers. However incapacitated was Dod Turnbull in person, his voice was not. They had to cut this short, with Janet taking them over to introduce to the provost.

They had barely begun to exchange civilities when the clatter of hooves, many hooves, sounded from the courtyard, raising eyebrows. Then into the hall strode Sir Walter Ker, backed by fully thirty supporters, spurs jingling, presumably one of them that accused Lancy Ker. John had heard of Jeddart justice, where the accused was hanged first and tried afterwards; this was perhaps Cessford's version thereof.

John exchanged glances with his wife. "Are all these necessary, Sir Walter?" he asked, gesturing.

"All are entitled to see a fair trial," he was told briefly. Cessford was looking somewhat askance at Janet Kerr.

"Perhaps the Turnbulls have more faith in an honest judgment?" that lady replied to his glance, with a half-smile. She won no smile back.

With the essential actors in the drama all apparently present, John saw no point in waiting, and nodded towards the dais. "Shall we proceed? Nothing to wait for now, I think."

There were a number of chairs on the platform, however devoid the rest of the premises, and John moved two of them a little way aside from the table, for the ladies, leaving three in place. He took the centre one, waving

Archie to his right, where Cessford appeared to be heading. They sat.

There was much chatter from the ranks of the Kers, so John thumped the table-top for quiet. "Silence!" he called. "I am Carmichael, now Warden of this Middle March. And this is a duly called court, under the authority of His Grace King James's regent. Here is my lord Earl of Angus, Lieutenant of the Border. And here, on my left, is Sir Walter Ker of Cessford, who will advise, and speak for the accused. Let the said accused stand forward."

A stir amongst the Ker mosstroopers and a small wizened man was pushed out, amidst grins and mock cheering, to John's frown even though Lancy Ker smirked.

"Quiet! This is a court of law, I remind all. With powers to punish any who may offend. Now, the accusers. Aid the injured man forward."

The three Turnbulls part lifted, part dragged the casualty to near his alleged attacker.

"Up wi' him! He can stand fine!" somebody shouted.

John slammed the table again.

"Now, the accusation first. Bedrule?"

That young man glared from the Kers to their chief, almost as though John was not there. He pointed. "This man, and another, came to the common grazing at Honeyburn in Tividale, and took three of Dod's stots. Marked with his mark. Two weeks past. Dod was told, no' far off. He and three others, Turnbulls, went after them. Caught up wi' them, near to Lanton. Demanded the beasts back. This was refused. Said that they were to make up for stots taken by Turnbulls from Morebattle Common. No' by him, Dod said. And when they were turning back the beasts, the Kers drew dirks. Yon Lancy stabbed Dod, a sore stroke. He could have slain him! We demand punishment. And compensation. I say that we . . ."

The rest was drowned in Ker denials and abuse.

"Silence! Silence, I say! Or I will close this court." John looked at Cessford. "Do you or your man wish to contest what has been said, thus far?"

"I do," the other said forcefully. "The Turnbulls are notour cattle-thieves. And notable liars, forby! Frequently raid Ker and other grazings. My folk are entitled to regain their beasts. And, if assailed, defend themselves. As happened here."

"Aye! That's a fact!" the accused Lancy yelled. "They had sticks, clubs, see you . . ."

"I never took a Ker beast in my life!" That was Dod Turnbull, from the floor.

John should have been provided with a gavel to beat on the table, for quiet. "Only speak in answer to my questions," he ordered, when he could make himself heard. "Or I will adjourn this hearing. You, Bedrule, you say that these three cattle-beasts were marked. Plainly?"

"Yes. Red and white ear-tags."

"So there was no question but that they were Dod Turnbull's beasts. They were being taken, not by mistake, but in deliberate theft."

"In retaliation," Cessford said. "For stots stolen by Turnbulls."

"Then should not the loser, this Lancy Ker or other, have sought lawful redress? Complained to authority, the magistrates, the warden, even yourself, Sir Walter? Not taken the law into his own hands. In especial, with cold steel in his hand!"

"That is not the custom, here on the border. Not for a few beasts. To trouble those in office. Folk serve themselves. Take their own justice."

"But not, surely, to the spilling of blood?"

"That was self-defence. Against attack by clubs."

"A lie! A lie!" Bedrule cried. "The sticks were to herd the stots round. With all the men mounted . . ."

"Speak when addressed, not otherwise," John commanded wearily. "See you all, there appear to be two offences here involved and claimed. Theft of cattle. And wounding with intent. We shall deal with each. Does the accused deny that the beasts were marked with the complainant's colours? Ear-tags. Therefore taking them was theft?"

"I had had stots o' mine stolen!" Lancy yelled.

"By the accused? This Dod Turnbull?"

"By his like!"

"That is no sound answer. You are not claiming that this man himself stole your cattle? No? Therefore, to take his was theft."

Silence.

"I take it, then, that the first offence is proven. Unlawful stealing of cattle. Now, the second charge. Wounding and bodily hurt."

"In self-defence," Cessford reiterated.

"How say you, Bedrule? Or your Dod! Did the Ker require to defend himself from your man's attack? Were the Turnbulls using their sticks, or clubs, on more than the cattle?"

Silence.

"I am to take it, then, that some self-defence was called for. But not with naked steel. If the two Kers were herding these three beasts, did they not have sticks also?"

Silence.

"So! We have it. The Kers could have defended themselves, in the unlawful stealing, with their own sticks. But this Lancy chose to draw and use a dirk. That is wounding with intent. How say you now, Sir Walter?"

That man sat forward at the table, looking almost threatening, fists clenched. "In haste, if attacked, a man may draw steel," he said thickly.

"Draw perhaps, but not stab!"

"If the Turnbulls were wearing dirks, as they likely were, and were attacking, my man was entitled to draw."

"Ah! And were they? Did you, or your friends, carry dirks at belt, or otherwise, Dod Turnbull?"

Silence.

"Answer me. Did you? This could affect my judgment."

From the floor Dod spoke, reluctantly. "I ay hae a dirk, aye. But I didna draw it."

"So-o-o! Then, I take it that we have sufficient evidence in this matter. On the first charge, I say guilty of theft of cattle. On the second, of wounding, guilty but with some possible warrant of self-defence in face of assault by more than sticks. That is my judgment." John glanced sidelong at Cessford, then at the accused. "You, Lancy Ker, have you ever faced court charges before? On theft or wounding?"

That man opened his mouth to speak, then shut it again, looking at his chief.

"I require an answer, Ker."

"What is this to do with it?" Cessford demanded.

"Much. As to penalties. As you will well know, Sir Walter. Having been a warden yourself. Since my appointment, I have been studying the *Leges Marchiarum*, the Laws of the Marches. And there are clear orders and distinctions as to penalties and fines laid down, for first, second and further offences. As instance, for the first conviction of a man for stealing cattle-beasts or sheep, compensation for each animal stolen, and a fine of one penny sterling for every nolt, stot or stirk taken; and one penny Scots for every sheep or lamb. But on second offences, the penalties are raised to two shillings sterling for the cattle and six pence sterling for the sheep. Therefore, this of any previous convictions against the accused is of some import."

There was some shuffling of feet and muttering amongst almost all these, but no spoken comment, even from Cessford.

"Do I take it, then, that since this Lancy Ker does not assert that this is a first offence, before all here as witnesses, in fact it is not?"

"We a' ken it's no'!" That was Dod Turnbull.

"Very well. I declare that the said Lancy Ker is fined in the sum of six shillings sterling, for the theft of three cattle-beasts, as a second or further offence. No compensation to Dod Turnbull for the beasts stolen, since they were recovered. And only moderate compensation for the wounding, of five merks Scots, to the injured victim, since the Turnbulls concerned have not denied that they also were armed with dirks as well as sticks, and a plea of self-defence has been put forward by the accused. This is my judgment. Payment of fine and compensation to be made within one month, on pain of imprisonment." John turned to Archie. "Have you anything to add, or contest, my lord?" And when that was answered by a shake of the head, he pushed back his chair and rose. "Session closed," he declared.

Cessford was looking up at him, narrow-eyed now. "You judge . . . heedfully!" he said, still sitting.

"That is my endeavour, Sir Walter."

They considered each other for long moments, before the older man rose.

Margaret limped across, Janet not far behind. She squeezed her husband's arm, words not required.

Cessford strode from the hall, waiting for none.

"That was well done," Janet said. "I salute the new warden! Most . . . judicious!"

"I was seeking to judge more than just those two offences, see you!" John said briefly.

"And Cessford had to accept it. You had him in a corner!"

"He will probably pay his man's fines. But that is no concern of mine."

Archie grinned. "I liked that," he said.

They waited there on the dais, to ensure that there was no trouble between the Ker contingent and the four Turnbulls. Bedrule made a somewhat questioning half-bow towards John, and then led his trio out, the injured man suddenly much improved as to carriage and fitness.

The Kers were clustered together exchanging views and comments, uncertain whether to look angered or relieved.

"I had not realised that I had wed a man of the law! And the Borders law at that!" Margaret observed. "I will have to watch my steps, my halting steps, with you, John!"

23

Just whose was the decision they did not know, but when the trio got back to Fenton and Tantallon, it was to find that the wedding of Archie and the Lady Mary was fixed for barely three weeks hence, St Drostan's Day, 14th December, almost a Yuletide nuptials. Not that this upset the bridegroom who, once the shock of the project had faded, had become much interested, even looking forward to so close association with that personable young woman. The ceremony was to take place in the Chapel Royal of Stirling Castle.

After much discussion over this, Margaret was concerned that the accommodation at Tantallon was such as suitably to welcome a new bride; and she was unsure whether Glenbervie and his wife, not the most responsive couple, would do justice to the occasion. Archie himself was not greatly put about over this, but bowed to his aunt's advice. So some time and effort was spent at the castle, making quarters comfortable and attractive, the bridegroom's normal rooms being scarcely apt or convenient, however magnificent the views therefrom. The required fine clothing also had to be ordered.

So, on 12th December, with the weather fortunately reasonable for the time of year, the four set out for Stirling, for Glenbervie was attending also, although his rather dull wife remained behind. They went only as far as Pittendreich that first day, to pick up Lady Douglas, who was not going to miss her grandson's wedding. The forty-mile ride did not seem to daunt her.

They arrived at the royal stronghold to find all in a stir, for large numbers of Erskines and Murrays had come to see the Red Douglas become associated with their families, and two of the most ancient earldoms of Scotland linked. They learned that the king himself was to grace the ceremony with his gangling, small presence.

Archie contrived an interlude alone with Mary that evening, despite the crowd of guests, and returned from it cheerful. He said that his bride was looking forward to going to Tantallon. She had had enough of being confined to the all but prison-like fortress above the teeming town.

Morton was not much in evidence at this stage, festivities and mixing socially not his preferred activity.

Accommodation for all the visitors, in addition to the royal and Mar households and regency attendants, being limited, Margaret had to share a bedroom with her mother, and John with Archie and Glenbervie. But the pre-nuptial feasting was excellent, the Countess Annabella seeing to that, and there were no grumbles.

Because of the monarch's presence, the Lord Lyon King of Arms took charge of the arrangements next forenoon, and everyone, even the bridegroom, was told exactly what to do, when, and where to go. The Chapel Royal was not large as churches went, and much ordering was necessary. John and Margaret, with her mother, were conducted by a herald to front seating near the chancel steps, this to the singing of a boys' choir. At least there were forms to sit on here, many churches being devoid of seating, unless the worshippers brought their own stools.

There was quite a wait before Archie arrived, ushered in with Morton, to stand at the steps nearby, waiting, and looking less than comfortable in his fine gear and his uncle's company. He had told John earlier that he would have wished him to be his attendant, but the regent had declared otherwise.

Then the Countess Annabella came to sit beside Margaret and her mother. John, through the singing, heard her explaining at some length to them that the service was to be conducted by the newly appointed

Archbishop of St Andrews. Word of this appointment was rife in the land of the Reformed Kirk, a strange installation made by the regent in the name of the king. Morton had discovered that, despite all parliament's ordinances, and those of the General Assembly of the Kirk, for reform of church government, it still remained a right and privilege of the crown to nominate bishops to any see left vacant for an indefinite period, as to be sure the primate's arch-bishopric of St Andrews had necessarily been, like so many another. And that archepiscopal see still had great wealth attached to it, mainly in lands, which no one was quite sure how to detach lawfully and take over. Morton had had no doubts as to how. He appointed an illegitimate cousin and reformed minister, one John Douglas, to be Archbishop of St Andrews; and the purely nominal incumbent promptly made over most of the lands and revenues therefrom to the regent, retaining only a modest residue to himself. How lawful, quite apart from ethical, all this was remained doubtful; but nobody had so far appeared to be in a position to change it, however great the fulminations of the Protestant clergy. And today, Archbishop Douglas was to prove his usefulness by performing this prestigious wedding. The countess reminded that the Reverend John was an ordained minister of the Kirk, whether or not he was a genuine archbishop, so the marriage would be valid and lawful.

The choir sang on, John wondering the more over his wife's brother.

Presently Lyon came forward again, to lead out from the former sacristy the celebrant, clad in magnificent archepiscopal robes, but failing, like the bridegroom, to look entirely confident therein. Bowing to the regent and all around, he went to stand before the communion table in the place of the previous high altar.

There was the blare of a trumpet from outside the chapel, which effectively silenced the choir, and all got to their feet. In stalked Lyon again, and two of his heralds, baton of office raised, and after them, almost at a run,

James Stewart, sixth of the name, King of Scots, his curious knock-kneed gait all too evident and causing him almost to stumble in his haste, as he peered round right and left in seeming alarm. Behind strode a very different figure in sober black gown, tall, stern, elderly, Master George Buchanan, former Principal of St Leonard's College, St Andrews, preceptor and tutor to the monarch, an unlikely seeming poet and dramatist, critically frowning at all and sundry but particularly, undoubtedly, at the archepiscopal celebrant up at the communion table.

Lyon led young James up to a throne-like chair at the side of the chancel, where the boy stood uncertainly, until Buchanan stepped forward, grasped the royal shoulder, jerked him round and sat him unceremoniously on the chair before going to stand a little way off, still frowning. Lyon looking at him all but outraged, turned and bowed low to the king, then to the regent, and nodding in the direction of the archbishop, raised baton high and cried, "God save the King's Grace!"

Rather falteringly, that cry was taken up by the congregation, as required.

Lyon then pointed his baton first at the choir, and then towards the door at the western end of the chapel, before going with his two supporters to stand behind the boy on the throne.

To the chant of the boy choristers, two other young people came in, to proceed up the aisle: John, Earl of Mar, and his sister, much taller than he, the Lady Mary, looking a deal more confident. Up to Archie and the regent they went, the bride, in white satin, looking radiant.

Everyone except the king remained standing.

The choir ended their chant, and Archbishop Douglas came down from his stance to commence the service. Standing before the four at the steps, he raised his hand high, and announced, in the Name of the Father, the Son and the Holy Spirit, that they were gathered together in the sight of God to join in the holy state of matrimony this man, Archibald Douglas, Earl of Angus, and this woman, the

Lady Mary Erskine of Mar. Marriage was an honourable estate, and represented in human kind the union between Christ and His Kirk. It was a worshipful joining in one, for the increase of mankind, and any children begotten therefrom were to be brought up in the fear and praise of the Lord.

This declared, he stepped back, and bowed towards Master Buchanan. Everyone, at Lyon's gesture, sat.

The preceptor and tutor strode over to the lectern, leant forward to clasp the Bible, open it authoritatively, and glared around him for long moments before launching, sonorous-voiced, into a reading from the Epistle to the Ephesians, on the sanctity of marriage, and the duty of husbands to love their wives, as Christ loved His Kirk, and wives to reverence their husbands. Emphasising the words with pregnant pauses between phrases, he made it sound more like a threatening than a blessing, and finished with three thunderous Amens. He remained at the lectern.

The archbishop, sounding mild after that, all but apologetic, moved forward again, to the bridal group, and asked, "Will you, Archibald, take and have this woman, Mary, to wife? To live together, after God's ordinance, all your days, to keep her in sickness and in health, forsaking all others for as long as you both shall live? Answer me, Archibald."

Swallowing, Archie croaked, "I will."

The celebrant then repeated the question and injunction to Mary, who replied with a clear affirmative, ending however in an incipient giggle.

"Who gives this woman in matrimony?" was asked.

"I do," her brother Johnnie said, and promptly stepped back, to glance round at his mother, grinning.

"In token of union, the ring. The unending circle of the love of God and man," the archbishop said.

Morton produced a ring and handed it to Archie, and likewise stepped back, but not so far.

Bride and groom moved together, as the celebrant turned to Buchanan at the lectern again.

They were treated to an all but ostentatious rendering of the Gospel according to St Matthew, the preceptor revealing himself to be a dramatist indeed, even though a demanding and challenging one, detailing Christ's exhortation to the Pharisees on the twain becoming one flesh, and what God had joined together man nowise to put asunder. Again the Amens.

There followed the plighting of the troth, word for word after the celebrant, the slipping on of the ring, slipping being apt, for the golden token almost fell to the floor, being over-large for the slender finger; and then the announcement that they were now man and wife, in the sight of God, and all there present as witnesses.

As the prayer of blessing followed, the couple kneeling, John and Margaret exchanged glances, remembering their own experience and emotions at the church of St Nicholas in Dalkeith those years before, and how blessed had been the results.

There was a general benediction. Then the bridal couple turned round to face the congregation, Archie sighing with relief, Mary smiling.

Johnnie Mar was starting forward, to head for the door, when Morton held up a cautionary hand and pointed to the throne.

James was sitting, watching all with those great eyes, clearly much interested. So interested indeed that he did not notice Lyon's respectful gesture that he should rise and be the first to leave the chapel. It was Buchanan who stirred the boy, striding over and waving.

James jumped up, and everybody else not already on their feet must rise. He followed Lyon down the aisle, beckoning Johnnie to come with him, which obviously was not in order but being a royal command could not be ignored. The two boys all but trotted out together, to the frowns of Morton and Buchanan.

Then it was the turn of the bride and groom, led out by the regent. Mary took Archie's arm now, and did the smiling for both, he looking only thankful to be getting it all over. John sympathised.

Outside, it was all congratulations to the Earl and Countess of Angus, Johnnie Mar asking his sister what it felt like to be a Douglas and a Red one at that, and charging her with nearly dropping the ring. She was chattering and laughing excitedly, with her spouse nodding but less eloquent and exuberant. The peremptory and masterful Master Buchanan, eyeing all severely, took King James by the hand and marched him off.

Thereafter the busy Countess Annabella provided her second banquet for the large company in the great hall of the palace wing, this a notably prolonged feasting, with entertainment interludes between the many courses, minstrelsy, acrobatic gypsies, jugglers, dancing, even a performing bear, all planned to take up the entire afternoon, for the actual wedding ceremony had been comparatively short and the day had to be filled in decently before the happy couple were escorted, in the accustomed fashion, to their bridal bedchamber. Fortunately, it being mid-December and darkness falling early, the delay did not have to be prolonged to any embarrassing extent, with at least the illusion of night-time evident. By which stage, perhaps propitiously, many of the guests were somewhat the worse for liquor, or indeed asleep at the table, so that it was only a proportion of the company which eventually rose to perform the time-honoured privilege of bedding the newly-weds. Archie had made it very clear beforehand, on John and Margaret's advice, and the Countess Annabella's approval, that he and Mary did not want the full ritual to be followed – that is, the men undressing the bride, the women the groom, and carrying them naked to the bed, to ensure that a full union was performed, before leaving the happy couple to it, a procedure which sometimes had the latter temporarily unable to achieve the desired demonstration. Conducting to the bedroom, yes, salutes to the pair there, but departure thereafter – that was quite sufficient. The Red Douglas's decision on this had to be accepted, however disappointed might be some of the guests.

So less than a score climbed the stairs to Mary's bedroom, where John and Margaret acted as ushers to ensure a not unduly delayed exit of the party, however little they were able to limit the advice and instructions proffered to young folk who were humorously presumed to know little about such matters physical.

Leaving them alone at last, a return was made to the hall table.

John had to put up with Glenbervie, snoringly the worse for wine, and an Erskine uncle that night as room-mates.

In the morning the bridal couple appeared to be fairly well pleased with themselves, and were able to fend off concerned enquiries as to headway in things matrimonial without too much discomposure, Archie now seeming the more confident of the two.

It transpired that the groom was set on getting his bride back to Tantallon as speedily as possible, indeed forthwith, Mary nowise objecting. With the bride's mother understanding, and no sign of the regent, it was not long before the five of them were off, Glenbervie electing to stay on at Stirling meantime.

Margaret and her mother got on well with Mary, exchanging female confidences in lowered voices from the saddle, and for his part, Archie confessed to John presently that females seemed to take longer to come to satisfaction in bed than did men; that is, at first, although later in the night matters improved. Was this quite usual?

In due course, the Carmichaels saw the younger couple installed in Mary's new home, she seeming delighted therewith and exclaiming over the locational and scenic prospects, and otherwise. With fond embraces they left them, then, and with promises of visits to come over Yuletide.

24

In the event, they saw a lot of the Anguses not only over the Christmas season but on into the new year, for Mary became as close to Margaret and John as they were to Archie, a happy development. It was clearly a successful and rewarding match, despite the match-maker, and Tantallon and Fenton being within six miles of each other, the newly-weds seemed to spend much of their time at the latter, to no complaints therefrom.

And not only Fenton, for Archie had become even more interested in land improvement with the acquisition of the further dowery lands from the Mar earldom which came with his wife, in Lanarkshire, Fife and even as far north as Moray. These last, which oddly enough included that other Pittendreich near Elgin, could be left uninspected meantime, awaiting more suitable riding conditions for long journeys; but the others were to be visited and their potentialities gauged, with John's and Margaret's advice as to gainful development. So there was considerable travel over the land that winter and spring, Mary proving to be a fairly good horsewoman, even if improvement there was also envisaged. The Carmichaels' Wiston property being none so far from the largest of the dowery lands of Alstoun in Lanarkshire, they were able to use this as some sort of model for what could be done beneficially in land use and in the training of tenants in that respect. Mary proved to be particularly interested in the beekeeping and its products and exploitation, saying that she would seek to concern herself with this, not so much the candle-making perhaps as with the distilling of mead and honey wine, as a general sweetener in much demand and for polish-wax and face-cream. She was delighted with the monkish brothers' chant on their especial item of relevant worship:

For Thy creature the Bee, the Wax and the Honey,
We thank Thee O Lord!

These excursions by the four were superseded in late March by a demand upon the Lieutenant of the Border for his intervention in an East March controversy involving the Homes, as any trouble there was bound to do. All along John had been afraid of something such, knowing the Home clan and its numbers and ambitions. The appointment of Sunlaws, or as he now was, Cowdenknowes, as warden, living as he did outwith the March, had inevitably aroused some disappointment and jealousy, especially amongst close kin of the exiled Lord Home; and now there was specific complaint. A notorious Northumbrian freebooting raider, one Farnstein, had been openly ravaging Home properties along the borderline and driving off cattle into the Cheviot fastnesses, where Robsons, Nixons, Charltons and the like scoundrels were aiding him, preventing repossession of the beasts, and Cowdenknowes, although complained to vehemently, was doing little or nothing about it beyond making a formal citation to Hunsdon, the English warden, who had done nothing about it either. Here was work for the Lieutenant.

Archie required guidance. John said that he would have to hold a meeting, with Cowdenknowes present, and the principal complainers, hear their versions of the situation and declare his decision, offering if necessary to support the warden in his protests to his English counterpart. Support, the other wondered? What sort of support could he give? A demonstration of armed power, John suggested. And with a smile, reminded him that one of his predecessors, the sixth Earl of Angus, had never gone to any important meeting without a tail of one thousand Douglases, men-at-arms and lairds. He did not suggest anything of that scale, needless to say; but men were available at the Red Douglas's will – which had Archie looking thoughtful. Did he mean at this gathering of Homes? No, no, he was told. Only if a confrontation with the English warden was called for. Although a modest escort of Douglases might well have a good effect on the Homes.

And where? And when?

Give them, say, ten days – that should be sufficient for a summons. As to where, Duns was the only fair-sized burgh in the East March, and in the heart of the Home country, probably that warden's seat of justice. But it had occurred to John that it might be politic and effective to use Home Castle itself. It was in theory now crown property, forfeited on its lord's exile for supporting Queen Mary. But it was reported that his son was still living therein. It might be no bad move to take it over for the meeting, demonstrating that the forfeiture meant something, and the realm's authority enforceable even though the castle was not actually occupied by the regent's men. A conclave held in Home Castle under the lieutenant might well give the Home lairds pause.

Archie was all in favour of that. He would send out messengers to Cowdenknowes and other senior Homes to appear before him at the castle in ten days' time. And have a party of his nearby Douglas tenants and herds to assemble, as escort. How many? Would one hundred serve?

Half that, John thought, would be adequate. It was only as a gesture after all, scarcely a threat.

So it was agreed. Agreed also that John would accompany Archie, to advise discreetly, although he had no actual authority in the East March.

Margaret and Mary would have liked to go with their husbands, but it was recognised that this probably would not be advisable, or there would be talk along the border-line that warden and lieutenant could not operate without their womenfolk.

* * *

On the second day of April, then, the pair set out at the head of some sixty Douglas supporters, many of them Lammermuir shepherds concerned over the in-gathering of the ewes for the lambing; this was not the best time to be away from their hills.

It was through the said hills that the party had to ride, due southwards by Garvald and over the heights to the upper Whiteadder, and down that river to Duns town, then across the Merse to Greenlaw on the parallel stream, the Blackadder, the adder in these names merely meaning water. Five miles south of Greenlaw, and between that village and Kelso, in the very centre of the Merse, rose the steep and isolated Home Craigs, on the rocky top of which perched the castle, a dominant landmark for miles around.

The riding, held back somewhat by the escort, not all of whom were as practised horsemen as were their leaders, had taken almost four hours, so that they were a little late for the meeting. They found scores of horses tethered at the foot of the craig, the Homes obviously out in force. Leaving their men to wait, at a suitable remove from the congregated Mersemen, John and Archie climbed the steep zigzag track up to the castle, alone.

Their approach having been entirely evident, they were met by Alexander, Master of Home, only son of the lord, and his brother-in-law, Sir John Home of Eccles, stiffly civil but scarcely welcoming. Led into the great hall, they discovered that many more Home lairds than those requested to appear had elected to attend, the hall crowded. From amongst the throng, one youngish man came forward to them all but thankfully – Sir John Home of Cowdenknowes, the warden. No doubt he had been having a rough passage hitherto.

No time was wasted in commencing proceedings, with Archie eager to get it over. There was no formal arrangement of dais-platform here, all just sitting or standing around the hall table, the master at the head thereof, not Archie who just had to seat himself where he could,

John beside him. The Homes were making it very evident that the Merse was their kingdom and this their capital. Cowdenknowes was allocated the foot of the table.

John had to beat the board for quiet. "Silence for my lord Earl of Angus, His Grace's Lieutenant of the Border," he commanded. "I am Carmichael, Middle March Warden. Accusations have been made that Sir John Home of Cowdenknowes, the warden here, is failing in some measure in his duties with regard to the depredations of one, Farnstein, an English cattle thief, and his associates. His lordship will hear the charges made, and the warden's replies."

This was Archie's first court hearing and he was scarcely confident. As a result, he spoke jerkily abrupt. "Who speaks on this charge?" he demanded.

"I do." That was the Master of Home. "We complain, and justly, that – "

John and Archie had discussed the possibility that this would happen when they had chosen Home Castle as the venue for the meeting, and decide on reaction.

"No, sir," Archie interrupted loudly. "You may not speak to it. You are the son and heir of the forfeited Lord Home. And although they, the parliament, did not name you in the forfeiture and exile, you are art and part with your father in the offence and the loss of right. And therefore as good as outlaw!" He glanced at John to see how he was doing; and at the approving nod, continued. "Indeed you ought not to be in this castle, which is now in the care of the crown. Let, let another speak to this."

"I do so." That was the Master's brother-in-law, Eccles. "I say that Sunlaws, who now names himself Cowdenknowes, is not serving us, in the Merse, as he should do, and as did my Lord Home, the previous warden, over our losses in beasts to those rascally English. It is grievous, worse than it has ever been, and still goes on. And we have received no help, gained no redress, complain as we have done. It is insufferable, I say!"

Archie actually grinned. "I would have thought that you Homes would have helped yourself, taken your own redress! As you have done in the past, all know, many a time."

There was outcry at that, some banging of the table.

"We are bearing with the new regent's policies," Eccles said, pointing. "He is for friendship with the English, the man. Nothing to be done to offend Elizabeth Tudor! Although she keeps our queen captive. So, no riding across the border, no fight with their thieves. So we forbear." That was said almost smugly.

Archie coughed, looking at John.

"Very proper," that man acceded. "All complaints and issues to be settled through the wardens. Without recourse to force. What has Sir John of Cowdenknowes to say?"

"Aye, the warden to speak," Archie confirmed.

Cowdenknowes appeared only too glad so to do. "I have made representations to the English warden, the Lord Hunsdon. Twice. He has not responded. What can I do, other?"

Various advices were given him by the other Homes, loudly and incoherently, most of them scarcely practicable.

Archie and John held brief conference.

"I say that you, Sir John, should yourself go to see Lord Hunsdon at Berwick Castle, where he is keeper. Tell him that if the raiding is not stopped, this Farnstein punished, and compensation for the stolen cattle not made, I, the Lieutenant, will have the regent seek redress from Queen Elizabeth's ministers in London. That should serve." Archie, looking round the hall, added, "The regent is my uncle!"

Cowdenknowes looked doubtful about this injunction; but most there seemed to approve, and said so.

"A wardens' meeting at Berwick, then," Archie reiterated. "Sir John to inform Hunsdon that he is coming, so to be present. If no satisfaction, then I act!"

"It might be the more effective if Cowdenknowes was

accompanied there by a number of those here present!"
John suggested, advice received with acclaim.

Thus briefly and with a minimum of contention the
matter was disposed of meantime, and the visitors able
to take their leave for the return journey, Archie quite
pleased with himself, but hoping that he did not have to
actually approach Morton over it all.

As it transpired, John's involvement in this East March
controversy was quite speedily translated into a more
personal concern, for only a week or so later he was
sent word by the provost of Jedburgh of trouble in his
own March over this same wretched character Farnstein.
It appeared that he had transferred his activities to the
Middle March, whether or not as a result of Hunsdon's
representations was not known. But he had, with supporting Northumbrian Marchmen, started to assail the
Jedburgh common grazings up in the Redeswyre area of
the Cheviots, to the outrage of the townsfolk, driving off
large numbers of their beasts. He appeared in fact to be
establishing something of a trade in stolen cattle for the
English marts rather than just casual raiding. Something
drastic would have to be done about Farnstein, of the
strange name.

John accordingly sent word to the English Warden
of the Middle March, the veteran Sir John Forster,
based on Hexham on the North Tyne, that he required
a wardens' meeting to deal with this nuisance and
troublemaker, and this as soon as possible. These joint
forgatherings, always held at the borderline itself, were
the normal method of settling troublesome disputes. As
well, meetings were held once a year, even when there
was no particularly grievous problem to deal with; and on
these occasions they usually developed into something of
a social assembly, with many of the folk on both sides of
the frontier attending, traditional and national enmities
temporarily put aside, with even pedlars selling their
wares and booths set up. Normally such were held in

early August, after the sheep-shearing and before the harvest, preoccupations for all Borderers. John decided that this Farnstein matter could not wait until then, and requested a prompt meeting with Forster, of whom he had heard not a little, as a character to be reckoned with. They had not met so far. He informed the Jedburgh magistrates of his action.

When a reply came from Hexham it was to the effect that Forster would be prepared to meet his opposite number. He suggested that this might well serve as the annual wardens' assemblage, instead of repeating the occasion a few weeks later. He proposed to meet at the Redeswyre, near the Carter Bar border crossing, on 7th July, when he would be prepared to discuss all relevant matters with Sir John Carmichael. The name of Farnstein was not mentioned in this response.

Inevitably there was talk and debate at Fenton Tower and Tantallon over this development, the more so when further word came from Jedburgh that additional cattle were being stolen, and two protecting herdsmen had been assaulted and injured up on the grazings. It scarcely looked as though Forster was treating the matter very seriously, any more than Hunsdon appeared to have done.

Archie declared that he also was going to be at this Redeswyre meeting. Could they insist that Hunsdon put in an appearance there too, even though it was not in his March? John said that he would suggest and request it.

The occasion offered an opportunity for Margaret to pay a visit to Janet Kerr at Ferniehirst, and to take Mary and introduce her to that friendly hostess, and in the height of summer. They would take the Carmichael children with them, and make something of a holiday of it.

So it was quite a party which in due course set out for the Jedburgh area a few days in advance of the projected meeting.

At Jedburgh itself, however, any holiday atmosphere was dispersed, the townsfolk incensed and making it evident. Their cattle were still being taken, and three more of their herders attacked and wounded. The burgh was perhaps unfortunate in that its common grazings were at a considerable distance from the town itself, this partly due to the topography of this Cheviot foothill area, and partly to the Ferniehirst property occupying most of the nearby ground. Other Border burghs had similar inconveniences, Hawick in especial having some of its commons, where all the inhabitants who wished to do so could pasture beasts, as far as fifteen miles away. The Jedburgh grazings, extensive as they were, lay well up the valley of the Jed Water and beyond, out on to the open Cheviot slopes of Crink Law and Bught and Stell Knowes summits, in Southdean parish, high, uninhabited ground rimmed on the south by the borderline itself. Since this frontier between the two kingdoms was not marked, save by the occasional cairn of stones, it meant that cattle from both sides were very apt to stray across on to foreign ground, despite herders' efforts; and many hundreds of beasts were involved. This was generally accepted and allowed for, but it did facilitate raiding and theft. And being so far from the town, tended to limit the number of herdsmen, usually an occupation for youths. That these were now in danger of attack much upset the burghers.

John promised to do what he could to right matters.

Janet welcomed them all, as ever declaring that she was glad of the company. Ferniehirst made a good place to visit indeed.

John held a more formal discussion with the magistrates and guild-brothers of Jedburgh, to garner details as to their complaints and losses. And they told him just where the wardens' meetings were held, and assured that a large contingent of the townsmen would be up there on the day, to give support. Seemingly this was normal procedure on these occasions, as it were days of truce, some competition indeed prevailing on both sides as to numbers and quality.

Janet was able to give them additional guidance as to proceedings, and especially as to Sir John Forster, a man to watch heedfully, she said. He was elderly, but no less dangerous for that, and had held the wardenship now for almost thirty years. Her husband had had continuing trouble with him. Thomas had always said that he was as cunning as he was unscrupulous. So John, and Archie, tyros at the game, were warned.

Margaret was vexed that it would never do for her to accompany her husband on this important duty.

They had not brought any Douglas escort on this occasion; and the Carmichaels did not go in for armed supporters; so Janet thought fit to provide them with a score of Kerr mosstroopers as tail, such as apparently would be expected.

Thus accompanied they rode off, on 7th July, to the well-wishing of the ladies.

Their way went due southwards by the banks of the Jed Water for some six miles, to where, at Camptoun, the river swung away westwards, and their road, rising steadily now, probed into the Cheviot Hills. There was another six miles of this climbing, through empty sheep- and cattle-strewn mixed moor and grasslands towards a distinct gap or pass in the hills between, they were told, Catcleuch Shin and Lumsdon Law, major summits; and here was the borderline, at Carter Bar, with the Redeswyre stretch of levelish ground just to the east. Beyond this lay the long descent into English Redesdale.

As they rode up to this pass area, John was astonished to find it crowded with men and horses, tentage and stalls, banners flapping, smoke rising from fires, almost like a fair, the stranger to behold after all the bare and empty hillsides, and this one of the loneliest stretches of the entire borderline.

Approaching, the first recognisable face was that of Turnbull of Bedrule, who hailed them cheerfully. So there were other Scots attending than just the Jedburgh ones. Some of the Kerrs pointed out Elliots, Scotts, Rutherfords, Kers and Pringles.

It was, however, the English warden whom John

and Archie looked for, if he was already present; and presumably a cluster of banners on staffs flying in the breeze in the centre of the encampment represented the quality. They dismounted, and pushed their way through the throng, Turnbull still with them.

That man duly pointed out Sir John Forster, a heavily built, grey-haired man with hanging jowls, sitting with others at a makeshift table of planks resting on boulders, drinking from pewter mugs. Their arrival was eyed warily, but there was no rising to greet them.

John announced that he was Carmichael, the Scots warden, and with him the Earl of Angus, Lieutenant of the Border, seeking Sir John Forster.

The elderly man nodded, looking more keenly at Archie that at John. He admitted his identity, and indicated his drinking companions, Sir George Heron of Chipchase, keeper of Tynedale, his deputy, Sir Francis Russell, and Sir Cuthbert Collingwood. Mugs of ale were proffered and accepted. They sat down beside the others.

Converse was stilted, to say the least, John getting the impression that he was looked upon as an up-jumped non-Borderer, inexperienced and of little account; and Archie, however resounding his name and title, too young to be taken seriously. It was scarcely a congenial meeting, however amicable the occasion was intended to be, with almost festive attitudes around them, and pedlars shouting their wares and others selling ale from laden pack-horses.

Presently, after a little of this, and his ale downed, John came to the point. "This of the man Farnstein," he said. "His depredations continue and have become intolerable. Complaints from the East March as well as this one – "

"Later!" Forster interrupted. "Wait until we hold our wardens' session." That was curt.

John did not appreciate the other's attitude, which was, apart from the personal aspect, dismissive of the Scottish warden's standing, to say nothing of the lieutenant's. He rose.

284

"My lord, if Sir John will inform us when he is ready, we will, I think, make our own enquiries. And give him time to produce this Farnstein."

Archie nodded, rising also.

"An arrogant character that! Janet Kerr said that he was cunning," John observed. "If so, he was uncivil of a purpose. Presumably to seek to put us in our place before all, and before any discussion. If so, he misjudges!"

"There was no sign of Hunsdon there. These English!"

They went looking for the Jedburgh representatives, to gain specific details of charges against Farnstein, but it seemed that these had not yet arrived.

Turnbull introduced them to various lairdlings of the March, some of whom had attended previous wardens' meetings and who said that, usually, when it came to the actual official exchanges, the two sides formed up facing each other, a short distance apart, with the principals in the centre, and any accused or witnesses brought forward to give their excuses or evidence.

They had not long to wait before a hunting-horn sounded, clearly a signal for proceedings to commence. There followed much movement, the breaking up of groups, some laughter and token fist-shaking, with the English massing on the south side, the Scots opposite. It was quickly evident that there were far more of the former, possibly double the number, at a rough estimate, John putting it at fully two hundred. Still no sign of the Jedburgh contingent, which was unfortunate, being the complainants.

When they saw Forster and his deputy and the other English notables coming forward to stand in the central space, John deliberately held Archie back from joining them.

"Let them wait!" he said. "Two can play that game!" He looked round, and saw Turnbull of Bedrule talking with Rutherford of that Ilk, and beckoned them forward. Lacking the Jedburgh provost and magistrates, it was best to have somebody to stand at their side.

After a pause, the four moved over to confront the Englishmen.

Almost before they halted, John was speaking, and loudly, determined to be seen by all to be making the running now. "I, warden of this March, and my lord of Angus, lieutenant, call upon Sir John Forster, English warden, to explain why measures have not been taken against the man Farnstein, a notable thief, troublemaker and attacker of herdsmen to their injury, and justice done upon them. This despite my complaints. I call upon Sir John to produce the said transgressor, Farnstein, and any of his supporting robbers."

Into the hush which received that, it was moments before Forster spoke. "I have received your complaints, Carmichael. But this Farnstein is not here. He has fled this March." That was flat, cold.

"Fled, sir! And you permitted him to flee? Where has he fled? To his own East March, where he has offended, as here, against Home cattle, to *their* complaint. To Lord Hunsdon. Is he here? I requested his attendance."

"I have no authority to summon the Lord Hunsdon. From a different March."

"What then is your answer to these charges? You have authority to control the English Middle March, and have the responsibility to do so."

"I do not need you to tell me my responsibilities, sirrah! I have been warden here since before you were born, I judge! If and when this Farnstein returns, he will be arrested and tried. Meanwhile, I have charges to bring against Elliot of Stobs and some others of *your* people."

John brought down his hand in a chopping motion. "Sir! I request that this of Farnstein be dealt with before other matters. The principal reason for this early meeting. You have not produced him, and we must trust that you will apprehend him in due course. But there is more to it than that. Compensation. Many beasts have been stolen, injuries inflicted. Due payment must be made in respect of these. Farnstein, we understand, has been selling the stolen beasts at markets. Even if he has fled, and taken his moneys with him, he will have house, goods, cattle of his own. Such must be constrained, as necessary. To make payment – "

"Do not tell *me* what must be done, man!" Forster exclaimed. "I will not be told my duties by any Scots upstart! Mind your words, sirrah! Enough of this . . ." The rest of the angry denunciation was lost in shouts and clamour from the ranks of the English behind him.

When he could make himself heard, hand raised high, John called, "This is a wardens' meeting, duly called, for discussion of a grievous offence, not for insults, Sir John. Have I your word that compensation for the Jedburgh cattle will be forthcoming? And for the wounds received?"

"I will hear no more of this!" Forster declared. "I did not come here to be miscalled and baited by such as you! It is enough!" And gesturing to his companions, he turned around, to stalk back towards the now gesticulating crowd.

"I shall make protest to the king's regent!" John's announcement could not compete with the English yelling. And as though Forster's turning back had been a signal for action, a couple of stones were thrown at the Scots four. None hit their marks, but these were followed by a positive hail of missiles, that stony pass in the hills providing ample ammunition. One did strike John on the shoulder, to no real hurt, but another drew blood from Turnbull's cheek.

Uproar ensued, the Scots behind the four surging forward and picking up their own stones as they came, the Kerr escort especially vehement. John and Archie had to duck down to avoid the efforts of their own throwers. The bedlam of yelling reverberated from the enclosing hillsides.

Then, above the shouts, a scream shrilled, and from close to the four. An arrow from a crossbow had transfixed one of the Kerrs, who fell to the ground.

Appalled, John stared – but not for long. He saw not a few on the English side raising crossbows and hackbutts, arquebuses, and fitting shafts, and priming to aim. He shouted, "Down! Down!" waving right and left, and flung himself flat.

Just in time, as a ragged flight of arrows came over, followed by a couple of shots from hackbutts, causing havoc amongst the Scots who had not been swift enough in obeying John's urging to throw themselves down.

In the initial panic, men sought to escape, some running after rising, others crawling away out of range on all fours or on their bellies. More stones and some arrows and bullets came at them, the English now seemingly accepting that the truce was over and their traditional enemies available, suddenly legitimate targets.

Getting back to the tethered horses was the prime urge, for all Borderers were at their best in the saddle. It was not flight that the Scots sought but retaliation. Most were able to reach their steeds for the opposition also had been dismounted and their horses well back. So there followed a brief spell, not of quiet, for the cries and shouting, and some groans, were as loud as ever, but of cessation of crossbow and hackbutt fire, as men sought their beasts. And by the course of events, the Scots reached theirs first, although leaving a few of their number on the ground.

John and Archie, unhurt, leapt to their saddles, and even before they were able to do so, some of the Kerrs, Turnbulls and others were mounted, and by no means pulling round to bolt, but reining forward for vengeance, before the English were equally ready for the fray.

John, although totally unprepared for this situation, knew what was expected of him, and waved his supporters into something of a formation, not a line but an arrowhead grouping, in the time-honoured and effective assault order calculated to divide up an enemy to prevent unified control, dispersing them initially in hoped-for confusion. All knew of this, to be sure, the enemy included, but in the general rush back, those mounted first, and formed up, had the advantage. It was a distinctly ragged V which advanced, John and Archie forming the apex, but it did represent some order and command, which could hardly yet be said of the opposition.

Most there, of course, at least on the Scots side, had not come armed, save with the habitual dirks at belt; but the Kerrs did have lances and swords, as required of an escort. They quickly formed themselves into the outer and assertive flanks of the spearhead, lances levelled, a potent array.

On they all pounded, the clan slogans of Kerr, Turnbull and Elliot shouted; and they had not much ground to cover before they were into the English. Forster and his group had not reached their horses, and although they were waving and calling commands, there could as yet be no defensive posture mustered. So they, the leaders, scattered, to avoid the Scots charge, and the arrowhead went plunging in and amongst them all, driving the desired wedge through in a drumming of hooves, breaking up the opposition into chaos.

So far, so good. But the real testing time had yet to follow; for it was one thing to lead a spearhead charge, and quite another, once through the enemy mass, to turn around in any sort of order and head back in effective further assault, especially with a mixed company like this, and come unprepared for battle. John had had some experience at Langside field, but this was Archie's first essay at warfare, save for tournament jousting practice, so he was of little use.

Amongst the alarmed pedlars and ale-sellers then, John sought to wheel his horsemen round, waving right and left to indicate a double-turn and a rejoining in formation thereafter. But that was more easily decided than effected. The turning process, amongst all the scurrying non-combatants and their pack-garrons, was less than co-ordinated, indeed was a disarray of rearing and plunging horses and cursing men, lances being now a handicap, all but a menace to all concerned, fugitives running and falling, John biting his lips in frustration, Archie himself no longer at his side.

The reassembling of his people took time inevitably, allowing for Forster and his companions to get themselves and their own people mounted and in some sort of order. So that it was not a struggling rabble but an armed assembly, however disorganised, which had to be faced, and numbering more than double the Scots strength.

John perceived that escape rather than confrontation was the sensible objective in their circumstances, the tide against them. The arrowhead again, then, to drive through the opposing mass, and then away, back to Ferniehirst and Jedburgh. There were surely not enough English to try to assail castle and town?

Urgently he got his people formed up, actually in better order than before, for they now all knew what was required, not only the Kerrs, who spurred their mounts into place, the lances forward as the desired steel-tipped hedge, Archie beside John again at the front. The latter raised arm high and brought it down in a sweep, pointing. They surged forward.

Had he come provided with sword and lance, John might have sought to drive directly for Forster and the others, in order to try to disorganise the leadership, favoured tactics always. But unarmed as he and so many others were, this was unlikely to be effective. Better just to drive through and away, if possible.

Charging men always have the advantage over those who wait for the impact. Forster would know that well, but had not had the time to marshal his superior force into any forward drive. So, in the event, the wedge formation again ploughed through the enemy, lances more menacing than thrusting, unhorsing a few but casualties minimal on either side.

Once out of the press and tumult, and facing northwards now, John pointed directly ahead, downhill for the Jed Water valley. None there sought to contest his decision.

But escape was not to be, not because of pursuit but

because there ahead, coming up into sight over a shoulder of the hillside, was a host of horsemen, banners flying, spears high, swords drawn, and yelling as they came.

"Jeddart's here! Jeddart's here!" the cry echoed and re-echoed. Jedburgh had come late to the meeting, but come in force, probably why they were late. And presumably some fleeing Scot had told them of the fighting as they came, and they were ready, eager to play their part, belated as it was.

So, faced with an entirely new situation, John did not hesitate but reined his people in, and indeed round, to face south again, so that, as the Jedburgh contingent, fully three hundred strong, came up, they were able to join them without them halting their onward canter. Positions were suddenly reversed indeed.

Spurring to ride alongside the Jedburgh provost and sheriff, John and Archie jerked out greetings but did not attempt any explanations or directions. It was obvious enough what was to do and what was required, and the Jedburgh men, living so close to that borderline, did not require guidance as to procedure, their swords, Jeddart staffs and lances indicating that. The combined force pounded on up to the Redeswyre.

The English were certainly caught unprepared. Instead of pursuit they were abruptly faced with attack, and by much superior numbers and fresh fighters. Forster and Heron sought to marshal a front of three sections, making use of the broken nature of the pass area, clearly so that the two flanks could turn and aid the attacked centre, or possibly the Scots themselves break up into three, lessening the impact. But their dividing was not entirely successful, with some confusion – possibly the effect of overmuch liquor consumed by many of the company, as might well have been the cause of the original outbreak of hostilities. This separating of the sections was still in process as the combatants met in violent clash.

This was not planned arrowhead or other formation, merely a headlong collision of men and horses, with no tactical manoeuvring. But the Scots, now in all but double the numbers of the English, were again the chargers, with the latter either stationary or moving over to the flanks. The result was inevitable, the defensive force overwhelmed, smashed through, driven back and dispersed. Where not overthrown by the weight of the collision, horses bowled over in screaming, lashing turmoil, men swept out of their saddles by those vicious Jeddart staffs, seven or eight feet long with hook-like heads of iron designed to act like shepherds' crooks but against mounted men, the defensive force was breached and scattered entirely. It was all over in a few moments, or at least victory was gained, even though minimal fighting was involved. Some individual battling did ensue for some time with the bolder spirits, but not a few of the survivors fled off down towards Redesdale, these hampered by the panic-stricken pedlars and their beasts.

There were casualties amongst the Scots also, of course, but few in comparison. Indeed no great numbers on either side suffered, although not a few were wounded by the staffs, swords and horse-falls and tramplings. It was no example of strategic warfare, merely elementary overwhelming by weight and concussion; but it was conquest, undoubted and complete.

John, himself somewhat dazed by the impact and speed of it all amongst the crush of lashing, rearing horses, flashing steel and noise, noise, sought to collect his wits and take charge, as was presumably his duty. He gazed around, seeking Archie, saw instead Forster himself unhorsed and bending over one body amongst many, of men and beasts, most lashing, stirring, crawling, blood everywhere. Reining over to his fellow warden, he stared down. No words were exchanged, but John saw that the fallen man was Sir George Heron, the deputy. He dismounted.

"Dead!" Forster jerked. That was all.

Archie rode up, apparently unhurt, with the Jedburgh

provost, both crying their triumph. Words themselves seemed totally inadequate, pointless; but John reached up to grasp his friend's wrist.

When at length, head shaking, words came, it was for John to gesture around. "Order!" he got out. "We must . . . win order!" He had to shout, the noise of screams and groans and yells still clamorous. He saw, hanging from Forster's shoulder, a hunting-horn, no doubt that which had signalled the official start of the wardens' meeting. Without asking leave, he whipped it over the other's head, and blew on it, loud and long, the ululating wailing sound penetrating the din and echoing from the hillsides. Men began to look whence it came.

John remounted his horse, but before doing so told Forster that he was his prisoner, ordering Archie to guard him, to see that he did not escape. He had much to answer for. Then he told the provost to bring his men under control, while he found Bedrule and some of the Kerrs to do the same, marshal their people, take charge, direct and order.

It took time, for the excitement and elation of victory was not readily calmed and overcome, plundering going on, won horses being argued over, some few individuals still fighting. But gradually some command was contrived, some rule and direction imposed.

A man announcing himself as Gladstanes of that Ilk came up with Sir Francis Russell, Forster's son-in-law, as prisoner; and another brought Sir Cuthbert Collingwood, slightly wounded. Heron's body was picked up and tied over the saddle of a horse, other corpses laid aside, very few Scots amongst them, for later burial. A large number of prisoners were rounded up, some injured more or less severely. There was no pursuit of the fugitives.

All this was not swiftly achieved, and it was late afternoon before sufficient order was established to make a move back down to Jed Water. After first protests by Forster at being treated as a prisoner, he maintained silence, although Russell, a son of the Earl of Bedford, apparently, kept complaining angrily. These and other notables were mounted, but well guarded, and with Heron's body with them, John and Archie and the Kerrs, and the Jedburgh leaders, set off ahead, leaving the mass of the prisoners to be marched northwards by the triumphant townsfolk, these apt to be calculating ransom profits.

It had been an extraordinary day, John's first wardens' meeting and Archie's initiation into warfare. They would have a deal to tell Margaret and Mary.

They, and the Kerr escort, left the others at the track up to Ferniehirst, telling the provost to confine Forster and his associates securely in Jedburgh Castle, not mistreating them but holding them fast; likewise the lesser prisoners when they arrived. They would make further arrangements in the morning.

The ladies, anticipating only a fairly humdrum account of the wardens' meeting, but interested in this character Farnstein, were agog over the news of the day's doings, concerned over the dangers their menfolk had undergone, and much impressed over the victory, Janet glad that her mosstroopers had been so effective. But Margaret wondered about the prisoners.

"What do you propose to do with them, John?" she asked. "You can hardly just keep them locked up, men of that standing."

"They committed a grave offence. Their men fired on us, and were not restrained. And at a time of truce. They attacked without cause. Drew blood. Failed to produce Farnstein. Forster in charge and responsible. After the fighting, we could not just leave them free."

"No, I see that. I but wonder, what now?"

"I will take them to your brother, the regent. Accuse them before him. For a Warden of the Marches to attack another, in truce, is no light matter. What Morton does about it is not my affair. But something such is necessary."

"My fine brother may not thank you!"

"He governs, in the name of the king and realm. And this was an offence against the realm as a whole, not only against the March laws. If he appoints me warden and Archie lieutenant, he must support us."

"No doubt you are right. But . . .!" She left the rest unsaid.

"What would you have me to have done?" he asked of Janet. "What would *your* husband have done?"

"I think that he would have brought Forster and the others here. Put them into our cellars for a while. Required payment as a form of ransom! Kept it all, as it were, in the Borders."

"This is where I, no true Borderer, lack guidance. Also, no cellars in the March to lock them in! But would not Forster's and the others' people then come raiding here, in force, to release them?"

"They might well, yes. They have done the like before this! And the Kerrs have had to gather to repel them."

"So we are back to more Border feuding! And I would not have them brought here, Janet. And probably bring down trouble on Ferniehirst."

"I have cellars a-plenty at Tantallon!" Archie put in. "Imprison them there. They will not win out of that so easily. Nor their folk win in, with my Douglases to deal with!"

"I think better to let the regent decide . . ."

They left it at that, the somewhat doubtful heroes of the day.

25

Next morning they borrowed a small group of the Kerr men again, to escort the prisoners and themselves to Edinburgh, or Stirling if necessary, or possibly only to Tantallon, where they could pick up a Douglas party instead. Margaret and Mary and the children would stay another day or two at Ferniehirst before returning home. John and Archie might well come for them, depending on the circumstances; otherwise more Kerrs would conduct them northwards.

At Jedburgh they found the town in high spirits celebrating their victory, even though they had not as yet received any compensation for their losses in cattle and injured men. John told the provost and sheriff to hold the rank-and-file prisoners meantime, in castle and town gaol. He was going to take Forster and his colleagues to the regent, and learn from him what was to be done with regard to all the captives. As for the body of Sir George Heron, probably, in this warm weather, it should be sent back over the borderline to some nearby English house or farm, and left for it to be disposed of as desired. Without warden or deputy on the English side of the March now, it might be some time before compensation claims from Jedburgh were paid or even considered. Patience would be required. He deliberately did not mention ransoming ordinary prisoners although he knew that would almost certainly be attempted.

Up at the castle on its hill there was but little exchange with the captives there. When told that they were to be taken to the regent, at Edinburgh or Stirling, they professed outrage and protest, but could do nothing to prevent it save make threats of suitable retaliation. John said that he knew his duty. He did not wish to offer them the indignity of being bound on horseback for their ride, but go they would; so if they gave their word not to seek to escape, they could ride freely, and he gestured towards the waiting Kerr guard eloquently. Recognising the situation, all five nodded their reluctant agreement, for there were two others added to the group by the provost, gentry, by name Ogle and Fenwick. This agreement would much improve the speed of the journey, for they would all be good in the saddle.

It was decided to go direct, by the shortest route, to Tantallon, there to exchange Kerrs for Douglases, and on to Edinburgh or Stirling the next day. So by the usual route north, to Ersildoune they went, there to strike off eastwards through the Lammermuirs, for Cranshaws and the Monynut Edge, to Stenton, where they were only some ten miles from their destination.

There was no converse with the prisoners *en route*, John and Archie riding ahead, the Englishmen in the midst of the watchful Kerrs behind. No doubt these were interested in what they saw of the land as they rode, especially after the Earlston of Ersildoune, which none was ever likely to have seen before, even the Kerrs, the Lammermuirs *terra incognita*, the extent of these sheep-haunted hills probably an eye-opener, far outdoing the Cheviots. What the Englishmen thought of Tantallon's towering bulk and threat, when they saw it on its cliff edge above the waves, would have been interesting to know.

At the castle they were confined, not in Archie's vaunted cellars but in respectable but securely locked rooms, Glenbervie and his wife much put about as to how to treat them.

The following day, then, after rewarding the Kerrs and sending them off, and collecting another escort, their ride westwards proved to be quite short, by comparison, for passing through Haddington it was learned, by a chance meeting there with Douglas of Whittingehame, a cousin of the regent, who said that he had been summoned to Dalkeith the previous day and so far as he knew, Morton was still there. So they had only another fifteen or so miles to go with their prisoners.

Presenting themselves at Dalkeith Castle, and seeing the earl's banner flapping from its tower-top, indicating presence, they left the Englishmen outside in the care of the men-at-arms, and sought the regent's audience. Morton they found with two of his illegitimate sons, eating, with no sign of his countess, when they were shown in.

"So, there you are, Archie! Aye, and you Carmichael man," they were greeted. "I jaloused that you would be away taking order in yon Borders. So what brings you here, eh?"

"We found order somewhat difficult to take, my lord," John said. "Both as regards the Homes and the folk of Jedburgh, all suffering depredations."

"You say so. But that's what you are there for, is it no'?"

"Order, my lord, is one thing – battle and bloodshed quite another! There has been serious trouble with the English, grievous assault and – "

"The English! You mean raiders? They're ay at it! Nothing new there!"

"Not raiders, no. Not what we are here for. Much worse. The English Warden of the Middle March, Sir John Forster. And his friends . . ."

"Eh? Forster. I ken him. What's this? What's this?"

"Fighting, Uncle – swords and lances! A battle!" Archie announced. "But we won!"

"Guidsakes, what's this now? What have you been at?" Morton actually glared. "Swords! Wi' Forster? What folly is this?"

"Folly indeed, my lord, and worse. An armed assault, at the borderline, at Carter Bar. We were attacked, arrows and shots. By Forster's people."

"Save us! What have you two been at? You're there

to keep the peace, no' to make trouble for me with the English."

"It was the English who made the trouble, not us. I called a wardens' meeting with Forster, in truce. As I am entitled to do. The Jedburgh cattle were being stolen, time and again, from the common grazings, and sold by a man Farnstein. Their herders there attacked. So we, the wardens, met at the Redeswyre, beside Carter Bar, on the border two days back. Forster did not produce the raider Farnstein, as I requested. Came himself, yes, with his deputy, Sir George Heron. But refused to hear our complaints. Dismissed them, indeed. And then his people started assailing us. First throwing stones. Then shooting arrows and hackbutts. It was – "

"Lord, you're telling me you've been in battle, man? With the English. Fighting. You and these Jedburgh rogues? This I'll no' have, by God!" John was interrupted.

"It was the English who started it, my lord," he repeated indignantly. "We were all unarmed, save for some Kerrs. It was a truce. Men fell. The shooting grew worse. We had to do something. So we mounted, and charged them. There were more of them than of us . . ."

"We ploughed right through them," Archie took up the tale. "Stopped their shooting. Then, then . . ."

"We had to turn back. They were gathering again, to assail us. Back through them and then flight. Down to Ferniehirst. And then the Jedburgh men rode up. Late for the meeting. But many of them, well armed. So we turned again. Attacked. And this time won the day. Some English fled, but we captured most. Including Forster. The deputy, Heron, had fallen, slain. Others were – "

"You captured Forster! And slew Heron! God in heaven, you did that! The English warden and his deputy! Have you lost such wits as you may have possessed?"

"We could have lost our lives!"

"Lives! Christ's death, man, you could be losing lives by the hundred by this error! War!" Morton had got to his feet. John had never seen him so angry. "You slew the deputy warden. And took the warden prisoner. Elizabeth's representatives on the border. Here's blunder, folly! And myself seeking to keep the peace with the Tudor, with the English! You do this!"

"We were attacked. What would you have had us to do? Should we Scots have bowed the head? Made no protest?"

"To take Forster prisoner! That hard man. And slay Heron!" The regent stamped the floor, his two sons now also on their feet. "What have you done with them? Forster and the others?"

"They are outside, here. Awaiting your pleasure."

"Out . . .? *Here*! You have brought them here? To me! Of a mercy – are you crazed quite? Deranged? Run mad?"

"They offended against our king's realm. Attacked His Grace's representatives in time of truce. So we brought them to the king's regent. Who else?"

They stared at each other in silence for moments.

At length Morton spoke, and pointed. "They are out there? Bring you them in to me."

Inclining his head, John turned and stalked out, leaving Archie with his uncle.

Down in the courtyard he told the prisoners briefly that the Earl of Morton would see them. Dismounting, they were led upstairs.

They found Morton's sons gone from the room, the two earls standing well apart, Archie looking disgruntled.

"Ha, greetings Sir John! And friends," the older man exclaimed, all but amiably. "The name of Forster is well known to me. It pleases me to meet you. But I grieve that it is in these circumstances, aye."

The captives eyed him doubtfully, unspeaking.

"I have heard o' the difficulty at yon Carter Bar. The failure to agree. Unfortunate, aye. I regret that it has come to this. That you have been . . . incommoded." Morton was speaking carefully.

Still silent, the Englishmen waited.

"To bring you here. All this way. See you, sit! Refreshment will be brought. There is wine." And he gestured to the table.

Obviously surprised, Forster glanced at his colleagues, then at John and, nodding, sat down, the others following suit. John and Archie remained standing. "These mischances will happen," Morton went on, sitting likewise. "Perchance action has been over-hasty. On all sides. Cross-border matters can be difficult. But such must not be allowed to damage relations between our two realms. You agree, Sir John?"

Now the Englishmen were looking questioningly at each other.

"What mean you, my lord?" Forster asked.

"I mean that what is of import, vital for us all, isna the theft o' a few stots, nor the petty feuding across the Marches, which has been going on for long. But peace and amity, aye amity, between the two kingdoms. No?"

Forster inclined his head, warily. "None can so deny," he said.

"So, this breach o' peace was unfortunate. But it isna beyond repair, I say."

"Bickering at the Redeswyre need not have had us brought here." That was Russell, undoubtedly something of a hot-head. "I am Sir Francis Russell, son of the Earl of Bedford."

"Ah – Bedford! A weel-kent name. My regrets that you have been so . . . misused, Sir Francis."

At those words and that tone, all five Englishmen again exchanged glances, and sanguine glances now.

"We also regret foolish, hot words and deeds, by some, at a wardens' meeting," Forster said. "But hold that Carmichael's action was, and is, over-great. Too much."

His companions nodded strong agreement.

"Perhaps, sirs. But in the heat of contest, such can happen. Blood was shed, I hear?"

"On both sides," Collingwood put in. "Those Jedburgh men were bent on mischief."

301

"They came *after* the first bloodshed," John declared. "We had already been attacked by your people. During truce. I do not — "

"Hot blood on both sides!" Morton interrupted. "Unfortunate. But it mustna be allowed to injure relations between the kingdoms."

Forster spoke up again. "I much resent being taken and held like some common thief. And brought here, prisoner. And my deputy slain."

"I regret that also. We must seek to put matters to right. Sort over-hasty actions . . ."

Servitors came in with food and more wine, and the captives found themselves being treated as guests. John and Archie, although not invited to do so, also sat, looking less pleased than did their former prisoners.

"See you," Morton went on, goblet in hand. "We must seek to right all this, with speed and the least upset for all. Here is how I see it. You, Sir John, shall best bide with me here, meantime. In fair comfort, mind. For my guidance, just. Your friends may return forthwith, whence they came. I will order that the prisoners at Jedburgh be freed. You to see that the payments for compensation are made, without undue delay. Eh? And I will send word to your queen, assuring her of Scots goodwill, and care that such Borders tiffs do not disturb the well-being o' the realms. How say you?"

John drew a deep breath, preparatory to speak out in protest, and then, at Morton's glare, thought better of it, Archie looking bewildered.

"I would liefer return with the others, my lord," Forster said.

"In due course, Sir John. But meantime you can aid me wi' your guid counsel."

The others, scarcely disguising their gratification, chorused agreement, raising goblets in acknowledgment.

But not John Carmichael. Abruptly he rose. "Have I your lordship's permission to retire?" he demanded.

"You have, Sir John, aye. Do that. I will send you word in due course."

Nodding curtly, John made for the door, finding Archie at his heels, no word said. Together they strode out, slamming that door behind them.

Down in the courtyard, they gestured for the Douglas escort to mount, and to take the Englishmen's horses with them – Morton could provide for such, out of his bounty. In the saddle, they all rode out from Dalkeith Castle.

"That was . . . beyond all!" John got out. "Folly, indeed – and worse! Shame! I would not have believed it, even of Morton!"

"What does it mean?" Archie demanded. "To do that to us. To let them all off. Treat them like friends. And us as of no account!"

"Would he call that statecraft, I wonder? Whatever he calls it, it is damnable! We, the warden and lieutenant, of his own appointing, to be made to look fools. And worse! I do not see me remaining warden after this!"

"Nor I lieutenant. But why? Why?"

"It is this of Elizabeth Tudor, I think. It is whispered that Morton is in receipt of a pension from her. As was Moray. If that is true, it could be behind it all. Safeguarding his English gold!"

"Could it indeed be that? Mere moneys?"

"I think that it might. If so, God help Scotland!"

In that state they returned to Tantallon.

Next day, uncaring whether Morton sent for them, they headed back to Ferniehirst, to spell out all their concern and anger before the womenfolk. Margaret forbore to say I told you so.

John was uncertain what to do about the Jedburgh folk. They would presumably be getting word, astonishing word, sent from the regent, to release the prisoners held, however little as to gaining their due compensation. But he felt that he personally had to make some

303

explanation to them. He still was the warden, however long he might remain so, and however inadequate he was proving as such. Janet said that he ought indeed to see the provost and magistrates, let them know that all this was not of his doing. If he liked, she would come with him, for they all knew her well, the wife of their principal laird, and would trust her. John thanked her, but felt that he did not want to seem to have a woman come to speak for him in the circumstances. He did not desire to appear even more feeble than he would already seem to be.

That evening they had long discussions on the situation, on Morton, the regency and the state of the kingdom, Margaret heartily ashamed of her brother. But she urged that her husband and nephew should not be too hasty in resigning their offices. There might be much that they still could do for the weal of the nation, which they would be unable to achieve as private individuals. John thought that it might not be a case of resigning anyway, but rather of dismissal.

In the morning he and Archie went down to the town, and had their difficult interview with the provost, sheriff and some senior citizens. They had no hesitation in putting the entire blame and responsibility on the regent; but that did not spare them distinct feelings of failure and ineffectiveness in their positions. They promised to do what they could in gaining compensation for Jedburgh's people, and the Homes also, but feared that, the way things were, the English would not pay a great deal of attention to their representations when not backed by the higher authority in Scotland.

They were received and heard more acceptedly than they expected, however fierce was the railing against Morton, their fighting side by side at the Redeswyre having created some sort of bond between them all. Perhaps Margaret was right again in advising them not to be in any hurry to give up their Borderland positions, in offence; they might yet be able to work some good for these people.

They left Janet to return to Lothian, with the family, next day.

26

Back at Fenton Tower, John found a message awaiting him, an order. He was to report to the regent at Stirling at the soonest, no details given.

He rode over to Tantallon to see whether Archie had received a similar summons. He had not. But that young man declared that he would accompany his friend nevertheless. Mary was anxious to see her mother and brother, so they would take her with them. John had little doubt that the interview would be less than pleasant.

At Stirling Castle, leaving Mary reunited with her family, and having paid their respects to the king, they both went in search of the regent. They found him in conference with some of his "tulchan" bishops. So they had to wait, John steeling himself for the meeting.

But when at length Morton accepted them into his presence, they were unprepared for his attitude. First of all he shook his head at his nephew, declaring that he had not summoned him. But he did not dismiss him. Then, almost genial for that man, he turned to John.

"So, Carmichael man, you have deigned to answer my call, eh? Taking your time!"

"We have been down in the Borders, my lord. Where our duty lies." John was not going to sound apologetic.

"Aye, no doubt. Well, I have a task for you. *You*, no' Archie here. He can watch over your Borders for you. It's further afield for you, see you. Aye, you're for England, my mannie. For London, just."

John stared. "London!"

"Aye, London. You're to go to the queen there.

Elizabeth Tudor. She's fell annoyed, the woman. Over this o' Forster and the killing o' Heron. Writes me an ill letter! Sends it up by hard riders. So we have to soothe her, calm her. I am sending you to do it, since you it was who caused the trouble, you and your Jedburgh loons!"

"But . . . but . . .!"

"Nane o' your buts, man! You're ay at it. I ken fine they provoked you, the English, at yon Carter Bar. But you overdid it, you did so! Taking Forster prisoner, and the others. Elizabeth's hot over it, sees it as an insult to her. I kent she might. That's why I treated them as I did, something kindly. More than they deserved, aye. But we canna afford to offend Elizabeth. No' at this pass. Her lords, her advisers, would be at war with us if they had their way. Always that's the English for you. And with the Catholics o' the north here, under yon Huntly, and the Hielantmen forby still threatening trouble, we canna afford war wi' Elizabeth's English. So, I sent Forster home, wi' a bit pat on the back. And some siller for Heron's widow. And you are to go to London, to Elizabeth. To tell her the rights o' it, and take her a bit present likewise."

John wagged his head, quite at a loss. "But why me to go to the queen? If she is angry over the Redeswyre affray – she ought not to be, for it was her people at fault – then I am the last one she will want to see. If she will even *see* such as myself, no great noble . . ."

"You are the warden responsible. And, to my cost, you are my own good-brother, my sister's husband. Some kind o' kin, to speak for me. You will take a letter wi' the royal seal o' Scotland on it. That will win you into her presence. And once before her, you will speak her fair. Tell her you, like mysel', desire only good terms, good relations wi' her realm, peace over the borderline. The bringing o' Forster and the others to me was only to save them from wild mosstroopers' assault, tell her."

"It was not!"

"Maybe no'. But you could put it that way, see you.

Best that way, make you look less the fool! And you my envoy, just. You'll do it fine, man. And you'll take her hawks."

"Hawks?"

"Aye, hawks. Falcons. I'm sending her two pair o' the finest hawks, trained for the hunting. A bit gift, see you. Women like gifts. And she goes hunting, they tell me. Better hawks than they'll breed in England, I vow! The Erskines have a right clever falconer. From Spain, trained by yon Moors. So you'll take them wi' you."

John looked at Archie, comment beyond him.

"Shall not I go with John? To aid him . . ."

"Na, na, he'll do fine on his own. What help would you be? You keep the Borders quiet for him — that's your task, as Lieutenant. Although how much use you are as Lieutenant I'm no' sure!"

"I'm to take hawks to Queen Elizabeth, my lord? As a gift? From me?"

"From *me*. To sweeten her. You have it? Aye, then, off wi' you. I've plenties to see to, with these bishops. You'll get the hawks from the head falconer downby. And no delay on being on your way, Carmichael — you're a one for delay! I'll have your letter sent to you within the hour — I've written most of it. It's only to get the royal seal. You're good on a horse, they tell me, so you'll be in London in four days, no? So no more buts, man! Off wi' you both . . ."

They went. It had scarcely been the interview anticipated.

They rode back to Fenton, each with a falcon, hooded and jessed, on their wrists, Mary included, a royal tranter with the fourth one. They had, of course, gone hawking occasionally, but neither of the men was particularly keen on the sport, which tended to be looked upon in Scotland as more suitable for women, Mary much more in favour. They felt distinctly foolish, riding thus, and in summer, with thick gauntlets.

But that was the least of it, to be sure. To say that John was disconcerted about this extraordinary mission thrust upon him was to put it mildly; aghast would have been nearer the mark. An envoy for Scotland's regent to the Queen of England! And an angry queen at that! Nothing in his rearing and experience had prepared him for such as this. That Morton thought him suitable for the task was in itself astonishing. Did he actually think more highly of his abilities than he seemed to show? John had heard about Elizabeth Tudor's glittering court, all her proud favourites and nobles. How, in heaven's name, was he to confront these? Forster and his like were one thing, but all these English viscounts, earls and marquises were quite another. Did Morton realise just what he was requiring of him? And did he have to do it, just because Morton ordered it? Yet the regent spoke in the name of the king, so that his word was a royal command and must be obeyed.

Archie had trouble with his hawk, a peregrine female, the largest of the four birds, a restless creature. The tranter – the third man in the sport of falconry, who acted as retriever of the birds and their prey in the sport, for after a kill they seldom would return on their own to their flier – said that if they gently stroked their hawks and spoke to them, they would sit quietly while being carried. But this did not seem to work with Archie's one, and he was glad to exchange it, presently, with the tranter's one. Clearly, on the long ride south to London, suitable arrangements would have to be made for these creatures' carriage. And they would need fresh meat, their daily food.

Mary, much used to hawking, evidently an Erskine partiality, laughed at her husband's lack of expertise.

They were not far on their way before John declared that he would have to make better arrangements for getting these wretched birds all the way to London. The journey was going to be sufficiently taxing, even without this problem. Morton had said four days, but surely that was scarcely possible? London was said to be nearly four hundred miles from Edinburgh. Eighty miles in a day would be good going indeed, with the best horses. And was there need for all this haste? Archie said that he would help in this, at least, provide a falconer and tranters from amongst his Douglas people, to act as escort as well, and he would mount them on the best steeds.

Back at Fenton, Margaret was much exercised over this odd mission of her husband's, and wished that she could have accompanied him, although clearly this was impossible, with the children to consider, besides it looking very strange. She much would have liked to see London town, indeed much of England on the way, even though she was not so keen to meet Elizabeth Tudor, who was reputed to be something of a female dragon. She hoped that John would survive the meeting! He would be away for two weeks at least, she judged. She would miss him. She loved her brother none the more for this peculiar charge. John must wonder indeed at the price he was still having to pay for his marriage.

She accompanied him over to Tantallon the next day, and they found that Archie had been as good as his word. Apparently Douglas of Kilspindie, near to Aberlady, was strong on hawking, the great bay there, with its saltings and tidal flats, excellent for the sport, wild geese, ducks and herons by the hundred, the thousand. He had sent his second son, Jamie Douglas, proficient with the hawks, who would be some companion for John on the journey, with a falconer and two tranters, and they would be well mounted. So that problem should be taken care of.

John was grateful.

As to route, no one could help him greatly, for none of their acquaintance had ever had cause to travel right down through England. Glenbervie had once had to go as far as the Northumbrian Tyne, on an errand for Archie's father, and declared it quicker, shorter, to go inland, not by the coast road and the Merse, but over Carter Bar into Redesdale, saving fully a score of miles.

310

John, liking young Jamie Douglas, a cheerful twenty-year-old, did not delay. The sooner he was off, the sooner he would be back. Margaret and Archie declared that they would accompany him as far as the Lammermuir watershed, at the Whiteadder, to see him on his way.

So, presently, farewells were said on the high ground of Gamelsheil, looking far over the Borderland to the distant line of the Cheviots, England. The hawks, at least, were now well looked after, and behaving remarkably well considering the pace of the horses. The tranters carried saddle-bags of pigeon meat for them. The five men settled down to hard riding.

It was strange, a couple of hours later, to be passing the Redeswyre and Carter Bar, scene of the cause of this mission, with little sign of the conflict now visible, save for some upturned red earth which might represent a grave, and some broken lance-shafts. They rode on down Redesdale past the Catcleuch Loch, empty country indeed. John had never actually been over the borderline here, but had been instructed by Glenbervie, who thought that they might get as far as Otterburn that first day. But it was, in fact, only mid-afternoon when they cantered past the scene of that famous battle of two hundred years before, when, as the ballad said, "a dead man won a battle", the said sad victor being the second Earl of Douglas, Archie's direct ancestor, carried onward into the fight against Hotspur Percy by his aides, although stabbed in the back. Jamie Douglas was highly interested to see this site, for the adjoining property to his Kilspindie was Luffness, where the man who had stabbed the earl in the back, his own armour-bearer actually, had been the son of that castle's keeper, Bickerton by name. The English called that battle Chevy Chase.

John found his new fellow traveller good company and easy to talk to although, at the rate that they were riding, converse was limited indeed.

They were threading hills most of the time, John interested to see the country from which the folk who tended to cause so much trouble along the Border came from, Robsons, Nixons, Fenwicks, Storeys and the like. It was all not unlike the Scottish side, needless to say, but less green, with more of heather, sedge and moss, the valleys narrower than theirs on the Middle March.

Quite pleased with themselves, the riders found themselves crossing the famous Roman Hadrian's Wall as dusk fell, a mighty barrier, now grass-grown, but very impressive. John had heard that Queen Elizabeth called it the Pechts' Wall, a corruption of the word Pict; which had its own significance, indicating that the English at least assumed that the Romans had built it to divide the northern Picts, or Caledonians or Albannach, the Scots' forebears, from the southern ones – which meant that the latter had dwelt once as far south as this, and further.

They halted for the night at an inn in Hexham-on-Tyne, a town well known by name to all Scots Borderers, as where the raiders had come from who were so soundly defeated at Hornshole, soon after the disaster of Flodden Field, sixty years earlier by the youths of Hawick, a feat of which that Scots burgh was inordinately proud, indeed celebrating it in its town anthem:

Teribus and Teriodin, sons of heroes slain at
    Flodden,
Emulating Border bowmen, ay defend your rights
    and common!

They had some difficulty with the innkeeper over those hawks, but eventually got them safely installed in a hayshed of the stableyard, with their pigeon meat.

John reckoned that they had covered eighty-five or ninety miles. But Queen Mary had ridden seventy-five miles in a day when she was less than well, so that they need not crow over-loud.

Next day it was due south over more hills, first into the valley of the River Derwent, then across into Weardale and Teesdale, unknown terrain now. The weather had deteriorated into a thin rain, but this only made them ride the faster. They would now be in Yorkshire, they assumed, so they were well out of the Borderland.

Wet but satisfied, after Swaledale and Wensleydale, they spent that night at Ripon, another eighty miles at least. Perhaps Morton had not been so far out in his calculations?

The third day took them down Swale to the Ouse, and none so far from York itself. The dales they had to follow, or more often cross, seemed endless; some they had heard of like Wharfedale and Airedale, but most unknown to them. Practised horsemen as they all were, they were becoming somewhat saddle-sore. And their mounts, bearing up wonderfully, must be wearying.

Nevertheless, their next day, the fourth, they covered more ground than ever, by Newark and the River Welland, to Stamford and on to Oundle on the Nen, not far off one hundred miles, this on account of the lower and more level terrain, rich, fertile country, the finest for crops and tilth that they had seen. The vales of Tyne and Peffer in Lothian could rival it, but, they judged, little else in Scotland. At Oundle they were told that they were little over one hundred miles from London. Five days, then, not four. Throughout, they had met with no hostility from the people, despite their Scots accents. The ordinary Englishman was evidently not the so evil character all had been brought up to consider him.

The last day's ride, by Bedford – where presumably that hot-headed Sir Francis Russell had come from, his father earl thereof – Hitchin, St Albans, Watford and Edgware, they came eventually to the Thames at Brentford – and they could smell London considerably before they reached it. Edinburgh could smell, yes, in its narrow wynds and closes, but on its seven hills and with winds off the Firth of Forth, these odours got dispersed. London, it seemed, was less fortunate, no hills worth the name in sight of the travellers, and the Thames no wide and windy arm of the sea.

Their approach to the great city was through populous

313

territory such as the Scots had never seen, villages, hamlets and communities running into each other. And so many churches, their spires and towers standing out everywhere. They could well appreciate now that England had ten times as many people as had Scotland.

It was evening as they entered the city itself, the supper-time fires sending up their clouds of smoke to create something of a pall over the tightly packed streets and alleys and lanes, the tenement houses reaching out balconies and projecting storeys the higher they went, often to all but hide that smoke-filled sky. People thronged everywhere, hung out of windows, children played and cried in the streets, mongrel dogs barked, vendors shouted, the noise, like the smell, all but overpowering. Edging their horses through it all was quite a challenge in itself, and treated as such by many of the citizenry.

John sought directions to reach Whitehall Palace, and got hooted at for his pains. The hawks also caused much exclamation and merriment. But eventually a young woman, after skirling the inevitable laugh at anyone requiring such directing, did inform them, and, it seemed, their destination was not very far off, and at this western side of the town, on the north bank of Thames between Westminster Abbey and Charing Cross.

Being by the riverside, the palace was not hard to locate, however difficult to reach by those crowded streets. They had to find some inn reasonably nearby, since they could hardly presume to seek to quarter themselves in the palace itself, welcome uncertain to say the least. However, London seemed to be full of taverns.

They found Whitehall, a huge and rambling establishment, near the waterfront, some parkland behind it. John was relieved to discover no lack of inns and hostels not far off. He should have anticipated this, for there would be many visitors to the palace who would not expect to be entertained therein. And since most high-born callers would come mounted, stabling would be required.

They found a suitable hostel called the Black Swan, with the necessary facilities, although the hawks, as usual, caused some doubts. But when told that they were for the queen, and from the regent of Scotland, the innkeeper became helpful and found the creatures a cellar.

Thereafter they made some enquiries of their host, ascertaining that the queen was in fact in residence, who to ask for on approach to the palace, when would be the best time to call, and the like. They were told that Her Majesty was apt to see special callers from her bed, or at least in her bedchamber – this with a smirk – of a forenoon, and had her midday meal in the early afternoon. So the best time to appear would probably be after that, in the late afternoon. They should ask to see Sir Thomas Parry, Deputy Master of the Household and royal treasurer, who would inform the queen of their presence and learn whether she would grant audience. As to those hawks, the innkeeper did not know.

They had quite a chat with this voluble but useful character before seeking their couches. He told them that this Whitehall had originally been York Place, the London seat of the Archbishops of York. But the late King Hal had taken it over at the Reformation, converted it into a palace much more comfortable than London Tower, greatly extended it and cleared a garden and park behind. He had some gossip to relate, inevitably, as to the royal customs and behaviour. He said that Elizabeth kept a lively court, court the right word, for most of the men thereat were for courting her, and not only for appointments, honours and suchlike. But the word was that she was still the Virgin Queen, even though she was renowned for entertaining some preferred ones naked, in her bath or *on* her bed, not in it – favourites like de Vere, Earl of Oxford, Dudley, Earl of Leicester, Sir Christopher Hatton, Sir Francis Walsingham, now Secretary of State, and Sir Nicholas Bacon, Lord Keeper. As to who to approach to gain the royal presence, Parry would advise no doubt, but probably Sir Nicholas Throckmorton, or even Burleigh himself, the Cecil. But if none of these was helpful, they could try to reach her through Kat Ashley, the First Lady of the Bedchamber, who was very close, often sharing the royal bed.

Somewhat bemused by all this, John sought his own bed, distinctly dreading the next day.

In the morning he and Jamie Douglas, after inspecting the various entrances and approaches to the palace, went sightseeing in the city, visiting Westminster Abbey to view the false Stone of Scone under the Coronation Chair, and the Tower of London, of ill repute. They looked in at two markets, one of fish and one of meats, the last with beasts there ready to be slain and cut up to order. The crowds everywhere, and the noise and smells, continued to preoccupy them.

The more urgent preoccupation took over, for John at least, in the afternoon, when the five of them set out for the palace, hawks and precious letter to the fore, the latter inscribed: "To Her Most Excellent Majesty, Elizabeth, Queen of England, Whitehall Palace."

The large wax Privy Seal it bore was at least impressive. Walking along the street with those hooded hawks at wrist attracted the usual attention and jeers.

John carefully chose the only entrance not manned by scarlet-uniformed Yeomen of the Guard, not wishing to be kept standing there in front of all viewers while possibly lengthy enquiries were made as to identity and business. They entered therefore into a side courtyard, rimmed with stabling and storehouses, and from this into an inner paved quadrangle, this lined with larders, food-stores and dairies, servants much in evidence. Of these John asked how to contact Sir Thomas Parry, Deputy Master of the Household.

Eyed somewhat askance, especially the hawks, he was advised to go to one of the other doors and ask the Yeomen. But he insisted that he had come thus deliberately, that he was an envoy from the regent of Scotland, and was not going to stand out there for all to gaze at, with these presents for the queen, while enquiries were made. Here at least they could wait in some privacy.

A little doubtfully they were ushered into a hot bakehouse, while a senior servitor went off to discover what to do with them.

It took some time for a haughty official of some sort to appear, who took not a little convincing that Sir John Carmichael was a fit person to proceed further into the royal premises – he had obviously never heard of a Warden of the Marches. It was the sight of the falcons which impressed him rather than these barbarous, ill-dressed Scots, evidently – he was of the class to recognise their worth. Stiffly he told the visitors to follow him.

They were led by various corridors and passages out of the kitchens and servants' quarters into progressively finer apartments and halls, the walls not painted nor tapestry-hung as at home but tending to be hung with pictures and portraits. Up a wide two-branched stairway they were brought to a door, on which their conductor knocked and then entered, leaving them outside and closing the door behind him. A number of elaborately dressed characters strolled past, considering them with eyebrows raised questioningly and passing audible comments.

Presently their guide reappeared and beckoned them inside. "Sir Thomas Parry," he announced, not the visitors' identity.

A short and tubby elderly individual, finely clad, sat at a great desk. He turned in his chair to eye them, but did not rise. Their usher stood behind them, as though prepared to show them out again.

"I am Sir John Carmichael, His Grace King James's Warden of the Scots Middle March of the Border," John announced, stiffly for him. "Come with word for your queen, from the regent, my lord Earl of Morton. And . . . gifts." And he moved forward, to present that heavily sealed letter.

The other raised his brows, took the paper, eyed it, transferred his gaze to the hawks, and cleared his throat.

"You wish me to convey these to Her Majesty?" he wondered, with a very Welsh lilt to his voice.

It was that accent which gave John the notion. "Ah, you are from our sister-land of Wales, Sir Thomas. Ap Harry, no? We have something in common, then. Our Cymric blood. For I am from the shire of Lanark, where once we spoke with the same tongue, I am told." It was a long shot, but it did find its target.

"Save us, here's some surprise! You speak our language, sir?"

"I fear not. It is long since Welsh, or the Cymric, was spoken in Scotland. But we were a part of ancient Strathclyde, a Welsh-speaking nation. Before Scotland became one. Our greatest hero, William Wallace, his family were so called for their Welsh-speaking."

"You say so? Carmichael, did you give your name? Carmichael. Myself, I come from Caerleon, in the shire of Monmouth. We have many car-names in Wales – Carmarthen, Carnarvon, Cardigan, Cardiff. And of a March, you said? We have our Welsh Marches also. But . . ." He stopped himself. "This is scarcely of any bearing on this of your coming here, I think. You say that you come from your young king's regent. With this letter. And . . . these birds."

"Yes, Sir Thomas. And to speak with Her Grace." John corrected himself. "Her Majesty."

"You seek audience, then? Personal speech?"

"I do. I have issues to relate, to explain. On which she herself wrote to the regent. My good-brother," he added, by way of emphasis.

"Your good . . .?" No doubt the other had never heard the Scots term for the relationship; but the brother was clear enough. "You are kin to the regent? But he is a Douglas, is he not?"

"I am wed to his sister, sir, the Lady Margaret Douglas."

"Ah!" Parry rose, clearly impressed now, as well as interested. "Come then, sir. We will see if Her Majesty will receive you. She is in the gardens, this fine day." He glanced at the other four callers. "These, with the falcons – they are to come also?"

"They require to, do they not? I cannot bear four hawks!"

"No. I will take you all, then." He dismissed the disdainful official.

So it was downstairs again and along more corridors and out by a rear door into a spread of formal gardens leading to an orchard with the parkland beyond. A number of men, and so far as they could see, only two women, were congregated at the orchard end, an instrumentalist plucking at a lute amongst the others.

The Scots were led out most of the way towards the company, and then signed to halt, while Parry went forward alone.

John was near enough to examine the group ahead. Which of the two women was Elizabeth he could not tell, both clad magnificently – as indeed were the men, the sunlight gleaming noticeably on much jewellery. Almost all the males wore short cloaks of velvet, barely reaching the waist, over what looked like satin tight doublets of varying colours, above trunk-hose, these puffed out widely but reaching only to mid-thigh, with silk stockings below, some with embroidered designs. Also most there, it was to be noted, wore garters below the left knee only, undoubtedly the prestigious Knights of the Garter.

They saw Sir Thomas bowing before the two ladies and gesturing back towards the visitors, this turning all heads in their direction. He had quite some discussion with the taller of the two women, presumably the queen, before bowing again, and backing away before turning to return to the Scots.

They heard a female voice calling out to some of the watching men, and two of these moved over closer to what must be their monarch.

319

"Her Majesty will see you, Sir John," Parry announced. "Come. But I think that these had best stay where they are, at this stage." And he waved back the four others.

Nodding, John went forward with the Welshman, very much aware of the stares of those superbly clad characters, much over-dressed in his opinion, certainly in comparison to his own modest garb.

But as he approached it was, to be sure, on the taller woman that his gaze concentrated, now flanked by two of the exquisites, the other female stepping back a pace. Elizabeth Tudor made an eye-catching figure, not only on account of the splendour of her attire. She held herself very straight, upright, fairly slender of person and with little of bosom, but wide of shoulder and narrow of waist. Her gaze was very direct, from watchful eyes, in a narrow and notably white face, above tight mouth and jutting chin. She was not beautiful, like her cousin Mary Stewart, but she was striking, formidable. She looked all the princess, her stature highlighted by the high divided ruff, pearl-studded, which emphasised her long neck, and by the jewelled corset which pointed down in a deep V almost to the groin, where it was flanked by the farthingale skirt expanded to wide panniers to match the puffed-out sleeves above. Her hair was back-plaited, with the front left uncovered, the impression being that it was dyed a reddish yellow. Elizabeth Tudor, however artificial her ensemble and adornment, was a figure to heed in more than her royal authority. It flashed through John's mind as he approached her how different was the appearance and impact of the two related monarchs of the realms.

"Sir John Carmichael of the Scottish Marches, Majesty," Parry presented. "Come at the behest of his brother-in-law, the Regent Earl of Morton."

John bowed low, and held out the sealed letter.

The queen took it, and handed it over unopened to one of the men, flicking a beringed finger imperiously, obviously meaning him to break the seal and open it. She was searching John's features and person assessingly.

"So you are he who had the effrontery to make captives of my representatives, in especial Sir John Forster. And slew his deputy, Heron!" she said, her voice steely. "I wonder that you dare to come into my presence!"

"My lord Regent believed, Majesty, that I was the best one to inform you of what took place that day at the Redeswyre. I come assured of Your Highness's honest judgment." He hoped that he sounded more assured than he felt.

"You are very bold, sirrah! When it could be the Tower for you!"

"Not, I dare to think, when you have heard the truth of it. And I come as envoy of King James's regent."

A snort from the elegant holding the letter.

"Well, let us hear you. But I will require a deal of convincing, young man! Slaying and taking prisoner my wardens is not to be wiped away by words. As I wrote to the Lord Morton."

"No, Majesty. But there are words and words, as none will know better than your royal self! There is truth, and there is merely the gloss of truth!"

"Out with it, then. I will judge which this is!"

"Yes. Wardens' meetings at the borderline are the recognised custom for settling difficult disputes where both realms are concerned. I sought this one, with Sir John Forster, on behalf of the folk of Jedburgh. At the Carter Bar – "

"I know all that, sirrah. Come to the point."

"Truce is always accepted on these occasions, Majesty. As it was that day. But the truce was broken. And by the English. Shots and arrows fired and stones thrown . . ."

"With good reason, no doubt!"

"Not so. Forster had not brought the culprit who had injured the Jedburgh people, was stealing their cattle time and again, and selling the beasts openly at market. Wounding their herders. He, Forster, said that the man Farnstein had fled. I said that it was the warden's duty to find and produce him. And to bring the due compensation.

321

He denied it. Then it was that the stones, arrows and shooting started. All from the English side. Forster did not attempt to halt it. Scots fell . . ."

"Forster says that there was provocation. I believe him!"

"I may have provoked by word, Highness. But not by deed, by force. It was truce. I was not armed. Nor most of my people. I blamed him, yes. But was I not entitled to do so. This of the man Farnstein was what the meeting was called for. And time had been given."

"Go on." It might be that John's admission of possible verbal provocation did help his presentation a little.

"We threw ourselves down, to escape the shooting. Some fell, wounded. We worked back. Then, reaching our horses and still under fire, we thought to charge the English. They were many more than ourselves. Wisest, I thought, to try to break up their ranks before we retired. To avoid a close pursuit. We drove at them and through. Then turned, to spur back. For Jedburgh and safety . . ."

"That is not how Forster tells it, young man."

"Perhaps not. Since his people were in the wrong. We fled. But we had not gone far when the Jedburgh riders came, late. Many of them, under their provost and magistrates. We turned back with them, my Lord of Angus, the Borders Lieutenant, with us. Would Your Highness have expected us to continue to flee? On Scottish soil!"

"It is not for *you* to ask questions of me, sir!"

"No. My apologies, Majesty. So, there was armed clash thereafter. And we had the best of it. Sir George Heron was amongst the slain. Many were wounded. Some English escaped, others were captured. Including Sir John Forster and Sir Francis Russell."

"Captured! There we have it! The affray, however wrongous, unfortunate, was perhaps understandable, to be forgiven. But to capture, to take prisoner and convey into your country, Forster and the others, *my* commissioners on the border, that was reprehensible, offensive, unforgivable!"

John had been fearing this, what Morton had warned of, the insult to the English throne implied, defiance of Elizabeth's authority. That man had said to claim that the taking into care rather than custody was for the prisoners' personal safety, against assault by the angry Jedburgh men; but that John was not going so to claim. Untrue, it would also be unfair to the townsfolk, who had made no such threats. Indeed, it could be proved false, in that he, John, had handed over the well-born captives to the provost and sheriff, to be housed overnight in the castle gaol, leaving them in Jedburgh's hands. So that excuse was not to be considered. What, then, to temper the queen's resentment? He had thought much on this, as he had journeyed south.

"Highness, something such was required of me," he said. "To have left the English leaders free could have made matters a deal worse than they were, brought about all but outright war, war on a much greater scale than this clash. Tempers were running high. Forster and his friends had been defeated, shamed. Would they have accepted it, done nothing more, if left at liberty? Almost certainly, I say, they would have gone back to their own territories, to Hexham and Corbridge and Haltwhistle, all upper Tynedale, and raised men, many men, to come back and wipe out this rout and shame, to win back their repute, make Jedburgh pay the price. Forster was a fighter always. Would he not have fought back, in the heat of his passion and humiliation? So, this had to be hindered, avoided. I saw it as necessary to keep him and the others under control, while tempers cooled. To bring him to the regent, who would deal with the situation wisely, better than I could, ensure that peace was maintained between the realms. Was I not right so to do, Highness?" That was a lengthy speech, but the best that he could do.

Elizabeth eyed him unspeaking for long moments; and waiting, John, himself searching her face for reaction, noted the slight scars under the dead whiteness of her skin, pock-marks.

323

The man on her left who held Morton's letter murmured something in the royal ear. She nodded.

"You cover yourself with much care, Sir John!" the queen observed, at length. "But why, then, did you have my representatives locked up in a prison like common felons?"

That was a poser. John racked his wits. At least she had called him Sir John this time, not sirrah. Was that some slight indication of compromise?

"Highness, was this misjudgment on my part?" he asked. "What was I to do with them? It was evening. They were angered, distraught, in no state for any accord or compromise. I could not take them into the house of Ferniehirst, where I was a guest of the Lady Kerr. They had to be held, or they would have been back over the borderline and rousing their people. The night had to be passed somewhere. Jedburgh Castle seemed best. Perhaps . . . perhaps I should have remained with them?" He threw that in as some sort of sop, scarcely hopefully.

"You almost persuade me that you are the innocent, Sir John!" Elizabeth said. "But not quite, I think! How say you, Edward? And you, Christopher?"

The handsome man with the letter shrugged. "The Lord Morton says here that he deplores the entire affair, Ma'am. Conceives it mishandled on both sides. And has sent this, his representative, here to convey his regrets and apologies. I cannot see other than that Your Majesty should accept it."

The other and younger man flapped a scented handkerchief. "Why should you concern yourself over it all, Ma'am? The behaviour of dolts and primitives! Off with him!"

"My lord Earl of Oxford would excuse you as scarcely responsible for your actions, Sir John! Sir Christopher Hatton appears to have me to overlook the offence. This once! Your regent is suitably . . . contrite, it seems?"

John all but voiced his protest, but thought better of it. But he had to make some answer, some comment.

"As to contrition, Highness, I would not see that as any stand of my lord's in the matter. Say concern and regret, rather. In token of which, mere token, he sends these hawks for your sport and pastime, Majesty. Two peregrines and two goshawks. Suitably trained." And he half turned, to wave behind him, hopeful that this would serve to ease what appeared to be the ending of the interview. He even risked a lighter note. "We have found them less than easy to transport for four hundred miles!"

"Ah, yes, the falcons!" Elizabeth herself almost seemed prepared to welcome an easing of the atmosphere. "Let us examine them." And, instead of ordering the birds to be brought to her, she waved John forward to conduct her to the waiting four Scots. Not only the two beside her, but all the other watchers of the scene, came after her, interested.

Jamie Douglas bowed, and John presented him as son of a Douglas laird. He and the others removed the hawks' hoods but kept their jesses secure. The birds eyed all with their fierce unblinking stare which offered no deference to royalty.

"Fine birds," Elizabeth commented. "Douglas falcons will be high fliers, I think!" Which sally brought forth suitably appreciative chuckles.

"Live hawks for dead Herons!" the cynical Earl of Oxford added, to the amusement of some and the frowns of others, including the queen.

"We shall test these out at our next hunting," she said. "Thank my lord of Morton. But he could have come with them himself, to express his regrets. After all, his predecessor, the Earl of Moray did so! But it seems that he can proffer favours, as well as receive them! You have my permission to retire, Sir John. Sir Thomas Parry will see to you." And she turned away.

All moved off with her, save for Parry, John left wondering at this abrupt end to the interview. Also considering that royal remark as to favours. Was this a confirmation that Morton was in receipt of some sort of English pension?

"Come this way, Sir John," Parry ordered.

Scarcely able fully to appreciate that this seemed to be the conclusion of the mission and ordeal, for that was what it amounted to, John and his companions were led back indoors, not through to the kitchen premises this time but to a front-facing doorway, where the hawks were meantime handed over to the less than confident guards thereat. As Parry ushered them out, John asked whether that was indeed all? Would the queen be seeking his further attendance?

The Welshman seemed surprised at the question and said that he saw no reason why she should. Save for perhaps a letter sent to the Regent Morton. In which case it would, no doubt, be delivered to wherever they were lodging. When told of the Black Swan, he raised eyebrows, but left it at that.

Both bemused and relieved, they made their way back to the hostelry, which presumably was not one of the class which Sir Thomas Parry would have patronised. At least they had not the hawks to consider any more.

That evening, with no letter arriving from Whitehall, their gossip of an innkeeper was agog to hear how his Scots guests had got on at the palace. He was given only very brief and general comments, but they did learn from him that the queen's so noticeably white face was kept that way by daily use of a compound of white of egg and powdered eggshells, this to attempt to hide the marks or scars of an early attack of the pox.

John waited until noontide next day, in case of a summons, or a letter coming from the palace. Nothing of the sort forthcoming by then, they set off on their long ride home to Scotland.

Had it been worth the coming, John wondered, from anybody's point of view? Was this how envoys and legates were apt to feel after their assignments? It had been an experience, certainly, and might indeed have turned out a deal worse. But he was only confirmed in the view that the private life was infinitely to be preferred to such as this.

His eventual arrival back at Fenton Tower was notable for the exchange of information. Margaret was eager to hear of all that he had seen and had taken place, particularly what he thought of Elizabeth Tudor. And for her part reported that Archie had exercised his authority as lieutenant by arranging a wardens' meeting between Cowdenknowes and the elusive Lord Hunsdon, which had resulted in some satisfaction for the Homes in particular and the Merse in general. And, more importantly and joyfully for her husband, that she was sure that she was pregnant again.

27

Husband and wife had some discussion on whether John should head for Dalkeith, Edinburgh or Stirling, to inform Morton as to the outcome of his mission, whether it had any sort of value, or the reverse. But in the circumstance, Margaret thought that there was no need to go. Her brother would send for him if he desired a report; but it seemed to her that John had merely been used as a sort of scapegoat, to clear Morton's own name, and to ensure that the pension from Elizabeth did not suffer. The national weal might have come into it, although she was not convinced that this was involved to any great degree. Let John wait. This, needless to say, suited his own wishes. There was plenty to concern himself with other than waiting on the regent.

It being now harvest-time, their lands and tenants were demanding their attention, with their improvements and introductions of new ideas and industry paying off – and requiring to do so, for labours as warden and envoy for the regent were not rewarded in terms of moneys, whatever they might represent in prestige. And the Carmichaels were ever concerned with their desire to purchase Fenton, not just lease it; and that would be costly. So many visits to their various lands and farms were called for, and usually, with no great distances involved, they were able to go together. Considerable satisfaction was, in the main, obtained, with ever new notions of development occurring to them, such as artificial terracing of their hillsides to allow cultivation, with drainage, an idea borrowed from their ancient Pictish ancestors; hide-tanning, and resulting from that, saddlery and harness-making. Enthusing their tenants and workers on the land was also a priority, with inducements provided.

John made a couple of journeys with Archie to the Borders. He recognised that he was Warden of the *whole* Middle March, not just the central Jedburgh districts; and that Kelso on the east and Hawick and Selkirk on the west were to be assured of his, and the lieutenant's, interest and concern. Neither of them really knew these areas well, and besides making their presence known in the various communities, they went exploring – and there was a deal more to explore than John, for one, had realised, in not only Ettrick and Yarrow but in the Borthwick, Ale and Rule Waters' valleys, and the high Cavers and Bonchester and Hobkirk regions south of Hawick, on the borders of the West March. By and large all this was a comparatively peaceful country, with less of raiding and reiving than to the east, although those hilly parts did tend to suffer at the hands of West March Armstrongs, Johnstones and suchlike freebooters. John promised to take such invasions up with the Lord Maxwell, his fellow warden there, if occasion warranted it. And Archie discovered Douglas lands of which he had never so much as heard.

So the weeks passed into months and autumn into winter, with Margaret beginning to thicken at the waist again – and still no summons from Morton, this far from deplored. Word of the regent they did have, for the realm was full of it. He was not popular, even though he claimed to be keeping the king's peace more effectively than had done any of his predecessors in the regency. It was what amounted to avarice which was the main complaint against him, allegedly on the realm's behalf, but undoubtedly much of the takings from taxes, imposts, dues and fines finding their way into his own coffers. Why this preoccupation with personal gain was not clear, even to his sister, for the Morton earldom was a wealthy one and he did not seem to indulge in expensive and luxurious living, although he kept a number of mistresses to compensate for his less than alluring wife. His unpopularity grew so bad that he was actually booed and catcalled in the streets of Edinburgh, where his impositions on the merchants and craftsmen were greatly resented, especially after he imprisoned a selection of them for non-payment of cess and levies. John even heard murmurings against him amongst the tradesmen, weavers and burghers of Hawick and Selkirk – not that any of this rubbed off on himself, John, his involvement in the Redeswyre affair, much talked of, helping to build his reputation as a good warden.

The twelve days of Yuletide came and went pleasantly, passed partly at Fenton and partly at Tantallon.

It was early March, with Margaret only another month or six weeks to go, when more serious news than the regent's mere unpopularity reached Fenton. It sounded as though the feuding and all but civil war, which was Scotland's curse and failing, was about to break out again, despite Morton's heavy-handed peace. Hamilton of Bothwellhaugh, the assassin of the Regent Moray, who had fled thereafter to refuge in France, had been brought back to Scotland by the Lord John Hamilton, second son of the late Hamilton chief, the old Duke of Chatelherault, who had died in January of this year. Bothwellhaugh was now said to be at Hamilton Palace in Lanarkshire.

This development acted of course like a spark to tinder, setting aflame the fears and passions of the militant Protestant and anti-Mary faction. It happened that the brothers, the Lords John and Claud Hamilton, were the most renowned fighters in matters military in the land, now that Kirkcaldy of Grange was dead; and they could raise up to ten thousand men if so they desired; they had brought six thousand to Langside, at which they had both fought brilliantly, almost the only ones to come out of that battle with credit. And to compound the threat thus posed to the ruling clique, the Lord John, Commendator of Arbroath, was now, since the death of his father, the nearest heir to King James's throne, grandson of the Princess Mary, sister of James the Third, his elder brother, the Earl of Arran, being insane and therefore debarred.

So why had this Lord John brought back Bothwellhaugh the assassin? The other assassin, of the Regent Lennox, the man Calder, had confessed under examination that that deed had been at the instigation of the two Hamilton brothers. Whether this was true or not, who could tell? Under torture men could confess to anything. Could it be that another assassination was contemplated – that of the Regent Morton? And were the Hamiltons now contemplating a *coup d'état*: get rid of the regent, take Stirling Castle, seize the young king and seek to rule the land; and in so doing threaten war with England, with French support, unless Queen Mary was freed and allowed to return to her throne? This was the picture which was so suddenly being painted by the lords who had succeeded the Lords of the Congregation. This to the land's major alarm.

That alarm was not long in being translated into action by some. Morton's own kinsman, Douglas of Lochleven, seemed to be taking the lead, demanding that the regent send a force to Hamilton to arrest the brothers, with Bothwellhaugh, before they could achieve any of their alleged objectives; and to back this demand, raised a force of twelve hundred armed men, with the aid of sundry lords, to help Morton enforce his will. It was said that the Earls of Atholl and Buchan, with the Lords Lindsay and Ruthven, were supporting this initiative, and the Campbell Earl of Argyll veering towards it. What Morton's own attitude might be remained in doubt.

John and Margaret, Archie also, like so many others, were inevitably concerned, the more so when the long-delayed summons arrived for John to report to Stirling Castle. Archie was not included in this call, but decided to accompany his friend.

They found Stirling in a state of tension, the ground west of the castle an armed camp. They had in fact difficulty in gaining access to Morton, the impression being that he was all but besieged in the fortress. Discontented, indeed angry, lords and lairds abounded. It was probably as well that Archie was with him, for a mere knight like John might have failed to get past the highly alert guards, whereas the Earl of Angus could not be kept out.

When at length they gained the regent's presence, it was to discover a very odd situation. Morton, however stern a regent, was not in favour of this muster and resort to arms. He had never been much of a soldier, preferring to enforce his will otherwise than by the mailed fist, however tight-clenched that fist could be.

"See you, Carmichael man," he said, "I want you to go to the Hamiltons. This folly has got to be halted. All this of armed hosts and swordery. We could have war in the land, full war, tumult, the breakdown o' all I have contrived. For if we go to fight the Hamiltons, on their own ground, nothing surer than that Huntly and all those rascally Hielantmen will be down from their north at our backs. And all the other Catholics rising likewise. Just what they've been waiting for. That's no way to order the realm. Wits and canny dealing, not cold steel, are the way to rule, I tell them. So I need you to go to see the Hamiltons."

"Me, my lord! Why me? I have no way with the Hamiltons. These great lords would pay no heed to such as myself."

"They'll heed, when you come to them from me, as my good-brother. I canna send one o' the lords. It's to be secret, see you. So no Archie! But you can go unbeknownst. I'm no' to be seen as in any negotiations with the Hamiltons, as regent. But we could come to an understanding! And spare the land much of trouble, bloodshed. Now – none o' your buts! You're the one for it. The man Killigrew, the English envoy, tells me that you did well enough wi' Elizabeth Tudor, yon time. When you use your wits you can serve none so ill. And you will be speaking for me."

"What am I to say to them, my lord? That will effect anything in this pass?"

"We're coming to that, man. See you, all this stir and upset has come about because that Lord John has brought back the scoundrel Bothwellhaugh from France. It has all arisen from that. Folk believe it's been done because the Hamiltons aim to have me slain, like Moray and Lennox, aye. Then to seize young James and take over the rule, maybe even the throne itself if they canna win Mary Stewart free from the English. *I'm* no' convinced that is their intent. But I want to know. You've to find it out, just. And you've to let them know, the Hamiltons, that I'm no' to be easily assassinated! I'm warned, and well guarded. And if there was to be any attempt at it, I'd make them pay! There are more Hamiltons in the land than are in Hamilton Palace and thereabouts! There's Hamilton o' Letham, Hamiltons o' Redhouse and Preston, aye and Innerwick, none so far from your Tantallon, Archie. And Hamilton o' Raploch near here, and Kincavil and Kilbrachmont. Others forby. Aye, and there's the women, these lords' own sisters. One, Jane, wed to the Earl o' Eglinton, and another to the Lord Fleming – that's Barbara. Och, there's plenty that we could use to teach these young lordlings where they stand!"

"You would have me to go to them making threats? Threats against their innocent folk, against their women?"

"Who said aught o' threats? Just to warn them that these could be endangered, if there was to be trouble. All of the name o' Hamilton could be at risk, they should remember. From the many who would use arms against them, presently assembled. Mind them of it! Aye, but here's an offer too, see you. Tell them that if they send yon Bothwellhaugh back where he came from, out o' Scotland again, I will overlook all this folly, accept that they intend me no ill, keep the peace with them. As well, I will advise the next parliament to cancel the decree against them that the Perth parliament passed these three years back, that they were behind the murders of both Moray and Lennox. That clearing them o' penalties, so that I could advise King James to create the Lord John a lord o' parliament, maybe Lord Arbroath, since he is

333

Commendator there. All that should win them over. You have it all, man?"

John wagged his head. "I have it all, my lord. But I am not happy to be given this task, sent to Hamilton, and made your mouthpiece. These high-born lords . . ."

"You went to a higher-born than these, did you no'? The Queen of England! And fared well enough."

"I was not there threatening. Merely explaining my own actions at the Redeswyre . . ."

"I tell you, you are *warning*, no' threatening, man! Do you never heed me! Go, and use your wits. But – secret, see you. None is to know of this, save the Hamiltons themselves. You heed that too, Archie Douglas! And no delay. I want you there – at Craignethan mind, no' Cadzow Castle, where they're dwelling now, Craignethan, near to Crossford, on the Clyde no' that far from Lanark. You'll ken it, you from Lanarkshire yourself. I want you there at the soonest . . ."

Dismissed, they did not linger in Stirling. Archie rode with John as far as Falkirk, where they spent the night. In the morning they parted company, John to ride due southwards by the high moorlands of Darnrig Moss and Slamannan and Fortissat, to pass well east of Glasgow and so reach the mid-Clyde valley, and Archie eastwards for Lothian and home.

The Hamilton lands amounted almost to a small kingdom on their own, and John was at least interested to see something of it. The Carmichael family, although living no more than fifteen miles from the castle of Craignethan, north-west of Lanark, this admittedly on the very eastern edge of the Hamilton territory, had tended to avoid it, their inevitable links with the nearer and rival great house of Douglas making that prudent, for the two lines were ever at enmity. And Craignethan had a doubtful reputation, having been built only some forty years before by the so-called Bastard of Arran, Sir James Hamilton, illegitimate son of the first Earl of Arran and guardian of the infant second earl, who became Duke of Chatelherault. This Sir James was a remarkable man, one of the cleverest in the land, perhaps too clever for his own good, and became Master of Works to James the Fifth, building many fine houses for the king and his favourites, but eventually being executed on the royal command for allegedly plotting to assassinate the monarch. At any rate, he had built for himself this castle of Craignethan, and it was reputed to be one of the most spectacular and unusual in Scotland, so much so that after its builder's death, the chiefly Hamiltons themselves had moved into it, from Cadzow their ancestral seat near Hamilton town, and seemingly were still based there.

So John did not head for the Hamilton "capital" but kept well to the east of it, making for the Clyde's central reaches not far west of Lanark, very attractive country, in its green, fertile and sheltered valley, after all the high, barren moorland that he had been crossing since Falkirk. In the vicinity of Crossford village he had no difficulty in finding Craignethan, for on the high western edge of the vale it dominated all, no tall stone tower this within a courtyard, but a great range of building in the form of a rectangular court occupying all the ground between the ravines of two converging streams, so the site was sufficiently strong; but the area within that outer court was filled with erections of various sorts, towers, separate houses and halls, platforms for artillery defence, barracks for retainers, a dovecote, a chapel, indeed all but a small town within those tall defensive walls. Because of the precipitous ravines on either side, the only way to reach this citadel was by crossing a single narrow and very defendable bridge with its own gatehouse, and thereafter a steep, zigzag climb to the castle.

John had to cross that bridge, but, strangely, he had no difficulty in gaining admittance through the gatehouse, the single guard on duty waving him through on his announcement that he came to speak with the Lord John Hamilton. The fact was that there was an air of assurance about all, including the village, the castleton and the approaches, which implied that it was unthinkable that any kind of hostility could arise here in the Hamilton's own country.

He rode on up that twisting track, passing men at work in repairing one of its flanking walls which had collapsed down into the ravine, these nodding to him casually. And up at the next gatehouse, that into the great outer court, he was not even challenged at all. He had never come across such an air of security and absolute certainty in any fortified strength he had visited.

In the courtyard men came and went, and on his dismounting one came to take his horse. When he asked if the Lord John was in residence, and if so could he be taken into his presence, another was called over and he was led through into an inner court, and to a handsome doorway, where a great bell was jangled, quickly producing a uniformed servitor. This individual did scrutinise the caller more carefully before gesturing him into the vestibule of the great square central keep, saying that he would fetch the chamberlain. He was left to wait. It occurred to him that the approach to the king's own presence at Stirling, or even the regent's, apart from the armed guards, was much less grand. This would rival Whitehall.

It took some time for an elderly individual, proudly clad and bearing himself with due authority, to appear, to ask Sir John's business. Told that it was with the Lord John Hamilton, he enquired further. He was curtly informed that it was a private matter of some weight, and left at that. Disapprovingly the other told him to wait further.

It was a lesser functionary who arrived presently to conduct John, by passages and a curious underground vaulted corridor, to a quite homely chamber in an angle-tower, by contrast, where two youngish men bent over a table, examining what looked like a map before turning to greet the visitor civilly enough. John wondered whether they were planning some campaign, these soldierly ones.

336

He had glimpsed the Lord Claud, the younger, before Langside. It was the other who spoke.

"Sir John Carmichael? Are you not warden of one of the Border Marches?" the Lord John asked. "You come far from your bailiwick, no? I am John Hamilton."

"I am here, my lord, at the behest of the Earl of Morton, the regent. Come . . . privily."

"The Regent Morton! And privily?" The brothers eyed each other. "What will my lord of Morton have to say to *us*, I wonder?"

"Much, my lords. So I am sent, no great one, that the matter may be secret. The regent would have it so."

"You intrigue me, thus early," the Lord John said. "What is so secret?" He was a good-looking man, tall and fair-haired, as indeed was his brother, of very similar appearance.

"There is much to make it advisable, my lord. Many in the land, and highly placed, are concerned that you have brought Hamilton of Bothwellhaugh back to Scotland. It is feared by not a few that the purpose thereof is to endanger the realm's peace."

"How so, sir? One man, and no great one, however questionable his past deeds."

"It is those past deeds which trouble many. The slaying of the Regent Moray. And, although *he* did not slay the Regent Lennox, there are fears that he was not unconcerned in that matter."

The brother spoke. "Bothwellhaugh was in France by then, sir."

"Perhaps, my lord." John hesitated. He could hardly say that these two themselves were suspected of being behind both slayings – and somehow they did not give the impression of being assassins. "But the untimely deaths of the two regents makes men fearful. The man Calder, who shot the Earl of Lennox, made . . . allegations."

"No doubt. Under torture a man may say whatever his examiners desire, sir." That was the Lord John.

"Perhaps. However that may be, fears are aroused.

337

Some, not a few, think that an attempt is to be made against the present regency and governance of the realm. This of Bothwellhaugh but a token of it."

"So?"

"Some believe it sufficiently to be mustering in arms, my lords. Some of the great ones. And they would have my lord Regent to act . . ."

"Act against us? The Hamiltons? We had heard word of something of this. But not sufficient to concern us. We have no plans to assail the regent. He should know that."

"He does not so believe. But there is much of pressure on him to move against you. In the past you have been strong against the Protestant lords in Queen Mary's cause. They fear . . ."

"Did not yourself fight for the queen, Sir John, at Langside? And your kinsman, the Lord Somerville."

"We did, yes. And still grieve for the queen. But we must face the situation which prevails."

"But do naught to better it? We hold that Her Grace must be saved. Freed from Elizabeth's grip. This is why I brought back Bothwellhaugh."

"You say so? To do what, my lord?"

"That is as secret as you say is your visit here, Sir John! We cannot have it talked of."

"What does the Regent Morton have you come to us for?" the Lord Claud asked. "You have not told us."

"Yes. He would have you to know that he does not judge you to be plotting his murder. Nor seeking attempt to seize the king and take over the rule, as these others do. But they press him hard. The Earls of Atholl and Buchan, the Lords Lindsay and Ruthven. And others. Even Argyll, it is said. So he sends me, privily, to seek your assurances, and to prove that you have no such intentions. He sends me, because I am wed to his sister."

"Then you have our assurance, sir."

John looked all but apologetic. "My lords, the regent will require more than but my word that it is so. He will have to

338

convince these other lords, Protestant lords, that it is so. That you are not threatening the realm's present rule. He would have you send Bothwellhaugh back to France!"

They stared at him.

"Is it so great a matter to ask? If you had no intention of using him against the regent. It would serve as a sign, a proof, that you are not planning any insurrection. For it was his return that has brought all this to a head."

"We cannot do that," the younger brother said. "He was brought for a purpose. Another purpose."

"That is . . . unfortunate. May I ask what?"

"This also is secret," the Lord John declared. "But if you, who fought for Mary, swear to keep it close, we might be able to tell you."

"My lords, I have to report to the regent. That is why I am here. If I cannot tell him, there is nothing to be gained."

The brothers considered him, and each other.

"So be it," the elder said. "If Morton can be relied upon not to divulge it."

"He will have to have something to tell the others."

"We perchance may think of something. Our aim is to rescue the queen!"

It was John's turn to stare. "Rescue . . .?"

"Rescue, yes. See you, Her Grace has now been at Tutbury, in Staffordshire, for long. In the charge of Talbot, Earl of Shrewsbury. He keeps her less close than some have done. She can walk in his gardens. At times, we learn, she has been allowed to go hawking with his folk. We judge this the time to attempt a rescue. And Bothwellhaugh to lead in it."

"But . . . is this possible? Deep in England. And why this man?"

"Possible, yes. But hazardous, to be sure. There are not a few English who would aid in it. Catholics. Squires. But they need a leader. And Bothwellhaugh, whatever else, is that. A man of action, resolute. Or he would not have contrived the slaying of Moray. So, we bring him back, to essay this. Told him that we will fight for his reprieve. Or, at least, for the repeal of the forfeiture of his lands, his lairdship, to go to his brother James, rector of Kerintoun. These lands, with Bothwellmuir, are in the midst of our's. This is not convenient! They are to be given to the Captain James Stewart, son of Ochiltree, to our loss. Bothwellhaugh, then, to lead in this great attempt. Thereafter, who knows. He may remain here, or go back to France, with the queen. He has agreed to essay it."

"But how may it be done? Staffordshire! Even if he gets to the queen and contrives her freedom from this house of Shrewsbury's, how to get her out and back to Scotland?"

"Not to Scotland. To France. At first leastwise. See you, Stafford is but a score of miles from the North Wales border, from the sea, at Flint. A boat. Bothwellhaugh to go in a vessel there. We have many, on the Clyde. Get the queen that score of miles, by night, to the boat. Then over to the Isle of Man, less than sixty miles. We will have a larger ship awaiting her there. And so to France. It is possible, more than possible. She could be at Man eight or ten hours after winning out of Tutbury. One of us would be there to greet her."

John could not but be impressed. It sounded feasible. But to get the queen out of Tutbury Castle?

"She has thirty of her own people, the Lord and Lady Livingstone, Leslie, Bishop of Ross, Mary Seton, even Willie Douglas who got her out of Lochleven Castle those years ago. Word to these, by one of the English squires, and they will have her in the gardens of the castle, hiding, at dusk. Bothwellhaugh will have horses at the nearby village."

What would Morton think of this attempt? He knew that the Hamiltons were seeking the queen's release – he had said as much. But how would he act if it was accomplished? He would not want her back in Scotland. But to France? That might be different. But could he tell the Protestant lords this?

"You say, my lord, that Bothwellhaugh might go back to France with the queen? If that was agreed, and the regent could tell the lords that he *was* for France again, that might serve. The threat removed. Nothing said of the queen."

The brothers looked doubtful.

"He, the regent, said that if you would have the man sent back, and declared your no intent to rise against the regency, he would seek to have your own penalties, enacted against you by parliament, lifted. And you, my Lord John, perhaps created a lord of parliament, since your elder brother cannot so sit, by reason of his . . . infirmity. As Lord Arbroath."

"He said that? How think you, Claud?"

The other nodded. "It would seem none so ill. Say that we will not promise that Bothwellhaugh will *never* come back to Scotland."

"That need not be stated. Will that serve the regent, think you, Sir John?"

"I would judge so, yes. I am to say that he should not tell the others of this move to rescue the queen. Merely that you have agreed to Bothwellhaugh's return to France."

"Yes. That is of the essence. For if these Protestant lords know of this attempt, you may be sure that they would warn the English. Someone would. And Mary would be put under stricter guard, possibly removed from Tutbury. So if this is told, our agreement falls."

"I shall so declare. I think that you may have no fear."

"Very well. So be it. Now, Sir John, you will have refreshment? Stay here this night?"

"I thank you, but no. A sip of wine perhaps. But there is haste required in this – Morton was strong on that. If I go now, I could be back at Slamannan, or even Falkirk, by darkening. And at Stirling before noon."

Mission thus speedily accomplished, John took his leave, approving of the Hamilton brothers, and they for their part declaring that they thought Morton fortunate in his good-brother. It occurred to the visitor, as he was conducted by the pair to the outer court and his horse, that somewhere in this great establishment was Bothwellhaugh himself, and also the mad Earl of Arran.

Morton received John's report well enough. He was never gracious, but on this occasion he was more amiable than usual, undoubtedly relieved.

"This of Mary Stewart's release – it will not succeed," he asserted, however. "She may be less closely guarded than heretofore, but Shrewsbury will have her well watched, day and night. It could well be the Tower for him if he let her go!"

"The Hamiltons deem it possible, my lord. They say that she has thirty of her people there with her, all but a court! Even that Willie Douglas who enabled her to escape from Lochleven Castle. They could perhaps disguise her as one of her women, win her out through the gardens by night, horses waiting nearby. Then on to the coast and their boat."

"I shall believe it when I hear tell o' it!"

"So long as Elizabeth is not warned! The privy undertaking is finished if she is!"

"Never fear. Only myself will know of it. And you, forby! And I will not speak, save that the Hamiltons agree that Bothwellhaugh goes back to France. So, if word gets abroad, it will be yourself that lets it out, man! None to know, not even Archie Douglas."

"I need no warning, my lord."

As John rode away from Stirling, he compromised with his conscience. He would tell Margaret the whole truth, only her. She would keep it to herself, that was sure.

28

Just when the rescue attempt was to be made had not been revealed. They waited long at Fenton Tower, and the days and weeks passed into months, and still no word of it came. And surely they would have heard if the queen had indeed been freed. So had it all failed? By Yuletide they had by no means forgotten it all, but had put it to the backs of their minds, whether the venture was unsuccessful, had been postponed or even abandoned, they knew not. No word came from Morton anent it, or on anything else. By this time the fears of a Hamilton rising had died away, and Lochleven's force dispersed.

Besides, they had other matters to demand their attention, in particular the birth of another son, another Carmichael, brother for Hughie and Elizabeth, Jamie, amidst much rejoicing. Archie was quite jealous, for his Mary showed no sign of producing a family. This child was as healthy and well-doing as the others, to Margaret's relief.

The wardenship kept John busy, although there were no major cross-border incidents to demand his intervention. So far as he knew, Sir John Forster had not been replaced; and when the annual wardens' meeting was due, he deliberately sent word that it should be held at the Deadwater Pass, unfortunately named perhaps, and nearer to Hawick, but at least avoiding unfortunate memories of the Redeswyre. He went, with Archie, nevertheless just a little apprehensive as to results, this time with a Pringle escort, but was relieved to find, when he got there, that Forster had chosen to be represented by his new deputy, one William Fenwick, surely a hopeful sign for the future?

Less auspicious for peace in the land was Morton's deteriorating relationship with the Kirk. His creation of those tulchan bishops had been a sore affront; and the appropriation of their diocesan revenues, which the presbyters claimed should have come to them, was even worse. The General Assembly of the Kirk, that May of 1576, passed a resolution of no confidence in the present regent, and urged non-co-operation by all parish ministers. This was a serious matter, for the incumbents of the hundreds of parishes had enormous influence on the people at large; and if hostility was being preached from the pulpits, much of the administration of the realm was made difficult, in particular tax and cess collection, already highly unpopular. And all this had an unfortunate, indeed grievous side-effect in that Master George Buchanan, a stalwart of the Kirk and the king's tutor, became markedly hostile to Morton, and his influence on the ten-year-old monarch obvious. The boy James, old for his years however much of a curiosity, became averse, clearly heeding his tutor rather than his regent, and this was inconvenient to say the least, for there was much in governance which required the royal assent and co-operation, even at this age, particularly the signing and sealing of documents, deeds, promulgations and the like, with many appointments needing the monarchial assent.

It was this situation which brought about John's next summons from Morton, to Dalkeith this time, not Stirling – typically no communication for months, and then an abrupt demand for his appearance. Since it was only to Dalkeith on this occasion, Margaret accompanied her husband. They would stay the night with her mother at Pittendreich.

Morton did not acclaim his sister's presence, but could hardly dismiss her. He explained the problem, denounced the Kirk ministers, and told John what was required of him. He was to go to see Master Andrew Melville at Glasgow, and seek to come to some agreement with him on behalf of the regency. It seemed that Morton had come to look upon his brother-in-law as something of a useful intermediary and negotiator.

John had heard of this Andrew Melville, son of the laird of Baldovie in Angus, probably the most influential cleric in the land, despite his having been domiciled on the Continent for some ten years and only returned to Scotland a couple of years before. He had held the Chair of Humanities at Geneva and had been rector of the college at Poitiers at the age of twenty-one, a strong Presbyterian divine. On return he had been promptly appointed Principal of Glasgow University at the instance of the General Assembly of the Kirk.

"This Melville carries a deal o' weight with these wretched ministers – none more so, I jalouse. And I need some aid with them. And with this Buchanan, who's turning the bairn James against me, which can be right unhelpful. So we must seek to win this Melville over, some way. You have proved none so ill at talking folk to see sense, so you're to go to Glasgow and talk with the man. Have him to see that he owes a duty to the realm, as well as to the Kirk!"

"Why should he heed me, my lord? I have no knowledge of Church affairs, no pull with the ministers . . ."

"You said the like yon time wi' the Hamiltons! And with Elizabeth Tudor, forby. I'll give you something to offer the man. Tell him that I seek good relations with the Kirk. That I am a good Reformer. That I am concerned with this present breach. Tell him that he should be my privy adviser just, on Kirk matters, a link with the divines. And a pension from the treasury to go with it!"

"A pension! For the Principal of Glasgow University!"

"Why for no'? Siklike can do with a pension as well as other folk."

"As *you* should know, James!" his sister put in.

"I know what men need to persuade them, woman!"

"Some men!"

"This Andrew Melville is notable," John said. "Has

held high office abroad. In Geneva and in France. Is he such as you can bribe?"

"Watch your words, man! I mislike bribe! It would be due payment for service to the state. Forby, if he didna want it for himself, he could give it to some good cause. You'll no' tell me that ministers dinna need siller, like lesser folk!"

"Why not do better, James? Tell him that, with his aid, you will see that some of your revenues from these bishoprics go back to the Kirk?" Margaret suggested. "You gain much from these, we hear."

"I need those moneys." That was brief.

"Would not the betterment in relations with the ministers, the easement of collecting dues and charges, more than make up for it? All over the land. Yes, and there is something else that I have thought on. The glebes. Every parish church has its glebe, its land, often many acres near to the manse. The divines seldom use that land, I have noted, save to pasture a cow or two. These glebes, well managed, could make much wealth for the Kirk. Our own parish glebe at Dirleton is but a wilderness of briars and thistles. Many like it, I judge. The old Church did better, with its monks' labour. John and I have been improving our lands greatly, making them give much greater yields, produce different kinds of tilth and worth, not just grain and crops and hay – honey and wax, mead and wines and the like. If that was put to this Master Melville, with, say, an offer to instruct, to guide folk of the Kirk in the way that we have learned to do, that might gain some approval?"

Her brother did not look greatly impressed, but John nodded approval.

"That is something that I could offer, in all honesty. It is well thought on. Our two former monks could lead in it. And others of our folk. Offer to instruct some of his students, who could then tell parish ministers. Here is a worthy design."

Morton shrugged. "The man will seek more than that, I say. If he does not like the name of a pension, call it

346

what you like. I'll have my Bishop of Glasgow set aside the tithes and church lands of one of his parishes, Govan perhaps. Tell Melville that he should come and see me at Stirling, one day. And soon. Aye, and while you're at him, say that when he comes to Stirling, he should have a word with that ill limmer Buchanan, the king's tutor. He could give you a message for the man. You could be seeing him the sooner, on your way back from Glasgow. To have the bairn James act better with me, be less difficult. For the good of his kingdom, say it. Kirk and state must work together for the common weal, tell him. Remind Buchanan of that!"

"Could not you, as regent, find a new tutor for King James?" Margaret asked. "If this Buchanan is so difficult."

"Do you think I havena thought o' that! But it is difficult, see you. He was appointed by Mar, the former Mar, keeper o' Stirling Castle and guardian o' James. Buchanan has links with the Erskines, and comes o' the Buchanans o' that Ilk. And he was close to Moray. Annabella o' Mar, the bairn's foster-mother, says that James is in right awe o' him, Buchanan. Like God, to him! A right hard God, the man! She says that to dismiss him would have James, at his telling, making a royal command of it not to. And even I canna disobey a royal command, folly as it may be. I have appointed a deputy, a Master Peter Young. But he's no' making much improve."

John wagged his head. "This is beyond me!" he said.

"Not if you have Melville's word on it. So see you to it."

The regent always made his dismissals very clear. But fortified by his wife's presence, John ventured a brief delay.

"My lord, the matter of Queen Mary's attempted rescue by the Hamiltons? We have heard no more of this. Do you know what has transpired?"

Morton glanced over at his sister. "She knows of this. So you did tell of it!"

"A man must have no secrets from his wife!" John said piously.

The regent snorted his comment. "God's pity! But it was as I jaloused. The attempt failed. Yon Bothwellhaugh tried it, aye. But they did not get Mary past the guards. Got so far, I heard, but not out to the horses. He took himself off, then. Contrived to escape, in the dark. Won to his boat. But she did not. Like I said it would be."

"Shrewsbury could not have been warned?"

"Not unless one o' you talked! Or the Hamiltons themselves."

John could not suggest that Morton himself might just possibly have been the informant, although he was prepared to believe it possible, earning his pension from Elizabeth. With Margaret he took his leave, promising reluctantly to make for Glasgow the next day.

They returned to Pittendreich, and to kinder company.

Margaret could scarcely accompany John to Glasgow, Kirk dignitaries apt to be fully as unappreciative of female interventions as was Morton. So he left her with her mother and proceeded on the forty-odd-mile ride to the west, by the Calders and Shotts, crossing the route, at Fortissat, which he had taken on his journey to the Hamiltons at Craignethan.

Glasgow was all but new territory for John, although he had been taken there as a boy by his father on a brief visit. It was not a large city, not half the size of Edinburgh or Dundee, but growing and becoming a centre for trade, outdoing Dumbarton as the Clyde shipping port. John's goal was not hard to find, for the town centre was clustered close round the towering cathedral of St Mungo, which stood out above the Molendinar Burn, where St Kentigern, or Mungo, and his mother Thanea or Thenew, had started it all in the sixth century. Indeed the site of the University College was still closer to that famous small waterway, at the Bell o' the Gate, off the

Drygate, this where had been the Lennox town-house in which the late Lennox's son, the Lord Darnley, had been sick and visited, somewhat reluctantly, by Queen Mary, nine years before, not long before his assassination.

John was astonished to find the so-called University College of Glasgow such a very modest establishment, not to be compared with Scotland's other university at St Andrews, with its three colleges, all greater than this one. Andrew Melville was no more hard to find than his premises, for he had only the one assistant and a mere dozen students, all apparently studying divinity as taught by Geneva. Was this the figure whose aid seemed to mean so much to Morton?

Melville, when he had freed himself from his pupils, proved to be a fine-looking, if hatchet-faced, youngish man, black-clad, no more than five years older than John himself, but with an air of authority which the latter could not hope to rival, despite the limited nature of his institution here. He accepted John's announcement, that he had come from and on behalf of the Regent Morton, with raised eyebrows.

"What has the Douglas to say to me?" he demanded. "I would say that we would scarcely speak the same language!"

"As to that, sir, I know not," John answered. "But you are both subjects of the King's Grace, as am I. And so have duties towards the weal of his realm."

"Ha! Is that the way of it? I hope that I will ever do my duty towards this kingdom. But that so long as it does not conflict with my duty to a higher realm than King James's!"

"M'mm. I do not think that the regent would ask you so to do, Master Melville."

"No? But he does ask something? And sends you here to seek it?"

John recognised that forthright talk was to be the order here. "Yes, sir. He seeks your aid. And is prepared to render payment for it."

349

"Payment? For my humble aid? Here is, I think, some strange play on words, Sir John."

"I think not, sir. The regent, by his appointment of these Protestant bishops, whom you call tulchans, and the taking for the treasury of some of their diocesan revenues, has offended the Kirk. And this is unfortunate for the realm. He wishes to be on better terms with the Kirk, and you are of much influence with its ministers. He cannot dismiss the bishops, but he can make other gestures towards the Kirk. Show goodwill. With your advice."

"So! He would have me sup with Satan, in order to win God's Kirk's sufferance!"

"I think that you misjudge, Master Melville!"

"Then show me how, sir. I am listening, at least!"

"Very well. My lord Regent would have you as his adviser, his link with the divines. For betterment between Church and state. And in return he will provide moneys, for the Kirk, from these diocesan revenues. In token of which he offers you some portion of the tithes and dues for one of the Glasgow bishopric parishes – he suggested Govan as possible, why that I know not." John took a chance. "For the benefit of your College of Glasgow here. And the training of new ministers."

The other eyed him keenly, assessingly, but did not speak.

"That would be but the first token of my lord's goodwill. Others, for other parishes, would follow, on your guidance. And there is more." Almost hurriedly John went on. "It is observed that the glebes of the parish churches are seldom made good use of. They could be a source of wealth to the kirks, of great aid to the ministers, if they were well tended and improved, to yield the best of the ground. We, my wife and myself – she is the regent's sister – have been much active in improving our lands. We have adopted many skills, more especially those used by some of the monasteries and abbeys of the old Church. The monks were strong on this, whatever you think of their faith! We have learned much from them, indeed

350

we employ two former monks. We have learned of good drainage of ground, using fields rather than long rigs, using the drainage to feed the tilth and give double crops, of better tillage, of the best grains and grasses to grow, and the like. And we have much advanced the farming of bees, producing wax for candles and polishes, honey and sweetening, mead and other wines. And . . ."

He paused, realising that he was all but gabbling in his enthusiasm, but saw that Melville was eyeing him intently now rather than critically. Encouraged, he went on.

"We, and the regent, believe that if the Kirk glebes, some of them quite extensive, were to be put to good use, then the ministers, and therefore the Kirk as a whole, would much benefit. All over the land there must be many thousands of acres of such ground, little used. We would be prepared to instruct in this, if scarcely all the ministers themselves, at least some. Or indeed your students here, in the college, who could then go out and teach the skills more widely. It would not greatly interfere with their principal studies. A day or two at a time. I have lands at Carmichael and Wiston, none so far from this Glasgow, east of Lanark."

"This is of much interest, Sir John," the other said, clearly impressed. "We will think on it. There are kirks and charges all over the land. It could be difficult to instruct many."

"Yes. But one could instruct another. Vie with each other. An on-going endeavour. At your General Assembly you could speak of it, recommend it."

"True. I see the possible gain. You would instruct the first students?"

"We, or our people. Think on it, sir. And when you come to Stirling to see and advise the regent, the furtherance of it all can be discussed. Next spring it could be in train."

"The good seed on the land! Here is a kind of worship, yes, which we may have neglected! I will certainly give thought to it, Sir John."

"Do, sir. And the sooner it can be started, the better,

no?" John struck while the iron was hot. "There is another matter in which the regent would value your aid, Master Melville, when you come to Stirling. It is over Master Buchanan, the king's tutor. He is very much against the Lord Morton – perhaps with some cause? But he is influencing the young King James against his regent. And this can much hamper rule and good governance, the regency requiring the monarch's constant aid and acceptance in form. It is unfortunate when the boy refuses his help."

"I can see that, yes. But what can I do?"

"A word with Master Buchanan, sir. He is in a strong but strange position. But he would pay some heed to you, the regent believes. He, Buchanan, was himself Principal at St Andrews once. The rule of the realm must go on however much some may mislike the lawful ruler!"

"Were you not kin of a sort to the Douglas, I might judge you less than enamoured of my lord of Morton your own self!"

John coughed. Perhaps he had been less careful of his words than was wise? "I spoke but in general terms, sir."

"To be sure. I will have a word with Master George when I see him. Although he is old enough to be my father! Remind him of the lesser kingdom's requirements! And the Kirk's advantage in having the regent's . . . better will."

"Then I thank you, sir. As will my lord. Now, I have kept you from your students for overlong . . ."

The other did not seek to detain him.

Back at Dalkeith, John found that Morton had gone to Stirling, so he had to ride on all the extra mileage. But at least the regent found no fault with his account, however much he sniffed and snorted at religious fanatics. John stressed that it was the improvement of glebe lands which had most interested Melville; and that he and Margaret would be happy to do all that they could to forward this project, the earl indicating that this was not anything in which *he* could be concerned, but willing to accede to it if it would serve any good purpose. He was more interested in Melville's reaction to the hostility of Buchanan, and when he heard that the man had been reasonably understanding, promptly ordered John to repair to the royal apartments and pass on the message to the tutor.

Far from joyfully, his brother-in-law made his way thither.

In fact, it was King James whom he came upon, at lessons with young Johnnie Mar, although the latter was drawing pictures of horses, deer, hawks, coneys and suchlike rather than translating Latin. James himself had laid aside his Latinity and was using his quill laboriously otherwise. Having bowed to a bent royal back without response, John thought to go and peer over the said back to see what so preoccupied the monarch, to discover that he was writing verses, not in Latin but in braid Scots.

"Sire, you are a poet!" he exclaimed. "Here's a wonder, at but ten years! This, this is your own? Not remembering some lesson? Some other's rhymes?"

"It's my ain," the boy declared. "We dinna get lessons in poesy!"

"Be praised for that!" his companion interjected from across the table. "The Latin's bad enough!"

"Johnnie hasna the gift," James informed, equally scornfully. "He draws beasties, just!"

"That is a different talent, perhaps, Sire. But, this is good." Peering down at the spidery writing, he read out:

David son o' Jesse, him as Kent the Lord,
Focht against the Philistines to promove the Word;
The heathen socht their fause gods the tulzie for to
    gain,
But David slew Goliath wi' a wee bit chuckie-stane.

"That is good. I like that."

"Och, the end's no' just right. Yon chuckie-stane isna right dignified."

"M'mm. I see what you mean, Sire. See you, how would *alane* serve? 'But David slew Goliath, outfacing him alane.'"

"Hech, aye. Ootfacing him alane. But . . . ootfacing's no' just richt, either. Say confoonding? Confoonding him alane. I like that. Are you a poet, too?"

"Hardly, Your Grace. But I have toyed with writing the odd rhyme, all my days. With little success, I fear. Just a line or two, here and there."

"I've scrieved a whole ode. To yon Brutus. His right name was Lucius Junius mind, the Brutus just meant imbecile. He pretended that he was mad, yon time, to save his life . . ."

"Och, spare us a' that again! No' again, Jamie!" Mar protested. "He's ay on aboot siklike, Romans and Greeks and yon folk, deid a thousand years!"

"And what is wrong with that, John Erskine?" a stern voice demanded from behind him. "You would be the better of doing the same! And get your years right, at the least. Nearer two thousand than one!"

John turned, to find the tall, frowning, elderly figure of George Buchanan in a doorway, pointing, and at him now.

"You are Carmichael, if I mistake not."

"I am, yes, Master Buchanan. Admiring His Grace's verses."

"I do not allow callers here to enter the king's presence without due permission, sir. I should have been approached."

John blinked. "I have the regent's permission, Master Buchanan. Moreover, I am His Grace's Warden o' the Middle March of the Border, and so have the right of audience." It occurred to him that this, perhaps, was not the most auspicious start for his present mission. "But I regret it if the custom is to inform you first, and I have not done so. In fact, it is yourself, my friend, whom I have come to see, not His Grace. But was ushered in here."

"Indeed. And what is your concern with me, sir?"

"I think that it would be best dealt with in private, Master Buchanan. If I have His Grace's permission to retire?"

"He's a poet, too!" James announced. "I tell't him o' my ode to Lucius Junius Brutus."

"Scarcely an ode, James. More odious than ode-like, I fear! This way, sir."

"I will show you it, when next you come," the boy said, unabashed.

"I will look forward to seeing it, Sire." And bowing, John followed Buchanan out into another chamber.

"What can I do for you?" that man asked curtly, closing the door behind him.

"I come at the regent's behest, sir. And with word from Master Andrew Melville, Principal at Glasgow."

"Indeed? Melville. I taught him at St Andrews, lang syne. Two very different senders, I think!"

"Yes. But both concerned for the weal of the king's realm. It is that which brings me here. Since you, Master Buchanan, must be likewise concerned."

"So?"

"My lord of Morton is aware that you can find fault with his rule and policies. As is, no doubt, your right so to do. But, since he rules for and in the name of the king, it is important that your fault-finding is not such as to affect His Grace. To cause him to be unhelpful in matters of state, where the royal assent and support is necessary."

"If the regent's rule is manifestly wrong, in the sight of God, then is it not my plain duty to inform the young king, sir!" That was all but thunderous, with sudden surprising force.

"You are His Grace's tutor. And, perchance, his pastor? But not his councillor in affairs of state, sir. There is a Privy Council for that, appointed by the parliament of the realm. And that council and parliament have appointed the Earl of Morton to rule on the king's behalf. The division is clear, no?" He paused, concerned that this interview

355

should bear some fruit, if possible, not become mere confrontation. "My lord would have you to understand, sir, that he bears you no ill will. And is prepared to further the Kirk's interests. In more ways than one. And Master Melville is to be his adviser. Moreover, I myself, together with my wife, who is the regent's sister, have agreed to help to give instructions to students, and thus to parish ministers, to improve their glebe lands to make them more of profit, produce wealth, yields, many at present being mere waste land."

"Glebes? Here is a strange concern! What moves you and the regent to this?" That sounded less than accepting.

"As I said, sir, the weal of the realm. Our duty, his, mine and your own."

"I do not need such as you to tell me my duty, young man!"

"I am sure not. I but answer your question – why. Why I offer this. And my lord also. Every subject's duty. We see Kirk and government should be at one in this. No?"

The other considered him for moments on end. "I will consider this," he said, at length.

"Do that, Master Buchanan. And I am sure that all will benefit. I bid you good-day. And see much benefit in your guidance of our young liege-lord."

Buchanan inclined his head, unspeaking, as John took his leave.

Out in the adjoining room again, the king was waiting for him. "See, sir, I dinna ken your name. But I've scrieved a bit poem for you. I've no' just finished it, mind. But you'll can dae that yoursel'. It goes this way:

The Laird o' Logie fell doon the stair,
    He'd counted ten, but there was mair.
The Lady Sue was at his back,
    She heard his screech and then the whack.
She lauched and lauched, at his said ado,
    But when he rose . . .

"I've gotten no further."

Seeking to keep a straight face, John took the scrap of paper, bending low. "I thank you, Sire, greatly. I shall treasure this. Perhaps, perhaps, it could end with:

> But when he rose, he shook his fist,
>   As to you, Lady Sue, you'd ne'er be missed!

"Will that serve? And my name, Your Grace, is Carmichael. John Carmichael."

"Hech, that's guid, guid! Ne'er be missed! Aye. When next you come, Carmichael sir, I'll show you my ode to Lucius Junius Brutus."

"I will esteem that a privilege, Sire. I thank you. Have I your permission to retire, once more?"

"Ooh, aye. Dinna be ower lang in coming back, mind."

John bowed himself out of the royal presence, and returned to Morton's quarters.

"I have seen Buchanan," he informed the earl. "Told him of your wish to work more closely with the Kirk. With Melville's help. He was scarcely forthcoming, but I think took some heed. And I won the young king's interest. He sees us both as concerned with poetry."

"Poetry!" Morton snorted. "Is that the best you could do wi' the bairn? You did better than that wi' Buchanan, I hope?"

"As to that, my lord, I am not so sure! But he says that he will consider. Whereas James urged me to come back. A royal command!"

"He did? Well, we'll see if aught comes o' it. Poetry!"

John made his escape.

29

The newly named poet did not have opportunity to exchange verses with his sovereign-lord for some considerable time, although he did pen a few stanzas for such occasion when it should arise, to Margaret's amusement but encouragement. She saw this as something to support, a link with their odd young monarch, however comical. The day might come when even such might prove valuable, kings being kings, whatever their peculiarities.

Morton made no demands that autumn and winter, although the same could not be said of the Borderers, who did not allow seasons, except perhaps harvest-time, to interfere with their preferred activities, especially in the matter of other folk's cattle. John, and Archie also, seemed to spend an undue proportion of their time seeking to smooth out the disputed ownership of flocks and herds. The more they saw of the higher areas of the Middle March, the more they recognised that it was a land most apt for the exchange of cattle, lawful or otherwise, empty hills but with fair grazing for hardy beasts, deep winding valleys and ravines, steep-sided hollows known as beef-tubs, where beasts could be hidden away securely, no evident boundaries and limits as to properties, even of the borderline itself, all an invitation to such as saw initiative as more compelling and rewarding than mere dull legality. Dealing with such activities was clearly a large part of a warden's duties.

Come early spring, John, and Margaret also now and again, had to become involved in their promised instructing activities with Melville's students, even though the two ex-monks did most of it. They found their pupils, on the whole, happy enough over it all, probably grateful to get away from classroom teaching of the Scriptures, dogma and Latin, out into the countryside. Most of it had to be done at Wiston, so Margaret could not be away from the family overmuch, although the land-improvement idea had been mainly her own.

These activities were overshadowed by a sudden storm on the national scene, and a protracted storm, this all but absurdly precipitated by purely personal avarice between the Earls of Morton and Argyll – although discontent with the former's rule by many of the lords and all of the Kirk had been building up, and this was only the spark to ignite the tinder. It so happened that Argyll had married the widow of the late Regent Moray, and with her gained the rich haul of jewellery, largely French, belonging to Queen Mary, which Moray had managed to grasp when his half-sister fled to England. There had been doubts as to where this treasure had gone; but Morton now got word that Argyll had it, and demanded its return to himself, as crown property.

Argyll refused, and conflict erupted. Conflict on a major scale, with little relevance to the jewellery, for others, many others, saw opportunity to better themselves and their causes by joining in. The Stewart Earl of Atholl in especial, who had always been inimical towards Morton, blaming him for the death of his friend Secretary Lethington; also the Gordon Earl of Huntly, consistently against regents; and, significantly, the Lord Glamis, the chancellor. These, with Sir Alexander Erskine, Master of Mar, young Johnnie's uncle and acting keeper of Stirling Castle for his nephew, acted. A great force from the north and the Highlands marched on Stirling Castle while Morton was at Dalkeith, and with Erskine's co-operation took over the castle without any difficulty, and with it, of course, the young king. And, with George Buchanan's help, got James to sign an edict declaring that he was no longer in need of a regent, the Earl of Morton or other, and with a council of twelve advisers would take over the rule of his kingdom personally, a parliament to be called in due course to homologate this.

So, abruptly, all was changed in the rule of Scotland, the nation at large bewildered.

The Carmichaels, and Archie Douglas, were of course much concerned. Not that any of them greatly deplored the fall from supreme power of Morton; but they could not but wonder what effect it all might have on themselves. Since it was the northern lords who had, in the main, engineered this coup, it was unlikely that they would think to interfere with the wardenships of the Marches. And the Kirk connection, the instructing of the students, could still go on, since that was for the good of the realm as a whole.

Margaret, although by no means seeking to support her brother's cause, declared that she did not see this new situation of governance lasting for any lengthy period. This because it was so largely of northern origins, practically all those involved coming from above the line of the Forth and Clyde. And by far the greatest influence, wealth and population of the land were based on central and southern Scotland. The Council of Twelve appointed to advise the young monarch, who was allegedly now ruling as well as reigning, had only one southern name on it, the Earl of Glencairn. Margaret did not believe that this could continue. The parliament, when it met, would be largely otherwise composed, dominated by members from the southern counties. It might not reinstate Morton but it would scarcely accept this present arrangement. It was interesting that George Buchanan had been co-opted as one of the twelve, no doubt because of his influence over the young king.

John wondered what that mission of his to Stirling Castle had served. Had it been but wasted effort?

Strangely as it might seem, Morton himself appeared to take his sudden downfall from supreme power with remarkable acceptance, more or less confining himself to Dalkeith Castle and the other Black Douglas possessions, and lying low. He was secure enough, of course, from any attempts at apprehension, with all the Douglas power behind him. His sister however said that he would just await his time and opportunity, that the pendulum would swing back, and if she knew her brother, he would not fail to swing with it.

A year passed, with little of event.

The parliament was not called immediately, to allow the new dispensation to settle in, consolidate and make the necessary new appointments — so, July of 1578. That would, admittedly, give time for others to move, likewise.

The Kirk did just that, calling an early General Assembly for the April preceding, with the proposal that Andrew Melville should become the Moderator thereof.

Queen Elizabeth made her moves also. Clearly troubled by the unseating of her pensioner, and disturbed by increasing talk of French negotiations with the Hamiltons for another Catholic assault on Tudor England, she sent up Sir Robert Bowes to Scotland to discover the full situation, and to see Morton. The rumour was that she was all but ordering him to come to terms with Argyll and the others, persuade them to expel Huntly and the other Catholics from their administration and unite against the Hamiltons and the French influence; that, or lose her favour and his pension.

Whatever the details of this mission of Bowes, results were forthcoming. In March, Morton rode, with a strong Douglas escort, from Dalkeith to Edinburgh, and there, at the Mercat Cross beside St Giles, announced with a flourish his resignation from the regency. He handed over the seals and insignia of office to the provost and magistrates, pointed out that his move was voluntary, and returned whence he had come — a peculiar but significant gesture.

Few in the realm, however, believed that to be the end of the story. Folk waited, wondering.

The General Assembly of the Kirk duly met, appointed

Melville Moderator, and declared that any suspected of Catholic leanings must be banished from positions of influence, in especial from the Council of Twelve. Huntly thereafter departed in high offence. His place was filled by the Lord Herries, Warden of the West March, which had John raising his eyebrows.

Throughout all this so critical period in the affairs of the land, no communications came to Fenton Tower or Tantallon Castle from the ex-regent. Morton only approached them, it seemed, when he required their services; and meantime apparently these were not needed. They by no means complained.

Only a few weeks before the parliament was due, however, John was summoned to Dalkeith. Although this was now no semi-royal command, he felt that he could nowise refuse to go. Besides, it would be interesting to learn what were his brother-in-law's views and intentions as to the current situation, and possibly the future. Margaret, as usual, wished that she could come with him, but forbore.

He found, of all things, Morton actually gardening, in the green strip between his castle and the River North Esk, very differently employed from anything seen before. Was this indicative of a new approach to life? It was not, it quickly proved.

"So you've come, eh? I've no' seen you this long while. Well, you're to go to Stirling again, Carmichael man," the earl announced, spade in hand. "Have you heard? Those ones have started to come to blows already! I kenn't they would. Johnnie Lyon, that's Glamis, the chancellor, has been slain. By Lindsay, Earl o' Crawford and his men. In the streets o' Stirling. A right tulzie! This so that Atholl can be chancellor! Aye, that's the state they're in now! So now I can act. I've been waiting for this. See you, I mind you telling me that you had won close to the king ower this o' poetry and siklike? That folly could be right useful now, daftlike as it is. You go to Stirling and say you come at the royal command. He tell't you, yon time, to come back, did he no'? They'll let you in, for the bairn is now ruling, in name leastways. He's twelve years! And I want something frae him."

"He is scarcely ruling, surely? Still being told what to do and say?"

"Aye, maybe. But he's in a different position, the laddie. If he wants something, and asks for it, there's nane can say him nay. And I want frae him a declaration, just. A declaration that he approves o' a' that I did and ordained while I was his regent. Approbation. Aye, approbation o' my rule in his name. And pardon for any bit offences which might have occurred by mischance. You have it? I've a letter here, saying it a'. You've to get James to sign it. I want this so that I can appear at the parliament they're calling, see you. They would, I doubt not, wish to hae me arrested there. But if I hae the king's approbation, signed and sealed, they'll no' can do it. Mind, I'll hae plenties o' my Douglases there, forby, to see I'm safe. But I want to speak at the parliament. So, you have it? Get your young friend, the king, to sign this paper."

John was by now used to staring and wagging his head at his brother-in-law, producing his buts. Now they were promptly interrupted.

"There you're at it again, man! You'll no' find this difficult. You've contrived much sairer errands than this. Talk your poetry wi' the laddie, and he'll sign this wi' nae trouble. See you, this slaying o' the Chancellor Glamis is just what was needed! Proof even to him, the king, that these who are now holding him are right rogues, and will stop at nothing! That's no' how I governed his land for him. The laddie's no' fool, despite his poetry! He'll heed you. But watch oot for Buchanan! He's no' got such a hold ower the lad as he had, mind, now James is ruling, or said to be. But he's on this fell council, and can still mak mischief. Now, when you've seen James, see you Johnnie Mar also. He could be useful, that one. Tell him frae me that his uncle Alexander Erskine, who ca's himsel' Master of Mar now, tell him he's a scoundrel. He'll likely be aiming to be the Earl o' Mar, no' just Master! Which could mean the end o' Johnnie! Tell him that. And he's only deputy keeper o' Stirling Castle – Johnnie's the right keeper, the Earls o' Mar ay are. So, tell him to be ready."

"Ready? Ready for what, my lord?"

"Ready for his uncle's ill will. To watch him. Aye, and ready for an improve, one o' these days!"

"Improve? What would that mean?"

"We'll see. Just tell him to be ready. Him and his friend, the king. Both the laddies. But watch you Buchanan. Your helping o' the Kirk wi this o' the glebes will help, aye. And working wi' Melville, who's now Moderator, will dae no harm. But watch him."

"What of the others, my lord? The earls. Atholl and Argyll and Crawford? Will they permit me even to see the king?"

"They canna stop you, man. That's the weakness o' their position, now. They're no' regents, as I was. They've hoisted the king up to the rule now. If he will see you, they canna forbid it. So long as the laddie remembers you and your poetry. Think you he will? It's a while back. And, to be sure, you're no' that important a man. Calling, you'll no' seem to threaten them."

"This is a difficult mission that you send me on, my lord. I cannot say that I like it."

"You're no' meant to like it! But it's for the guid o' the realm. The guid o' young Jamie Stewart himsel'. He's in right ill hands at this present. You'll be helping to win him oot o' them."

"And yourself back in power?"

"Who said that? I'm consairned for the laddie. Both laddies. So – be off to Stirling the morn. And bring back this letter signed, see you."

John rode home to Fenton, as usual after an interview with Morton, very thoughtful. He would have to look out his scraps of poetry . . .

* * *

Next midday, at the gatehouse of Stirling Castle, he announced, more confident-sounding than he felt, that Sir John Carmichael, Warden of the Middle March, was calling, by royal command, to see His Grace the King. And he added, to the mystification of the guards, that he came to see the Ode to Brutus. Tell His Grace so. He had to repeat that twice.

He had a considerable wait, but eventually he was admitted and conducted to the royal quarters. And there he was surprised to find James Stewart waiting for him at the outer door, papers in hand, eagerly watching his approach from those soulful eyes.

"You've been lang, lang!" the boy cried. "I tell't you to come soon. Why did you no'?"

Bowing low, John sought for suitable excuse. "Sire, I have the Middle March to warden. And the Kirk students to instruct. And lands to tend. I could not conceive that mere poetry, verses, of mine, could mean so much to the King's Grace, who is so busy with ruling the land."

"Poesy is right important. Is it no' the rich fruit o' the ripest minds, as yon poet Chaucer said? I've been awaiting you, Sir John. I've scrieved mair – much mair. Hae you?"

"Some, Sire – not a great deal. Nor great verse, at all. But some. I regret the delay. But I cannot just call upon Your Grace at any time. I am a man of small consequence and mark. Today, my lord of Morton has sent me . . ."

"Och, him! He's no poet, that one! I dinna like the man. I dinna like maist o' them! They're ay at me to dae this and dae that, sign papers, mak appointments. For themsel's, mind! But, see, I hae my Ode to Brutus to show you. Come awa' ben . . ."

John followed his liege into the usual classroom, hoping that he would not find Buchanan there. He did not, but Johnnie Mar was, the two boys ever together, however ill assorted a pair. John saw some difference in them both, for the passage of the months.

The Earl of Mar eyed the visitor with less of welcome. "Another poet!" he said. "Rhyming words mean nae mair than the others, do they?"

"They do, they do!" James asserted. "For those wi' wits to hear them! And it's no' just the rhyming. There's the lilt and the scan o' it, forby."

"I have a word or two for you, my lord. Scarcely poetic perhaps. Hereafter," John said. "From the Earl of Morton."

"See you, here's my ode," the monarch interrupted. "You can tak it wi' you. It's ower lang to read and right appreciate here."

"But, Sire, I cannot just take away your lengthy poem! All your work and care and thought . . ."

"Och, I've scrieved oot this copy for you, Sir John. I've had it awaiting you this while."

"This is most kind, most generous. I cannot feel that I deserve it." John took the papers, somewhat grubby. "Myself, I have brought you only a few verses. Some on the cliffs of St Ebba's Head, near to where I live. And another on the Border reivers. I am not very proud of them, I fear."

James eyed the first offering, and read aloud therefrom:

> The craigs and cliffs, the boiling tide,
>   The screaming fowl on wings spread wide,
> The dizzy drops, the fearsome heights,
>   The scene which e'en the brave affrights;
> Saint Ebba's nuns chose as their fate,
>   As refuge from the heathen's hate,
> To worship God in that wild place
>   They tamed the wildness with their grace.
> So let us all the lesson learn,
> From savage scene we need not turn,
> So long as faith in heaven above
>   Brings down on us the balm of love.

The boy, apt to slobber, especially when excited, with a tongue rather too large for his mouth, sucked in. "That's right weighty. Aye, weighty. But Maister Buchanan wouldna like the bit aboot St Ebba. He's right strong against saints!"

"St Ebba was not a Catholic saint, I think, Sire, but a Celtic Church one. There are saints and saints! What of our patron, St Andrew?"

"Aye, that's true."

"Those cliffs and craigs?" Johnnie Mar asked. "Whaur are they? Are they mair fearsome than this castle rock?"

"I would say so, yes. Higher. Sheerer. And with the seas breaking below. It is a wild coast between Dunbar and Berwick. But this of Master Buchanan . . ."

"I wouldna show that to him, just the same, Jamie!"

"How fares he, your tutor, with the new rulers?" John glanced apologetically at the king. "The new *advisers* of Your Grace?" He laid down the papers on the table. "This Council of Twelve. He is on it, I understand."

"He says that they dinna heed him enough." That was young Mar. "Or the Kirk. The Campbell, yon Argyll – they dinna agree. Nor yet Atholl."

"I think that they do not agree even amongst themselves, these lords? They slew the Chancellor Glamis, one of them. And there are tales that Ruthven and your uncle, my lord, are at odds."

Johnnie nodded. "Aye."

"So, they are scarcely an improvement on my lord of Morton's rule?" The boys exchanged glances. Neither spoke.

"In Lothian, we do not hear of all that goes on here at Stirling," John said. "But the word is that all is not well with the Council of Twelve. Or eleven, now!"

"They bicker amongst themsel's." James nodded. "Maist o' them."

"And you, Sire? You now are ruler, in the name. Are you better placed, more content with all, than before? Under Morton?"

The boy shook his head.

"And you also, my lord of Mar? What of you?"

"I dinna get to say much."

"No? Your uncle, Sir Alexander, Master of Mar? Does he not take heed of you? He is strong on this council."

"No." That was said with a scowl.

"He is deputy keeper here, only. *You* are keeper of Stirling. So!" John looked from one to the other. "The new rule, in fact, is no better than the old. Worse, in fact? My lord of Morton at least did not permit this bickering and dissension, this feud and strife. And killing. Even though you scarcely liked him!"

"He let us be. We didna see that much o' him. A right sair man. But nane so ill at the governing, I jalouse."

"And he kept your uncle in his place, no?"

"Aye. My mither says that Morton had a right heavy hand. But he could keep the peace."

John was rather ashamed of himself over thus manoeuvring the youngsters into these admissions, the attitude which he needed. "There is to be a parliament at the beginning of July," he reminded. "Much may change thereafter. My lord of Morton will seek to right matters, to limit the power of these eleven, possibly to replace some of them. And to ensure Your Grace's royal will as supreme. And that you, my lord, are accepted as keeper here, your uncle put in his place."

"I, I am no' sure aboot the ruling," James said doubtfully. "I'll need help, just. Maister Buchanan ay tells me to dae this or dae that. And, whiles, I dinna want to. And the others tell me different . . ."

"Yes, I see how difficult it is for you, Sire. But, after a parliament, it will improve, I think."

"Can a parliament change it a'?" Johnnie demanded. "They meet and talk, and then they're awa' for hame! And we're left here!"

"The parliament can appoint Lords of the Articles to carry out its will. And the king in parliament is supreme. So matters should be much bettered. The lord of Morton means to see to it. That is, if . . .?"

The boys looked questioningly.

"If he is able to attend the parliament!" John went on carefully.

"Might he no'?" That was James.

"This council might try to debar him. They fear him. Accuse him of misrule. Misruling the kingdom while he was regent. Might well even try to arrest him. They would fail in that, for he has his many Douglas guards. But they could bar him from appearing at the parliament, claiming that he has committed treason against Your Grace."

"He hasna done that!"

"Could they bar him?"

"They could, yes. From attending. Speaking. Calling them to order. But . . . not if he had the king's personal order to attend."

"Eh?"

"See you, Sire, he has given me this letter. For you to sign, if you will. It says that you require his attendance at your parliament. And that you approve, in the main, of his actions while he was Your Grace's regent. And that if he committed any offences against your will, then he has your royal pardon. If you will sign this, then none can stop him from joining and speaking at your parliament." And John produced Morton's letter. "Your signature, Sire, and the way is clear. Will you read it?"

"Aye." The boy ran his eye over the quite brief wording, which said little more than John had stated. "Will my name on this serve, just?"

"Morton believes that it will, Sire. Now that you have the rule, in name."

"Och, well." James went round the table to pick up a quill and the ink-horn, ever on hand where that boy was, and came to sign the paper without more ado.

Sighing his thankfulness, John blew on the ink to dry it. "Now, Your Grace, to kinder matters," he said. "Tell me what poetry you have been writing since last we forgathered. And, do you write other than verse? Not just your lessons and the like, for Master Buchanan. But legends, accounts, tales?"

"Aye, I do. I've scrieved stories o' the past. Aboot my ancestors. And thae Picts and Norsemen. Aye, and Romans. Witches, forby. And the like."

"He's ay at it," Johnnie declared. "And nane to read it but himsel'! For I'm no for it a'!"

"Perhaps you would be better of it sometimes, my lord Earl! Do you write nothing but your lessons and the Latinity, and so on?"

"No' me. I'm for better employ! Archery. Quarter-staff. Hurly-hackit. Hawking. And the like. Jamie's no' guid at them . . ."

"I can use my time better, Johnnie Mar! Some o' us are gien wits! To use. Some dinna use them. Hurly-hackit! Sliding doon a hill and climbing up again! What's the guid o' that?"

John coughed. "You have not told me of your poems, Sire."

"I've done ane on the fowls o' the air. And how they fly. They a' fly differently. I can watch them frae the castle cliffs. It goes:

> The birds of the air take wing,
> The crows that croak . . ."

"Ooch Jamie, no' that again!"

> "The birds of the air take wing,
>   The crows that croak and the larks that sing;
> Flapping, swooping,
>   Flailing, sailing,
> The wind availing:
>   Winging, swinging,
> Sliding, gliding,
>   The breeze providing
> The birds of the air soar high
>   But men, even kings, they cannot fly."

"Excellent, Sire! Most . . . observing." But John also suddenly had had sufficient. For he heard voices from the next room, and he thought that he recognised George Buchanan's harsh tones. He had no wish for an encounter with that man, here and now. "Your Grace," he said, "I fear that I must be gone. I have overstayed my time and your royal patience. I have far to ride. Have I your permission to retire?" He was pocketing Morton's letter, and the royal ode in his doublet.

"I had other rhymes to tell you, Sir John."

"If I may come another time, Sire. Less long delayed, I hope. I leave these few verses of mine with you – poor things. May I go?" He was already backing for the door.

"If you must . . ."

Bowing, John escaped, scarcely proud of his behaviour and achievement.

Riding down through the town and heading eastwards, he wondered whether he was, in fact, improving his sovereign-lord's state and well-being by helping Morton to regain some power in the land. He was allowing himself to be used, yes – but for good? Or ill? He owed that boy back there his allegiance, but more than that, regard, even verging on fondness now. His duty was to James Stewart, not James Douglas. Could the two tally? He must endeavour to see that they did, if at all possible. What could he do, to that effect?

He got scant thanks from Morton, at Dalkeith, however glad the latter might be to have that royal signature of approval. Armed with that, he could make progress. John Carmichael, armed with his copy of the Ode to Lucius Junius Brutus, wondered which was the most valuable? He was astonished, and touched, that his young monarch had actually written out a copy for him . . .

30

It did not take long for Morton to make use of his piece of paper, at any rate, although hardly in the way that he had indicated to John. It was Archie who brought the news to Fenton, only a week later, in much excitement. He was to assemble his Red Douglases and ride to Stirling, where they would be joined by Lochleven and the Black Douglases, there to make a show of force, this to aid young Mar, who had been sent instructions as to how to bring down his uncle, the master, and take over the castle for the king.

Surprised at this development when he had expected only a perhaps dramatic appearance at the forthcoming parliament, which was still a couple of weeks away, John, who had not been sent any word of it, asked what reasons Morton had given his nephew for this challenging display of Douglas might, and how willingly Archie was acceding to it. He was told that it was to ensure the king's freedom from these council lords and to topple Erskine from control of Stirling Castle, and to put young Mar therein; also to arrange that the parliament would be held there, at Stirling – for apparently the said lords were now calling it at Edinburgh instead, and Morton deemed that as suspect, and to be countered, recognising that he was less than popular in that city. Archie saw all this as worthy of support, and hoped that John would accompany him on this venture, even though he had not been summoned to do so.

John felt that he could hardly refuse. Moreover he saw himself as having some responsibility towards the two boys at Stirling, over and above his due loyalty to the monarch;

after all, presumably it was his convincing of James to sign that letter of approbation which had triggered off this new move of Morton's, together with his condemning of Erskine's taking over of the keepership of the castle, which was involving young Mar. So he agreed to go with Archie, Margaret privately urging him to see that her nephew did not do anything over-rash, with all these armed men.

So two mornings later, he presented himself at Tantallon, where he found four hundred Red Douglases assembled and eager for whatever their earl required of them. They rode, with little delay.

This was a new experience for the two friends, leading a large armed force to challenge an entrenched authority, very different from the Redeswyre embroilment and other Border ridings. John was far from easy in his mind about it all, although Archie enthused. Why was Morton himself not leading this venture?

Four hundred men, even Douglases, ride less swiftly than does any small party, and that night they got only as far as Falkirk, still some sixteen miles from Stirling. And it was there that they had a visitor, in the person of Douglas of Lochleven who, it transpired, had another five hundred Black Douglases waiting in the cover of the nearby great Tor Wood, the cover so useful to Bruce before Bannockburn. It seemed that he had expected the Angus contingent at least two days earlier, his men becoming restless. He said that he hoped that young Mar would be playing his part in this endeavour, for even nearly one thousand men, such as they now had, would be ineffective in taking Stirling Castle without some co-operation from within the citadel itself. Morton's message to this Lochleven was that Johnnie Mar had received his instructions. Clearly the ex-regent had been busy enough mentally even though he was not leading this enterprise in person.

In the morning they rode on into the depths of the Tor Wood, a forest covering many square miles, where, passing sundry Black Douglas scouting parties on the lookout for them, they duly joined Lochleven's host. A potent force indeed, they headed on through the glades and shaws of the wood for Stirling. John was very much aware of the significance of all this territory in Scotland's story, not only the Bruce and Wallace connections, but here had been fought the Battle of Sauchieburn, where James the Third and his son, to be James the Fourth, had changed roles, the former to be slain and the latter to take the vow which had eventually led to the calamity of Flodden Field.

When at length they emerged from the last screen of the trees, it was to see the mighty castle rock of Stirling soaring before them less than three miles off. It certainly looked, from here, no fortress to subdue without a prolonged siege. Would young Johnnie Mar be able to aid them effectively?

In fact they joined the Earl of Mar sooner than expected, for, their approach visible for a considerable time before they reached the town, he and some of the guard had come down to meet them, the youngster in a state of great elation. The castle was his, he announced proudly. No need for their hundreds of Douglases!

Bubbling over with satisfaction, Johnnie told them how he had achieved the victory. He had declared to his uncle that he was going hunting and hawking on the meanders of Forth, and the latter acceding, he had gathered a company of Stirling men outside the castle, and turning back, had ridden in again with them and quickly captured the master, the garrison, which much preferred the nephew to his uncle, not interfering. So, with a minimum of fuss and delay, perhaps the strongest citadel in all Scotland was taken – and by a boy of twelve years.

Archie, with John and Lochleven, much impressed, rode up to the fortress with the excited boy, to find James in a state of fear and uncertainty. He had a great dread of violence in any form, and apparently there had been some minor skirmish when the master was captured and locked in a cell, and the king had seen a young man wounded. So John found himself allotted the task of calming and reassuring the monarch, to Johnnie's scorn, poetry the obvious pacification.

It was an extraordinary situation. Here they were holding the royal fortress, and in effect the king's person, Archie, Lochleven, Johnnie and himself, with the key to power in the land in their hands. What to do with it? All had, of course, been planned by Morton, and that man had to be informed. Lochleven sent a couple of his men to Dalkeith with the news.

George Buchanan did not take all this any more calmly than did James Stewart. He had no actual authority at Stirling Castle other than as the king's tutor, but he had influence; and he deplored the sudden rise to power of one of his pupils, Johnnie now conceiving himself as freed from Buchanan's strict regime, and showing it. So the clash was not so much over who controlled the great citadel as who controlled its keeper. Fortunately, perhaps, Archie had the means of dampening down this confrontation. Morton had told him, as a mere aside, that Buchanan was in receipt of a pension of one hundred pounds from Elizabeth Tudor, as indeed had been John Knox, information relayed by Sir Robert Bowes, the English envoy. Not only that, but that Master Peter Young, the assistant tutor, had refused an offer of the like. So here was something to use, a stick to beat the old man. Buchanan would certainly not want this information passed on, in general, or to his Kirk colleagues in particular. So Douglas of Lochleven was given the task, which he quite relished, of telling Master George that this was known, and declaring that it would be noised abroad if Buchanan did not forthwith resign his tutorship and leave the castle, Master Young to replace him. Now aged seventy-four and not quite the man he once had been, the veteran capitulated and agreed to pack his bags and leave – to the great relief of his sovereign-lord James and the triumph of Johnnie.

Morton took three days to arrive, to the surprise of John and Archie. He was, no doubt, much pleased with the success of his plottings and plannings, but he scarcely showed it, critical as to details. However, he did explain to Archie and John what had delayed him. When he had heard that the king and Stirling were in the hands of his appointees, he had gone to Edinburgh, or at least to Craigmillar Castle outside the city, and had invited Atholl, Argyll, Montrose, Glencairn and Lindsay to meet him there, the place well guarded by his Douglases. They had come, and he had informed them of the situation, but apparently not in any aggressive fashion, indeed further inviting them to join him for the night at his house of Dalkeith, where they could discuss the future roles of all concerned. This they had all done, with what agreement Morton did not declare. But having seen his illustrious guests well fed and wined and off to their beds, he had promptly left Dalkeith at first light, for Stirling, leaving the others to their slumber; and here he was. Unsure as to the point of this manoeuvre, his hearers were given no fuller information, save that he had ordered the parliament to be held at Stirling, not Edinburgh, this in a week's time. Whether the lords he had left at Dalkeith would attend was another matter. Yet Atholl was the chancellor, and ought to be in charge of it.

Morton did make another and surprising statesmanlike move. He came to terms with the captive Sir Alexander Erskine, Master of Mar. On condition that he in future supported him, Morton, he would be released, allowed to leave Stirling, and actually appointed to be keeper of Edinburgh Castle instead – or so Morton would recommend this last to the forthcoming parliament. Erskine, needless to say, agreed with the proposal, and departed forthwith. So they had got rid of two awkward characters, meantime at least, and peace of a sort descended on Stirling Castle – not that peace was ever very evident when James Douglas was around.

John Carmichael, who was not there by the earl's command anyway, sought permission to return home, although Archie was commanded to stay, his Red Douglas force a useful precaution in case of unforeseen eventualities.

But John's request granted, he was told to return for the parliament, where, his brother-in-law said, he could sit as Warden of the Middle March.

Thankfully that reluctant conspirator set off back to Fenton. Margaret would be intrigued by all he had to tell her.

That very significant parliament of July 1578, held in the great hall of Stirling Castle, was very much Morton's own, although he was no longer regent. He did not reclaim that style and title, acceding that the king, present in person, now ruled as well as reigned. But with no sign of Atholl to chair the meeting, he acted chancellor himself, and so conducted all from the dais near the throne, on the edge of which chair young James sat, in some agitation, after being ushered in by the Lord Lyon King of Arms to a flourish of trumpets.

This was John's first parliament and, unsure where to sit in the crowded hall, he took a lowly seat at the back. It was noticeable how empty were the earls' benches at the very front, Angus, Mar, Erroll, Buchan and Cassillis being the only representatives. Morton's tulchan bishops were out in force, and there was a fair proportion of the lords and a good showing from the counties, sheriffdoms and royal burghs.

Morton started the proceedings by humbly requesting the monarch to declare that this was a right, proper and duly authorised parliament, of his own royal calling — which James did in something of a gabble, although he had to be prompted to end up with the announcement that he had appointed a new Council of State to advise him, the president of which would be his well-beloved James, Earl of Morton.

That done, all was in order for matters to proceed.

Despite the presence of those bishops, to keep the Kirk from taking offence, the accustomed prayer for God's blessing on their deliberations, followed by a brief sermon, was presented by a black-robed divine, the Reverend

Duncanson, the Stirling minister, who then retired to the minstrels' gallery to watch, and no doubt report in due course to the General Assembly of the Kirk.

Morton then began by announcing the names of the new Council of State. But there was an unfortunate interruption. The Earl of Montrose and the Lord Lindsay, sent by Atholl and Argyll from Edinburgh, marched into the hall, to shout out that, since this meeting had not been called by the chancellor, the Earl of Atholl, whose duty and privilege it was to do so, then this was no true parliament but an unauthorised gathering, and any motions and decisions which it might pass would have no validity in the law of the land.

In the uproar which followed, Morton moved, frowning darkly, over to the small king's throne to speak vehemently into the royal ear, before banging his gavel on the chair back for silence.

When this was obtained, James haltingly declared that the chancellor only issued the summons to a parliament in the name of the king. And if the king was present in person, it was therefore a true parliament.

The newcomers' contention thus disposed of, Morton ordered Montrose and Lindsay to take the seats they were entitled to, but any further matters they might wish to raise must be put forward in the due form of motion and seconding, to be debated and voted upon, that when discussion was opened.

The pair hooted, but went to their respective benches. They had not done the anti-Morton cause any good; but it did indicate that the opposition was not dead, only dormant.

Morton then went on to announce the names of those proposed for the king's new Council of State, these with His Grace's approval. The first, Archibald, Earl of Angus, Lieutenant of the Border, who was now to be promoted to be Lieutenant of the Realm. Then John, Earl of Mar, son of the former regent and keeper of this castle. Then the Abbot Commendators of Cambuskenneth and Dryburgh, both Erskines. Also, to John's surprise, still another Erskine, none other than the Master Alexander, at Edinburgh Castle. Clearly Morton was seeking to make sure that that powerful family were now firmly attached to his cause.

Douglas of Lochleven was the next name put forward, and here the Lord Lindsay jumped up to protest that these were men of no repute and standing. The lords of parliament ought to be strong on any council to advise the monarch . . .

Angrily Morton ordered him to sit down. "Think ye, sir, that this is a court of churls and brawlers? Take your own place, and thank God that the king's youth keeps you safe from his resentment!"

"I have served the king in his minority, as faithfully as the proudest among ye," Lindsay cried. "I think to serve His Grace no less truly in his majority!" He then strode from his seat on the lords' benches to leave the hall, being rejoined by Montrose – although thus departing from the presence of the monarch without royal leave could carry an accusation of *lese-majesty*.

Shaking his head, Morton resumed his nominations for the council. The High Treasurer, Sir Thomas Lyon, brother of the late Chancellor Lord Glamis, he proposed. And the Lord Maxwell, Warden of the West March.

John drew breath, hoping that this last was not an indication that other wardens were to be appointed – for almost the last thing that he wanted was to become one of Morton's council, or indeed to any other position in the governance of the land, his wardenship quite sufficient. Of course, Maxwell was married to the Lady Elizabeth Douglas, a cousin of Morton's . . .

Fortunately, the further announcement was that such other appointments to the council should be left open meantime, in the hope that certain members of the former regime might recognise where the best interests of His Grace's realm lay, and be prepared to co-operate. He, Morton, would advise that the names of the Earl of

Montrose and the Lord Lindsay be specifically excluded from any such appointment, because of their display of disrespect for parliament; indeed that they be ordered to confine themselves to their own houses meantime, for the nation's weal. Were these nominations, already approved by the King's Grace, accepted and agreed by the parliament?

There was no dissent expressed by the assembly — scarcely to be wondered at after that example of what happened to dissenters — even though no enthusiastic reception was evinced either.

Morton proceeded to ask homologation of the demission of the regency and the king's acceptance of personal rule and government, together with approbation by His Grace of all that he, Morton, had done as regent. This was also accepted by the delegates, even though some eyebrows were raised.

The next business was the continuing danger to the realm of any Catholic uprising in favour of the release of the former Queen Mary, this the more possible in that the Kings of France and Spain, together with the papal state and sundry Germanic dukedoms, were threatening joint action in the matter as challenge to England. The house of Hamilton was, of course, foremost in this matter in Scotland, and steps would have to be taken to limit its ability to cause trouble, with parliament cautioning the Lords John and Claud Hamilton. Was this agreed?

Some show of enthusiasm was evinced for this, at least, from an almost wholly Protestant company.

Having gained all that he presently required, Morton threw the meeting open to motions, proposals and assertions from the delegates in general. The rest of the session was devoted mainly to the many items of central and local government which required parliamentary sanction and authority, John making his only contribution with a suggestion that the keepership of Liddesdale and Hermitage Castle should be detached from the wardenship of the Middle March, whether added to the West March or kept as a separate entity, it being an unsuitable duty, too far distant from the former. The Lord Maxwell seconded this proposal, and the matter was deferred for the new council's decision.

Clearly the acting chancellor was now concerned to wind up the proceedings as soon as was decently possible; and very soon thereafter he sought the king's permission to adjourn the session, James only too eager to accede. So the Lord Lyon summoned his trumpeter, all rose, and the monarch was led from the hall at all but a shambling run.

Thereafter John, as ever anxious to get off home to Margaret and the family, found himself summoned to the royal quarters to discuss poetry with his liege-lord, James of course having noted his presence over that matter of Liddesdale. The king informed him that Johnnie Mar was getting too big for his boots; and with Master Buchanan gone, was treating him as though *he* was the king now. John sympathised, but said that Johnnie would be puffed up meantime with his sudden rise in status, but would no doubt calm down presently. And His Grace could, after all, order him by royal command to behave more suitably.

Versifying took over.

John had no orders from Morton to detain him at Stirling – unlike Archie who was required to remain. John foresaw that he would be a deal less in the company of his friend from now on, for as Lieutenant of the Realm, which was in effect commander of the royal forces, the Red Douglas would be apt to be kept close to Morton. Which was a pity. He hoped that Archie, like Johnnie Mar, would not grow too big for *these* boots . . .

When next he heard from the lieutenant, at Fenton, however, it was to learn of major happenings, and his friend uncertain whether to be pleased with the way things went, or the reverse, far from becoming over-lofty. It seemed that, when Montrose and Lindsay had got back

381

to Edinburgh, they had, in their wrath, persuaded Atholl and Argyll and the others there to rise against Morton's resumed sway – and rise in arms at that. Raising a great host of seven thousand men, they had marched north from the capital for Stirling. Word of this had reached Morton, oddly enough, by the mouth of none other than Sir Robert Bowes, the English envoy, who had ridden fast from Edinburgh with two prominent Kirk divines, to seek to mediate, declaring that armed confrontation, indeed civil war, between the two factions could be disastrous not only for Scotland but for the Protestant cause generally. The last thing that his Queen Elizabeth would desire was an encouragement for the Catholics, backed by France and Spain, to rise in arms, led by the Hamiltons. Her Majesty was not paying pensions to members of both sides to have this happen. He urged Morton to come to terms with the opposition, and offered to act as mediator, the Kirk representatives aiding him.

Morton had seen the point of this, never indeed one to involve himself in armed struggle; but had not wished to seem to bend to the threat of war, any more than to yield up any of his newly recovered power. So he had ordered Archie to lead a hurriedly mustered force, mainly Douglases Black and Red, to meet the challenge, but taking Bowes and the ministers with them, to try to reach some sort of agreement with the Atholl-Argyll party, even going so far as to offer these two earls, possibly also Montrose and Lindsay, seats on his present council. Thus early had the new Lieutenant of the Realm found himself propelled into action.

The two forces, the Edinburgh one the larger, had met at Falkirk, Bowes and the divines riding ahead under a white flag, another extraordinary situation, the Douglases occupying the high ground at the southern edge of the Tor Wood. And the mediators had proved their worth; of course, Bowes had a powerful weapon in his hands, pensions, whatever the Kirk's contribution. In the event, the lords had seen their bread as best buttered by coming to an agreement, Atholl, Argyll and Lindsay accepting seats on the council – although Montrose had scornfully refused – and turned back their host for Edinburgh, a victory of a sort for Morton, and most assuredly for Elizabeth Tudor, that dispenser of bribes.

John's comment that the bribe-dispenser was perhaps less to be condemned than the bribe-accepters had Archie shrugging. At least he had not had to fight, and there had been no bloodshed. Margaret agreeing, said that there could be worse uses for English gold, however humiliating for Scottish pride.

So now Morton sat reasonably secure in Stirling Castle, governing the land again, although he kept his force of Black Douglases mobilised and ready at Loch Leven, none so far off, just in case.

John and Archie could turn their attentions to the Borderland again, since it seemed that the latter was still lieutenant thereof as well as of the realm. During all this preoccupation by their betters with national affairs, who knew what the mosstroopers, March-riders and cattle-reivers had been up to?

31

In fact, the months that followed proved to be fairly
peaceful for Scotland, at least on the surface, Morton's
rule stern and grasping but effective in the short term.
Seethings underground there were, and always would be
in that land where feud and unrest were endemic; but
the remainder of 1578 and much of 1579 saw no major
upheavals, and Archie was not called upon to lead any
armed campaigns such as Morton himself recoiled from,
however busy Borders activity kept him and John.

The latter, now thirty years old, had more on his
mind than wardenly duties, of course, for he was still
co-operating with the training of Kirk students in land
improvement and utilisation, as well as seeking to reap the
productivity of his own properties for amassing the funds
he required for the purchase, rather than the leasing, of
the Fenton estate, and improving the accommodation of
the tower. Margaret was pregnant again, and her family
preoccupations prevented her from helping John greatly,
save with advice.

A new call upon John's time developed that early
summer of 1579. Morton had difficulties in his dealings
with the young king, who had never liked him. He had
no knack of coping with the growing boy and yet needed
his co-operation in the rule of the land. Learning that
James was developing a taste for hawking, but jealous of
Johnnie Mar's prowess at the sport on the meanders of
Forth nearby, Morton got the notion of rehabilitating the
royal hunting-seat of Falkland, in Fothrif of Fife, where
James could pursue his hawking without the other boy's
challenging company, thus also serving to get the young

monarch from under his feet, as it were, yet available when required. But he had to be very carefully guarded there, for whoever held the king held the country, and there were always folk prepared to exploit the fact. So – Douglas guards. Archie found himself appointed keeper of Falkland Palace, to add to his other responsibilities, with frequent spells thereat. He also found James less than easy to deal with, and tended to seek John's help, whom the king continued to look upon as a friend, and in more than mutual fondness for poetry, this something missing from Archie's make-up. So there were not a few visits to Fife, fortunately of fairly easy access by one of the Tantallon boats from North Berwick harbour, a mere couple of hours' sail across Forth to the nearer havens for Falkland. John, in the circumstances, had to nurture his versifying abilities, with Margaret's encouragement.

That summer was well past, and an active one, when the precarious peace of Scotland was again threatened. And this time it was by Morton's own doing, even though he was spurred on from over the border. It was the Catholic threat again, which was worrying Elizabeth, with the word that the Hamiltons were receiving messengers from France, coming secretly by sea to Ayrshire havens. Something had to be done about it.

Lieutenant Archie was sent for, and told to take a Douglas force down to the Clyde valley and to apprehend the Lords John and Claud Hamilton. Just like that. Archie was less than happy about this. When he suggested that John should accompany him, the latter asked to be excused. He had no quarrel with the Hamiltons, and indeed had rather liked the brothers when he had visited Cambusnethan. In something of a quandary, for the order came as a royal command bearing the king's signature, Archie could hardly refuse to go; but John came up with a suggestion of his own. Why not send a messenger ahead to warn the Hamiltons that a royal-ordered force was on its way to apprehend them, and urging that they fled the scene, preferably overseas. John could send the secret courier, if so desired, and send him only a day ahead of the Douglases, so that the brothers would not have time to muster a defending force of Hamiltons, of whom it was said that they could raise some five thousand, given the time. Archie jumped at this offer, and it was all arranged.

So the lieutenant's host, with Lochleven acting second in command, in due course arrived at Cambusnethan Castle to find their birds flown and no real opposition offered, anticlimax indeed. Hamilton of Merton, left in charge, with a few others, to look after the mad Arran – Bothwellhaugh had fled with the brothers – was taken back to Morton at Stirling, Lochleven insisting on this. Morton was probably well pleased with this outcome. He had made his gesture. He made another, however, promptly hanging Merton and the others without trial on a charge of treason, by conspiring with the French and Spanish against the King's Grace – this presumably calculated to please the Protestant lords.

It did not please Archie Douglas, who was indeed much upset. Nor did it please Atholl for some reason; he was known to have leanings towards Catholicism, and had been friendly with the Hamiltons. He had been the least co-operative of the lords, and now did not hide his dislike and distrust of Morton and, being chancellor, this was awkward. He named the hangings of those Hamiltons a grievous offence, and used it to stir up opposition against Morton.

Archie, a worried young man now, told all this to John. He did not want to be blamed in any way for the deaths of his former captives. And he was sure that Atholl was planning to bring down Morton if possible, and these hangings were being used by him. John thought that no one would hold Archie in any way responsible; after all, if he had desired to get rid of his prisoners, he could have executed them when they surrendered at Cambusnethan.

His friend hoped that John was right. He was being tied ever more closely to his uncle, pushed into prominence, and with very little desire for it. He was but seldom at home with his Mary now. He had to go back to Stirling the very next day to attend a great banquet which Morton was laying on, this allegedly to celebrate the fall of the house of Hamilton, and the sinking of the Catholic cause in Scotland. John had not been invited to attend this great occasion, to no complaints on his part.

He heard about it, however, in due course – all Scotland did, and not because of its magnificence, the king and all the highest in the land being present, save for any surviving Hamiltons. It was quite other which gripped the nation's attention. The Earl of Atholl had taken ill thereat, and died shortly afterwards. His personal hostility to Morton known, and that man's ruthlessness so recently evidenced, poison was immediately suspected. The Black Douglas mocked this, saying such rumours were the work of the basest of his enemies. But when the whispers continued to circulate, with details as to Atholl's last agonies, and with the countess demanding a post-mortem, Morton, to quell the canards, ordered physicians to examine the corpse and prove them groundless. The doctors duly cut open the earl's body, and came up with the declaration that they could not positively deny the possibility of poison. One of them, by name Preston, presumably more concerned than the others to clear Morton's name, showed his contempt for his colleagues' feeble verdict by declaring that there was nothing in the contents of Atholl's stomach to indicate poison, and to prove it bent down to lick the said contents with his tongue – whereupon he quite quickly collapsed and all but died.

This dramatic development did nothing to allay the accusations, to the fury of Morton, who retaliated by hanging a couple of rumour-mongers to still the gossip. John began to wonder whether his brother-in-law was losing his grip.

That wondering increased rapidly thereafter, and oddly, aided by the arrival of two newcomers on the scene, both coming from France, but unconnected apparently. One was the Lord d'Aubigny, Esmé Stewart, a Lennox kinsman and cousin of the murdered Lord Darnley, grandson of the third Earl of Lennox and son of the governor of Avignon in France and Captain of the Garde Ecossais, a brilliant, talented and handsome courtier, who, it was said, had been invited to Scotland by the king himself, not only because of his relationship to James's father, Darnley, but on account of his poetic abilities. The other was also a Stewart, Captain James Stewart of Bothwellmuir, second son of the Lord Ochiltree, who was renowned as a soldier on the Continent and who was married to the late Atholl's daughter Elizabeth. Also, as it happened, brother-in-law to the late John Knox. It was alleged that he had returned to his native land at the behest of his wife and the countess to avenge the death of his father-in-law. These two, in their different spheres, were set to have a major impact on affairs, on Morton's affairs in especial. However unrelated was their coming, if it was so, they quickly got together, with mutual interests other than their Stewart blood.

The captain's impact was the more immediate. He set about avenging Atholl without delay. He announced that he had evidence to convict Morton of implication in the murder of the Lord Darnley a dozen years before, the king's father; and since Darnley had been given the crown matrimonial by Queen Mary, this constituted high treason. He demanded trial.

This, of course, however old a story, was as grist to the mill of Morton's many enemies and would-be supplanters. Safe from Morton's grasp in the Highland fastnesses of Atholl, he began to spin his web of intrigue. And the other Stewart, Lord of Aubigny, picked up the weft and woof of it. He was kin to Darnley; and his closeness to the king, not only in blood, gave him major influence. The Stewarts began to assail their old enemies, the house of Douglas.

Archie's anxieties grew. He sensed no personal animosities towards himself, but he was a Douglas and associated with Morton. How could he distance himself from his uncle in all this? John advised burying himself meantime in the Borderland, perhaps in the remote Hermitage Castle, where Morton would have difficulty in reaching him.

Fortunately their kinsman himself appeared to be lying fairly low in this situation, no doubt hoping that these temporary clouds would blow over. Esmé Stewart's influence with the king was something which he could not dismiss however, and had to be reckoned with. Morton, in recognition, did seek to come to terms with Aubigny, advising James to award him the family earldom of Lennox and invite him on to the council, this involving not a little arranging for there was already an Earl of Lennox; but he was a former Bishop of Caithness, and a recluse, taking no part in national affairs, so he was bought off with the nominal royal earldom of March. Esmé Stewart took his seat on the council as seventh Earl of Lennox. How much good that would do Lennox remained to be seen.

The new Lennox did not delay in demonstrating his increased authority and sway with the king. He saw Stirling as something of a prison for the now thirteen-year-old monarch, and therefore for himself, and persuaded James to order a move to his capital's palace of Holyrood – this contrived while Morton was temporarily incapacitated at Dalkeith with an injured knee received while dismounting from his horse. And at Edinburgh the king was able to assume a much more monarchial role, and to become more approachable by other lords who had found difficulty in reaching him at Stirling.

Morton suffered another loss of support that summer of 1580 by the withdrawal of Sir Robert Bowes back to England, to be given a new appointment. Bowes had been a useful go-between and adviser, and was not immediately replaced.

James Stewart was developing all but an infatuation for his kinsman Lennox. Inevitably an isolated and lonely youngster, his falling out with Johnnie Mar had left a further void; and this gifted and intellectual newcomer more than filled the gap. Moreover, he appeared to be a man of considerable wealth, and had brought with him from France, whether his own money or otherwise, much gold, alleged to amount to forty thousand *louis d'ors*, and seemed to be prepared to spend it on the king. The royal treasury ever empty – Morton had seen to that – the boy had always lacked luxuries, fine clothing, the best horses, hawks and the like. Now he gained them, and was grateful. In return, he made Lennox governor of the royal castle of Dumbarton, to give him a foothold on traditional Lennox territory, and moreover created him Lord High Chamberlain.

The other visitor, Captain James Stewart, was nowise left out in all this, becoming Lennox's lieutenant and part of the royal entourage. That is, until he went back to France that autumn, speculation rife as to what this implied.

In these circumstances, John Carmichael saw little or nothing of his liege-lord, although James was now based a bare twenty miles from Fenton Tower. He was sorry about this, in a measure, for he had come to have some fondness for the strange boy, quite apart from his loyal duty to his sovereign. But he recognised that Earl Esmé's poetic abilities, infinitely superior to his own, had quite superseded his efforts on the king's behalf, apart from all else. Besides, John was sufficiently busy, not only with his warden's duties and the running of his properties, and family affairs. His father had suddenly died that summer, and John was now Carmichael of that Ilk. This did not greatly add to his wealth and possessions, for the Carmichaels were not a rich family; but it did mean that he had to visit his old home frequently, and its estates, and to ensure that all went reasonably well with his mother, his sister Mary now married and away. The old lady would have liked him to come and live at Carmichael, but he much preferred Fenton, as did Margaret. Fortunately his brother Archibald, at Eastend, was nearby and could keep an eye on their mother. Some advantage in becoming head of the family did accrue in that he inherited just sufficient extra moneys which, added to his own accumulated savings, enabled him to purchase the Fenton estate, to his major satisfaction. Now he and his were secure in their chosen home.

Margaret had produced her fourth child, to further rejoicing, another boy, to be named William. Archie Douglas was the more jealous, he and his Mary remaining childless.

The family went to pass that first Yuletide after her husband's death with John's mother at Carmichael – this amidst rumours of governmental stresses. John was thankful that he seemed to have become fairly detached from all such. He prayed that this would continue; but feared that the same could not be said for Archie at Tantallon.

John was back at Fenton only two days into January when Archie brought him the portentous news. Morton was fallen, a prisoner in Edinburgh Castle, his gaoler Sir Alexander Erskine, Master of Mar, whom he had made keeper thereof.

In a state of excitement and agitation, not unmixed with alarm, Archie recounted events. On the last day of the old year Morton had called a council meeting, held at Holyrood, the king present, with Lennox, Argyll, Montrose, Lindsay and the rest. They had barely commenced proceedings when an usher had entered, to announce that Captain James Stewart of Ochiltree, of the King's Guard, urgently sought audience. Morton had said that this was no occasion for such appearance, but James had ordered that the captain be admitted. Stewart had entered, and hurrying past Morton's seat at the foot of the long table, had gone to kneel at the king's chair at the other end, and pleaded for His Grace, and all others, to hear him. He came to announce that he had proof positive that the Earl of Morton, here present, had been art and part in the murder of His Grace's father, Henry, Lord Darnley.

He was therefore guilty of highest treason, and should pay the price.

In the uproar which followed, with Morton outraged, denying such grossly wicked charge by this nobody, the captain, also on his feet again, declared that he had brought the proof of the treason with him, and from France. If His Grace would consent to make pardon of Sir James Balfour, bearer of that proof, and involved in some degree in the dastardly murder at Kirk o' Field, he would forthwith bring him in before them all. King James, obviously not entirely unprepared for all this, nodded acceptance, and the council, in a state of ferment and clamour, reacted variously. The captain went to fetch in an anxious-looking man of middle years, Sir James Balfour, carrying a paper. That paper had been a bond, signed fourteen years before by Morton and the late Earl of Bothwell, Douglas of Whittingehame and his brother Alexander, now a Senator of the College of Justice, the High Court of Scotland, and Balfour himself, agreeing that it was necessary for the realm's weal that the queen's husband should be got rid of by whatever means was necessary, and that the signatories bound themselves to mutual support and aid in carrying out the project. This signed at Whittingehame in January 1567.

Read out, and presented to James, with Morton declaring it forgery and shameful artifice, and clapping hand to sword, Captain Stewart reached for his own blade, and it had looked like coming to bloodshed then and there in the royal presence. But Argyll, Montrose and Lindsay had demanded that Morton be arrested and held in custody while this dire charge was enquired into; and Lennox had advised the king that the meeting be adjourned. So James had been hurried out, and Morton conducted to a secure chamber and locked up, Archie's voice the only one upraised against this. Later his uncle had been transferred to an Edinburgh Castle cell.

John and his wife heard it all grim-faced. Margaret declared that she judged that it had all been contrived by

Lennox to bring down her brother. The accusation might well be true, as to the bond and signature, for Morton was known to have been much against the arrogant Darnley and friendly with Bothwell; but it was an old story to be bringing up now. Nevertheless she did not see how her brother, clever as he might be, was going to win out of this toil, for young James could scarcely be seen to condone the assassination of his own father.

John was more concerned for Archie himself, whom these days was being seen as ever closer to his uncle, and now well aware of his vulnerability. Lying low in all-but-impregnable Tantallon Castle seemed advisable meantime.

So, in effect, extraordinary as it might seem, the newcomer Lennox had the king secure, and would be all but ruling Scotland. And he was a Catholic, to be sure. Apart from all else, what would Queen Elizabeth think of that?

It did not take long for the northern kingdom to find that out, the Protestant Tudor never lacking in spies to inform her. She sent up a new and authoritative envoy, Sir Thomas Randolph, with urgent instructions. And to reinforce her views, she ordered the Lord Hunsdon, English Warden of the East March, to mobilise maximum armed force in the north of England, to ensure that no Catholic influence prevailed over the borderline.

John, along with the other wardens, found himself dispatched to their Marches to ready all Borderland strength to repel possible English invasion, Archie, unsure of his position, remaining behind.

Abruptly all was changed.

32

Midwinter was no time for armed struggle in hilly country, and no actual invasion materialised, although the threat of it remained, with constant probings by small English parties over the borderline. Elizabeth's Randolph, a tough character and much less diplomatic than Bowes had been, made very clear what would transpire if there was any overt Catholic upsurge in Scotland, with or without King James's nominal acceptance. There were even suggestions that if such occurred, the boy's mother, the still captive Queen Mary, would promptly be executed.

In the meantime, the other captive, James, Earl of Morton, was transferred to Lennox's fortress of Dumbarton on the Clyde estuary, for added security, while arrangements were made for his formal trial. He was permitted no visitors.

Captain James Stewart was rewarded for his so effective efforts by being created Earl of Arran, the insane Hamilton earl being rated as incapable of holding such dignity, and his brothers being forfeited – this partly to reassure Queen Elizabeth that there was no intended Catholic uprising with Hamilton involvement. Stewart's mother had been the daughter of the first Hamilton Earl of Arran. By April he was also a Privy Councillor and Captain of the Royal Guard.

With tension slackening in the Borders, as elsewhere, aided by a rumour almost certainly deliberately spread abroad that the king himself was seeking to convert his friend Lennox to his own brand of Protestantism, the March wardens felt sufficiently confident that there was going to be no invasion to relax their armed mustering arrangements. John was able to return to Fenton.

He found Archie Douglas, still at Tantallon, in a state of much concern, instructions having come to him from the new governing authority. Was he still Lieutenant of the Realm? Lieutenant of the Border? Even keeper of Falkland Palace? The king, based now at Holyroodhouse below the heights of Arthur's Seat, with all the surrounding hillocks, parkland and lochs to hunt and hawk in, did not appear to require frequent visits to Falkland over in Fife. Did he require himself, Archie, in any capacity now? Or was his relationship with the imprisoned Morton making him no longer acceptable? Not that he particularly wanted any of these appointments; but he did want to know where he stood. Would John, whom the king used to look upon as some sort of friend, go and try to find out the position?

That man was distinctly doubtful about such a mission, but could not refuse. He did not know whether James Stewart still looked on him fairly kindly – after all, he was wed to Morton's sister. He had not been replaced as warden admittedly. But would this Lennox, whose poetic abilities were reputedly sufficient to enable him to laugh at John's feeble efforts, even allow him to enter the royal presence? Margaret thought that there was no harm in making the attempt, nor in taking with him two or three versifying efforts which he had produced in the interim.

So, on a May morning, John rode the score of miles to Edinburgh, less than confidently.

At Holyroodhouse he found all markedly different from the Stirling ambience, the fortress might replaced by the palatial, no drawbridged moats and gatehouses to get past. Guards there were, but these were less challenging, and when, in the forecourt, John announced that he was Warden of the Middle March come to report to the king, he was not kept outside but conducted into a chamber off the inner courtyard and told to wait while His Grace was informed.

It was some time before there was any development.

But eventually he was taken upstairs and through a series of handsome intercommunicating apartments, to an ante-room, and again left alone. He could hear voices from the next room.

He had not long to wait now before a further door opened and a handsome, splendidly dressed and smiling man of about his own age strolled in, to make a hand's flourish.

"Ah, Sir John Carmichael it is, I understand? From the Borders?" this striking personage said, with a marked French accent. "His Grace tells me that you are a poet. I am Lennox, chamberlain here. I hope that your visit to the king presages no grievous problems? I have heard of your Borderers, and their unruly ways!"

"No, my lord. I come in loyal duty, but with no problems of that sort," John answered. "Nor can I claim to be a poet, save by His Grace's charity! I come seeking . . . guidance."

"Do not we all so seek, *mon ami*, in one degree or another? Come, His Grace will see you."

John was led into what appeared to be a library, tables spread with papers and open books. James sat at one of these, quill in hand, undoubtedly at his preferred employment. He looked round, those great eyes enquiring all but anxiously, as John bowed low.

"Aye, Sir John," he said. "I've no' seen you this whilie."

"No, Sire, to my loss! I crave Your Highness's pardon if I intrude."

"I'm scrieving a piece on yon David and Goliath. Cousin Esmé here's right helpful. It's in the French, mind. I'm no' so guid at the French as at the Latin."

"I marvel that Your Grace can devise either. I could nowise so aspire."

"Och, the Latin's no' difficult. The words can ay rhyme, and there's a bit scan to it. But the French . . ."

"His Grace seeks to convert *me* to his Doric!" Lennox declared, pulling a face. "I find it worse than Greek!"

"It's no' so sair as the Gaelic. You'll never win roond yon, Esmé!"

John, looking from one to the other, knew relief. The atmosphere here was anything but hostile, and this Lennox seemed amiable despite all the polish. But would the reason behind his visit change all that? He was hesitant to announce it.

"Hae you brought any new verses for me?" James went on, pointing the quill at him all but accusingly.

"I have, Sire. Three. But they are poor things. One on the Lammermuirs – the sheep-strewn hills. One on the days of the week and how they gained their heathen names. And" – he took his chance – "one on the fowls of the air around Tantallon on its cliff-top." He glanced at Lennox. "Tantallon is the castle of my lord of Angus, my wife's nephew." There it was out, the gauntlet cast.

"Aye. Angus, yon Douglas. The Red one. He's no rhymster, him!"

"We have not all been given your talent, Sire. But he is a loyal subject of Your Grace, and concerned to serve you well."

"He's yon ill Morton's nephew, forby. For Sir John's wed to Morton's sister." That was a reminder for Lennox, but not said to sound like an accusation. "He's keeper o' Falkland."

"Ah, yes. The Earl of Douglas . . ."

"Na, na – Angus. He's chief o' the Red Douglases. Earl o' Angus. Morton's the *Black* Douglas. They're different. Mind, Douglas is just *dubh glas*, in the Gaelic, meaning black stream. It was the river they took their name from, I jalouse."

"M'mm. Difficult."

"My lord is unsure as to his position, Sire. Now that my lord of Morton is, is no longer assisting your rule. He is, or was, Lieutenant of the Border. And was made Lieutenant of the Realm also, later. He desires to know Your Grace's wishes in these matters."

James looked at Lennox questioningly.

"What mean they, these styles?" that man asked.

"Och, the Borders one's just to keep a bit eye on the three March wardens, Sir John one o' them. Lieutenant o' the Realm, I'm no' right sure. There had not been one until Morton made it, that I ken o'. It's no' the Earl Marischal, who aye commands the forces o' the crown — but the present one's just a laddie, mind. And it's no' the High Constable — that's Erroll. It was maybe to command until the right Marischal comes o' age. Angus led against the Hamiltons, did he no'?"

"Yes, Sire."

Lennox shrugged, continental-style. "It is confusing, no? I think that you should hold this of the kingdom's armed command open meantime, James. Until . . . later. Will that upset the Earl of Angus, Sir John?"

"No, my lord. He never sought that position. Does not see himself as leader of armies. The Border lieutenancy is different, more judge than marshal."

"That's right," James agreed. "The command o' armies is best held by, aye. Johnnie Mar would hae it, if he could — but I'm no' so sure! But the Borders is right enough."

"So my lord remains Lieutenant of the Borders and Keeper of Liddesdale, Sire? And what of Falkland?"

"Aye. He's as guid as any other at Falkland."

"So there you have it, Sir John," Lennox said. "Is this Angus your friend, as well as your wife's nephew?"

"He is, my lord. A good friend. His Grace can rely on him."

"Aye, then," His Grace said. "Plenties o' that! Your rhymes, see you. We'll hae a look at them."

"May I leave them with you, Sire? Rather than read them now. I am nowise proud of them, and would prefer my poor efforts to be scanned in my absence!"

"Hoots, man, be no' sae nice!"

Lennox came to John's rescue. "I understand our friend's concern, James. Myself, I fear your royal judgment at times!"

John cast him a grateful glance. "Besides, Sire, I am

interrupting your own more important writings. I crave your forgiveness and seek your permission to retire."

The king waved his quill towards the door, and bowing, John made his escape, Lennox patting his shoulder as he went.

Outside, John decided that he liked Esmé Stewart, and that probably his coming had been to Scotland's benefit, since clearly the king all but idolised him. Now there was good news to take back to Archie.

Nothing had been said about Morton's trial for treason.

Something was said, however, a few days later. An officer of the Royal Guard, from Holyrood, arrived at Fenton Tower bearing a spoken, not a written, message for Sir John Carmichael. It was to the effect that it was probably wise for the Earl of Angus not to be present at the forthcoming trial of his uncle, on the first day of June, eight days' time. Let his lordship know it. In the circumstances it might be advisable for him to be gone before then to some destination sufficiently distant, perhaps across the borderline, where he could not be reached and called upon to appear, either as another earl at the trial, or as a witness for the Earl of Morton. That was all, the warning carefully attributed to no named sender.

John had no doubts that the sender was Lennox. And that it was to be heeded. There might well be a plot by Douglas enemies, Argyll, Montrose or others, to seek to embroil Archie in the trial in some fashion, to his hurt. He rode for Tantallon within the hour.

Two days later Archie was on his way southwards, ostensibly to confer with the English Warden-General, the Earl of Northumberland at Alnwick Castle, his opposite number, on unspecified Borders business. Mary came to stay meantime with Margaret at Fenton.

33

Scotland waited with tense anticipation for the day of the great trial. There were mixed feelings about it. Morton had never been popular, his stern rule, taxation and avarice gaining him few friends; but he had managed to keep the peace better than any of his predecessors, and had come to terms with the Kirk despite his tulchan bishops, which had been only instituted as a method for grasping their diocesan funds. He had kept the Catholic cause under control – and their new leader was a Catholic, Lennox, strong on the French connection and hostile to the English. So folk waited, wondered and debated.

The vital day of decision was to be 1st June, and the scene to be set at the new tolbooth of Edinburgh, erected some years before at the south-west corner of St Giles Kirk in the High Street. The ex-regent would be tried by a panel of his peers, an earl of Scotland traditionally entitled to face the judgment of his fellow earls, these, to be sure, carefully chosen for the occasion, and none friends of the accused. There was not much room in the tolbooth for spectators, but John Carmichael claimed the right to attend, as a warden, when he heard that the Lord Maxwell, of the West March, was taking part although not an earl, presumably not given a vote. Margaret was doubtful as to his wisdom in going at all, but he felt that he had to be there, he who was only warden by her brother's appointment; also did he not have a duty to report the proceedings to her thereafter, also to Archie?

Edinburgh's narrow streets were packed to overflowing on that fine summer's day, the citizens being joined by many from the countryside. Two troops of soldiers had been brought in to ensure order, and to prevent any possible rescue attempts by Douglases; so the tolbooth was well guarded, so well that John had some difficulty in gaining admittance although he arrived sufficiently early. He eventually found a seat in the gallery, with none other than Douglas of Whittingehame, brother of the Senator Alexander, the alleged principal actor in the murder itself, on the same bench only two seats along.

When at length the judges filed in, led by Argyll, Lord High Admiral, it was noticeable that Lennox was not one of them, despite it being he who had undoubtedly engineered Morton's downfall. The new Earl of Arran, Captain Stewart, was there however, with Montrose, Erroll, Buchan, Glencairn and Eglinton. The Lords Maxwell and Lindsay also came in, presumably as advisers. Clearly the king was not to be present. They all took their seats behind a long table.

Then, to a roll of drums, Morton was led in by members of the Royal Guard under the selfsame officer who had brought the warning message for Archie to Fenton Tower, named Stewart appropriately. The prisoner betrayed no fears, no evident concern, indeed paced up to the other side of the table with dignity, reddish head held high. Almost scornfully he eyed the panel, but did not speak.

Argyll took charge. "James Douglas," he said, in the musical Highland voice which so belied his character, "you are brought here, before your fellow earls of this realm, to answer grievous charges of highest treason against the crown. There are no fewer than twelve heads of indictment against you, dating from various periods; but the major one is that dealing with the murder, in the year 1567, of King Henry, Lord Darnley, who wore the crown matrimonial, as wed to the then reigning Queen Mary. The others commence with the assassination, in the presence of the said queen, of her secretary, Signor David Rizzio, in the Palace of Holyroodhouse, that in the year previous, 1566, in March . . ."

The guard-captain coughed. "My lord of Argyll, and

my lords, His Grace the King sends here his order that the Earl of Morton, here present, is to be tried on the one main charge only, that of the death of His Grace's father, King Henry, Lord Darnley. That alone. Here is his written and sealed command." And he placed on the table a folded paper.

There were drawn breaths all over the hall, not only from behind that table. What did this signify? John's guess was as good as any, that there might well be matters in those other eleven charges which could implicate persons in wrong-doings which were now better forgotten. Was this of the clever Lennox's contriving?

Argyll, clearly put out, picked up the paper, to scan it and pass it to his fellow earls, while Morton eyed them all keenly.

The Campbell cleared his throat. "To proceed, as His Grace commands. You, James Douglas, are charged that, on a date in the years 1566 or 1567, you signed a bond, along with others including the late Earl of Bothwell, declaring that Henry, Lord Darnley, should be slain, this for purposes best known to yourself. He, wearing the crown matrimonial, and father of the present king, was duly murdered at Kirk o' Field, in this Edinburgh, on 10th February, 1567. This, then, is highest treason. Can you deny it?"

"Proof?" That single word was barked by Morton.

"Proof there is – the signed bond. Bring in the witness, Sir James Balfour."

One of the guard went to lead in that individual, a lawyer, who had been Clerk Register and President of the Court of Session before fleeing to France. Even from the gallery John could see that he held the paper in his hand. Standing beside Morton but not looking at him, he bowed to the panel.

"You, James Balfour, hold the paper bearing the signature of the Earl of Morton, here present?" Argyll said.

"I do, my lords."

"Why has it not been brought to notice before this?"

"I had it with me in France, my lord. And have only recently returned."

Morton snorted.

"Who has seen and vouched for this signature as the accused's? Of sufficient stature for this court's acceptance?"

"The highest, my lords. The King's Grace himself. Who knows my lord of Morton's signature well. As his regent."

So there it was, why James and Lennox were not present, the monarch not to become involved as a witness before the panel. But why was the bond itself not produced?

There was silence for moments on end as men considered the implications – not only those behind that table. It was Morton himself who broke it.

"My lords, why waste your time, and mine, thus?" he demanded. "I did sign a paper, those many years ago. I have signed a host of papers, before and since! That paper said that the Lord Darnley was a danger to this realm's weal, and to the queen's authority, even her continued occupancy of the throne, and that he should be removed therefrom. Many agreed then that this was so – some here present!" And he eyed his accusers one by one. "I, at least, made honest judgment of the situation. Darnley, wed to the queen by folly, should go. He had written to the Pope, the King of France, and to the Cardinal of Lorraine, her uncle, declaring that she was dubious in the Catholic faith, and that she should be deposed for looking too kindly on the Protestant cause, and that he, Darnley, should be raised to be King Regnant of Scotland. This, that year of 1566. Was my judgment wrongous? My signing of the paper that he should be removed was nowise faulty, and did not make me in any wise responsible for his murder at Kirk o' Field those months later. It was a statement of concern for the realm, the newly Protestant realm, and the Queen's Grace, not a pact to slay."

"You ask us to believe that!" Argyll demanded.

"It is truth. Bothwell had proposed the death of Darnley,

earlier, but I said no to it. I merely signed that he should be removed from power."

"Removed! How removed, he, the queen's husband, but by death!" Argyll looked along the line of his fellow lords who all nodded their heads. "I say that you should be convicted of counsel, concealing and being art and part in the king's murder. Is it not so?"

There were cries of agreement from the panel.

"Art and part! Art and part!" Morton exclaimed, his hitherto calm and dignified stance momentarily deserting him, at this failure of his appeal in the direction of the Protestant cause. "God knoweth the contrary! God knoweth, I say!" And he struck the table more than once with his fist.

Although there was some stirring throughout the hall, there was no relenting on the part of his judges, their decision most evidently made beforehand. As the accused sought to control himself and recover his composure, Argyll, with more nods from his colleagues, stood to pronounce verdict and sentence.

"It is the decision of this court that you, James Douglas, are guilty of complicity in highest treason, in the murder of King Henry, Lord Darnley. For which dire offence against His Grace's father, you shall yourself suffer death, this by being hanged, drawn and quartered. This on the morrow."

The silence which greeted that verdict lasted for long moments, Morton motionless, all there whatever their views and sympathies stricken by the awareness of the so sudden downfall of supreme power in the land to that dire and ignominious end. Then the condemned man threw back his shoulders, and head as high as when he came in, without another glance at his judges, wheeled about and strode for the door, so abruptly that his guards had to hurry to catch up with him.

Even the panel of his judges seemed at something of a loss now, for a space, before they all rose, and filed out.

John sat there for longer. Hanged, drawn and quartered!

The fate of only the most wretched of felons! Margaret! How was he to tell Margaret of this?

Outside the tolbooth he was just in time to see Morton, mounted but hemmed in by a strong troop of soldiers, being led off down the High Street for Holyrood.

Little as he relished the duty, John was back in Edinburgh next day to witness the execution. It was to be held at the Mercat Cross at noon; and if it was possible, the city was even more crowded than ever for the occasion. John had difficulty in getting anywhere near the said cross, which was in fact close to the tolbooth, after his twenty-mile ride, until he saw the Lord Maxwell gaining access thereto, and, attaching himself to his fellow warden's party, managed to win reasonably near to the scaffold. Maxwell informed him, without comment, that the king had cancelled the hanging, drawing and quartering, ordering that Morton was to die by decapitation, on the Red Maiden.

This was ironic, to say the least, for this so-called Maiden was a guillotine introduced by Morton himself, a tall machine of posts supporting a sharp steel blade, weighted, which could be hoisted by a rope and then loosed by the executioner, to drop down, within grooves and in great force, on the neck of the unfortunate victim, guaranteed to sever head from trunk without any possibility of a botched stroke from an axe. John saw this grim contrivance had been erected on the scaffold platform, at a height to allow maximum observance by all who wished to see.

Maxwell disappearing into the tolbooth, John had quite a lengthy wait amongst the jostling and noisily excited onlookers, with street-hawkers peddling their wares and almost a holiday atmosphere prevailing – which seemed unsuitable indeed, little as he or probably anyone there loved the ex-regent.

At length, shouts from down the High Street heralded developments, and presently lance-bearing soldiers clearing a rough way through the throng arrived with, in their midst, the doomed earl, flanked by black-robed divines on either side, not mounted this time. He had been made to walk up the mile from Holyrood to his death, like any criminal.

Now that he was present, a hush fell on the crowd as he was conducted to the scaffold and ordered to climb the steps. He held himself, not proudly but with no cowering or shrinking, dignity retained. On the platform he stood alone, looking around him calmly, the two ministers remaining at the foot of the steps, with a burly character who was presumably the executioner. The same captain of the guard went into the tolbooth to fetch the men who had condemned the prisoner.

The great ones duly appeared, and had some difficulty in finding room to stand round the scaffold, the guards having to clear a space for them, John being one of those forced back somewhat. He did not know whether Morton, in his gazing, had recognised him amongst the sea of faces.

Argyll, in charge again, signed for the ministers and the executioner to mount to the platform. John insinuated his way forward to Lord Maxwell's side. He had noted that again Lennox was not present, not that he had expected the young king to be there.

"He takes it all well enough," Maxwell observed.

"What would you expect? He is the Black Douglas, is he not?"

The divines were speaking with Morton, one of them the prominent Reformer, the Reverend James Lawson. Then there was an interruption. The new Earl of Arran, Captain Stewart, came halfway up the steps, to call Morton down to him, and there requested him to tarry while his confession, made earlier at Holyrood to the ministers, was set down in writing and brought for his signature – an odd demand, in the circumstances. Clearly Morton so considered it.

"Bethink you, my new lord, that I have far other things now to advise upon. I am about to die. I must prepare for my God. These good men," he pointed to the ministers, "can testify to what I have spoken." And he climbed back up.

After a word with Lawson, he turned to face the people. "Hear all," he said, sufficiently loudly to be heard by many. "I have confessed to some foreknowledge of the death of the Lord Darnley. Let that be sufficient. I die this day, in the profession of the Gospel as taught by the Kirk of Scotland. I exhort all, if you look for the favour of heaven, to hold to the same." That said, he turned to the executioner.

However, Lawson, holding up a hand, commenced to pray louder still, in ringing tones. Morton, shrugging, sank down on his knees, face bent to the boards there before the Maiden, and remained thus until the minister finished, and provided a general benediction. Then he rose and shook the two divines by the hand, and then the hand of the executioner also. But when the latter was for binding his wrists behind him, Morton shook his head, and went to kneel again, this time at the guillotine itself, to lean over and carefully place his neck at the centre of the block.

It was still not sufficient. Lawson produced a Bible from beneath his robe and proceeded to read some verses of Scripture apt for the occasion, as the executioner took the fatal rope in his grip, and most watching held their breaths.

As the reading ceased, with an Amen, Morton added, from his awkward position, "Lord Jesus, receive my spirit!" the last words of a strange man in this stage of his life, for, with a jerk, that rope was pulled, and the massive blade, released, descended with a scraich, greased as it was, and the reddish head was neatly parted from the sturdy body in a sudden fountain of blood.

A great corporate sigh went up from the watchers. John found that he had to wipe a tear from his eye, little as he had loved or even esteemed this man who had had so great an effect on his life. But Morton had died well. And who knew, the great Judge above might well assess the Black

Douglas a deal more kindly than had most there, including himself.

All waited while an iron spike was brought for the executioner to pick up the bloody bearded head and impale it on the sharp point, to be affixed, as Argyll commanded, to the topmost pinnacle of the tolbooth gable, for all to see and remark upon hereafter, while the still twitching body was taken down to be laid in a fish-cart, to trundle up the mile or two to the Burgh Muir and be buried in a pauper's grave.

So ended the last of Scotland's regents.

John did not linger in the city. His thoughts in some turmoil, speaking to none there, he rode back to his wife and Morton's sister. How much to tell her?

EPILOGUE

The death of Morton and the rise of Lennox was the end of one era and the start of another, this last really marking the commencement of the rule of James the Sixth, as distinct from his reign. Esmé Stewart himself did not long maintain his sway, however, the Protestant cause triumphing, the new Arran turning against him and throwing in his lot with Argyll and his party. Lennox was forced to return to France, although his son, Ludovick, did return to Scotland in due course and became very influential, years later.

John Carmichael came back into the royal favour, and in time was appointed Captain of the King's Guard, was sent as an envoy to London to negotiate with Queen Elizabeth, and later was one of the ambassadors who went to Denmark to arrange the marriage between King James and the Princess Anne. Because of these activities he could no longer function as Warden of the Middle March; but in 1598 he was made Warden of the West March, in lieu of Maxwell. This appointment did not last long, for in 1600 he was murdered by one Thomas Armstrong, a mosstrooper, when leaving a football match between the obstreperous Marchmen. He was greatly mourned, for he was renowned as one of the best wardens ever to have sought to control the Marches. By that time he and Margaret Douglas had had three sons and four daughters. His descendants became Earls of Hyndford – and there is still a Carmichael of that Ilk at Carmichael.

Archibald, Earl of Angus, had a more chequered and much shorter career. In opposition to Arran and in co-operation with the Earl of Mar, he eventually helped to oust Arran and free King James to control his own realm, however oddly. He did not long survive this success however, dying in 1588, his death "attributed to sorcery". He left no offspring.

Mary Queen of Scots, after nineteen years of captivity, was executed by Elizabeth the year before.

In 1603 King James, aged thirty-seven, on the death of the Tudor, succeeded to her throne to become the first monarch of the United Kingdom, putting an end at last to cross-border warfare, however much feud and mayhem continued amongst the Marchmen themselves. One of the strangest characters ever to mount a throne, the Wisest Fool in Christendom nevertheless was the only King of Scots, or of England either, never to go to war.